# Courage

A Story of Love and Friendship

Disko Praphanchith

# CONTENTS

# PROLOGUE

A cigarette. Jenny wanted a cigarette.

She wanted one because she never really tried one, wanted one because she'd always envied those who had the opportunity to smoke one. It was a phantom craving, a lascivious longing, an addiction that existed deep within without having tasted the actual physical. Just hearing the word itself was addicting, its consonants like a knotted word of perfect blended tight cacophonies: cigarette, cigarette, cigarette. Jenny wanted a cigarette. No, she *needed* a cigarette right then. Thinking about it made her dizzy, made her weak, made her envision it like a passionate longing of good sex after a long season of drought.

Tom would never let her have a cigarette, though. His rules were much too stern for that. If Tom told her to do something, she did it. If he told her not to do something, she did that too. If she ever disobeyed him on either occasion, well, then, things got a little rough for her, and Jenny no longer spent her time wondering about cigarettes. What she thought about instead during those times lying in bed after doing something he didn't want her to do (or *not* doing something he *did* want her to do) was whether or not she could go to work the next evening, whether or not she had enough concealer to cover up any new bruises, and whether or not she would come back home smelling like freshly brewed black coffee and hash browns again.

She always smelled like diner food whenever coming home in the morning. Tom hated it. He always called it something horrible to her face, something like That Smell or That Shit Stink, and always made her take a shower before going to bed with him. Which was fine, Jenny agreed; she did smell like wasted grease-shit at times, and hated the smell herself. Just that, sometimes, if he was irritable—or just in one of his BAD MOODS again, something that was always in caps—he got mad at her, and liked to express his anger at her so that she knew he was angry. And Tom always made sure she knew when he was angry.

*God, I want a cigarette. It looks like blood.*

Splashed residues of red covered her fingers and trailed down her wrists; heavy patches of it marked her face. Globs of it smeared her legs and patterned the white surfaces of her naked feet.

*It looks like blood, but it isn't. It doesn't feel like blood, doesn't taste like blood. It doesn't even smell like blood. It actually smells kind of good.*

The left side of her face throbbed with aching fire. Half her face felt lopsided and fat where Tom had struck her, and the skin there stung like acid from the searing touch of tears.

A bruise was coming on soon.

*He didn't have to do that,* Jenny thought miserably again. *He didn't have to rub it all over my face, didn't have to call me stupid again. If he'd just slapped me and let me cry, if he'd just yelled at me, cursed at me, I'd be...I'd be okay. Everything would just be okay.*

She shuddered. She curled her legs in against herself and sobbed.

It was cold tonight—just so cold. The only things she had on tonight were a pair of blue shorts and a white tank top. There was a greasy pizza box lying next to her on the floor; next to it were two wine glasses with their contents spilled out on the carpet. Even in the darkness Jenny could see their color, and thought suddenly of cold, dark, frozen veins. A slice of pepperoni pizza lay next to the wine glasses.

*He didn't have to that,* Jenny thought again. *All I wanted to do was surprise him with dinner. God, why do I always* mess up?

Something loud flowed heavily from the dark. It was Tom. He was washing his hands again. In the kitchen, Jenny thought; where else could it be? She could picture him with bloody hands in the dark and with his shoulders hunched over the sink. Globs of tomato sauce stained his nails; rivulets of bright red swirled down into the sink. Like a calculating murderer having cleaned up after his latest victim, Tom scrubbed his hands diligently in an effort to remove all the evidence of blood from his fingertips.

*Only it's not blood,* a voice whispered. *It's tomato sauce. Stop thinking that it's blood! That's disgusting!*

Jenny brought her hands up and closed her eyes. Warm tears spread down her cheeks and tickled her chin. Revulsion filled her.

*Look at me,* a sickening voice whispered, *look how pathetic I am, look at what I'm doing. I'm crying on the floor with tomato sauce spread all over my face and tasting it in my tears. Look how disgusting I am. Look how I'm just crying in the dark!*

Another voice came to her ears, whispering: *You're crying blood, Jenny. And you know it.*

She shuddered. She rewrapped her arms around herself and sobbed against her knees, curling them tight against her chest. If Tom saw her like this—sobbing, wet, subdued and submissive, covered in tears and bundled on the living room floor with sauce smeared all over her face—he'd get mad at her again, snap at her, yell at her, hurt her, do something worse to her to make her stop. She was a mess, her hair plastered all over her face like black stringy webs of spaghetti. Even her bare feet were messy, covered in sauce and looking like she had splashed around in a puddle of…well, blood.

Tom hated weakness.

*Suffocate yourself,* a voice whispered. *Suffocate yourself, Jenny, bite down on your tears. Don't let him see you crying like this, don't let him catch you. Just soak your tears, Jenny. Just bite down on your knees, and soak your tears.*

Jenny whimpered. She tightened her arms around herself and squeezed her eyes shut, letting tears slide down her legs.

Where was he? An eternity had passed with there being no movement from the kitchen. What was he doing? And why was he taking so long? Was he considering getting something? Was he actually thinking of getting *something?*

*Oh please,* Jenny moaned, *don't let it be the roller or knife. I know I'm not supposed to think that about my husband, but please, don't let it be the knife, don't let—*

Tom Acworth's figure appeared at the doorway. Jenny let out a cry when she saw him and realized she'd squeaked out loud. There was nothing in his hands.

"Your feet are dirty."

She didn't say anything. She scanned his face and quickly turned away, terrified at the dull rage in his eyes. Sauce stains patterned the inner sleeves of his suit; dark bands of sweat laced the collar of his shirt. And his breathing, though faint at first after having turned off the water, now became deep and clear, sounding heavy and slow, like a mammoth predator gazing wonderingly at wounded prey. He'd taken his tie off, Jenny saw. It now wrapped tight around his hand just below the ridges of his right knuckles. It looked like a newly designed gentleman's brass-knuckle spotted with blood.

*The reason my feet and legs are dirty is because you were using me as a piñata just now, remember Tom?*

"Did you shower yet?"

"No."

His eyes narrowed. Jenny hugged herself and braced for him to yell at her. He hardly ever yelled her—it wasn't his style—but when he did, it was always with a loud sharp bark that hurt her as much as his fists against her jaw.

Tom slowly made his way over and knelt next to her on the floor. Jenny pressed herself against the wall and backpedaled away with her feet. Small imprints of red between her toes smeared the carpet. A soft, voiceless whimper accidentally escaped her as he took hold of her hands.

"Clean this mess up," he whispered. "Now. Do you understand me?"

She nodded. She said nothing as he studied her. Jenny was sure that if Tom wanted to break her fingers, he could do so—*would* do so—in one single effortless movement with his hands, snapping all of her bones and joints collectively in one horrible single *snap!*

"Yes, Tom," she whispered. "O-o-okay. I will, Tom."

"Afterwards take a shower. Do you understand?"

"Yes. Okay."

"When I come back down, I'm not going to see any more pizza stains, will I."

Jenny shook her head. It hadn't been a question. "No," she answered meekly, "you won't, Tom."

"Good."

He got up and left her.

That was it. Nothing more. No more shouting, no more hitting, no more pizza in the face. He just stared at her, drew back a lock of hair from her eyes, and walked back upstairs to their bedroom, leaving her there on the floor.

*What did I do so wrong?* Jenny cried. *God, why did this happen to me? Why couldn't things just go the way I planned them?*

Slowly, reluctantly, and even painfully with new aches and sores in her knees, Jenny soberly picked herself up from the floor and walked over to the two giant wine glasses. Her toes accidently stepped into a cold puddle of wine and she pulled back with a quick shudder. The feeling was like moist hair to her feet.

She placed the glasses on the dining room table and stared at the pizza box. Grease stains, thick as bruises, soaked through its cardboard skin.

*I hate you,* Jenny thought sourly as she bent down and picked up the box. She flipped open the lid and saw two remaining pepperoni slices inside. *I hate you so much, God. I hate how you always have to look at me even when I'm crying, hate how you'll always see me in the dark. Why can't you just leave me alone? Why do you always just look at me?*

Crying—and still with globs of tomato sauce on her cheeks—Jenny silently reached for the two pizza slices, sighed, and bitterly ate them in the dark.

PART I

The apparition of these faces in the crowd;
Petals on a wet, black bough.


--Ezra Pound
"In A Station Of The Metro"

# CHAPTER 1

Red Moon's Diner always stank of freshly grilled hashbrowns and buttermilk pancakes. It was what the place was commonly known for. Those who frequented the diner could only in brief describe these qualities, as to do so otherwise out loud would be to state the already obvious and mundane. The floors were black and white: They checkered endlessly in an uneven alternating square pattern that came to an abrupt halt at purple-grape colored walls. The walls themselves were decorated with ribbon streaks that were colored yellow and pink, blue and red, orange and green. The floors were polished so clean that the ceiling lights glared upward from the floors like menacing clown eyes. On the eastern wall near the back was a black-and-white picture of a young Elvis Presley hanging next to a framed photo of Marilyn Monroe. Other innumerable American celebrities adorned the wall: There was James Dean posing as if he were a rebel without a cause; a Paul Newman alongside a sensual Elizabeth Taylor; a contemplative Montgomery Clift trying to find his place in the sun; a beaming Doris Day, an Audrey Hepburn, Susan Hayward, John Wayne, and a plethora of others. Dark red leather booths surrounded white butcher block tables and gave view to a parking lot overshadowed outside by an autumn night.

Jenny stood leaned forward at the front counter of Red Moon's Diner with a hand supporting her chin. Her other hand drummed absentmindedly away as she stared blankly out at the windows. A strand of hair drifted down in front of her eyes. She blew it away, idly, and uttered one small puff that served as a sigh.

Red Moon's was slow tonight. Jenny supposed she was thankful, but really, she didn't care. All feelings of hope and desire had been abolished long ago since beginning to work here. She'd gotten accustomed to it all now, the myriad activities that belonged to this world. The clock, the customers, the occasional opening of the diner door as announced by the small ringing golden bell—these were all things part of her day-to-day permanent existence. Occasionally there was some mild chitchat in the back between the two cooks, Ted Kessler and John Rhodes, and other times Abigail Rogers and Nora Rhys were there to speak with her when on shift together, but for the most part, Jenny found herself alone, occasionally with nothing.

The pungent, acrid, and often times, *revolting*, odors of the diner were the second quality to this meager existence. Jenny had grown so accustomed to the smells here that she supposed *not* having an immunity to the thick, syrupy smells of grease-oil and fat would have made her seem abnormal. The coffee that was brewed here hung heavy and thick in the air; the savory smells of grilling hashbrowns and bacon strips saturated the senses. There was the hot aroma of deep-fried onion rings and grilled pork meat, of tender pork chops smothered in Swiss cheese served with French fries, of fluffy buttermilk pancakes cooking on the morning grill, mouthwatering sautéed mushroom hamburgers, and hot chili-cheese hotdogs. The smells were revolting, but almost pleasantly so, teasing the guilt triggers of the mind. The scent of fried steaks and crisp golden French fries were all hell to her hair, and Jenny suspected it was the same for all the other girls that worked here. Tom had ventured into Red Moon's once and had almost gagged, declaring that the place smelled like Clogged-Up Arteries Shit. Jenny had frowned when hearing his words. She'd been surprised at how hurt she'd been. Though she offered no strict feelings of loyalty to those at Red Moon's, she'd felt as if her husband's words had been inadvertently directed at her. Tom deemed it necessary that she make her hair clean before going to bed with him. He not only deemed it necessary, but strictly *demanded* it, forcing her to always shower for an hour or more whenever coming home in the early morning. She had to be clean for him. She just always had to be so, so clean.

"Jenny?"

"Hmm?"

"Watcha thinkin'?"

She turned around and saw Abigail Rogers near her shoulder. Golden locks bounced playfully near her ears. Her Red Moon's uniform made her look incredibly small and doll-like. The sight was unbecoming for reasons Jenny couldn't explain, and she suddenly wished Abigail hadn't come up to her.

"Thinking about what I'm going to do later this morning," Jenny muttered, referring to the clock near the windows. It was ten past midnight. "That's all."

"Oh! That's nice. You know, I started this exercising routine at the gym with my trainer. He's cute and all, and we've been going through these steps for a diet and stuff. His name's Dean."

"Great," Jenny grumbled.

"Yep, it is. I mean, I don't think I really need to diet and stuff, but it's about being healthy and energized, you know? It ain't all being skinny. Being on a diet means to be healthy on the inside and out, and…"

Jenny let her go on, her temples hurting, the blood behind her eyes swirling like black poisonous whirlpools. She checked the clock again and sighed when seeing the time. Less than ten seconds had passed since Abigail began ranting to her—it felt like ten hours already. There were only three of them on shift at this hour at Red Moon's. The other woman—Nora—was out on medical leave due back in two days. Abigail had her own frivolous mannerisms and Nora had hers. With Abigail, it was the constant chit-chattering whirr of a blabbering mouth. With Nora, it was the constant skin-peeling sounds of her magazines and cork-popping sounds of her bubblegum. Jenny didn't know which she loathed more. The two usually left her alone when together at the counter, but now that Nora was on temporary leave, Jenny found herself acting as a substitute for Abigail's frantic babbling.

"…people eat dogs?"

Jenny turned towards her. "Hmm?"

"I asked, do you people eat dogs?"

Jenny stared at her. An earnest, if not childlike curiosity filled Abigail's eyes then, creating a bloom of pity in Jenny's chest. She sighed. She collected herself, and said patiently: "No, Abigail. We don't eat dogs. That's just a cultural myth."

"Oh! Well, that's great then. Cause like, no offense, but eating dogs is kinda…you know, weird. I mean, not to say it's absolutely *wrong* or anything, just that, I couldn't *imagine* eating my cutie Spencer back at home! He's so cute, Jenny, you know what he did last night? He got this ball for me that I threw down the stairs, right? And like, while he was hopping back up the steps…"

Jenny smiled, nodding as she did so, mentally forcing Abigail's voice away. She politely turned back to the windows and expressed another inward sigh.

Yes. It was true—she was a 'they' according to them. It was a 'they' that was plural and singular, a word that signified a 'them' and an 'us.' After all these years she still was just a foreign 'them.'

*If you want, Abigail,* Jenny thought sourly, *I can ask you to forgive me for being Korean. I can ask you to forgive my small eyes and black hair, ask you to forgive my small frame and ethnicity and background, ask you to forgive my ability to speak bilingually. I'm sorry that I'm bicultural, and I'm sorry that I sometimes fail to fulfill everyone's stereotype of being an Asian woman. What will you ask me to forgive you in return?*

The anger—so familiar, but so old now—registered in her chest, set ablaze, and then quietly died as fast as it appeared. The fire left embers in her heart; it was a feeling Jenny supposed would never abate. She felt no self-loathing then, but only a feeling of outward pity for the world.

It was a common theme at the diner: Red Moon's one and only 'exotic' waitress ready to serve and please all of Boise's hungry customers! Come and see the foreigner, the exotic beauty that has come to work for us! There were no glares here, no tantrums; there simply were condescending looks with patronized smiles and affable friendships built by fetishisms. There was no slander, no hate; there simply were pocket-voids of ignorance supplemented by cultural stereotypes that acted as knowledge. She was not the talk of the town, but rather, the quiet fascination of all American men.

Embers in her heart. Just simple embers.

*When I married you, Tom,* Jenny thought quietly, *I saw how you once looked at me as an exotic object. I heard once how you joked to me about your friends, how you once used the term 'her people' when describing me to your family. And yet, still, I can't hate anymore, and have only enough energy to pity. We've gotten over it, but it still rests in my heart, Tom. Do you understand? As an Asian woman, as a woman, as an object, as a noun, it still hurts my heart.*

Headlights cut through the parking lot. Jenny rose from the counter and placed several pins in her hair. Abigail shouted "Oh, we have customers!" and Jenny automatically grabbed the water pitcher beneath the counter, filling it with ice. She muttered, "Thank God," and waited for the door to open.

\*\*\*

They had three customers that morning. Two were an elderly couple while the other was a large middle-aged man who seemed to want to only flirt with Abigail whenever she was near. They ordered quickly, and soon Jenny was back at the front counter again drumming her fingers along with Abigail by her side.

An hour passed.

"Hey look, Jenny!" Abigail shouted once the diner had emptied again. "It's your tall, dark, and handsome! Look at that!"

Jenny lifted her eyes. Her heart dropped at what she saw and sweat broke out across her forehead. A shudder passed through her.

*Not again,* she thought quietly. *Please God, not again. Not this morning.*

The doors to the diner opened and a man in a black overcoat entered. Jenny watched silently as he made his way past the counter and took a seat near the windows. His walk was deliberate; Jenny saw how his gaze stayed determinedly forward without a glance towards her direction. Thin lines of murky water trailed beneath his shoes and stained the checkered floor. Jenny shuddered at the prints. The words *flesh wound* came to mind for whatever reason she couldn't understand, and another abrupt breaking of gooseflesh spread down her arms. She'd expected the man's leather shoeprints to be bright red for some reason, not muddy brown. The loud squeak of his shoes reminded her of crying babies.

*A cigarette,* a cold voice whispered. *I'd like to try a cigarette just for once. Tell him it was tomato sauce.*

She shuddered.

The man was Red Moon's newest habitué. He'd begun coming to the diner three weeks ago. He came in early every Monday, Tuesday, and Friday morning and took the same red booth near the windows. He usually came in about 2 a.m. and rarely spoke to the other girls. His gaze instead was mostly secretive and turned towards the dark where he seemed to contemplate far-off thoughts. Jenny recognized the demeanor as a false display of convoluted demureness—she understood with all her heart he frequented the diner just for her. His passing by her whenever entering the diner, his stoic expressions whenever she was at his table, and his tendency to charge the night with dispassionate stares—Jenny knew it was a tactic meant to belie his inner yearnings for her.

He left two fifty-dollar bills on the table after finishing his meals, and always, written on these bills, were the letters *J.J.* This had announced to all the girls at the diner—even those on the afternoon and evening shifts—that he was a romantic admirer undertaking the enchanting ceremonies of love. Because of this, Jenny knew, wild gossip and intense speculation had begun flourishing around her.

*J.J.* The man always left money for her with the letters *J.J.* written on

17

them. And when seeing the letters, Jenny's heart always hurt.

"Boyfriend's here again," Abigail said cheerfully from the side, "and right on time, too."

Jenny sighed and tied her hair into a ponytail. "Don't remind me," she said wearily. "God, he comes in so much these days! Why can't he just go somewhere *else* looking for a girl, huh?"

"Ah, come on now, Jenny. Where *else* would a handsome guy like him go and find a pretty gal like yourself?"

"The Shining Tilt is open a lot these days, I hear."

Abigail pouted at her. "You're not a hooker, Jenny," she said. "Don't compare yourself to those people. Now, go on. Go and serve the man before he gets hungry."

*Funny way to put it,* Jenny thought, but didn't say. She grabbed her notepad from the counter and walked to where he was sitting. Her pumps clanked loudly against the floor as she walked. A voice whispered to her, saying a second time: *Tomato sauce. Just tell him it was tomato sauce.*

"Hey there. Welcome back. Same as usual?"

The man raised his eyes. He regarded her, briefly, steadily. A quiver a fear passed through her. "Please," he said flatly. "That would be fine."

Jenny forced a smile. She said "All right," and turned around.

*That's right*, she thought, as she pocketed her notepad and walked away, *keep staring, I know that you are. I don't care if it's my ass or what, but I know that you're staring. It's all that you're going to get, okay?*

"Jenny?"

"Same as always," she muttered to Abigail. "What else would it be?"

Abigail looked at her. "You're mad right now, aren't you?"

*Well, I'm certainly not jolly right now.* "I'm just...I don't know. Do you mind if you gave me a few minutes, Abigail? Like five or something? I just have a lot on my mind right now, and I'd really like to be alone to think. Just tell Ted or John that Jenny's *secret admirer* is back, and that he wants his usual."

Abigail frowned but didn't say anything. She muttered the words "Okay then," and turned away, golden locks bouncing.

Jenny watched her go. She held her head for a minute and sighed. She massaged her temples and stared at the countertop in front of her, feeling hot blood pulsating behind her eyes. She looked up. She frowned.

*Goddamn it. I forgot to fill his water. Fuck me.*

She grabbed the pitcher from under the counter, filled it with ice and water, and walked over with another tight smile on her face. "Sorry," she said as she poured. "I forgot your water. Or would you like something else to drink instead?"

"No, that's fine. Thank you."

She watched as he took a drink. He set the glass down and stared at her. She stared back.

"If there's anything else, Abigail and I are here to serve you. All right?"

He nodded. Jenny gritted her teeth together and flashed another smile. She turned away.

"Jenny."

She spun around. Her hair whipped around her shoulders and slapped her in the face.

"I—Yes?"

He reached up to the sides of his face. In that moment, Jenny's heart exploded and sweat broke out on her neck. "I don't want to be rude," he said slowly, touching his cheek. "But you have a mark here."

The smile on her face disappeared. A thought

*(how does he know my name how does he)*

*(the nametag duh he read)*

screeched through her head and her cheeks flushed hot, her breath catching suddenly in her chest. She opened her mouth to say something but then closed it, the words suffocated in her throat. Her tongue turned dry. Everything around her spun out of whack for a quarter-millisecond, and the water pitcher nearly dropped out of her hand.

"I—excuse me?"

19

"Just right here," he said. "A small patch of something. You have something on your face, Jenny."

She reached up and touched her face. Her fingers felt a slight bump on her cheek and her heart suddenly stopped. She pressed it with a sweaty palm and grimaced. It was a bruise.

*Oh God, don't let him see, don't let him see, please don't let—*

"Oh!" she cried. She put on a surprised laugh. "Yeah. That's…um…I don't know what that really is." She patted her cheek and pretended to wipe it off. "Is it gone now?"

He looked at her. His eyes narrowed, and an old

*(familiar)*

solemn look filled his face.

*He knows I'm lying,* Jenny thought frantically. *Ah God, he knows I'm lying, he knows I'm trying to*

*(sauce just tell)*

*act false around him. Just look at his eyes, just look at his face, look at the way he's pitying me and—*

Another voice spoke to her, freezing her blood cold.

*You ate those two pizza slices last night, Jenny. You know you ate them.*

Gooseflesh crawled down her back; something cold pricked the skin on her arms. An involuntary shudder broke through her and her nipples hardened.

"Yeah," the man said thinly. He glanced at her face. "It's gone now, Jenny."

She breathed a sigh of relief. "Oh. Well, thanks!" she cried. She forced another reassuring smile and turned around.

Her feet carried her drunkenly back to the front counter; pumps clanked loudly against the floor. She slammed the water pitcher down and ripped the pins out of her hair. She felt his eyes gazing at her from behind, into the back of her shoulders, and gnashed down on her teeth to keep from turning around. She could hear Abigail with Ted and John in the back laughing in the

20

kitchen; their laughter was like an ice pick in her ears, digging and sharp. Jenny made her way to the bathroom, heard again the odd, uneven beat of her feet as they carried her from the main area of the diner, and found the door.

She slammed the door shut behind her, rested her back against it, and shuddered uncontrollably as a hammer-beat rhythm thundered away in her chest. Warmth flooded her eyes.

*Don't cry, don't cry, whatever it is you do, just don't* cry.

Jenny wiped her face and stumbled to the sink. Her hands clutched the sides of the sink where bone-white burst from her knuckles. She stared breathlessly at the mirrors and panted.

Yes, there it was. There was the bruise just as he had shown her, right there on the fat swell of her left cheek. Any passerby would have seen it as an odd lump on her face, an uneven bulge that had come about from a disastrous time at the orthodontist. It bulged there on her face beneath a thin layer of concealer and foundation. White finishing powder had smoothed it to an eggshell white.

How had he seen it? *Why* had he seen it? Makeup had been an art inadvertently loaned to her by Tom, and was something she'd learned how to adopt and perfect long ago. Why had he gone on and *seen* it?

*Go to hell*, Jenny thought sobbingly. She stared at herself in the mirror and bit down on her lip. Dark red lipstick coated her lips; murky aqua eyeshadow patterned her eyes. The red made her lips look voluptuously plump like the curving swells of a summer plum, and the blue adorning her eyes made it seem as if she were in a permanent salacious grin. Dark eyeliner pulled her eyes back into tight Korean teardrops.

*God, I look so ugly tonight—just so ugly. No wonder he saw my bruise. Tom would be so mad if he knew what happened. Jesus.*

Trembling, Jenny reached over and grabbed a paper towel from the wall dispenser. She sniffled as she wiped her tears and painfully swallowed a buildup of thick phlegm. She threw the paper towel away once she was done and stared at herself in the mirror a second time. Raccoon ringlets of mascara smudged her eyes. She sighed. After a moment, she cried, and let the teardrops slowly run down her face.

***

The diner was empty by the time she left the bathroom. Abigail stood at the counter, doodling on her notepad.

"There you are!" Abigail cried once she spotted her. "I was wondering where you went."

"Just had to use the restroom for a bit," Jenny said, smiling. "No biggie."

"Your tall, dark, and handsome just left, you know. I think he was sorta disappointed you weren't there to talk with him."

"That's fine. He'll be back next time."

"Left another present for you."

At this, Jenny's phony smile disappeared, and another cold feeling filled her stomach. She uttered a nonchalant "Oh" and walked towards the booth where the man had been sitting. A Country Fried Steak with mashed potatoes sat idly untouched at the table; condensed water droplets covered the sides of his drinking glass, the ice cubes, having partially melted.

Jenny removed the plate and found two crisp bills lying on the table. She reached out with a trembling hand and collected them, feeling something sigh deep inside of her. When she unfolded them—two fifty-dollar bills smelling clean and recently withdrawn from an ATM—she saw two letters neatly written on the upper corners. The letters read: *J.J.*

# CHAPTER 2

She arrived home at five o' clock that morning. When she stepped into the house, she kicked off her shoes and heard the loud grumble of John's Honda Civic disappearing into the night. The headlights momentarily flashed through the windows and sprayed the walls with a white surprising glare. John often gave her rides because his home was just another two miles in the same direction east of Crescent Rim. Jenny had a license, but owned no private vehicle herself. She took a cab to the diner whenever Tom was on his business trips, and supposed it was just one of the many—though less than subtle—ways he emotionally (and, perhaps, psychologically) tamed her.

Pain throbbed through her feet as she entered the house and closed the door behind her. Jenny forced herself into a ball on the floor and sat back against the door. She drew her legs in and pressed her forehead against her knees. An ache began in her temples. It was an ache filled with lead, *hot* lead, molten lead, throbbing lead, weighing inside her head like a massive pendulum swinging back and forth in the dark. Jenny sobbed for a few minutes (though not really—no, not really. They were just hoarse gasps in the dark), and then picked herself up when she was done.

She walked barefoot through the dark and stopped in the living room. A red eerie light blinked in the center of the living room. It was the answering machine.

*It's probably Tom*, Jenny thought numbly as she walked over and pushed the PLAY button. *He's probably calling to say he won't be back until tomorrow evening again and that he's out of Boise.*

The answering machine whirred to life.

"Jenny."

*Bingo.*

"It's me. Look, I'm getting held up at the office again and Bradley is meeting me tomorrow at noon. I need you to fax me the Whittingham documents when you have time tomorrow morning. I need them before two o' clock. I'll be back Friday. Thanks. Love you."

The message ended with a dull beep. Jenny shuddered at the abrupt stop and hugged herself.

The wine stains were still there. Even in total darkness of the living room, one could make out their original shapes spilled across the carpet. The stains looked like splattered gunshot wounds. *Grape juice*, some part of her wanted to say, but was unsure. Another part of her mind laughed when seeing the stains, and said wryly: *All that's needed now is a chalked outline of my body lying on the floor.*

Jenny shuddered. She closed her eyes for a minute and swayed quietly on her feet. She turned around after a few seconds and headed for the stairs.

She took her pants off midway up the stairs. She grabbed the pins in her hair and tossed them to the side. Soon she was undoing her blouse, slipping out of her underwear, unhooking her bra, and then was fully naked by the time she reached the second floor. She trembled when a cold draft of air touched her skin, and realized, with an odd sense of bitter irony, that her nakedness in the dark like this was quite liberating, freeing…*good*. In this moment of cold blindness and dark, there was nothing but the metaphoric securities of being carried in the protective wombs of a fading night.

*Who would have thought,* a voice whispered from somewhere behind her, *that being naked like this could feel so good? That this nakedness was actually warm, comforting…safe?*

She reached the bathroom and stepped into the shower. She turned on the hot water and waited for it to burn her skin. She'd kept the lights off.

Tom would be back soon. His message hadn't indicated when, but it didn't matter—he would be back soon. The physical conditions of the house fell on her shoulders where she was meant to maintain all that was already faultless and clean. She would clean; she would work. She would tidy what had become unruly due to minute moments of neglect, and take care of all that seemed imperfect. Tom was keen with his nose and knew if she ever cheated on him with her shower. He was also uncannily aware with his sense of sight and could detect any imperfections she failed to correct. He liked things pristine, Jenny knew; he liked things *cleaned*. In Tom's world, men were beautiful clean creatures endowed with superb qualities. *Business*men, then, were even cleaner, and required stupendous amounts of effort to properly maintain themselves. A perfectly set smile with full white teeth, a strong dominate jaw-line with chiseled chin and stern nose, broad shoulders, clean-cut and expertly jelled hair—all of these, despite their grand and immense importance, fell subordinate to one simple Tom rule: If it didn't *smell* clean, then it was just *shit* clean.

Tom had to reteach this lesson to her a month ago. Back then, the days had been quiet and serene. School had ended, and Teacher Tom had momentarily retired from instructing. Had Jenny been a good student? She had been—indeed she had been, and summer school had no longer been an option on Tom's mind. Her status as a student was mediocre, but her efforts were grand. There were, of course, occasions where he still tutored, but these moments were breathlessly brief. There were, for example, moments where she'd clumsily trip over her own tangling feet and spill water across the carpet, other moments where she'd mindlessly load their laundry together without removing her lipstick, and other times when she slammed the door too loudly when returning home from work and woke him up in bed. There were fleeting moments where she failed to remove a coffee stain from his business suit, foolishly uttered a stupid comment in front of his clients, and other times where'd she forget the essential rule of having absolutely NO food or drinks in the car. So, yes—while school was out of session and Tom no longer taught as an instructor, he most certainly still *tutored*, and what he tutored were lessons primarily consisting of hard, cold, dreadful stares in the eyes, a warning slap to the face or thighs, a simple pinching of the arms or breasts, or a quick palm-slap to the cheek. Nothing more. Excluding the ridiculous act of sharing a 'romantic' evening together eating greasy pizza and drinking cheap wine (an act so obscene that Tom had dubbed such an occasion as 'pornographic' in his mind on the night he'd smeared pizza in her face), there were no great urgent lessons that needed to be learned, and Jenny had proven herself to be a satisfactory pupil.

All of this changed last month when Jenny had been making breakfast in the kitchen. She'd been scrambling eggs then. Tom always asked for scrambled eggs when considering his breakfast meals. It was a demand that seemed mind-numbing and meticulously typical: three slices of sizzling Italian pancetta peppered bacon, two links of plump Swaggerty's Farm breakfast sausages, and three cracked Wilcox Family Farms' Omega 3 eggs. His choice of drink was always Tropicana Full Premium orange juice, no pulp. Pulp had a strange aftertaste to it. Jenny always made sure to follow these rules.

"Jenny, babe. What's this?"

She'd turned around with a happy smile on her face and a light giddiness in her heart. Her impression was that he'd say something congratulatory to her for waking early that morning and cleaning the kitchen. She'd vacuumed the day before and had scrubbed the bathrooms to utter perfection. The Acworths had a large estate that was quite generous for any middle-class American, and the cleaning of the drapes, the dusting of the tables and shelves, changing of the bed sheets—the vacuuming of the carpet, taking out the trash, washing the dishes—and the scrubbing of the bathroom tiles had all been untold labors unto themselves. And yet, Jenny had done it all for him, and had been delighted (if not relieved) when she'd been praised for her efforts.

She turned around expecting a surprised smile on his face. What she saw instead was a dull look of rage in his eyes and their pillow cases in his hands.

They were the same pillow cases they used when sleeping together. Jenny knew instantly what she'd done wrong.

"Jenny."

"I…I forgot!" she stammered. She quickly ran over. "Oh jeez, I'm so sorry, Tom, I'm so sorry. Jesus, I was just so tired last night, I didn't think of taking a shower before sleeping. I know, I'm sorry, my hair smelled so bad last night, but--"

He backhanded her. The blow came out of nowhere and smashed the left side of her face, sending her to the ground. Her limbs tangled together like a broken puppet.

*Don't hurt me*, her mind whimpered. *Oh, please, whatever he does, don't let him hurt me, don't let him hurt me, please, God—*

"Wash these, Jenny. I want you to wash these. Do you understand?"

She nodded. A pulsating throb radiated from the corner of her left eye. She brought her hand to her face and felt one side swell with fire. "Please, Tom," she sobbed. She tried looking at him. "I didn't…I didn't mean to. I'm sorry. Please."

He stared at her. Jenny sobbed again and drew herself into a ball. His rings—they hurt so bad when he smacked her like that.

"Do you remember the Rahmans?" he asked her. "Huh, Jenny?"

She nodded. She didn't really, but it was stupid to say otherwise.

"And do you know that the Rahmans are close partners with Mr. Lassek?"

"Tom, please. I said I'm sorry. My face…"

"The Lasseks are at the top of the chain, Jenny! They're *top*. Do you understand?"

She nodded.

"I'm going to meet Mr. Rahmans and his family tonight. I'm going to dress in my best business suit and offer them the best deal they're going to see. But do you know what might hold me back from making that deal, Jenny?"

27

Jenny shook her head. He threw the pillow cases at her.

"*This* Jenny. This right here. No salesman makes a sale if they smell like this. Do you understand? Do you think I can go to sleep smelling like wasted grease shit and then wear a suit to work and expect to make a sale? This shit smells so bad it can't even be washed off at the cleaners!"

He stomped his foot down. Jenny squealed. She backed away and huddled against the leg of their dining room table.

"Wash these," he told her again. "Wash them, Jenny. And make them clean, do you understand? Make them clean. And next time you decide to come home smelling like that stupid diner place you work at, next time consider: What will *Tom* think? What will he have to say once he starts smelling like his stupid wife? Okay?"

Jenny nodded. She watched soberly as he walked back up the stairs and stared at the pillow cases. Tears ran down her cheeks. She carefully got up and gathered the cases, clutching them to her chest.

Stupid. She'd just been so goddamn stupid again. He had *called* her stupid, and Jenny supposed he'd been right, although being called stupid still hurt. In ways she couldn't explain, being called stupid like that was akin to being hit in the face with a blunt fist that broke one's nose. Perhaps the pain was much worse; perhaps the pain was so horrible that only analogies could be used to describe the pain. When said with a snarl, being called stupid was a deep cut to the heart that stabbed directly beneath the skin. The marks on her face healed after a few weeks, but the nature of words…they sank deep beneath the rings of mascara and by-passed thick layers of foundation. Concealer could not conceal the hurt of words, for words rang forever in one's memory. His fists made it hard to breathe, hard to live, but they were bearable. Manageable. But words…words could not heal like skin.

*You hurt me, Tom,* Jenny thought soberly, clutching the pillow cases, *not just with your fists, but with your words, too. Do you understand? Do you understand how much words weigh? You may not understand, but I do, and I have to take it so much in my heart. I woke up this morning trying to please you, made you breakfast, and now…*

Jenny's heart stopped. Her face went blank and her eyes widened. She dropped the pillow cases to the ground and ran back to the kitchen.

"Oh, God, no, no!"

She ran over and switched off the stove. Sparks of bacon fat jumped from the frying pan and stung her arm. She screamed. She flinched backward and sought desperately for a rag. Not only had she left the scrambled eggs to go dry and ruin, but she'd also forgotten all about the bacon strips. They lay crispy and burnt looking like shortened muscle appendages shriveling into decaying worms.

Tom didn't like his bacon too crispy.

"Jesus, not today, not today, please God, *not today!*"

She found a rag on the counter and wrapped it around the handle of the frying pan. There was no sense to what she was doing—any other sane person would have just let the boiling pan settle, pour the waste out, and remake breakfast. But today her heart was in a panic and her mind was in overdrive (not to mention that her face was swelling fat with pain too), so when another splash of burning oil popped out and burned her hand, Jenny screamed again, dropping the entire pan of sizzling bacon on her feet.

"*OH GOD, NO! NO, PLEASE!*"

Hot oil burned her toes. Jenny screamed and jumped into the air. One bare foot came directly down against the hot surface of the frying pan, causing her to howl.

"Jenny?"

Tom's voice. Somewhere upstairs in the bathroom.

"Jenny, what's going on down there?"

"NOTHING!" she screeched. "Nothing! Everything's fine!"

She hobbled to the sink and turned on the water. She brought the rag up, placed it under the rushing faucet, and then desperately wrapped it around her foot. She sat back for a minute and cried, pounding her fists on the kitchen tiles.

*This can't be my life anymore. It just can't be. Please, God, was I really born to suffer all of this?*

Ten whole minutes passed before breakfast resumed again, and by then, Jenny's foot had grown red and tender on the sole. Had Tom spotted her slipping around crying, he'd have it in mind to do more than just teach her a lesson: He would have brought her to detention. And if detention wouldn't teach her, he would have brought her to boarding school—and no doubt too the boarding school of his choosing would have closely resembled the shape of a hospital.

But Jenny was lucky. Tom was a man who liked things *cleaned*. His time in the shower was like a man performing a religious ceremony.

"These look great, babe," he said to her once he was done. He sat at the breakfast table and looked at her. "Something wrong, babe?"

Jenny shook her head at him. She did it in a tentative, shy way. She simply offered him a brief waning smile and told him quietly: "I burnt my foot." When asked where, she'd shown him her foot, now wrapped in a bandage. Tom frowned at her. She needed to be careful, he told her. Also—had she washed the pillow cases yet?

"Love you, Jen," he said once he was at the doorway. Jenny nodded and let him cup her face before kissing her on the cheek.

"Love you too, Tom," she whispered as he walked away. "I...I love you too."

***

The glass doors drew back, and Jenny finally stepped out of the shower. She reached blindly for a towel and felt her fingers touch something soft and light hanging on the wall. Silence followed as she dried herself in the dark.

Yes—Tom said he loved her that day. He had whispered it in her ear like a terrible secret. And when he'd come back from work later that afternoon, he'd been gentle when making love to her, caressing her breasts this time, not cruelly squeezing them, telling her that he was sorry if he'd upset her. And Jenny had, like always, ignored his last remark, telling him to just hold her, to stop talking, and to let him take her away so she could become drunk with the dark.

He'd said he loved her that day.

Dim flickers of violet crept through the curtained windows and spilled darkly along the marble floor. Morning was here. Jenny dried the last bits of her hair and threw the towel to the floor. She hesitated. Why should she care? Tom wouldn't be back until Friday. All her clothes tossed out on the stairs, her partially dried and fully naked body in the dark—these were *hers*, weren't they?

*Crazy*, Jenny thought as she turned off the bathroom fan. *Just…going crazy with what little happiness I have. Christ.*

She left the bathroom and entered the hallway. Like before, she kept all the lights off as she walked, and, like before, she walked freely and naked in the dark. She entered their bedroom, found their large king-sized bed, and flopped down with a happy sigh.

*He knows you've been crying.*

Jenny groaned. She rolled on her side and drew in her legs.

*The man*, her mind whispered, *the man at Red Moon's. He knows you've been crying.*

*I don't care. Leave me alone. Tired.*

*Crying…the man…he knows you've been crying.*

Fading. Yes, she was fading. She was just fading away from the world. The blankets beneath her body felt nice and cool while the darkness around her was quiet and heavy. She was fading. Just fading.

*The man…he's…he's always there, that man, he's always…*

*there that man he's always*

*always he's*

*there he…*

*he…*

*he—*

31

# CHAPTER 3

—felt a sense of dread in her chest that morning as the bell rang.

Jenny raised her head. She stared at the clock in front of her and closed her textbook. A heavy feeling plummeted into her stomach as she heard the bell, and she released a dull, heavy, miserable sigh.

Morning. Morning was here. And with it, the beginning of the week as announced by the early hours of Monday.

The bell echoed in Jenny's ears and traveled slowly through the acoustic hallways of Evanston-Woods High School. The sound was not jarring and was not sharp: It instead produced a soft tonal *bing...bing...bing* echo that was reminiscent of an entrancing lullaby before sleep. Jenny hated the sound. Her eyelids drooped whenever hearing the noise, and her heart sighed with a quiet sobriety. Rather than jolt her awake with agitation and nervousness, the bell only produced a life-threatening calm in her that made her want to sleep through her all classes.

It was *not* a great thing to hear.

The bell signaled the beginning of Ms. Karens' IB Senior History American class. As Jenny heard the soft bings of the morning bell begin to fade, she turned her head to the side and watched despondently as the doors opened. Students filed through the doors one by one, shadows of unhappiness beneath their eyes, their shoulders uneven, fat overstuffed backpacks lugged across their backs. They grunted and grumbled when making their way towards the tables. Zippers unzipped and buttons unbuttoned; the IB class of 2005 stripped off their raincoats and autumn sweaters with an almost solemn ritual. It was a grim ceremony Jenny had observed frequently since enrolling in Ms. Karens' IB class: The sight of her classmates settling down for the morning while stripping off their outer wear always reminded her of ancient warriors preparing for battle. That her warrior-classmates were simply weary-eyed teenagers did not belie the irony: EWHS's mascots were the Soldiers, and those who entered class this morning seemed anything but.

Outside, oceanic gray clouds painted Seattle's skies with a bleak morning shade.

Ms. Karens' IB class began at 7:30 a.m. and contained twenty-five students. Jenny, of course, belonged to these twenty-five, but she was not part of the IB world proper. The IB program was the International Baccalaureate program. The program was, according to colloquial lips of passing students, the educational *elite* program that was reserved for *only* the most intelligent and brightest of students. Jenny didn't know if she belonged to this category.

Those who partook in the program found themselves breathlessly bombarded with incalculable amounts of schoolwork. Those who could only withstand a few IB classes prided themselves as partial-IB students, while those who found the thought of sleepless nights and endless hours of note-taking masochistically wonderful prided themselves as *full*-IB students. Jenny, of course, was the former. She was enrolled in Ms. Karens' IB American History class as the only partial-IB student, and found her position incredibly forlorn and lonesome (there were only a hundred or so full IB students at EWHS). It was common to have partials and fulls intermingled in the same IB classes. Somehow, though, Jenny had ended up as the only partial-IB student in Ms. Karens'.

She didn't like the IB Program.

*Lonely,* Jenny sometimes thought when staring out at the windows. *I'm surrounded by over two thousand people at this school, and I only have enough thought to say that I'm lonely. Why does it rain so much in Seattle? And why do I care?*

It was times like these—times where staring outside the windows seemed like the most natural, the most desirable, perhaps, even, the most sorrowful—that the loneliness in Jenny's chest took on a sharp poignant point of realization, and she'd cruelly be reminded of the shape of her eyes again. Moreover, in this somber silence of staring out at the thin naked autumn trees as the only partial-IB student, Jenny would be reminded of her *ethnicity.*

She did not giggle; she did not chirp. She did not follow the latest Korean dramas online, and gave no thoughts at all to the Korean Wave that was now so overwhelmingly sweeping through all of Asia. She took no quirky pictures of herself with her cell phone, did not pucker her lips to appear obediently cute, and did not follow the latest fashion trends, styles, celebrities, or music that came from her "homeland." She carried no purse with her, and she wore only typical black-gray sweaters to school with regular old skintight jeans for girls. Nearly all her clothes were from The North Face online store.

Conversation always regressed into awkward pauses whenever with her Korean kinsfolk at lunch. These pauses were slight and hardly overt, akin to the subtle interrupted heartbeats before a startled gasp. Jenny noticed them, though. She noticed them, and whenever with her 'friends', she'd always see indistinct signaling going through the table. Glances went her way and scrutiny went through the eyes of her Korean friends; conversation shifted into slight alternate directions. The eyes that scrutinized her wondered openly if trust could be maintained with a girl whose face was clearly derived from South Korean descent (which was a radically different derivation from those in the North, apparently), and whether or not  trust could be given in return. The glances moreover blatantly wondered how much of her upbringing in America had Americanized her, and—perhaps this being the most crucial question of all—whether or not she still retained the ability to speak her native tongue.

Several weeks ago, Sarah Ryu had approached her in the library and asked to speak with her. Sarah was a girl Jenny once regularly saw at church, but was someone she hardly ever spoke with. She was in full IB. She was also Korean.

"Mind if we speak in the conference room?" Sarah had asked, somewhat conspicuously. Her voice was charming but also a bit demanding. Jenny thought there was a bit of urgency in it as well.

"Um, sure," Jenny replied. "Okay."

They found one of the study rooms in the library, and Sarah slowly closed the door. Jenny watched with a suspicious frown as Sarah placed her laptop bag on the table and removed her backpack.

"Have you been busy these past few weeks?" Sarah began. "Like, I don't see you at church anymore."

Jenny stared at her. She scanned her round face and saw a deliberate expression in her eyes. She released a sigh.

The church Jenny attended—or rather, once attended—was a Korean Presbyterian Church located in Mountlake Terrace, west of Lake Ballinger. It was a medium-sized church that served as the focal point for every local Korean community north of Seattle. The church—having no true name other than what colloquial tongues called the Second Korean Presbyterian Church in Mountlake Terrace—was situated in a wooded area next to a preschool. Sermons were given both in Korean and in English with the latter meant to reach out to younger people.

Pastor Oh had given a sermon last week entitled "The Greatest Gift." This "gift" was a gift that needed not be reciprocated or held in debt, Pastor Oh had taught them. It was a gift given freely with all thoughts of altruism held sound in the giver's mind. It was not the free lending of money or the lending of a helping hand. The Greatest Gift, in fact, was the Word of God, and Pastor Oh had been adamant of how great this gift was. This gift was so great in fact, that Pastor Oh had asked for volunteers to stay behind to make a special oath to deliver this "gift" to others. Jenny had remembered seeing Sarah staying behind with several other members of her youth group. Jenny didn't know what they were doing, but suspected that they were performing an initiation of some kind.

She'd stayed away from church since then. There was life to live, and since life was filled with so many gods already, Jenny decided that it was just better to live life without any gods to worry about, gift or not. Her parents had regarded her decision with basic apathy. Now, apparently, it seemed like her jealous God wanted her back.

"I've just been busy, that's all," Jenny said, carefully eyeing her. Sarah stood directly between her and the door. "I'm kind of struggling to keep up these days."

"Yeah, I hear that. Being a senior sucks right now in IB."

Jenny watched as she removed something from her backpack. She cringed when she saw what it was. It was a Bible.

"Do you remember Pastor Oh's sermon a few weeks ago about the Greatest Gift?" Sarah asked. "The last time you were at church, I mean."

"Um. Kinda."

Sarah removed something from the inner pages of her Bible—a frown cut through Jenny's face. It was a white notecard with dark boldface font printed on both sides. The title of the card was clear to Jenny even from where she stood across the table. It read: THE ROMANS' ROAD.

"If you don't mind," Sarah began, "I'd like to, like, say a few things to you before you leave. I haven't seen you at church these days, and I'm kind of getting worried. You know?"

Jenny said nothing. She waited for her to go on and realized that she was waiting for a signal. "Okay," she sighed dully.

Sarah said: "Pastor Oh told us that the Greatest Gift one could give to someone else they loved was the Word of God. Well, I'm here to say that I love you, Jenny Park, and that I see you as an older sister. Because of that—and because it seems like you've lost your way a bit and are no longer attending church—I'd like to read for you something that Pastor Oh taught us. It's called the Romans' Road, and it's supposed to be the sharing of salvation. I'd like to read it to you so that you remember what the Good News is about again."

Sarah cleared her throat. She brought the card in front of her face and held it at arm's length as if giving a formal presentation. She said: "The Romans' Road clearly defines who needs salvation; why they need salvation; how God provides that salvation; how we receive that salvation; and the results of salvation. Romans 3:10 to 3:12 begins with: 'As it is written: There is no one righteous, not even one; there is no one who understands; there is no one who seeks God. All have turned—'"

"Stop."

Sarah looked up. "Stop?"

"Just stop it," Jenny said. "I've heard it all before. You don't need to read it. I know it already."

Sarah frowned at her, her eyes quickly darting back and forth. She said, "Right. Um, I know. But I really just want to read it to you again so that you'll remember what it means to—"

"I already know. Thanks, but you don't have to read it. I got it, Sarah."

Another sour look went through Sarah's face. Her lips pursed together and her cheeks went fat. She said again, "I think it's important if you heard this though. It's the most important thing you'll ever hear, Jenny. I'm doing you a favor."

Jenny stared at her. A cold feeling of hurt entered her chest. She eyed her, thoughtfully, carefully, even almost pityingly, and said to her: "You're not doing me a favor. And you are *not* doing this out of love for me, Sarah."

"I *am* doing this out of love for you. I love you because I—"

"No, you're doing this because Pastor Oh *told* you to!" Jenny cried. "You're doing this because it's your *job*, something that you hold as your Christian *duty!* If you really did love you me, you would have loved me out of your own freewill! You would have come to me without seeing me as a...a...*means* to your ends. You would have been sincere!"

"But I'm *trying* to be," Sarah said back. "Jenny. Calm down. Can't you see that I'm doing this *because* of God's love? God is the ultimate form of love, and He—"

"*You're loving* for *Him instead of loving for your*self!*" Jenny shirked back. Hot tears tickled the bottom of her eyes. "I thought you came up to me wanting to speak to me and be my friend. I thought that…that you'd ask me about my day or whatever, ask how I was doing without taking out your Bible. Now I see you just care out of duty and obligation. You don't care to love. You can't even *care* to love without even being ordered to do so. If you needed to have some old book tell you how to love, have a community of people direct you to love, then you never loved authentically as a human being!"

Sarah gaped at her. Her eyes bulged out wide like fat beetles on her face.

"You've lost sight, Jenny," she said quietly. "I'm so sorry seeing you like this, but you lost sight of God's teachings. You don't get that I came to you today because I love you, and because of this love wanted to give you the ultimate gift of salvation. I wanted to *save* you."

"Do you love a *dog* so much you begin treating it like a *cat?*"

Sarah's mouth dropped. Disbelief filled her face. Her eyes searched Jenny's face for a minute, and a hot flash of embarrassment spread through her cheeks. The statement had been said in Korean.

*There it is,* Jenny thought bitterly. *There's that look of surprise again when people realize I can speak Korean. There's that look that brands me as an outsider from Korean culture. It's the same look that Americans have when I speak English, looks that are surprised that I can exist in two worlds. I'm meant to be Korean but am told that I have to conform first; I'm meant to be American but am told to be a stereotype first. Where do I exist, and where can I find someone just to appreciate me for who I am?*

"When you love your *dog*," Jenny continued, still speaking in Korean, "do you force it to be a cat? Do you teach it how to meow, how to eat fish? Or do you just love it naturally and let it be its own thing, *loving* it as it is? Do you love your dog like a cat because people tell you to, or do you love it because it's simply your friend?"

"We're not animals," Sarah said back. Her voice had gone quiet. There'd been a momentary pause before speaking. "And…and I'm not trying to love you out of…of obligation. Or duty."

*And yet you come to me telling me what Pastor Oh has taught you without having once asked about my day,* Jenny thought coldly. She shouldered on her backpack and walked towards the door. *You don't even know about my struggles in my IB classes, Sarah, don't even know about the problems I have at home or about how lonely I am. And now you say you love me. You can't even think for yourself without having someone else telling you how to think.*

"I chose to love *you*," Sarah cried. "Don't you get it? I *chose* to approach you today Jenny! I chose to decide to bring you God's Word and love you. I just want to *help*."

"If you choose to love," Jenny shot back, "why do you have to love like a Christian? Why can't you love me as a person? Is being human not good enough for you?"

Sarah said nothing. She just stared downward and lowered her eyes, unable to answer. Jenny stepped towards her.

"Move out of the way, Sarah. I need to go to class."

"Wait. What can I say to make you come back to church with me? What can I make you see Pastor Oh again and—"

"I'm older than you, Ryu Saerom. *Move.* I'm giving you an *order*."

Sarah's eyes widened and her lips sucked back into her mouth. A clear look of hurt—so obvious now, there between her eyes—cut through her brow as an ugly frown. She'd spoken in Korean again. Only now this time she'd uttered Sarah's Korean name and called herself older.

Sarah moved back and lowered her head. She stayed silent.

"If you really need to be told to love, then you're not capable of loving at all," Jenny said. She opened the door. "And if you have to be told to be friends with someone, then you're not a trustworthy friend. Love shouldn't be a duty, Christian or not. It should be about choice."

"But I wasn't trying to do—"

Jenny stepped out of the room, slamming the door shut.

Wicked scorn had greeted her the following day. And with it, a cold poisonous reproach that made Jenny feel unsafe sitting at her usual spot in the lunchroom. Conversation had lagged; sly glances had shot her way. There'd been delivered whispers covered by cupping hands, sly plastic smiles delivered in her direction, and jubilant fake laughter at things not funny. All the girls at her lunch table spoke in high-pitched falsetto Korean, but when they switched speaking into English, their voices dropped to a basso profundo American slang. Dark glances stole her way whenever their voices changed. They were derisive and accusing, those voices, intentionally mocking, and were, in part, a mockery of her own voice when speaking English.

Jenny had gotten up from her meal and gone to the bathroom. She'd cried in the bathroom. She'd locked the stall door behind her, sat on the toilet, and cupped her hands to her face, smothering her sobs. She'd cried like that for half-an-hour with warm salt in her mouth, and swallowed what felt like a gallon of snot in her throat. She'd skipped sixth and eighth period that day (Evanston-Woods High School revolved around an alternate even-odd day schedule with one hour and thirty minute classes), and had gone home to cry some more in bed.

She didn't eat in the lunchroom anymore.

***

Barks of laughter erupted behind her. Jenny jerked in her seat and turned around, jarred from her thoughts.

Mark Padamada and Anthony Pagaliluan high-fived each other in the back of class. They laughed at nothing in particular, and cried out loudly, "Hell yeah, man!" They sat backwards in their chairs leaned against the wall. Five other boys sat with them, their sneakered feet resting comfortably on the table. When Jenny turned around to see what had startled her, all she saw in their direction were uneven grooves of rubber soles pointed her way.

40

Their laptops were out and set on the table between their feet. Jenny couldn't hear exactly what they were all listening to, but thought it was another random YouTube clip they'd found to amuse themselves. Maybe it was porn.

*Happy,* Jenny thought quietly. *When with friends, people are just happy even when they can just be idiots. When alone, though..., you're just yourself as an individual when alone, and always just lonely. Being yourself always means to be lonely. This is the sacrifice needed for individuality.*

"Dude, Ms. Karens is coming, Ms. Karens is coming!"

Jenny turned her head. She looked to the side and saw her teacher making her way through the flex area towards their classroom. An uneasy flip-flop went through her stomach. She spotted sheets of paper in her teacher's hands, and realized they were quiz papers. Her teacher had come late to class to print out a quiz.

*Fuck me,* Jenny thought weary. She closed her eyes and pressed her hands against her face. *This is going to hurt. This is going to hurt my grade so bad.*

The doors to the classroom opened, Ms. Karens entered, and Jenny let out a tired sigh.

\*\*\*

A mild gale began when school let out. It cut through Jenny's sweater and chilled her skin, causing her to shiver. She walked through the school parking lot with her arms folded under her chest and kicked aside a few straying leaves that swirled around her ankles. Strands of hair blew wildly around her shoulders and brushed her ears.

Students rushed by and crowded the parking lot. They got into their cars and sped away, eager to get home. Jenny heard a few shouts beside her, a few laughs, and occasionally heard the thunderous sound of blasting music from booming speakers. There were mechanical grunts that erupted to the sides as engines started, some more rambunctious calls across the lot, and soon the parking lot was alive with zipping vehicles and honking horns. It was all a loud spectacle to Jenny's ears.

*Look at how many people leave school together as friends,* she thought somberly. *Look at how many of us carpool with one another, laugh with one another, and just go home with one another. And look how sad I'm sounding to my own ears when speaking like this, as if I had nothing better to do than feel sorry for myself. Self-pity sneaks up so cheaply.*

She thought of Sarah again, and in thinking of her, released another heavy sigh.

The religious Korean community drew heavily from western traditions derived from Protestantism and Roman Catholicism. Those who believed in these two religious sects were vast. Jenny had completed a research essay in her IB Junior Psychology class, and had found, to the bewilderment of her own perceived understandings of the world, that thirty percent of her native South Korea strictly adhered to one of the aforementioned religions. Another twenty percent subscribed to Buddhism, while the final fifty percent were irreligious. Of the latter, "small religions" such as shamanism, Taoism, and Confucianism fell into the irreligious category.

In 1958, David Yonggi Choi founded the largest Pentecostal church on Yeouido in Seoul, South Korea, called the Yoido Full Gospel Church. The church since then had become the largest Pentecostal Christian congregation in South Korea—as well as the entire *world*. A recent article by Robert Muller in *Modern Christians of Today* focused on Samuel Lee, executive director of World Wide Korean Mission Associations. The article had compared Western missionaries to that of South Korean missionaries. Already, South Korea had equaled the number of American missionaries, and was soon predicted to surpass their western counterparts in the near future. In a *BBC News* article simply titled *S. Korea's Religious Zeal,* James M. Stanwood wrote of South Korea's religious fervor, and of the nearly unyielding passion South Korea had for sending their missionaries into hostile environments. These 'hostile' environments, apparently, all belonged to the Muslim world. The article had been brisk. It had simply declared at the end: "Korean Christians know no bounds. Nearly 1,000 missionaries are sent each year overseas to places all over the world with little rest, little hesitation, and little cultural sensitivity."

In other words: Her Korean identity necessitated that she belong to a religious order. Always.

Her encounter with Sarah Ryu last month had been minor. The malicious glares she'd received at the lunchroom by her Korean kinsfolk, aside from the painful loneliness they offered, had been mild. Her most severe encounter (perhaps "clash") with her Korean religious identity had occurred three years ago when she was fifteen. At that time, it was Pastor Hwang who led the Second Korean Presbyterian Church. Pastor Hwang often came by to observe the English sermons and regularly taught the Korean sermons on Saturdays. He was an older gentleman who wore his features like battle scars: Angry eyebrows shaped the daggered look of his eyes; heavy wrinkles gave his expression a permanent pit-bull scowl. When speaking, his voice was heavy and demanded respectful listening from all those around him. Rumors said Pastor Hwang was a once-upon-a-time boxer who had won numerous boxing titles in a very-long-ago Korea. The rumors didn't surprise Jenny. The bulk he carried beneath his robes was hardened middle-aged-man muscle—not fat—and she could see at times the muscles of his forearms naturally bulging when rolling up his sleeves.

He was a brutish man. He was also the man who would punch her in the face and break her nose for questioning God.

As was the custom when finishing praise, all those who wanted to stay behind in church and speak with their youth leaders did, and Jenny on this occasion had forced herself to remain. The reason was simple: A recent death had just occurred in her family. Her *imo*, her maternal aunt, had just died in Korea, and her mother had been devastated. Her *imo* had been heinously struck by a driver and killed in the accident. It was a stupid accident and stupid death; Jenny hated the driver for making her mother cry. Her parents had plans to return to Korea to attend the funeral while she remained in America with a family friend (her parents wouldn't allow her to skip school). In the meantime, though, Jenny wanted answers. Her *imo* had been a practicing Buddhist before she died. She did not believe in Christ. That meant she was in Hell.

"Why look, everyone! It's Jenny! Jenny Park!"

Jenny offered a timid smile and nodded her head as a slight bow before entering the room. Her youth leader—Kim Sungmin—waved at her and gestured for her to sit down. The youth group sessions were regularly held in the preschool part of the church. Drinks were provided with a few snacks on the small table near the center of the room, and a cluster of chairs had been brought up to the front. Sungmin stood near the chairs and beamed at her. He indicated for her to take a seat and gave her a quick grin when she sat down. He held a Bible in his hands.

"Finally decided to let God speak to you, huh, Jenny?"

Jenny nodded. She thought for a moment, and then was at a loss of words. She bit her lip and felt an unsettling silence fall around her. Curious eyes darted her way. There were sixteen in her youth group, and most already knew of her apprehension toward God. To them, she was just an uneven seventeenth.

"I just thought…I don't know. I just thought I'd come by and say hi and stuff."

"Well, great!" Sungmin said. "We could always use more believers in this room. Welcome back to the pack, Jenny!"

Awkward claps spread through the room as Sungmin urged everyone to cheer. Jenny asked: "Is Pastor Hwang going to be coming by soon?"

"Indeed he is, Ms. Jenny Park. Stay for a while, and let's all praise God together!"

Weary groans filled the room.

They spoke of God, read from the Bible, sang some praise, and then spoke more of God. They discussed the parable about the sower and the seeds, chatted about current affairs in the Korean entertainment world (anti-fans were just *shit-crazy*, declared one person), prayed for each other's problems, and then spoke more about God again. Jenny sat quiet all throughout and stared continually to the side.

Where *was* Pastor Hwang?

"The quiet type, right, Jenny?" Sungmin said to her, breaking her thoughts. He gave her a light grin "I apologize if my lessons aren't as powerful as Pastor Kim's."

She turned her head. "I...no. No, I'm sorry, that's not it. I just was hoping for Pastor—"

The door opened. Pastor Hwang appeared.

"Pastor Hwang!"

Sungmin approached the pastor with a smile on his face. Before he reached out to shake the pastor's hand, he lightly bowed his head, greeted him in Korean, and said: "Please, right this way. We've been waiting for you."

"Good boy," the pastor said, speaking briefly in old, rugged, and broken English. "Good day today."

Jenny watched as the legendary pastor made his way over and sat down in a chair. She was surprised to see the pastor wheeze a bit as he sat down, and was even greater alarmed when, instead of sitting upright and rigid in the chair, he gradually slumped backward with a tired slouch. His feet stuck out like two dead black birds from beneath his Geneva gown.

Jenny eyed him carefully. She heard herself think, *Pastor Hwang is dying,* and chided herself. Gooseflesh spread through her arms.

The final reading of the Bible began. Afterwards, Sungmin introduced his group to the great pastor. Sungmin spoke in English, and Jenny saw the eyes of her youth group gazing curiously—but not appreciatively—at their eldest church leader. Finally, toward the very end, Sungmin allowed them to ask questions.

"Is it true that you were once a boxer, Pastor Hwang?" a girl, Lee Jungyoon, asked. "Others have said you were. I don't want to be impolite, but I'd like to know too. Um, sir."

Sungmin translated the question. Pastor Hwang smiled (or scowled, Jenny thought). He said, "Ten years I boxed," in slow, lengthy English. "I won a lot."

Nervous laughter followed. Several others raised their hands and asked similar questions. Pastor Hwang graciously answered.

Jenny looked around her and frowned at her peers. Here in their midst was an authority figure, that, presumably, was closer to God than all of them, and now her peers simply wanted to know how many boxing matches he'd won? They wanted to know how often he went back to Korea, which were his favorite cuisines, and how old his children were? None of them were brave enough to ask questions about *God*? Were they really that afraid of the *truth*?

Jenny rose from her seat. She rose so lithely that she herself barely realized what she was doing. Those around her who felt her move became silent, and stared.

"Pastor Hwang," she said evenly. She spoke in Korean. "I have a question to ask."

The pastor looked at her. He regarded her briefly, and then said, "Ask away, daughter," with a gesture of his hand.

She asked, "Is it true that only through Christ we will find salvation?"

"Yes."

"And salvation is eternal life with God."

"Yes."

"What about those of us who don't believe in God?"

A suspicious frown crept through the pastor's eyes, further scarring his already withered face. He said thickly: "It is clearly stated in the Bible: Those who do not accept Jesus Christ as the true and ultimate Savior are condemned to Hell. This is the unfortunate consequence that befalls anyone who does not choose to hear the Word of God. This is why we are here: to help spread the message of God to our brothers and sisters on earth."

"There are those in this world who will never hear the Word of God."

"Yes."

"They will die and go to Hell."

"Yes. It's unfortunate. This is why it is imperative for us to spread the Word of God to all corners of the world."

"Pastor Hwang—all of our Korean ancestors are in Hell."

Silence followed, sharp and cold as a bladed edge. Jenny went on.

"Our grandparents' parents are in Hell. And all of our ancestors before them are also in Hell because you say they are. Everyone before the arrival of Christianity in Korea is in Hell because of you."

Sungmin rose from his chair. "Jenny."

"You say it's our mission to spread the Word of God to all corners of the world. You say it in the present tense because you believe in the future. But Pastor Hwang—what about the past? What about the countless *millions* of people who lived before us who had their own cultures, own traditions, own religions? Is it really fair to say they all went to Hell when we don't even properly know about their customs?"

"Sit down, Jenny," Sungmin said to the side. "That's enough now."

"Who are *you*," Jenny cried, ignoring him and pointing a finger at her pastor, "to say that we know so much about the world when we don't even allow ourselves to study the religion of others? Who are *you* to say that we know everything in the world and beyond it when science and history have proven countless times that all of our stories are wrong? Who are we to say we know better than anyone else that's *human!*"

"*How dare you point at Pastor Hwang!*" Sungmin shrieked. He grabbed her. "Are you *crazy?* What do you think you're *do*—"

Jenny threw off his hands and turned back to the pastor. Rage was building, thick and hot, but it was not a maddening rage. It was a hurt rage, an offended emotion, something that was not blind, but alert and aware. It was the same type of rage a child has when being lied to. It was the same type of rage a young girl has when being told she must be alone in this world simply because she wishes to be unafraid.

"Jenny, stop right now! Just *stop*, what are you trying to—"

"God created the world. He allowed it to be populated with countless millions of people. Each of these societies had their own religions, and yet, God *still* had the audacity to say that none of these societies will be saved simply because they did not believe in Him. He purposefully sets up laws declaring that *only* certain individuals can be saved whilst knowing *millions* of people have different religions! He populates this world knowing that many of His children will die and go to Hell! How is this all-loving? How is this *fair?* He makes a place called Limbo *just* to set aside millions He knows will never hear His Word? What a convoluted being we worship!"

Pastor Hwang said nothing. He simply sat in his seat and eyed her, his arms folded, his pit-bull scowl deepened. His eyes did not leer and his gaze did not shift. He seemed to only be studying an opponent before making the first strike…or intently observing wounded prey about to enter his realm.

"Before Christianity gained stable ground in East Asia, there were *millions* of indigenous Chinese people who had their own laws and customs. They practiced their own religions and had their own beliefs. Yet *you,* and *God,* and every other Christian all say that they were *wrong*, and that they are in Hell, that they have failed to be saved. Millions of *Indian* people currently have their own ritual and practices, and you *still* say they will go to Hell when they die. You and every follower of Christ say this so casually as if each and every one of you can comprehend the history of other societies and the sheer number of years and peoples that constitute it.

"Millions of people who were Chinese before Christianity reached China died and went to Hell according to God's law; how does God account for that? *Millions* of Mayans and Incas and other indigenous peoples of the Old World lived and died before the first European missionaries came to their land—did they go to Hell too simply because they never heard of *Christ?* Are all Christians that naïve of world *history?* God made the Incas just so that they could burn in *Hell?*"

Sungmin grabbed her, again, this time taking her by the collar of her sweater, choking her, pulling her back—and then Jenny simply batted his hands away again, vaguely aware that wide eyes were staring at her, that mouths were opened, that shocked and astonished faces had spread through her audience. She hadn't meant to make a scene, and she'd only momentarily forgotten where she was. She simply had zoned in on Pastor Hwang with a crystal-sharp rage and unleashed everything that had been inside of her: God, the contradictions, the lies, the falseness, her loneliness, everything that seemed wrong in the world.

Jenny stared at him. She breathed. She felt Sungmin next to her but knew he wouldn't touch her again. His hands were just so incredibly weak. Almost girly.

Pastor Hwang, having suddenly sat straight in his chair all throughout, grunted, and slowly rose to his feet. He approached her. Jenny took one step back. She stared at him.

"You have much more reading to do, young daughter," Pastor Hwang said in a thick, raspy voice. "You seem to need much more guidance when it comes to understanding God's Word."

"I go to history and science class," Jenny said back steadily, "and in those classes, we're allowed to question. We're not told how to think, but *allowed* to think. I've read the Bible already. Reading it has me believe less in God."

Pastor Hwang grunted. It was a disgruntled and annoyed sound. "Do you think no other Christian today knows the innumerable problems that come with living in our modern world, daughter?" he asked her with a sneer. "Do you really think we're that naïve and ignorant?"

"So much that the Church purposefully has to distort the Bible to fit with modern-day thinking and science every few years, yes I do. I *do* think you are all ignorant."

Gasps sounded behind her. There'd been numerous other gasps before, Jenny was sure, but it was only on this occasion did she hear it.

"Do you think you're being brilliant right now by speaking so disrespectfully to me?" Pastor Hwang asked. "Do you really think you gain anything from this?"

"I think…I think I gain my freedom from your ignorance," Jenny said. Her voice had momentarily faltered, but she remained where she was.

The pastor laughed. It was a short laugh, cold and curt. It was almost a scoff. "Little girl, you don't even know what freedom means. How do you think that by defying God you become free?"

"I become free because I no longer abide by anyone's law."

"You are a troublesome little girl. Your parents should be ashamed to have raised such a despicable daughter like you. Speaking so elegantly as if knowing so much—nothing but rubbish. Now, if you'll excuse me."

He turned to leave. Jenny watched him go, her heart heavy in her ears.

She remembered the wheeze he'd given when sitting down then, the sudden slouch when in his chair, and the almost glassy gaze his eyes had given when momentarily catching his breath. It hadn't just been an exhausted gesture, but one internally pained. His wheeze—his own breathing seemed to be eating him. Had Pastor Hwang used his sleeve to wipe his brow because it'd been so hot, or because something inside of him was burning? Arthritis? Cancer? Something else? Was the gravity when sitting down *that great* for a man who once had bouts in the rings as a boxer?

"*I think you're a coward!*" Jenny screamed. Out of the corner of her eyes, she saw the rest of her peers visibly draw back. "Pastor Hwang! You're turning your back on me because you're a coward!"

Pastor Hwang stopped. He stopped so suddenly that his gown wavered past his ankles. His feet had only carried him two steps before Jenny shouted behind him (*And look how slow he walks*, Jenny vaguely thought; *look how slow he moves. Something's wrong with his body, something is breaking him down inside*), but now he turned back, dark flames in his eyes.

"*What* did you call me?"

"I…I said I think you're a coward. You—"

Jenny stopped herself, watched as he strode back, and swallowed again. He seemed two meters taller than her now. She came up to his chest, but his bulky shoulders made her look small and weak.

"How dare you. How dare you even *begin* to say that to me. Not because I lead this church, but because I am your *elder*. Just how *dare* you!"

Quivering, Jenny said: "I...you're a coward because you won't answer my questions. You won't answer my question because you don't have the answers and won't admit it. You...you just walk away when I assert something about your god and expect me to remain ignorant."

"Question? *What* question? What sort of thing are you—"

"When I said God was unfair for creating millions of people just so that they could go to Hell!" Jenny screamed. "He allows us to worship false gods and then penalizes us for it! It's convoluted!"

"You little, mouthy, *bitch*." More gasps from the side. Jenny barely heard them. "Do you think you know more than me simply because you have the confidence to *shout*? You fool! It's not God's fault that sinners turn away from Him! It's to *them* that the blame falls! God gave us freewill to *choose* our destiny because He loves us! Surely a girl as stupid as you can understand this."

"When He created the world—"

"He gave mankind freedom to choose! You stupid brat, you understand nothing! God didn't just create the world, populate it, and then make laws about salvation to condemn everyone! He gave us freewill to choose whether or not to love Him! That's how great He is!"

"But those ancient civilizations that never believed in God—"

"Bah! Will you always default to your stupid 'ancient civilizations'? The past is the past—that's all there is to it!"

Jenny glanced down at his hands and saw that they were shaking. The tremble was slight, but there. Not just a tremble from anger, but something else. Just something else.

"If the past is the past as you say," Jenny said, "then God is unjust, and all the ancient Egyptians, Mayans, Chinese, and everyone else that once existed deserve to harbor hatred in their hearts for being lied to. This wasn't

51

an act of freewill—this was an act of deception. For how could they have known about God's freewill if Christianity wasn't yet developed?"

"That mouth of yours had better—"

"And there is no such *thing* as freewill!" Jenny screamed. "Not when God is declared as omniscient! If He is omniscient then there's no freewill, for He already *knows* which one of us will love Him or turn against Him! If He's totally omniscient then that means He already *knows* which one of us will go to Heaven and Hell! There's no great plan for us, no destiny, no calling— God already *knows* everything! We praise Him for nothing!"

Pastor Hwang glared at her. His eyes searched her face, and he said nothing.

*There,* Jenny thought suddenly when seeing the flicker in his eyes, *there it is, there's that thing everyone gets in their eyes when they realize something they've never thought of before destroys their world belief. There's that look when they realize that something about their logic is wrong. It's not a paradigm shift—it's a paradigm collapse.*

"God knows which of his children will turn against Him because He is omniscient, and yet He still punishes them. When creating the world, God already foresaw the many religions that would come up in this world, and yet, He still punished those who practiced them and sent them all to Hell. He doesn't test our faith and doesn't test our strength because He already knows all of us. He's just a liar. Every god in the past has just been a bunch of lies."

Another flicker of uncertainty. And then, this thought, almost as frightening as Pastor Hwang's massive size: *Why hasn't he used any Bible verses to argue against me?*

"When…when people ask about your boxing career," Jenny began again, voice shaking, "they rarely ask about why you switched to join the church. It wasn't a calling, and it wasn't a fulfillment. It was an accident. Wasn't it?"

Jenny felt the entire room pull back from her. Sungmin, her youth group, everyone—it seemed as if all her peers had suddenly taken a breath to hold and stealthily crept away. More than silence now surrounded them; it was a silence filled with tight fear and disbelief.

"You…you left boxing to find God only because you had to," Jenny continued, "not because you wanted to. Something happened to your body and made you retire. That's it, isn't it? You're…you're slowly dying. You've tried to turn to God but found that God doesn't offer real answers. So you just lie to us. You lie to yourself and you lie to your children at the church. You, after all these years, developed a complex where you love being worshipped by the church and love it when we look up to you for answers, like how you were a boxer once. But now that you're older and your disease has returned, you're suddenly weak again and afraid to face the truth of God. You're afraid of—"

He struck her in the face.

Blood exploded from Jenny's nose—her nose broke. The soft tip of her nose cracked and a rupture of blood flowed backward into her throat. She opened her mouth to scream and then stopped when a thick, coppery taste of blood flooded her mouth. Tears and salt gushed down her cheeks. His fist collided so hard with her face that the bones in her neck popped; teeth ripped the inside meat of her cheeks.

Jenny screamed and felt her feet tangle beneath her. Tears and blood and snot clouded her vision. Soon she was reeling, tittering, falling to the side and sticking her arms out blindly for balance. The ground rushed up and slammed her in the chest, stealing her air. She let out a sudden gasp and felt more blood stick in the back of her mouth; red caked her lips. She let out an agonized whimper, rolled on her side, and cupped her broken nose.

*Hit me*, she thought incoherently. *My pastor hit me.*

She cried. A pathetic sob escaped her lips, and Jenny just cried.

Pastor Hwang made his way over, and Jenny cowered into a ball. She saw his black-shoed feet approaching and the wavering edges of his gown. She whimpered in fear and tried to draw away. Black hair tangled her vision and matted her cheeks; blood and tears dripped into her mouth.

"You are a loudmouthed little *bitch*," Pastor Hwang muttered as he approached her. He sighed, and carefully lowered himself on his haunches, using his thighs as support. He stared at her. Jenny stared back. Her eyes bulged with terror. "Like a bitch, you bark so annoyingly and loudly. Like a bitch, once you are kicked in the stomach, you go off to whimper in the corner, hoping to gain sympathy and forgiveness from your master. How pathetic."

What almost appeared to be a smile went to his face. It was a frown.

"What say you, daughter? Why have you gone silent? Before, you were so confident—look at you now. Cowering and whimpering on your side. What happened to all your bravery?"

Jenny swallowed. Globs of blood trickled down her throat. She grimaced, and tasted a thick mixture of salty mucus.

"You…you hit me," she gasped. "You're not…you can't do that. My nose…you—"

He gripped her by the hair. Jenny shrieked. She felt his fingers dig into her scalp and felt her forehead stretch and scream with fire. His grip was like iron, ugly and cruel like an eagle's grasp. He pulled. The roots to Jenny's hair stretched. Tears bled from her eyes. She screamed.

"*Stop! Stop it, stop it, it hurts, it* hurts!"

He lifted her face and suddenly pressed his lips against her ear. Sweet smells of herbal medicine and spices radiated from his body.

"You think you know everything because you're still so young," Pastor Hwang whispered. His voice came out scratched and rough against her ears. He was almost kissing her. "But you don't understand anything at all about this world. So let me tell you something right now, daughter. Your parents don't love you; they are disgusted with you, and think you're filth. You disrespect them and everyone else around you, and so have brought them humiliation and shame. Your entire family despises you."

"*Liar!*" Jenny sobbed. "You're lying! It's not true, *it's not!*"

His hand tangled deeper into her scalp. Jenny snarled.

"You don't know how ashamed your parents are for having a single, worthless, and troubling girl like you. They suffer because of your idiotic antics, and hurt inside for having to raise you. You bring nothing great to your family. You're nothing but a waste. You're just a girl."

He slammed her face back against the floor. Jenny let out a cry and felt the carpeted floor slam against her forehead. She brought her hands to cup her face and curled her legs into her chest. Her knees reached her chin, and soon she was sobbing against denim skin. She shuddered.

"I'm going to retire to my home now," Pastor Hwang announced calmly. His voice was far away, a thousand kilometers behind her. Jenny trembled when she heard his voice.

"Yes, Pastor Hwang."

"Make sure everyone here is satisfied and that they go home safely."

"Yes, Pastor Hwang. I will. I…I'm so sorry about all of this. I—"

Jenny heard footsteps moving away, and then the slow opening of the classroom doors. Silence followed.

"Jenny. Get up."

She opened her eyes. Sungmin was gazing at her. He had a frightened and agitated look on his face.

"*Get up.*"

He reached down and pulled her up. Jenny sat dazed on the floor and looked numbly around her. Blood flowed down her face and into her mouth. She stared at her youth group. She stared at *all* of them, all of those around her, and saw only frightened looks in their eyes, eyes that shamefully turned to the side when met by hers.

"Why didn't any of you help me?"

There was no reply. More tears spilled down her face.

"Why didn't any of you just *help me?*"

Sungmin gently hooked his hands around her and pulled her up. "Come on, Jenny. Let's go."

Jenny threw his arms off. She sobbed, and swallowed another thick pocket of blood.

After a while, Sungmin dismissed everyone to go home, told everyone to keep quiet (though of course, this was a ridiculous command), and eventually gathered his Bible and backpack to leave. Jenny sat on the floor by herself as everyone left, feeling nothing but bitterness and loneliness.

*** 

Pastor Hwang hung himself a year later. The news had spread fast, and while the church did all it could to hide the facts of Pastor Hwang's suicide, rumors persisted. Jenny listened to all these with open ears, though in her heart (as well as her mind containing the memory), there was only coldness.

Rumors said Pastor Hwang hung himself in his own home. He'd become depressed. Rumors told of how he'd lost his faith at the very end and could no longer find any reason for believing, and so had killed himself to rid his mind of the torment. They said he hung himself with his own belt strap.

There'd been a note. This too had just been words with speculation, but Jenny had no reason to disbelieve it. The note had been short. It had been written in Korean, and had said simply: *To my family and my church—my sons and daughters, brothers and sisters, wife and friends. I am sorry. There is no God. I've tried looking for Him in my heart and have found nothing. I have lived a lie. I am a coward.*

Jenny said nothing when she heard about the note. By then, she was too hurt and too tired to care, and only hoped that Pastor Hwang's family would find some sense of closure. After a brief period of confusion at the church, Pastor Oh came along, and everything regarding the suicide was forgotten.

Only Jenny remembered.

*** 

A horn blared her way.

Jenny jerked from the sound. She saw a yellow Mustang hurtling her way and quickly stepped to the side. The Mustang honked a second time—"Walk a bit faster, won't cha!" the driver shouted—and then was gone, speeding out of the lot and screeching through the gates. Jenny frowned.

*I'll watch where I'm going if you obey the freaking speed limit,* she thought sharply. She sighed. She continued on her way through the lot and observed again with jejune interest stray leaves collecting near her feet. She had, like always, parked in the back again. The lot was nearly big as a football field.

Her parents had fought after hearing about the incident between her and Pastor Hwang, of course. Their bickering at home had become a thing almost procedural. Jenny accepted their arguments bitterly as a teenage girl could, though in her heart, the sounds of her shouting mother and sighing father always hurt her. They snapped and snarled at each other, always accusing the other of failing to raise an obedient daughter. Jenny had even listened to their bickering once while secretly sitting at the top of the stairs overlooking the living room. This had just been a few hours after the incident with Pastor Hwang. They hadn't argued what to do about the pastor, hadn't talked about pressing charges, and hadn't even discussed the time in the emergency room at the hospital—they just argued about their daughter, about her, *Jenny,* wondering which had done wrong as a parent, accusing the other of failing to provide proper parental supervision. Their reputations were tarnished now, Jenny's father bellowed; how were they supposed to show their faces at church? Wouldn't it have been so much better if they had raised a *son?* And like always, when hearing this last part, Jenny had, with warm tears in her eyes, retreated back to her room to cry.

"Hey, Jenny! Hey, what's up!"

Jenny turned her head. She frowned at what she saw and released a breathless sigh. "Kooper," she said heavily. "Hey."

Steven Kooper jumped from the back of his Ford pickup and slowly made his way over. A goofy grin spread across his face. His varsity jacket stretched the width of his 5'10" football frame and stopped at his doublewide gorilla shoulders. An almost haughty gait came with his walk as he stepped towards her. The waist of his jeans clung low to his thighs and revealed the upper bands of his white boxer briefs. A white Pittsburg Steeler's cap sat snuggly skewed to one side on his head; tuffs of blonde hair poked out from under the edges.

Jenny grimaced when she saw him. Had she been carrying her textbooks, she would have held them protectively over her chest with a wary regard. Indeed, she only brought her arms up to hold herself when he neared, and cupped her elbows. A sweet, sparkling, and almost head-aching odor came from his direction. It was the smell of Old Spice having been copiously sprayed on the meaty and sweaty body of a hormonal teenage boy that frequently slammed himself against *other* meaty, sweaty, and hormonal teenage boys on the football field. The smell was repugnant and sharp. Jenny grimaced a second time.

"Jenny," he cried cheerfully. "What's up, girl! Need a ride? I'm sending Matt and Jacob home, and we thought we'd ask another person to join."

Jenny glanced past his side and saw two other boys in the back of the pickup. Varsity jackets covered their shoulders. They tossed around a football and whistled wildly when two female students passed by. Jenny raised an incredulous eyebrow.

"Thanks, Kooper," she said calmly. "But I have a ride. Maybe another time."

"You sure, Jenny? Cause I can drive you anywhere you want."

Jenny stared at him, dubious, guessing that he'd been trying to make a sexual connotation. He grinned at her, and said again: "Jenny, has any guy ever told you that you were cute?"

"No."

"*For real?* Dude, Jenny, you're like, hella cute. In a classy way, you know?"

Jenny darted her eyes to the sides, hoping to find someone she'd recognize. The absurdity of her situation fell on her like a crushing hammer blow: She knew nobody. No one could help her and she had no friends. She was alone.

Everyone knew Kooper's name, of course. Evanston-Woods High School wasn't so great that it could rid itself of typical clichés. Jenny saw Kooper sometimes in the hallway with his rambunctious herd of football friends. Like migrating wildebeests crossing the river, they were a spectacle of their own, and required wary gazes when letting pass. They enjoyed taking up the hallways with their massive bulks and liked to announce their presence with meaty howls. They did not torment and they did not terrorize; as far as Jenny knew, EWHS had no bullying problem. Like wildebeests, they were large and proud but still gentle herbivores. Officer Richards drifted between classes to ensure order most of the time, and acted very much like a lazy crocodile that monitored the hallways with a close reptilian eye toward Kooper and his gang. Kooper was in her chemistry class.

"Like, you're from China, right? Or like, Japan?"

"Korea," Jenny said quickly. Sweat formed on the back of her neck. "I'm from Korea."

"Oh, nice! I love Korean food. You guys use metal chopsticks, right?"

"Um...I—"

"Hey, you know a good Korean place nearby for like a lunch or something? We could take you, you know. Matt and me. Dude, we love Asian food! There are just so many Asian places here in Seattle, you know?"

"I don't think...I mean, Korean food—"

"Kooper. Hey."

Jenny spun around.

Her heart thundered in her ears and her chest tightened. She hadn't realized she'd been holding her breath until she turned around, and even then, she'd let out a loud gasp when hearing the voice, sucking air from her lungs. Her hair whipped around her shoulders and hit her in the face like a mild slap of feathers, and for just a brief second, she saw no one behind her, thinking that she heard a random noise. But when her heart settled down—and when the last tendrils of black hair slid from her face, tickling, almost like a caress of leaves—she saw a boy standing behind her with one hand in his pocket and the other hand holding a notebook against his thigh. She vaguely recognized him to be from Ms. Karens' class, but couldn't quite pinpoint his name. Daniel or something. Maybe David. He stood there behind her with a stoic look on his face.

Jenny's heart pounded.

"D, baby, what's up!"

Kooper pushed her aside (literally), and opened his massive arms. He enveloped D—Daniel/David—in his arms and gave him a big crushing hug. Daniel/David winced back, and returned the gesture.

"Still captain of all your classes I hear!" Kooper said, letting him go.

"Still running back for the team, I hear," David/Daniel said back.

Kooper laughed. He flung his head back and let out a yelp that was produced heartily from the stomach. "Yeah man, barely! Shoot." He rewrapped one big arm around Daniel/David's shoulders, and said to Jenny: "See this boy right here? This boy Daniel be my lifesaver! Best tutor ever. Made physics a piece of cake and got me my first A. That's what's up with this boy!"

Daniel gently peeled off his arm and politely stepped to the side. He said plainly: "I think you kind of did it all by yourself, Kooper."

"No way, man. All those equations and formulas to memorize? Shit! I thought I was going to get a nosebleed seeing all those numbers. Ya know?"

"Yeah," Daniel said stilly. "Sure."

Kooper laughed a second time. He said, "Anyway. Jenny and I were just talking about getting some Korean food after school. You in for it, Big D? Want some sushi?"

"I never said I wanted—"

"Actually, Jenny and I were going to go home together."

Jenny turned toward him. "*What?*"

Daniel stepped next to her and slipped his hand out from his pocket. He nudged her, and Jenny recoiled, not understanding what he was doing. "I'm driving her home," Daniel said. "I'm her newest physics tutor. We're starting today."

Kooper glanced at them. His eyes traveled from left to right, and his smile briefly diminished. A thought seemed to go through his head (a thought that was, sadly, not very fast or smooth, as his face for a few seconds went mind-numbingly blank), and then he suddenly grinned at them.

"Oh, *daaaang!* I hear you D!" He paused and winked towards Jenny. Jenny grimaced with disgust. "Hey, all right, I catch you. My bad, Jenny. I didn't know you were already with D the man." He turned his face toward Daniel. "Score, baby, you hear?"

"Loud and clear," Daniel said. His hand went to touch her, and Jenny again flinched away. Daniel turned toward her. He frowned at her, made a slight, discreet nod in Kooper's direction, and pressed his lips together.

*Oh,* Jenny thought. *Okay.*

"I'll see you around, Kooper," Daniel said. "Take care."

"Will do, Cap," Kooper replied. And then to Jenny: "He's a keeper, Jenny. He's gonna go far while people like me just stumble in the gutter."

A frown passed across Daniel's face. It was a frown barely there, light as it was subtle, and Jenny realized it was a hurt frown. She suddenly felt sorry for him, and realized his frown made him look ten years older. Handsomer, even. Deep.

"Don't say that, Steven," Daniel said. "We'll all make it eventually. We have to."

"Nah, not me, D. Jocks like me only get one moment in life. Afterwards, we just fizzle out. It's the American way."

Jenny, still noticing the frown on his face, stepped next to Daniel, and took his hand. She said gently, "Daniel's right, Koop…I mean, Steven. Keep working hard. You'll be okay."

Another smile went across Kooper's face. It was a thin smile, sad and even. He eyed their held hands. "You two look good together," he said. "Ya'll be good now, kay? And have fun too. And, D, remember—use protection, bro!"

He turned around and walked away, laughing as he did so. Jenny noticed an increase step in his pace and realized that he no longer swaggered.

"Sorry about that," Daniel said. He let go of her hand. "Kooper's a good guy. Just loud sometimes."

"No, that's fine."

She stared at him. She looked at his face and noticed his eyes again. They were brown. Like syrup, almost.

"Thanks for that. I was scared that I was really going to have to take a ride with them."

"No problem."

She stuck her hand out. "My name's Jenny Park. Thank you again."

He looked down at her hand. He laughed at her. "After having held hands, you want to shake now?"

"Is something wrong?"

"No, not really. It just seems odd."

He shook her hand.

"Daniel Fischer. Nice to meet you, Jenny Park."

"You're in Ms. Karens' right?"

"Yeah."

"In the back?"

"Yeah."

"Oh. Okay."

She stared at him. He stared back. A brief flicker went through his eyes, and Jenny realized she was still holding his hand. She let go, embarrassed. "So, um. How did you do on the quiz?"

"Don't really know. Hopefully well."

*Psht. So modest,* Jenny thought. *It's obvious he knows he aced it. He's just saying that to me to sound polite.* "Yeah, well, I think I flunked," she said flatly. "I got my butt kicked today."

He smiled at her. It was a sad smile, thin and waning, and Jenny realized it was another one of those rare smiles only briefly given. It was a good smile. "Maybe you should study more, Ms. Park," he said, shrugging a bit. "Tests are only going to get harder."

She said: "I'd like to. But IB is giving me a headache. I can't even sleep regular hours anymore."

"Welcome to the club then. The Losers' Club."

"Ready for that Civil Rights presentation this Friday?" she asked.

"I guess. Like everyone else though, I'm probably going to start this Thursday night and procrastinate until the end."

"Oh yeah, me too. I always end up doing all of my homework last minute. It kinda sucks."

"Yeah."

"Yeah."

A light wind blew, rippling her hair. Fresh smells of sweet strawberry drifted from her shoulders, and Jenny was suddenly conscious of the scent traveling towards his direction. She hoped her hair smelled good.

"Do you plan on working on it by yourself?" Daniel asked. He brought a hand up to scratch the back of his neck. His eyes slightly lowered from hers when speaking. "Or, like, do you prefer working alone?"

"Oh. I...actually, I haven't even thought about how to start the project yet. I usually work alone on things."

"Ah. Okay."

"But, like, I think having a partner would be good for this project. Since it's a major presentation and all."

He looked at her. She looked back.

"Want to work on the presentation together then?" he asked slowly. "Like, only if you want to, I mean. Research, and stuff."

"Yeah. I think...yeah, I think that would be cool."

"Really?" His eyes widened. "Oh. Well, okay then. Um...do you want to meet tomorrow sometime?"

"I have a free period during fourth. We can meet then."

"The library then," Daniel said. He smiled again. It was a relieved smile. "I have a free fourth too. I'll meet you in front of the doors and we'll work together at the computers. Okay?"

"Yeah." She smiled at him. "Cool."

"Cool."

They smiled timidly at each other.

"See you around then, Daniel," Jenny said. "It was good meeting you today. Thanks again for the whole Kooper thing."

"No problem, Ms. Park. I'll see you tomorrow."

He turned away with one last look, and Jenny watched curiously as he strolled through the parking lot by himself. Had there been a cloudless sky today with afternoon sun, Jenny was sure his shadow would have stretched far from the heels of his sneakers.

She felt incredibly buoyant then.

*Daniel,* she thought, as she began walking towards her car again. *Daniel Fischer. Well, okay then. I'll see you tomorrow in the library, Mr. Fischer. I think I just made a friend.*

Jenny got to her car and started the engine.

# CHAPTER 4

As always when returning home from school, Jenny followed a typical routine. She took off her backpack as she entered the house, kicked off her shoes, stuffed her shoes in the closet, and, finally, peeled off her socks. She'd walked barefoot to the kitchen to dine on whatever snack it was her mother had left for her (usually rice with dried seaweed wraps, or even a small plate of kimchi), and ate in the cold silence of the house. When she finished, she would go upstairs to drop off her backpack in her room and check online for any new updates for her classes. This was usually followed by a much-needed afternoon nap. Afterwards, she'd wake up several hours later at ten or eleven, sit on the edge of her bed with a grouchy pout, tiredly turn on the lights to her room, and start her homework. If luck was with her, she'd finish her homework by four in the morning. If not, she'd pull another all-nighter and suffer another day at school with red droopy eyes and bloodless, exhausted looks. Her mother sometimes left dinner for her downstairs. If not, she'd have to serve herself another cold plate of rice.

It sucked being in IB.

Jenny finished her bowl of rice and cleaned it under the faucet. She grabbed her backpack and climbed the stairs to her room. Her parents were out, and this too was typical. Her mother came home usually an hour after she arrived, and her father always returned in the evening. How they always mustered enough energy to find something to bicker about at the end of the day, Jenny didn't know.

Her parents fought more regularly these days. They were fights that always brought a tightness to the heart. It hurt knowing that their bickering was borne out of themes she had no control over. It was a fact: Her parents wished that she'd been born a boy. That she'd been born a girl had brought bitterness to her parents, Jenny knew. That she was quiet, slow, often perceived as lazy and struggling in her studies only provided fertile ground for her parents' animosity toward one another. Had she been the type of girl that knew something in the world, a girl that was assiduous and intelligent, her parents' angst might've lessened. Had she been a Korean girl that allowed herself to become subordinated by culture and religion, then perhaps her parents would have regarded her with a better (*kinder*) light. She was none of these things though, and knowing how often her parents praised the children of their friends hurt Jenny as much as seeing her Korean classmates glaring at her during lunch. Jenny supposed, for her father, at least, some of his animosity toward her mother was also misogynistic: He probably found fault with her mother for having birthed him a daughter instead of a son.

Slight as these thoughts were (but oh, this too was a lie. None of these thoughts were slight at all, for Jenny had struggled with them for years. They were only slight in that they barely touched the surfaces of her mind, and were treated tentatively like fragile glass whenever allowed to manifest), they were not without evidence and were not just random conjectures. Her time with Pastor Hwang had helped solidify this notion of classical patriarchy and slight sexism—it was then that Jenny realized her parents didn't really love her.

She'd gone to the bathroom after everyone had left her on the floor and after the blood had stopped flowing. She'd gone to the bathroom with her head tilted forward and with harsh gasps spilling from her mouth. Blood still collected evenly in her throat despite the position of her head, and the sensation was sticky like hot mucus, making her shudder every time she swallowed. The pain momentarily returned with devastating force when she was in the bathroom—the pain felt like rusty nails shoved up her nostrils. Bolts of metal pain throbbed across her face and blood smeared her lips like

66

dried rusty paint. Jenny gingerly washed off all the blood she could and watched impassively as it swirled down into the sink as a bright pinkish color. She stupidly touched her nose to test the pain and wailed out loud when the broken bones grinded together, sensitive nerve-endings scraping cruelly against uneven ends. She cried breathlessly for five minutes and swallowed, breathing haggardly through her mouth. Her face looked fat and bloated in the mirror.

*God, what if I look like this for the rest of my* life?

She walked out of the bathroom and went to the main office to call her mom. There, Sungmin stood waiting for her, a somber, if not sad frown spread across his face. He looked as if he'd just suffered the news of a lost loved one.

"You shouldn't have done that, Jenny," he said to her when he saw her. "You don't know how much trouble you've caused."

Jenny stared at him. Before she could say anything, Sungmin reached forward and offered her something. Jenny stared at it, suspicious, and then felt a slight gratitude of thanks. It was an icepack.

"Thank you," she muttered thinly.

Sungmin said nothing. He watched as she placed the ice pack against her face. She called her mother on her cellphone, and the two stood together in awkward silence. Jenny eyed him carefully from the side. He fumbled with random items in his pocket and stared down at his shoes.

"Stay out of trouble, Jenny," he said after what seemed like an eternity. He glanced at her, frowned, and then walked away. He spoke in Korean. "I mean it. Think before you talk, Jenny. And don't question God so much. It just brings more trouble than good."

Jenny watched as he rounded the corner of the building. He returned a few seconds later on his bike. Jenny realized then that Sungmin had a small crush on her, and that today she had given him a reason to stop.

Word was like fire in the Korean community. News of her encounter with Pastor Hwang had spread to all ears of the church within less than two hours. When her mother had picked her up, silence had invaded the car, thick and piercing. Jenny kept quiet in the back seat with a sour pout on her lips.

"Omma."

Her mother's eyes went to the rearview mirror. They gazed at her, like two black frozen orbs. She said nothing for a moment and then refocused her attention back on the road.

"Omma? *Mom?*" More tears spilled down Jenny's face. "He...he hit me first! I didn't do anything wrong, omma! He...he...he *broke my nose when all I wanted was to ask questions!* He broke my nose and pulled my hair first, and he said bad things to me. He said that—"

"Enough, Jenny." Her mother's eyes snapped at her from the mirror. "Just be quiet. You've caused enough trouble for today."

Jenny pouted and sat back in miserable silence. She cried.

Dr. Kim x-rayed her nose and found that it was mildly fractured. This hardly lightened Jenny's mood (what the hell was *mildly* fractured anyway?). The doctor prescribed Advil and Tylenol, and told her to elevate her head when sleeping. He told her she was lucky it hadn't broken. Her mother thanked the doctor with a quiet smile, though Jenny had noticed a certain briskness about her mother. Dr. Kim also attended the same church as they did. Their story was that she'd stupidly run into a wall.

"Omma—"

"Go upstairs, Jenny. Just go upstairs and think about what you've done. I'll call you down when dinner is ready."

Jenny lowered her head as she entered the doorway. She said quietly: "Omma. I did this for you. I...I stayed behind at church today for you because I wanted some answers. I wanted to see you stop crying. I wanted auntie to be okay now that's she's gone."

Her mother stared at her. She sighed. "Jenny-ah," she said wearily, "go upstairs. Go upstairs to your room and just rest."

Jenny sniffled. She silently lowered her head, removed her shoes, and climbed the stairs.

Her father had returned home that night tired and exhausted. The mood he brought into the house that evening hadn't helped things. As always when her parents fought, Jenny snuck out from her room and sat silently near the banisters at the head of the stairs. Sometimes she saw her parents' shadows on the living room walls and ceiling. Other times, she saw the top of their head as they stomped back and forth in a maddening display of rage. Tonight though, there were just loud sighs and mild accusations, a great change to the often loud, blaring noises they made when yelling at each other. They sat on the family couch speaking to one another in distilled whispers.

"…supposed to be your duty as a woman and mother, Jaewha."

"Oh, *please*, Yongsook. Don't put all of this blame on me! You're her father too, aren't you? You think all because she's a girl she has to rely on me all the time? All because you're a father you think you can't console our daughter as well?"

"What do you do in your spare time after work all day, huh, Jaewha? At the very least you can teach our daughter some basic manners."

There'd been a pause, and Jenny had waited anxiously to hear what her mother would say. She said: "I wished that we had had a son."

"Yes," her father replied with a sigh, "me too. Life would be so much easier if we had a son."

Jenny let out a loud sniffle. She brought a hand up to wipe her nose and felt jolts of pain spread through her face. She winced before getting up again. She crept quietly through the dark and retreated to her room.

\*\*\*

Yeah. She was a girl. It was something Jenny realized and knew she could never escape. It hurt realizing what she was, and it hurt worse seeing how everyone always had to remind her what she was. Her "friends" at church, her "friends" at school—they all silently told her what a *real* girl was supposed to look like with their salacious red-painted lips and darkly decorated mascara-eyes, and they all told her how a girl was *supposed* to act. Sometimes Jenny sighed to herself when thinking about her sex—and, sometimes (just…sometimes), she sat quietly in the bathroom and cried in the dark.

It sucked being in IB. It sucked even worse being a girl.

\*\*\*

Jenny rolled on her side and opened her eyes.

An aqua-green glow spread along her nightstand and dimly splashed the carpet. The clock read 11:45 p.m. in dull, black, digital numbers. Outside, a bone-clattering noise battered the windows as a swift wind blew through the hollows of the house. Jenny groaned when seeing the numbers. She'd slept for almost nine hours.

*God,* she moaned. *I feel so bloated. It's like I gained fifty pounds or something. Why did I wear my school clothes to sleep?*

She threw the blankets off and rolled out of bed. It hadn't been just the wind outside that had pulled her out of her sleep; there'd been a sudden slamming of the door downstairs too that had rocked the house. Her parents were fighting again. Jenny could hear their screams from below like distant war shouts. She swung her legs to the side and let her feet touch the floor. She rubbed her eyes again and let out a low, exhausted sigh. She moved drunkenly from the bed and went to turn on the light switch. She stopped, decided against it, and just stood there in the dark.

She opened the door to her bedroom. Light fell against her face. With a kind of despairing jolt, Jenny realized she'd left her shoes and socks scattered all over the foyer again, and groaned miserably a second time as she walked through the hallway. Her mother always gave her hell with her socks. She chastised her constantly about how unkempt she was, and always wondered out loud if she'd ever make a good housewife. This last part of her mother's belittling, of course, hurt Jenny the most.

*No wonder someone's mad tonight,* Jenny thought wearily as she neared the bathroom. *I guess I'd be mad too if someone always left their dirty socks in the entryway of my house. Gross.*

A crash erupted from the living room, stopping Jenny cold. Her skin turned hard and the hairs on her arms rose. Gooseflesh spread through her back. The sound had been sharp and defining, cutting suddenly like exploding glass. Jenny waited, breathed slowly, and jumped again when another loud crash sounded from the living room. Her mother screamed downstairs.

"*...go and take your* fucking *money and spend it all on that fucking whore!*"

Jenny's blood froze.

She ran to the head of the stairs and saw her parents standing in the living room. Her mother's back was to her. Her fists were balled and she clutched a piece of paper in her hands. Her shoulders shook. There was a suitcase next to her, and when Jenny saw this, her heart stopped. Her father stood there too, his tie loose, his jacket draped over one arm of the living room couch, sweat plastered across his forehead. The desk lamp usually found on the living room table was shattered into a dozen pieces next to the fireplace along the wall. Sharp, pink ceramic shards glared upward from the floor like jagged shark's teeth.

*What?* Jenny thought. *What? Omma*...what's *happening?*

"You hypocritical whore, Jaewha," her father spat. "Don't tell *me* what to do with my money when you yourself spend so much time at the casinos with other men every Fri—"

"Oh, and do I sleep with them, Yongsook! Do I stick my dick into them and e-mail at night calling them my *sweetie?*"

Jenny stumbled down the stairs. Her lungs plunged up and down in her chest and her bare feet stomped loudly against the steps. "Omma," she cried. "What happened, what's going on? What—"

"Go back upstairs, Jenny." It was her father. "This doesn't involve you."

"But...I thought I heard—"

Her mother pointed a finger at her. "*See,* Yongsook? See this one here?

71

She's so dumb and naïve she doesn't know *anything* that goes on around this house anymore! You call yourself a father, Yongsook? You can barely teach your own daughter. You just fail as a husband!"

"**SHUT *UP!***"

Her father's voice rocked the house. Jenny hunched her shoulders and felt another tight ripple of gooseflesh spread through her back. She watched as her father tore off his glasses and thought that he would suddenly go and smack her. Red burst through his cheeks and green veins throbbed against his temples; black patches of sweat layered the areas around his neck.

"What do you want, Jaewha?" Yongsook asked, sighing now. He crushed his glasses in his palm. Shards of bloody glass stuck out between his fingers. "You want to leave, is that it? You want to be a coward and leave this house right in front of your daughter?"

Jaehwa's eyes widened. She barked a sharp sound of laughter, and cried: "*Daughter?* You call this girl here our *daughter?* Don't do that family emotional horseshit crap on me, Yongsook! You loathe her as much as I do! She hasn't done *anything* to contribute to this family! All she does is whine and complain and eat what I feed her. And you want to call her our *daughter?*"

Jenny's ears flushed hot. Warm stringy tears spilled down her face and blood blushed her cheeks. "*Omma,*" she cried, reaching out and taking hold of her mother's arm, "please…please stop it, you're scaring me. Don't scream anymore, I—"

Her mother threw her hand off. "Don't touch me," she spat. "Don't you *dare*, Jenny. Do you know how long I've been feeding that mouth of yours? Do you know how much it tires me just to keep you *alive?* How long will we keep you around just so you can abandon us? How long before you become a woman and then a wife? Were you the type of girl I could be proud of as a mother, I'd hold you in my arms and say how much I loved you!"

"*Omma-ni.* Please…mom, don't, I—"

"Do you want to know how depressed your father was when he found out you were a girl? Do you know that he blamed *me* for making you a girl?

72

Huh, Jenny? Did you know that? Do you know how much your father *loathes* you?"

Jenny shook her head, not caring. She closed her eyes and clutched her mother's arm. Tears and snot spilled down her face. "Please," she sobbed, "I'm sorry. I'm sorry, *je-song hamnida*. Mom, I'm sorry." She slid down to her knees. "Please, forgive me, don't be mad, I'm sorry, I'll do better in life, I—"

She slapped her. Jaewha's hand came out of nowhere and smacked Jenny across the cheek.

Jenny's head snapped to the side and her sobbing stopped. There was a sharp inhale of breath, a sharp cry of surprise, and nothing more. A lock of hair fell across her face.

"Stop it," Jaewha hissed. "Stop groveling. I'm tired of hearing your voice." She turned to her husband. "Leaving now would bring you the greatest pleasure, wouldn't it, Yongsook? After all our years of marriage, it's me leaving that'll make you the happiest. Am I right?"

Yongsook said nothing. He shrugged his shoulders and threw his broken glasses on the couch beside him. Thin red crept between the cracks. "You leaving won't make a difference," Yongsook said. He took out a handkerchief from his pocket and began wiping his hand. "You're just as worthless as a wife and mother if you were to stay."

Jaewha sneered. She turned to her daughter and said, "Here you are, Jenny. Take this e-mail and learn what nearly twenty years of marriage can amount to. Maybe you'll be able to avoid some of the mistakes we made."

"Omma, please, don't—"

Jaewha threw the note at Jenny's face and grabbed the handles of her suitcase. Jenny reached out and grabbed her mother by the arm.

"*Please*, mom," she sobbed. She crawled on her knees now. "Don't go like this, please, I'm sorry. I'll do better, I promise, I'll do better, *please*—"

Her mother reached back and dug her nails into her scalp. Jenny shrieked. Jaewha flung her off and whacked her with her purse, striking her in the face. Jenny screamed as one of the metal clippings on her mother's purse slashed her in the eye. She fell painfully against her left arm and made a piercing wail as it twisted awkwardly under her weight.

"Goodbye, Yongsook," Jaewha said at the doorway. She fished for her keys and gripped them with a tight, bony fist. "When you fuck that whore of yours, I hope you know she's faking it. She'll always fake it with you."

"At least she knows what to do in bed," Yongsook shot back. "Goodbye, Jaewha. Leave before the rain starts. You don't like to get your hair wet."

A ghost of a smile came to Jaewha's lips. It was an almost cruel and ghastly smile. She turned her gaze back down at her daughter. She sighed. "Be careful in life, Jenny," Jaewha muttered. "Be careful whom you marry."

She turned around and closed the door.

"Mom! Mom! *Omma*, please—"

"Be quiet, Jenny."

Jenny stopped herself. She turned around and saw her father massaging his temple with his bloody hand. Small droplets of red ran down his handkerchief and made it look like dangling pieces of meat. Jenny watched in horror as he used it to wipe his forehead. "Stop screaming. You're giving me a headache."

"But what are we supposed to do about mom? What—"

Her father's eyes snapped open. Jenny stopped herself. An honest, confused, and even weary look went to Yongsook's face as he stared at her.

"What about her, Jenny?" he asked plainly. "She's gone now. Why do you care?"

Jenny lowered her gaze and stared at the floor. Her breathing hitched in her chest and another scratching sniffle escaped her lips. The sound of her mother's car started, and soon only screeching tires could be heard in the distance as she drove away. Her left eye throbbed and her arm still hurt.

Her father made his way towards the door. Jenny raised her head.

"Daddy?"

"Going out," Yongsook muttered. He shrugged on his jacket and studied her. With some dismay, Jenny realized he'd cleaned the blood off his glasses and put them back on his face. Cracks decorated his eyes. "Don't you have homework to do, Jenny?"

Jenny shook her head. She swallowed, tried to say something, and then watched somberly as her father opened the door. A cold draft blew into the house.

"Appa, where—"

The door closed.

Jenny listened as her father started the engine and put the car in reverse. She heard the engine revving, the tires screeching, and then, finally, nothing more.

Outside, a strong gust of wind battered the windows.

*Why did this happen, God?*

Jenny wrapped her arms around herself and sniffled. Snot and tears streamed down her face while black strands of hair stuck to her cheeks.

*I'm sorry God. Please, just bring my mom back. I'm just so sorry about everything. Please, please, just bring my mom back.*

Sobbing, Jenny brought a hand to wipe her face and cried alone on the floor.

# CHAPTER 5

Rape.

It was a word that always occurred to Jenny whenever staring at the rain. It was a word that was mysterious and cold, dark and quiet, foreign as a brief touch given by a stranger's hands. The word came to her mind whenever hearing the beating raindrops overhead, whenever the sky was dark, and whenever the stars were rare. Sometimes when the night was cool and the rain had stopped, a fine white mist would rise from the ground and enshroud the parking lot in a thin cocoon, giving the illusion of an eternal haze. The windows at Red Moon's Diner would turn opaque with late autumn frost, and Jenny for a minute would imagine herself in hell. There were no crickets to ward off the silence. Jenny supposed they froze to death in the autumn or something.

"Said Spencer was supposed to be okay in the next few days," Abigail said next to her, scooting up to her side and putting a pin in her hair. "I don't know why, but I think the vet likes me. When I came to visit, he told me I had nice eyes. Isn't that a weird thing to say?"

"Yeah," Jenny mumbled. "I guess it is."

"I mean, it would be cool and all to date a doctor, even if he is just a vet. I mean, not that I have anything against vets. Just that, you know, they treat animals. That's kind of…"

She went on, and Jenny blew a lock of hair out of her eyes.

*Rape. That's what it looks like, that's what it looks like outside the window. It looks like rape outside. For some reason, seeing the midnight rain reminds me of rape. Why?*

Three boys stood outside the diner, their bodies huddled under the fluorescent lights. Falling sleet had turned to soft rain and made their raincoats slick with melted ice and shine. Their breaths released hot and dry into the nightly air. They laughed and elbowed each other, gawked at each other, slapped each other, and produced low, brassy laughs that echoed through the windows. Jenny watched them with a dumb envy. She was jealous of their laughter. She imagined their faces even though their backs were turned, and suddenly wished to be with them.

They were smoking. All three of them, just a trio of dumb college boys huddled together in the rain, doing nothing but laughing and smoking. They exposed their faces to the night and puffed out a plume of gray cigarette smoke that dissipated into the dark. Cigarettes. They were smoking cigarettes. And Jenny longed to be with them.

*Last night I had a dream. Last night I had a dream that I was back in high-school, and there were various faces and names that I remembered. Last night I had a dream, and in that dream, there'd been a confused little girl that had just wanted to find her place in the world because she was just so lonely. There was Ms. Karens, my history teacher, Pastor Hwang from church, my mother and father, and just…just so many other things I can't remember. Seattle. Last night I had a dream about Seattle.*

"…likes this yellow chew toy that Ernest gave him one summer, and when he threw it across the yard, Spencer ran after it and stepped on this rake, and…"

*Life. In ten years from now I'll be almost forty. In ten years from now my face will have gotten older with more wrinkles and heavier eyelids. My cheeks will have drooped and my hands will have become weaker. I will look back on my ten passed years and wonder how I've come to this place in life, finally realizing that no amount of makeup or fashion I wear on my body matters. I will realize fashion is useless; I will realize makeup is in vain. The makeup I put on my face to look clean and beautiful, the fashion that I wear on my body to hide the bruises and look feminine—I will realize it was all in vain, for fashion does not stop the onrush of time, does not guarantee me friendship or love, and does not stop me from aging. Nothing stops me from aging. Fashion and makeup are false—why can't I realize this now?*

77

*Why am I so afraid of the rain?*

*(rape it's what i think of when i hear the rain rape it's what)*

Jenny shuddered. She turned to Abigail to see if she'd spoken, and realized she hadn't. The voice had sounded like Tom's, but that was impossible. Tom was away and wouldn't be back for another night. The voice had belonged to someone else. Just someone else.

"Thinking about your man again?"

Jenny jumped at the sound.

"Yes, Abigail," she said sharply with a frown. "That's most definitely what I'm thinking now. My tall, dark, and handsome. What else could it be?"

"See? I knew you liked him! It's good to admit these feelings."

*How about I admit some feelings about you then,* Jenny thought, but didn't say. "What do you think those boys are doing there?" she asked, gesturing toward the doors. "They've been standing there for like an hour."

"Hmm? Oh, them?" Abigail squinted and held a hand up. Jenny snorted. As if she were blocking out some glare from an imaginary sun or something. "Looks to me they're just hanging out and smoking. Nothing wrong with that, right?"

"They could be doing something."

"Oh? Like what?"

"Like...well, I don't know, but they could be. Shouldn't you go and ask them what they're doing?"

Abigail looked at her. She cocked her head to the side and scanned her face. "Are you okay tonight, Jenny?" she asked lightly. "You're really out of it."

"No," Jenny replied, shaking her head. She sighed. "I guess I'm not. I didn't get a good night's sleep last night."

"Oh, I see. Period?"

She frowned at her. "*Dream*, Abigail," she said curtly. "I had a weird dream last night. That's all."

Abigail giggled. "Oh, right! I knew that. You know, the funny thing about dreams, they say it tells a lot about you. I wonder if dogs dream? Because you know, they say that when a dog is asleep and it's wagging its tail, it's supposed to mean…"

Jenny rolled her eyes, sighing a second time. She returned her gaze back toward the windows and stared out at the rain.

Smoking. Yes, those three boys were just smoking. And oh, how she longed to be with them.

An hour passed. In that time the boys left the diner and the rain dissipated. What was left in their place was a familiar thin white haze that overtook the surface of the parking lot and formed thick frost on the windows. The clouds above concealed the moon and hid the stars.

The door to the diner opened, and Jenny raised her head. Her blood froze. Abigail elbowed her in the ribs and giggled.

"Hey, it's your tall, dark, and handsome!" she whispered. "Why is *he* here again? Guess he's getting braver coming in here, huh? Maybe he's here to ask you out on a date. That would be something, wouldn't it?"

Jenny ignored her. She watched as the man took his regular seat at the window and felt gooseflesh ripple across her skin. He took off his jacket as he sat down and blew into his hands. Droplets of rain speckled his hair. Jenny thought of morning dew when seeing his hair and hated it. He set his hands on the table and waited.

*Tomato sauce,* a voice whispered. *If he asks, tell him it was tomato sauce. Tell him it was tomato sauce, tell him it—*

*God why is he here again, why is* he *here? He shouldn't be here tonight, he was here last time, he shouldn't* be—

"…me to approach him?"

She turned around. Abigail stared at her with a slight frown and a thoughtful look in her eyes. Her eyes were earnest and sincere, but Jenny felt as if they were untrustworthy too, as if she'd suddenly heard her thoughts.

"No," Jenny replied, grabbing a pitcher from underneath the counter. "I got this. He wants me anyway."

"Sure?"

"Yeah. Yeah, I got it. Thanks though."

Abigail shrugged, letting it go.

*Same as usual. It's just going to be the same as usual. Literally. I'm going to ask, "Same as usual?" He's going to say, "Yes, please," and I'm going to turn around, he's going to keep staring at me, maybe at my ass, he's going to get his Country Fried Steak, and everything will be okay. Everything will be*

*(please don't say that please don't)*

*okay. Okay?*

"Hey," she said as she poured him his water. "Nice to see you here. Same as usual, right?"

"Yes. Please."

Jenny nodded. She scribbled his order down and offered him a wide smile.

She was able to take four steps away when his voice suddenly spoke up behind her, freezing her in her tracks.

"Jenny, wait. We need to talk."

***

The man tipped a hundred dollars every time he entered Red Moon's Diner. He didn't know why he did this; he just did it because he didn't know what else to do. The role of the waitress, the role of the policemen, the role of actor as hero, and the role of the model as fashionista—these were all examples of actors and actresses living a life of bad faith. We all act in bad faith, the man thinks; we all act when frightened before life and the truth.

*I enter a world of play and see before me a false world-stage occupied by faces that do not wish to be here, he thinks as he enters the diner. With my words, I cast them appropriate roles and allow them to exist as they do through a mutual understanding of bad faith; I take a grain of rice and call it a meteorite. Men will wear masks to hide their responsibilities in life; women will wear makeup to cover their bruises. We are all afraid to face the world in which the audience before us may be unkind and mute, and so, take roles to appease their minds while denying our true selves. But life goes nowhere once the curtain closes; these roles provide us nothing in the end. To laugh, to cry, to perform on stage— doing so before a group of strangers does nothing when these strangers are just as voiceless and faceless as the dishonest actor.*

The woman that served him every night has marks on her face; the man saw them every time he entered the diner. He knew what they were, those marks, and knew that she desperately tried covering them up every morning with makeup on. He imagines her standing naked in front of the mirror because of those marks; he imagines her frightened and afraid. Shamed, even, disgusted with herself. He sees her helpless and in pain, lost and pitiful because of those marks, and wonders why, when so easily visible on her face, no one else cares to notice them. She looks ugly, the man thinks; just so ridiculously ugly. He hates the lipstick on her lips, the eyeliner that decorates her eyes. He hates everything about her face, and wished dearly for her to free herself, to wash her face, the makeup, the tears, the bruises, the shame and all.

He'd come in weeks ago and had spotted her behind the counter. Her eyes had caught his when just barely inside the door, and they'd both stopped. Small flares of burning pink had gathered beneath her eyes and given her face a hot helium glow. She'd walked away after a minute and had gone back inside the kitchen while he'd stood there bewildered and frozen. She didn't serve him that night. She'd come out only when he was shrugging on his jacket about to leave.

He had seen her eyes, though. Before she turned away, he'd seen the shape of her right eye, and had thought it looked like a piece of wet tissue paper hanging haphazardly from the corner of a battered eye socket. Its skin was pulled down millimeters lower than her left, seemingly torn from her face, quivering like loose dead muscle. He understood then. He understood, and so, without fully being aware of what he was doing, he'd reached into his wallet, pulled out whatever he could find, and casually thrown it out on the table. It was two fifty-dollar bills. He'd taken a pen from his pocket and written the letters *J.J.* on them.

*Jenny*, he thinks, *oh, Jenny. You're so much better than this. What happened to you?*

"Hey," she said as she poured his water. "Nice to see you here. Same as usual, right?"

"Yeah. Please."

She scribbled his order down. "A few minutes, okay?"

He nodded. She smiled at him, folded her notepad, and walked away.

*Stop her*, a voice whispered. *Stop her before she walks away again. Just stop her before she walks away.*

He sighed. He turned his head to the side and closed his eyes. A memory had entered his mind. Just some old memory where everything had been good and warm. Just some memory from the past.

*Stop her. Stop her before she walks away, stop—*

"Jenny, wait. We need to talk."

She jerked to a stop. The move was so sudden that the ice cubes in her water pitcher made a clanking noise as they collided with one another. Bits of water spilled from the edge.

"Sorry," she said as she turned around, "what was that?"

"Talk," the man said. He rose from his seat and slowly approached her. "We need to talk."

"Oh. I'm on shift right now. Maybe next—"

"You can't even spare five minutes?" he asked sharply. "There's no one here, Jenny. It's just you and me."

He walked closer. Jenny took a step back and felt the surface of her forehead collect with sweat. Her mouth turned dry.

"Jen—"

"No." She took another step away from him. "Don't come near me. Don't you *dare*, do you understand? I don't know you, okay? I don't know you, have never seen you in my *life*, and don't—"

"Stop acting like that, Jenny. You—"

"Stop saying my name like you *know me!*" She slammed the water pitcher down on a nearby table. "Just stop! Get the hell away from me! Just leave me alone and go back to *wherever you came from!*"

She swallowed. She stared at him, breathless, and wiped her eyes. She turned around and suddenly felt a hand on her wrist.

"How could you have turned out like this?" he asked. "How you have changed *so much?* How could you do this to yourself, what—"

"DON'T FUCKING TOUCH ME!"

She threw his hand off.

"Go away! I don't need you anymore, I don't need you *here!*"

She slapped him. Her hand whipped through the air and made a loud *SMACK!* against his face.

The man's head snapped to the side and tears blurred his vision. Part of her ring had cut into his cheek; a small slash opened below his cheekbone, spreading hot like embers.

"*Go away,*" Jenny moaned. "Why don't you just go away and leave me alone? What did I ever do to you to make you *do this to me!*"

He stared at her. He said nothing, and watched again as she turned away. The burn on his cheek began to fade.

"*Jinyoung.*"

Jenny jerked to a stop. Her body froze, and her shoulders became rigid at his voice.

"Look at me, Jinyoung. Don't walk away from me again."

She turned to him. Dripping mascara slid down her face like black tears.

"What do you want?" Jenny sobbed. "What do you just *want?*"

"I'm going back to Seattle tomorrow," he said. "I have to leave. Come with me. Leave Boise and just come home with me. Please."

Something small and light flickered through her eyes. It was quick, barely there, lost in again under a sea of black and brown.

"Go away," Jenny whispered after a moment. "Just go away and leave me alone. I don't want you here."

"Jinyoung—"

*"DON'T CALL ME THAT! DON'T EVER CALL ME THAT AGAIN!"*

She brought her hands up and gripped the sides of her head. Pathetic sobs escaped her lips.

"Don't call me that. Don't you *ever* call me that ever again, do you understand? Just don't."

He gazed at her, thoughtful, pitying, hurt. He could see another woman at the counter out of the corner of his eye. ABIGAIL her nametag read. She stood frozen and wide-mouthed, her eyes bulged out fat on her face. A hand had come up to her neck while the other hand had disappeared beneath the counter. Telephone, the man guessed. Police.

"Is this what you want?" Jenny spat, ripping off her wedding ring. She had to snarl as she pried it off, wrestling it off her finger. She cried, threw it at him, and heard it bounce somewhere on the floor. Another hoarse sob escaped her.

"Just go away, Daniel," Jenny whispered. She brought her arms up to hold herself and turned her face away. "Just go away before we call the cops. Please. For me."

Daniel gazed at her. He said nothing and silently turned away. He gathered his jacket and reached into his wallet. He threw two bills onto the table and sighed, wishing that he could face her. The makeup on her face was disgusting.

"One last time, Jenny," he said quietly. "Just come back with me. You don't need to be here. You won't have to be afraid with me. I promise."

Jenny lowered her eyes, shaking her head. "Go away, Daniel," she whispered again. "Please just go away. Leave me alone. I don't know you."

Daniel brushed past her. He said nothing as he moved past but briefly touched his hands with hers. Jenny recoiled at the touch—but, before she drew back, she let his fingers firmly hold hers.

*I should have let you go, Jenny*, Daniel thought as he opened the doors. A cold pocket of air hit his face. *I should have let you go. I should have just let you go and let you die in my memory as someone I once knew. I'm sorry for ever hurting you. Just so goddamn sorry.*

At the edge of the light—the light separating the night and dark, the fluorescent glows of Red Moon's midnight shine and autumn's cold chill—thin snowflakes drifted slowly from the sky and fell around Daniel's feet. Daniel lifted his face and closed his eyes, letting them land against his face. After a few seconds, he was out of the diner's shadow, and back in the dark.

\*\*\*

Jenny sank to the floor and wrapped her arms around herself. She felt Abigail holding her and whispering in her ear. Extra tears smeared her cheeks and forehead, and Abigail's sugary bubble-gum breath spewed in her face, suffocating her.

"Ted? John?"

There was some clatter from the kitchen, some sound, and then the approach of shoes.

"Think he's gone now," Ted said.

Abigail nodded, retaking Jenny in her arms. "Jenny? Are you okay?"

Jenny shook her head. Shivers ran through her body and forced her to hold herself tighter. Her face was a mess, makeup oozing down her cheeks. She wiped her face and sniffled.

"Bathroom," she whispered. "I think…I think I'm going to throw up."

She got up and felt Abigail's arms drop away.

"Do you want to call the pol—"

Jenny shook her head and stumbled towards the bathroom.

She barely made it. She ran towards the stalls on uneven clanking heels, opened the door, and crashed down on her knees before a violent torrent of vomit exploded from her mouth. A horrible liquid burn of morning waffles and cheap French fries ripped through her throat and scorched her tongue. She heaved, retched, and vomited a second time, feeling her chest muscles tighten, her stomach squeeze, her throat burn. For a moment, the pressure in her chest was so great she couldn't breathe, and the world around her dimmed to uneven colors. Jenny sighed when she was done, haggard in the cheeks, sweat drenching her face. Another upheaval of vomit surged through her throat, and she held it back, swallowing, burping. Murky vomit-yellow from the toilet splashed her face.

*Oh, Jesus Christ, it's all over my face, it's everywhere on my lips, it's like that*

*(blood)*

*tomato sauce from two nights ago. It just smells so horrible.*

She pulled away from the toilet and leaned against the wall. Cold tiles touched her neck and cooled her skin. She leaned her head back and closed her eyes, gasping. *I'm going to die,* Jenny thought frantically. *I'm going to die if I puke again. My chest can't take it, I can't breathe when it rips through me, my stomach just hurts so bad. Christ, it smells.*

The bathroom door opened.

"Jenny? Jenny, are you all right?"

"Go away, Abigail. Leave me alone."

"You sure you're okay?"

*No, Abigail. I don't think I am anymore. I don't think I ever was. But who are you to care when you don't even know me?*

"Five minutes," Jenny yelled back. She kept her eyes closed as she called out again. "Just five minutes, Abigail."

There was a slight pause, an "okay," and then a slight muffled sound of feet moving away.

Jenny pulled the pins out of her hair and let out a deep, shuddering sigh. She reached over and flushed the toilet. Foul, fetid smells of fresh vomit and toilet water filled her nose. She let out another sighing gasp, leaned her head back, and felt the world slowly slip away.

# CHAPTER 6

Daniel opened his eyes and realized there was a silence in the room. It was a deep silence, sharp and invading, ringing in his ears like a loud afterthought of some distant clap. Splashed sounds of raindrops periodically punctured the silence while thin, slight, indirect sounds of notebook paper brushing against each other whispered in the back. The sounds to Daniel reminded him of denim-skin jeans slowly being peeled from naked legs, of the removal of skintight garments from the body, and of the eventual revealing of flesh that was fresh, taut, smooth…skintight. Quiet yawns sounded around him while loud, rusty, and mechanical shrieks split the air as students shifted in their rotating metal stools. Fists muffled autumnal coughs, and loud sniffles sounded through the tables. Daniel grimaced when hearing the sniffles. He imagined a thick slip of phlegm running down his throat as someone hacked behind him.

*Silence*, Daniel thought quietly. *The sound I hear around me is silence. Despite the noises I hear, there's a silence to everything, and right now I'm hearing it.* Feeling *it*.

Physics equations littered the whiteboard in front of him. Graphs, unit numbers, complicated diagrams, substituting coefficients, and Greek letters denoting special functions and constants all screamed wildly at him in a colorful myriad fashion. The whiteboard now looked like a splattered rainbow mutated into thousands of different numbers.

Daniel turned his head towards his physics teacher. He asked calmly: "Sorry, Mr. Domen. What was the question?"

"I asked, Daniel," Mr. Domen said, rather patiently and kindly, "if you'd be so kind to find the wavelength and frequency of the equation up on the wall. Don't forget to find the velocity as well."

Daniel raised his eyes to the board. The equation

$$y(x, t) = (0.35m)\sin(10\pi t - 3\pi x + \pi/4)$$

had been written there for him to solve. He stole a glance toward Erika, his table partner.

"Sorry," she whispered. She gave him an apologetic shrug. "I tried to wake you. You can use my notes if you want."

Daniel waved her off. "That's fine," he said.

He approached the whiteboard. His sneakers squeaked and his footsteps lagged; another blanket of silence seemed to fall on his shoulders as he approached the board. He was suddenly aware of the entire class staring at him.

*I didn't even do the practice problems last night*, Daniel thought mildly. *I just stayed up reading and thinking. I don't know what I'm doing up here.*

He grabbed the calculator that was near the whiteboard and punched in what he hoped were the right values. His other hand went to grab a blue Expo dry-erase marker.

"Go ahead and solve for maximum magnitude of the transverse velocity of the string too, Daniel," Mr. Domen said behind him.

Daniel punched in a few more calculations, wrote his work step-by-step on the board, and circled his answer. He announced: "Maximum velocity is ten-point-ninety-nine meters per second."

Mr. Domen looked down at his answer sheet. He nodded, satisfied, and asked the class: "Anyone disagree?"

Silence answered him.

"Any questions?"

More silence.

"Does everyone understand the steps Daniel went through to get his answers? Maybe, no, sorta?"

More silence with a few nervous nods.

"Well, okay then. Thanks, Daniel."

Daniel returned to his seat and sat down with a heavy sigh.

Mr. Domen neared the board. Now noise exploded through the classroom as everyone hastily opened their notes to scribble down whatever it was they could. Binders clapped open, sheets of paper ripped from notebooks, and tight, dull, tapping fingers hurriedly typed away as those with laptops sought to record word for word Mr. Domen's lecture. Coughs and sniffles persisted while the rain outside dulled.

"Nice job," Erika said to him as he slumped back in his chair. "You looked bored up there."

"I'm always bored in this class," Daniel said back heavily. Erika's smile disappeared.

"Yes, well…" She turned away. "We all can't be smart like you, Daniel Fischer. Some of us have to actually suffer before we can have what you have. Not everyone is so privileged."

Daniel looked at her, hurt. He tried to think of something to say, but managed nothing. He said finally, "Erika. I didn't mean—" and stopped when a bunch of papers were handed their way. Erika took one of the sheets and placed it in her binder. Daniel watched sourly from the side and then passed the rest of the sheets away. He didn't have a binder. He also never did any of the practice problems.

"Are you going to be tutoring again this Friday after school?" Erika asked him lightly. She kept her face from him. "For the upcoming quiz next week?"

"Maybe. I have to tutor Maria and Savannah for chemistry tomorrow. And then there's Kooper."

"Ah, Kooper. I heard he's still on the team because of you."

Daniel said nothing. He watched quietly from the side as she brought her nose to her paper and scribbled her name down. She was ignoring him.

"Erika."

"Hmm?"

Daniel opened his mouth, closed it, and then paused. He just stared at her and felt another poignant ache in his chest. Unraveling holes decorated the sleeves of her sweater; washed-out blue colored the thighs of her jeans.

"Nothing," he said quietly. "Sorry."

Erika looked at him. A thoughtful look went to her eyes, and then she went back to her notes, shrugging.

\*\*\*

Daniel sat alone in the school's library conference room an hour later with nothing in front of him. He sat leaned back in his chair with his eyes closed and his face directed towards the clock along the wall. Once in a while he would open his eyes to read the clock, but for the most part, he kept his eyes closed. He was tired this morning. Outside, rain fell, hitting the cement surface of the courtyard like impatient tapping fingers. He'd opened the blinds behind him to let a leaden light into the room, and now a dark somber gray lit the walls. He'd kept the lights off when entering.

Beyond him, outside the room, sounds of printing paper and rushing feet filled the library. It was lunchtime now. It was A lunch.

*I am here doing nothing,* he thought quietly. *I am doing nothing here, and in this boredom that seems pleasant, I am in anguish, for this moment of freedom reveals to me my own loneliness. Moreover, this moment of freedom reveals the hectic lifestyle of the world around me, where I in this brief moment of enjoying the rain am able to realize my freedom at the expense of others. And it hurts. This freedom now temporarily gained? It hurts because it reasserts my loneliness. No one here is with me in this moment of peace.*

He thought of Erika and the look she'd given him before turning away. The look hadn't been defiant or malicious, but rather, doleful and hurt. It was a look he saw often when with his peers; it was a look he always hated. He recalled the holes in her sleeves and the faded coloring of her jeans, jeans that were too tight, jeans that were withered and faded, jeans that he remembered on her legs two years ago. Her hair smelled like spicy burnt autumn leaves, and she owned no more than a few pairs of fluffy woolen

90

sweaters, hand-me-downs bought at cheap clothing stores. He'd wanted to apologize to her, but he knew that his voice would have sounded insincere when speaking.

Smart. She had called him just so, so *smart*. Daniel hated the word.

*In this dichotomy called intelligence and its opposite*, he thought sadly, *the one called intelligent is always made superior before the venerating eyes of the inferior. Words that supplement the Individual are words reflected back onto the Speaker, for in order for the Speaker to utter words toward the Individual, the Speaker in their mind must already have formulated the opposite of their words before speaking. In order for this world to call me "smart" or "intelligent" or whatever it is they call me, they themselves must already in their minds have a standard of what is "smart" and "intelligent," and must by default admit to themselves that these are things they are not when loaning me these words. I am "smart" because the Speaker admits they are not as smart as me when saying these words; the standard is established in their words whenever speaking. Just as one cannot call another "boy" without acknowledging the opposite "girl" in their mind, their praise for me is at their own expense.*

He opened his eyes. Shadowy globs decorated the walls of the conference room; continuous soft rainfall echoed behind him. The globs along the walls were shadows belonging to the rain outside, and they speckled the room like soft bruises.

*I hate this. I hate this dichotomy, I hate this feeling of always having to be seen as smart, hate hearing how people always talk about me. I want to be my self. I hate how I can no longer make a human mistake without gasps or wide-eyed surprise by my classmates, hate how I can't just be free and allowed to want normally like a human being. I'm smart only because those around me degrade themselves for my sake, and am smart only because those around me are not my equal. Saying this will have me sound conceited and pretentious without the world realizing that I mean it that the individual can exist without the dependency of the other. I shouldn't have to be the dependency of my peers; I shouldn't be made to be so alone right now. I just want a friend. I just want a friend who doesn't care about "smart." Should I strip down naked for you, Erika, and tell you that fashion doesn't matter, you would penalize me for patronizing, wrong me for insulting you.*

The memory that came to mind then was of Francis Lagabas jumping up and down in his IB Anatomy/Physiology class with a mid-term exam held in his hands. He waved his exam wildly above his head and danced like a madman through class. He had scored a ninety-six on the exam while Daniel had scored a ninety-four. The news to Francis was akin to winning the lottery.

"I beat Daniel Fischer!" he shrieked. "I beat *Daniel Fischer! I beat Daniel Fischer! Hell yeah!*" Those around him laughed and applauded with awe. Some looked in Daniel's direction and told him: "Looks like you're slipping, Daniel."

Daniel had frowned. A sense of hurt had grown inside him like a thorn stuck in his side. He'd thought to himself: *Why is everyone so happy over this? Do they really see me as that great? Jesus, Francis, you and everyone else at this school could be smarter than me if you all just studied. I'm not better than you. All of you here, all of you who praise me and think so highly of me…I'm no better than you.*

The moment had put him in a somber mood that had been interpreted as cold jealously. In order to compensate, Daniel had smiled wildly at everyone around him and offered jokes to the side. He hated himself at that moment; he hated having to lie with a smile on his face.

Steven Kooper had approached him last month asking if he'd be his physics tutor. Daniel at that time had taken a few tutoring positions to pass the day and earn extra credit. He'd spoken with Mr. Domen asking for a tutoring position, and had done the same for Mr. Holton, the instructor for IB Organic/Inorganic Chemistry. Both had said sure.

He'd gone to the printing office and taped a few posters on the walls leading to the Great Hall. The posters had been brief and his background description terse: It simply stated he was a mathematics tutor who also taught physics and chemistry. It also stated that he was a senior.

"Are you Daniel Fischer?"

He was reading a book in the library. He looked up upon hearing the voice, and had seen a nervous, timid, and even frightened Steven Kooper at his table. He placed his book aside.

"Hey. Yeah, I'm Daniel. Can I help you?"

Kooper showed him one of the posters he was holding. "Um. do you do that tutoring thing for physics?"

"Yeah."

"Oh. Sweet. Would you mind if I asked you for help?"

Daniel glanced at him, curious, and felt an overwhelming sense of sadness.

Steven Kooper stood at his table towering with his 5' 10" frame, yet the expression on his face was reminiscent of a ten-year-old boy lost and scared at the toy store. He wore his Oakland Raiders cap skewed to the side with the brim just jutting over his right ear, and had his varsity jacket from last year's season draped over his shoulders. His jeans hung low and folded at the ankles; his beltless waist sagged toward his thighs.

*Naked,* Daniel thought incoherently. *This guy in front of me is afraid to become naked. Should someone strip him of his varsity jacket, remove his cap, take away his swagger, eliminate his height, he'd have nothing, and this is why he looks so nervous when approaching me. Without his reputation, without this high-school, his shoulders, his hands, he has nothing, and he at this moment when looking at me for my help realizes this. He isn't proud of himself. Football season only lasts so long. At this moment of brief hesitation seeking help from another, he realizes this. He realizes it when seeing me seeing him. Fashion just means nothing.*

"Sure," Daniel said pleasantly. He tried offering another smile, but felt it grow insincere on his face. "I'm Daniel."

"Steven, but I like to be called Kooper. Like, just to keep things cool and casual." He paused. He looked at him. "Like, do you mind if we start today? Like now?"

Daniel nodded, said sure again, and told him to take out his physics textbook.

They worked together for an hour in the library. Kooper muttered dry curses here and there, and Daniel watched quietly from the side. He pitied him. It was a feeling he hated when felt, but was a feeling impossible to ignore. There were tattered holes on the shoulders of his jacket, some loose stitching on his back, and faded coloring on his arms. Daniel knew that the jacket would eventually become useless in life. *All* varsity jackets, in fact, would eventually become useless, and it hurt him that so very few realized this.

"Damn, man," Kooper said after a while. He took off his Raiders cap and swiped a hand through his hair. "I dunno. Could we go over on how to do it again?"

"Sure," Daniel said. He tried grinning for him. "No problem."

They drilled through a few more practice problems and then stopped when Daniel told him he had to go to class.

"We can meet tomorrow," he said, gathering his notebook. He didn't have a backpack. He rarely carried anything to school these days. "I'll be here in the library at the same time if you want."

Kooper nodded, rubbing his face and titling backward in his chair. "Man," he sighed. "This shit is tough. I don't get how you get stuff like this. Einstein stuff, you know?"

"I just try," Daniel replied. "It's tough for everyone. We'll practice again tomorrow. You'll be okay."

"Wish I were smart as you, D. It'll be cool to have a brain like yours. You don't mind if I call ya D, do you?"

Daniel said nothing. He just studied the earnest regard in his eyes and felt hurt inside. Finally, he said: "Sure. D's fine. Call me that if you want."

"Sweetness. I guess I'll catch ya tomorrow." Kooper gathered his things and stood up. He grinned. "Guess I'm kinda just a dumb jock to ya, huh, D?"

Daniel said nothing. He stared at him. He said: "You're not dumb, Kooper. You just…you just don't know the material. That's all. Everyone begins school not knowing the material. That's why they call it learning. That's why they call it life."

The grin on Kooper's face lightened. "You know what, D? You're a pretty cool dude." He slapped one meaty hand against his back. "See you tomorrow. I'd like to get some genius off of you sometime. Peace!"

Daniel watched as he walked off.

Kooper eventually received his first A in physics because of him. And, because of him, he'd been able to play in the Big Game. Daniel didn't care what the "Big Game" was (nor did he care), but was just glad that Kooper had done well on his exam. Kooper had called him later to say thanks.

"D! D baby, what's up!"

"Kooper?"

"D! Hey man, what's happening!"

A hurricane echo of shouts and cheers sounded in the background. Daniel winced and pulled the phone away from his ear. He could hear other voices in the foreground and another thunderous roar from the crowd. An eruption of clapping sounded behind him.

"Hey, man! I just wanted to call ya and say thanks! Thanks for everything, D! *We kicked ass!* We kicked ass, my man, and it was all because of you! You hear that, D? *It was all because of you, brotha!*"

Daniel nodded, understanding. He was calling right after the game. He was calling him to say thanks for not having him flunk out from the team. He was calling probably not even out of uniform yet. Daniel was touched.

"No problem, Kooper," Daniel replied. "Don't thank me. Thank yourself."

There was another holler behind him, another raucous of male laughter, and then Kooper was saying: "Yo, D, I gotta go now. I'll catch ya later, man. I just wanted to call and say thanks, buddy! Thanks for everything!" There was one last *whooo!* and the phone went silent in Daniel's hand.

Daniel stared at his cell phone for a moment and then snapped it closed. He gazed out the window above his computer desk and let out a thin, forlorn, sigh.

Days later, Kooper would come to him again and hug him in the middle of the hallway, thanking him with tears in his eyes for another A on a pop-quiz. Daniel would hold him back, smile as best as he could, and feel again that tight, poignant pain in his chest whenever Kooper slapped him on the back.

"Good for you, Kooper," Daniel had whispered. "Just…good for you."

***

The bell rang.

Daniel jerked opened his eyes and felt a quick tremor spread through his back. Gooseflesh tightened his arms. He glanced around the room, startled, thinking that he'd heard a voice.

There was nothing.

Outside, hurrying feet rushed by the conference room doors and threw darting shadows through the blinds. Daniel sat back with a sigh and raised his eyes to the clock.

12:30. A lunch was over. It was time for B lunch now.

*I can skip class,* he thought distantly. *I can skip class, and me not being there would be exactly the same as if I were there. There is just nothing right now.*

Jenny. It'd been her voice he heard, her voice that had come with the soft tonal bings of the bell. Thinking of her made the gooseflesh on his arms tighten all over again.

*Where are you, Jenny?* Daniel thought distantly. *Why aren't you here? What happened to you last week, why aren't you here at school? Last week when we met together at the library, you…you just felt so light in my arms. You were just so light when I carried you.*

A shudder broke through Daniel, forcing him up from his chair. He didn't want to think about her. He didn't want to think about her, and yet, he still couldn't throw off the image of blood on her lips, the image of vomit on her face, blood on his shirt, the scent of tears against his neck. He'd held her last week with her sobbing in his arms. He'd half-carried her to the bathroom and had just held her while she shuddered uncontrollably against him.

*So light,* Daniel thought quietly again as he opened the door. He stepped out of the conference room and walked out of the library. *Last week when I had held her, she just felt so light in my arms. Jenny. What happened to you last week? Why were you crying?*

As Daniel walked to class, he allowed his mind to replay what had happened last week, blackening his thoughts.

\*\*\*

They met each other last week outside the library as promised. Jenny stood waiting for him with her back against the wall and with her arms folded beneath her chest. Her eyes were dark. Daniel spotted her from the end of the hallway and felt a slight giddiness pick up in his chest. Butterflies fluttered nervously in his stomach. He set his feet to a walking pace and slowed his breathing, hearing his heartbeat in the loud background of his ears. His ears flushed hot.

Jenny. He was going to meet *Jenny* soon, and the anticipatory thrill that filled him then was like a dull toothache that needed to be badly soothed. He'd noticed her since the beginning of the year, of course, and knew that other boys noticed her too. She was quiet in the classroom and always with a pensive look in her eyes, eyes that Daniel admired whenever catching a glimpse of their dagger-like shape.

She sat near the front in Ms. Karens' IB American History class and always presented her backside to him. She wore plain black North Face sweaters and jeans most of the time. Whenever she bent forward to read from her textbook, leaned over to pick up her backpack, or simply just stretched her hands up for a full yawn, a sliver of naked back would slip loose from between the waist of her jeans and sweater, revealing a patch of smooth skin. A trace of white cotton underwear sometimes presented itself, but it was mostly the smooth flesh of her lower back that captivated Daniel, made him watch her, *want* her, admire her. Her face to him was a quiet solemn beauty that evoked images of burnt autumn leaves.

He'd spotted her several weeks ago standing in the hallway near the vending machines. This had been in October, right when everything was turning bright gold with autumn. He'd frowned when seeing her then, thinking that she spent most of her time eating lunch at the "Asian table." He'd walked past her in the hallway, inconspicuous, and headed for the stairs, taking time to glance at her over his shoulder. Her eyes were red and her cheeks pale; dark hollows formed on her cheeks, and the black silky wave that was usually her hair hung around her shoulders frizzled and unkempt.

*Tired,* Daniel thought as he walked past. *She must've pulled an all-nighter last night. She just looks dead-tired this morning.*

She stepped toward the vending machine. Daniel turned around, watching as she inserted a dollar into the bill slot. She punched in a few keys on the number pad, stood back, and waited. She bent down after a second and reached in to collect her item. Daniel waited, half-anxious and anticipating, wanting to see whether or not her sweater would pull up from her waist and reveal that smooth slip of naked back again. She reached into the vending machine and took out what looked like to be a blue bag of M&Ms. Daniel raised an eyebrow at her, curious. She clutched the bag of M&Ms and suddenly made her way toward him.

Daniel started. He briefly caught sight of her eyes and had one alarming moment where he thought she'd spotted him. He casually turned around and headed up the stairs. There was a small drinking fountain on the second floor, and Daniel quickly went to it, turning his back. He felt her behind him and took in two big thirsty gulps. She walked past and Daniel slowly lifted his head. He thought for a minute, hesitated, and then decided to follow. As he moved behind her, he noticed the slight sway of her hips again, the ample shape of her thighs, the skin-tightness of her jeans, jeans so tight, he could make out the bulge of her cell phone in her pocket.

That he was temporarily stalking another student hadn't yet entered his mind—he was caught in a paroxysm of unbroken curiosity that seemed to cut off all logical thinking to his brain, shackling his feet toward one direction. As she walked, he slowed his steps and let her move ahead, trying hard to match her footsteps with his, trying hard not to breathe too loudly. Part of him chided himself for allowing his eyes to fall to her ass, while another part of him chided himself for chiding.

He followed her until she was in the hallway between E and D-200. There, a small boy sat on the hallway floor with wooden blocks in his lap. When Daniel saw this, he stopped, and backtracked several steps. He watched as Jenny approached the boy and smiled. It was a kind smile. The boy raised his head and then Jenny showed him the bag of M&Ms.

The boy's face lit up and his mouth dropped open; a cheer spilled out. He raised both hands at her and chirped happily as she shook the bag.

*What are you doing, Jenny?*

The boy was Michael Lamb, the one and only student enrolled in Special Ed. at Evanston-Woods. Daniel saw him sometimes limping through the hallway with his Scooby-Doo lunchbox and wide-eyed gawking face. It was unknown what type of degenerative disorder Michael Lamb had, but Daniel knew that it affected his physical shape and that it was incurable. His fingers were gnarled and crooked at the joints; his gait when walking was biased to his left foot, and his back had a horrible hunch. His limbs sometimes randomly twitched, and his foot dragged along the floor. He had crutches, Daniel knew, but very rarely did he see him using them. When he spoke, a loud, honking croak reverberated from his throat and became nearly inarticulate to those who heard him. He sat in random places in the hallways sometimes, but was usually between E and D-200 where the Special Ed. classroom was located.

*What are you doing, Jenny?* Daniel thought again. *Just what are you doing upstairs here during lunch? What are you doing with Michael?*

As if to answer his question, a door in the hallway opened, and a heavy-set woman stepped out. It was Mrs. Stevens, Michael Lamb's caretaker and personal assistant. She had a large face and long curly hair that fell past her shoulders. Daniel usually saw Mrs. Stevens with Michael carrying colorful bags of medicine and snacks against her bosom. She made sure Michael entered his classes on time, fed him his specific diet, changed his clothes when necessary, and did everything else a caretaker was meant to do. Daniel thought Mrs. Stevens was a nice lady. She also taught ESL.

As he watched, Jenny jerked with surprise and took one step back. She hid the M&Ms behind her back and stared at Mrs. Stevens. A look of guilt flushed through her face. She said something then, something Daniel couldn't hear, and slightly bowed her head. Daniel could only imagine it was an apology.

Mrs. Stevens slowly stepped out. She smiled at Jenny and placed a gentle hand on Michael's head. She ruffled his hair. She smiled and said something that diminished Jenny's worried look. Jenny offered a light, timid nod in return.

Slowly now, and with one foot forward, Jenny offered the bag of M&M's to Mrs. Stevens, and allowed one, small, shy smile. A surprised look went through Mrs. Stevens' face. She reached for the bag of M&Ms and took it with a grateful smile. Then she looked down at Michael and said something that made him cheer and nod his head. She turned back to Jenny, and a look of warmth, sadness, and pity filled her eyes. She said something else then. Daniel didn't need an interpreter to know what was said.

*Thank you.*

Jenny lowered her head and bowed, doing it shyly, quietly, slightly, barely lowering her head so that it seemed nothing more than a deep acknowledging nod, an embarrassed yet modest shrug. She gave Michael one last look, smiled, and waved him goodbye. Michael cried out joyfully in return.

Daniel stood where he was and watched as she approached him. He scanned her, and this time when she was near him, he refused to turn away. She lifted her eyes at him and their gazes locked. She regarded him, briefly, steadily, and then turned away. She walked past him.

Daniel turned to look back at Michael and Mrs. Stevens. The two of them were smiling and laughing. Michael had his crooked hands up and was asking for an M&M. He cried out happily as Mrs. Stevens spoke to him and uttered loud piercing caws that filled the hallway.

*This is it,* Daniel thought suddenly. *This is something I can never do. What just happened before me…I can never do what just happened, never do what she did. No matter how intelligent, no matter how praiseworthy…I just can never do what she did.*

Later at the end of that same day—right before the bell rang, just seconds before school let out—Daniel thought back to that big blue bag of M&Ms and Michael's jubilant cry, and smiled.

It was a forlorn smile. It was a humbled smile.

***

Daniel wanted to ask her about Michael. He wanted to ask her how she helped others without objectifying and degrading them, how it was possible to help those in need *without* pitying and hate. How was it possible to objectify freely? And how was it possible to retain a sense of self while still interacting with others in this world? He wanted to ask her all of this—he just wanted to be with her. "Hey," he said as he approached her. He felt a goofy grin go to his face and tried to surpass it. He hadn't noticed she was without a backpack today. "Ready?"

Jenny looked at him. At once, all of Daniel's light giddiness plummeted, and his heart went cold. Her eyes—they were red this morning. They were not only red, but tired as well, straining to stay awake with a glassy, dazed stare. Dark patches of purple stained the bottom of her eyes; oil covered the swell of her cheeks. The partial bangs above her eyes were ruffled and messy.

"Daniel," she began. "Hey. Look, I'm really sorry, but…but I can't work with you on the project anymore. I have to go home."

He stared at her. She lowered her eyes again and began picking at the sleeves of her sweater.

"What?"

"Yeah. Look, I'm sorry, but something…something came up with my

101

family. I won't be in school for a few days, and like…look, I'm just really sorry. Maybe we can work on something else. Okay?"

She scanned his face, waiting, hoping, wanting to see anger. Anger was good, anger was kind—anger would help deflect penetrating questions and leave him with his own thoughts, scornful or not. If there was pity or hurt, then she would feel guilty, and guilt…guilt was something her heart couldn't bear at the moment. There already was just so much of it.

"Is everything okay then?" he asked. A concerned look came across his face, hurting Jenny. "Like, with your family and all?"

"Yeah. Yeah, everything's cool." She sighed. "Look. That's all I wanted to come here and say. I'm…I'm sorry again for having stood you up like this after you helped me yesterday with Kooper. If I figure stuff out at home, then maybe I'll come back, but it isn't likely, and, like, Ms. Karens…"

Her voice faded. A student walked by and headed to the C flex area, leaving them alone in the hallway. Fourth period was starting; everyone around them had disappeared to class. The feeling that followed was an eerie silence filled with a strange tension of coldness and dread. The vending machines next to them came to life with a startling hum.

*A dead silence*, Jenny thought incoherently, *it's a dead silence we're hearing while alone in the hallway. Every school has one, but no one hears it. Only certain people can hear it. Only people like…like Daniel, I guess.*

"Yes?"

She jumped at his voice. It sounded much louder now, now that the hallway was empty. It sounded much closer as well, and Jenny realized that in their moment of silence, *she* had stepped closer toward *him*.

"'Yes?' What do you mean 'yes'?"

"You were saying. About Ms. Karens?"

"Oh. Right. Look, Daniel, I've already spoken about my situation at home to Ms. Karens, and she's going to let me off for a few days. That's why I came to school today. I'm sorry, but I…I just won't be around."

*Her situation*, Daniel thought quietly. *Why does she always refer to it like that, like it's something so far away yet still close to her? What happened last night with her family?*

"And Ms. Karens really said she was cool with all of this."

"Yes—"

"And you're really just dealing with stuff at home?"

*"Yes!"* she screamed. *'I* already told you! *Yes, yes!* I already spoke with her this morning! Can't you hear? Jesus, why do you keep asking—"

Jenny stopped herself. A look of hurt and surprise filled his face and her heart skipped several beats.

"Goodbye, Daniel," Jenny said quickly, turning around. She brought a hand up to wipe her nose. "I don't want to see you again. I'm sorry for yelling."

"Jenny—"

She walked three steps and felt a hand on her wrist. "Look, I'm sorry-"

*"Don't touch me!"* She threw his hand away. "Don't touch me Daniel, okay? Just don't! Just LEAVE ME ALONE!"

Something hot burned her eyes.

*Please not again please I'm sorry God please don't let me cry don't let me cry in front of him I'm sorry just don't let it be like LAST NIGHT AGAIN.*

"Jenny, hold on a minute, wh—"

"Just *don't,* okay, Daniel? *Don't.* Just…just leave me alone, why can't you?" She pushed her hands against his chest. "What did I ever do to you? Huh? What? You're like this…this guy who I don't even know, and already, I hate you. I just…just…"

She slid to her knees.

*My head…I'm so tired. Ah, God, I'm just so tired.*

Blood trickled from her nose. A cold bleed sped down her upper lip and traced its way to the inside of her mouth.

"Jesus, Jenny."

She heard him but didn't see him. She couldn't tell where anything was anymore.

"Jesus. Jenny, come on, get up, you're all right, you're okay. I've got you, Jenny, I have you, come on…."

He grabbed her by the arms.

"Jenny—"

She shook her head. Tears rolled down her face. "I can't," she sobbed. "I just can't. Daniel—I just *can't*."

"Shh. It's okay. It's okay."

He wrapped his arms around her and felt her face sink into his shoulder. He sank down with her to the floor and held her close. Blood smeared against the collar of his shirt; a hot smell came from the top of her head. It was a wonderful smell. It was a heavy smell, thick and exotic almost, like the perfumed scent of spicy cinnamon.

*She's so slim*, Daniel thought suddenly. *She's just so slim in my arms.*

"I'm not like this," Jenny cried. "I'm not, okay? I…I don't just go crying like this, I'm not trying to use you or anything like that, I don't *use people*—"

"Shh, it's okay, Jenny, it's okay. Don't cry, everything's okay."

She hit him on the shoulder. "*Please* don't say that," she begged. "Please don't. Okay? Cause it's *not* okay with me, okay? Nothing can ever be okay anymore. I know I'm supposed to love my family and stuff, but like…I just *can't*, not when they hate me, not when they won't love me, not when…when…"

She sobbed again. Daniel held her, rocking back and forth with her on the floor. Blood stained his shirt. It had a cold scent to it, smelling like cool liquid metal. Most had smeared on her face and around her mouth, giving her a disgusting clown-like quality. He patted her on the back and whispered in her ear, telling her that it was all right, she didn't need to cry anymore, he wasn't going anywhere, stop crying, stop crying, Jenny, stop crying, she didn't need to cry.

"And like…last night too, right?" she sobbed. "Like, *everybody* fought and stuff. My mom and I…*God*, Daniel, why can't my parents *love* me anymore? Why can't they just love me as their daughter?"

"Don't say that Jenny. They love you, you know they do. They—"

"I'm going back to Korea soon, Daniel."

There was a pause. Jenny felt him pause, felt him hesitate, felt him go rigid against her. And then she felt him rubbing her shoulder again, whispering in her ear (so close now, now that she could almost feel his lips against her): "They love you, Jenny. Believe that. Okay? Just...just believe that. Everything will be o...everything will be all right. Everything will be all right."

He cradled her, holding her close to his chest so that she could wipe her bloody nose. Eventually, her tears subsided and her shaking stopped.

"Get up Jenny," Daniel said after a few minutes. It felt they'd sat for hours together on the floor. "Come on. Please, we have to move."

She shook her head at him and sobbed something he couldn't hear. He hooked his arms under her and helped her to her feet. "Please, Jenny. Come on, I have you. You're all right."

He steadied her, felt something wet against his neck, cringed, and half-carried her to the girl's bathroom in front of the C flex area.

"Jenny—"

"Okay," she said weakly. Her voice was thick and broken. "I'm...okay. I..."

She stepped in and let the door close behind her. Daniel stood where he was and waited, dimly aware that his heart had picked up to a thunderous beat in his chest. He looked to his left and right to see if anyone was passing by, and saw no one.

*Jesus. There's so much blood on my shirt. It looks like I killed a puppy or something, or suddenly went crazy and tossed paint on me. Jesus.*

He grimaced. A large wet stain of black blood soaked through the left side of his collar. The rest of it trailed down his shirt in small delicate patterns of red droplets, splashing here and there like squashed spiders. A cold metallic smell came from the blotch closest to his neck. He shuddered when he picked up its smell. The word *sentient* came to his mind for whatever

105

reason when smelling the blood, making him think that it was alive somehow, conscious even, breathing on his shirt.

*Her smell. It's* her *smell that I'm smelling, it's* Jenny's *smell. Ah, God, I'm smelling* her, *I'm smelling Jenny on my shirt, I'm smelling* her *blood while it's on me, smelling something that came from* inside *her. God, what…*

A horrible image suddenly resurfaced in his mind where Mark Padamada, Anthony Pagaliluan, Francis Lagabas, Ryan Pham, and Dan George had all beckoned him into the library's conference room last year. He had a large gap in his schedule then, and had spent most of his time in the library. Francis had opened the doors to the conference room just as he was walking by and waved him over.

"Daniel! Daniel, hey captain, check this out!"

He'd been presented with a darkened room with laptop monitors set around the tables. The monitors sprayed the walls with a bluish hue, and a loud mechanical whir filled the air. The blinds had been drawn, forcing the light outside through bamboo slits against the walls of the room. Daniel frowned when seeing the laptop monitors. His heart dropped, and he knew instantly what was going on when he first stepped in. Francis shut the door behind him.

"Daniel, dude!" Anthony waved a hand. He sat back leaned in his chair. "You wanna see something cool?"

"Not really…"

They laughed, and Francis wrapped an arm around his shoulders, leading him toward a table. "Been hitting the books, Cap?" he asked. He pulled a chair out for him. "Take it easy, man. You only live once. Gotta have stress relievers now and then, you know?"

Daniel nodded. He gulped, and took the chair as politely as he could. He knew already what was on the laptops; the noise was clear and defining. Mark sat to his side, his eyes glued almost comically to the screen. The lights illuminated his features like a hideous pumpkin. Sweat broke out across Daniel's forehead.

"*Eew!*" Dan George cried. "Ah man! All over her face too! What the hell? God, I hate it when they gotta show the guy's dick all like that. Why can't they just censor the guy's parts and let us just see the girls'?"

They all laughed. Ryan Pham said, "Duuude! I know, right? God, it's hella nasty to see that sometimes. And like, you know, it's *hella* weird to see it when the camera shows all the girls swallowing it and stuff. It's like they swish it all around their mouths and make it like white caramel or something—"

"Yo, Anthony, show Daniel some of your stuff, man," Francis said. "Come on, he just got here. Show the one with the girl with big-ass tits and the huge Mexican guy. I swear, that girl is *hella fiiiiine*—"

"Oh, shit! Ugh, that's hella *weird!*"

All the boys jumped over to Mark's screen. Daniel waited, unsure. He glanced around and then gradually got up with the rest of the boys, heading slowly towards Mark's screen. What else was he *supposed* to do?

*Just one glance*, Daniel thought as he made his way over. *Sure. Why not? Just…fuck it. Whatever.*

"*Ugh*," Mark said again with a quick shudder. "*That's* what girls go through when they go through their period? Dude, that's hella nasty!"

"Shit," Ryan said, "I knew they bleed and all, but I didn't know it looked like *that.*"

Daniel walked behind Mark's shoulders and peered at the screen. What he saw then made him frown and his stomach lurch. He hadn't expected this.

A close-up view of a woman's vagina smeared with blood appeared on the screen. Thick coats of red stuck on the inside of her thighs and smeared deep in between the crevices of her crotch. Blood stained parts of her pubic hair with most of it soaked through the white silk sheets part of the background. There was a pair of white cotton panties to the side of the bed; blood stained the panties.

*Jesus*, Daniel thought coldly. *It looks like rape what I'm seeing. For some reason, this picture of an unknown woman's vagina makes me think of rape.*

"Gross dog, why'd you even look this shit up for?" Dan George asked.

"Man, I was just curious! We're all learning about this in anatomy and physiology class, and I was like, 'Oh, I'mma go and check this out to see how it looks.'"

"Dude, it looks like she pissed cranberry juice or something."

They all laughed (it was a nervous laughter, stiff around the octaves, and tight in their voices. Daniel was the only one not laughing).

"Sick, man. Look at her underwear. God, no wonder women are all pissed off at this time when they have their periods. They'll probably be all thinking they gotta buy new shit at the mall because they keep on bleeding every month."

Laughter struck them. Daniel kept his eyes on the screen and pressed his lips together. He traced the blood on the white sheets and studied the curving thighs of the woman. *This is not a violation and it is not an objectification,* he thought distantly. *What I'm feeling now in terms of disgust and dismay is culture suddenly falling against me and weighing me down. This is a picture, solely a picture with a woman going through her menstrual period, but I at this moment am feeling disgust at my own self for wanting to objectify her. This is a picture, nothing more, and my knowledge of the female body will tell me simply that this is a natural process all women go through— but the shadow behind me, the shadow called CULTURE and SOCIETY, will say that I am objectifying this woman whereby my biases of my own sex are revealed to me in contrast to what is presented before me. We cannot look at bodies objectively any longer in this society for we Americans are sensualists. I feel culture against me at this instant of staring, and know that my disgust is not something inherent or visceral, but loaned and social. I am disgusted at this picture because I am disgusted at myself—I become disgusted by society. Had this picture been presented in a museum, would my feelings of self-disgust been lessened? I hate this picture. I hate what this picture does to women and what it does to men.*

*Rape. We really are raping this woman with our eyes. But I wonder—what is it that this woman is doing to us?*

These were the things that raced through Daniel's mind as he stood there waiting for Jenny with her blood on his shirt. He was horrified; he was disgusted. There was no difference between the blood on his shirt and the blood on the woman's thighs—they both had been given from *inside* the body. The only minute difference was a quality of the physical and of the *right now*. The woman's blood had no effect on him. He could not smell it, touch it, taste it. It was a representation of a reality having occurred sometime in the past made false again by becoming a digital image. But Jenny's blood—it was on his shirt at this *instant*, there for him to smell, feel, touch...taste.

*The blood from the unknown woman,* Daniel thought silently as he looked down at his shirt. *It's similar to the blood from the picture, the same color, the same pattern. Only instead of some random individual, it's Jenny's blood, it's Jenny on my shirt, her blood, someone I know. I have Jenny bleeding all over me, it's her wet smell I'm smelling. This blood is something I know, something that I can call personal. Language simply belies the physical touch of truth—menstrual blood, virgin blood, nose blood, blood-blood. What do I have on my shirt?*

A second voice suddenly spoke up in his mind. It was chirpy sounding and sharp, stating simply: *Daniel! You have to hurry and get your notebook in the hallway! Remember your notebook, Daniel? You left it in the hallway! Hurry and get it before someone steals it! Also—do you know what time it is? You're going to be late for English!*

*Crazy,* he thought. *I'm just going fucking crazy.*

He tapped his knuckles against the door. "Jenny? Jenny, are you all right?"

There was nothing. He knocked again, harder this time, and said, "Jenny. Please let me know if you're okay."

There was still nothing.

Swallowing, Daniel placed his hand on the handle and pushed open the door. A loud flush filled the girls' bathroom just as he was about to call her name again. It was followed by a sigh, a horrible female-retching sound, and then the thick, splattering sounds of splashing water. A loud clanking sound

109

followed, some sobbing, and then heavy gasping. He saw a pair of blue jeans knelt before the toilet.

"Jesus, Jenny."

He closed the door behind him and ran over to the stall. Images filled his mind: Jenny with her entire face bleeding, her eyes dripping with blood, blood caked around her lips, blood spilling down her nose, her face fat and swollen; Jenny sitting with vomit on her mouth, her head reared back, her white neck exposed, her small breasts heaving and struggling to breathe, the crotch of her jeans stained with blood black as poisonous berries; Jenny with white vomit all over her lips, her eyes closed, revulsion on her face, and Dan George again, Dan George crying from the side: *Eew! Ah man! All over her face too! What the hell?*

Daniel slammed the stall door open and found her leaned back against the wall with a trickle of vomit on her lips. Her eyes were closed; her hair was in disarray over her face. Sweat gleamed on her neck. A slight, delicate, paper-thin movement traveled through her throat as she struggled to swallow. She'd taken some toilet paper and tried to wipe her nose, Daniel saw; smudges of blood marked parts of her face like faded fingerprints. A bit of red still ebbed from her nose.

"Daniel. I'm…sorry. I'm not trying to…I'm not trying to make—"

"Shut up." He reached out and grabbed several long rolls of toilet paper. He began wiping her face. "Just shut up, Jenny. Just shut up, okay?"

She nodded. She started crying again. Daniel gently wiped her lips and cleaned her cheeks. A horrible, fetid stench bloomed from her mouth as she spoke. It smelled like sour orange juice and spoiled oatmeal.

"I'm so sorry. I'm sorry, please, God, I know…I know, this shouldn't be happening, I'm sorry I'm like this, but I don't—"

"Shh, Jenny. Don't talk, okay? Just don't talk. Come on. Please."

"Can you forgive me?"

He paused. He'd wiped part of her mouth and was about to wipe her cheeks again when she muttered those words. Now he suddenly stopped and stared at her. "Don't, Jenny," he said firmly. "You don't have to say that to me. Okay?"

"But…please, I'm…I'm asking you if you can forgive me. I've messed up everything for you—"

"Don't," Daniel said again. "Just don't. You have no reason to say sorry to me. No reason, whatsoever. And don't pretend you do, because you don't."

"But your shirt—"

"*Screw* the damn shirt, Jenny! Jesus, listen to you!" He knelt in close and threw the toilet paper away. He gently grabbed her by the shoulders. "God, Jenny, don't say that you're sorry to me anymore. You got that? You have *no* reason to say those words to me. Why do you act like you've done something wrong and need me to forgive you? God, just let it go. Please."

She sniffled. It was followed by a serious of hiccups and gasps. "I'm sorry," she said again. "I'm sorry, I really am. I know you don't want me to say those things, but I am, I really am. Just that my mom…" She wiped her face. "I always have to say it. I always have to say it to them, I always have to say it. I always used to have to say I'm sorry. Just that, last night it didn't work anymore, and now nothing *makes sense…*"

Daniel held her and patted her back. "I know, Jenny," he said. "I know." He rested his chin on her head and closed his eyes. "It's fine, Jenny. I know."

"Will you sit here with me?"

"Yeah. I'm not going anywhere."

"Okay. Okay, thank you."

He nodded again and closed his eyes, grimacing as he heard her hiccup with pain. He thought about saying something but then decided against it. He just sat there and held her, feeling awkward and scared.

They sat like that, for perhaps ten minutes, and in that time, Daniel wordlessly began wiping her face again. Jenny said nothing as he cleaned her. She just kept her eyes closed all throughout, and when she felt another urge to vomit, quickly swallowed it, feeling a horrible wet burn in her throat.

"Daniel?"

"Yeah?"

"I think…I think I got some of it on my shirt."

"Yeah," he said. "I know. It's fine."

She shook her head. "No," she said. "I mean…here." She reached into her jeans and pulled out her car-keys. "Mazda," she said weakly. "Two-thousand-five. Dark green. It's in the back. I always park in the back."

"Are you sure?"

She nodded. She said, "I think…my gym shirt should be there. It's a shirt I bring to school sometimes after P.E. It should be in the backseat."

He took the keys from her. "Will you be okay?"

"Yeah. I need to sit here for a minute. Alone. I don't think I can walk yet."

"I'll only be a few minutes then," he said. He stood up and suddenly heard his knees crack. "I'll be back, okay?"

She nodded. Daniel thought she was going to say more, but then watched sadly as she closed her eyes again. She turned her head away. It looked like she was sleeping.

Daniel pushed the bathroom door open and bolted down the hall. He pumped his legs as fast as he could and eventually made it to the parking lot (he had to be careful when running. Officer Richards sometimes roamed the hall, and he had to stop to grab his notebook. The voice inside his head was *mad, mad, mad!*). Dry autumn wind blew against his face as he dashed through the lot; sparse slants of sunlight broke through the clouds. With some quiet bewilderment, Daniel realized it had only been yesterday since he met her here. The time felt like ten years ago.

He ran to the very end of the parking lot and spotted a small green Mazda next to an old Cherokee. He quickly ran over and unlocked the doors, failing the first three times because his hands shook so badly (the idea of pressing the UNLOCK button on the keychain never occurred to him). There, in the back seat just as she said, was an old rumpled t-shirt. Fresh

112

smells of taut leather and cinnamon filled his nose as he opened the door.

Daniel grabbed the shirt, slammed the car door close, and hustled back towards the school.

"Here," he said once he was back inside. Hoarse gasps escaped his mouth as he spoke. Amazingly, no one had entered the bathroom while he was away. "Jenny?"

She opened her eyes at him. "Thank you," she said weakly. "I…thanks, Daniel."

"Yeah. It's nothing."

She took the shirt from him. "Do you…do you mind if you turned around for a minute?"

He nodded. He turned away at her request, and saw out of the corner of his eyes naked shoulders as she stripped off her shirt and donned on her grayish tee. JESUS LIGHT OF THE WORLD was on the back of the shirt with big, black, bold capital letters next to a green-colored hillside with a sunrise in the background. When she turned around, LIFE THROUGH CHRIST was written on the front in similar big, black, bold capital letters, accompanied now with an outline of a cross in the middle.

"Okay?"

"Yeah. Better. I think. I don't know." She hesitated. "Can I say something to you?"

"Of course, Jenny. Anything."

"I know you won't accept my apology, but…still. I'm sorry. I'm sorry, Daniel. And…and I'm really thankful too. For everything."

Daniel said nothing. He watched sadly as she went back to the wall and sat on the floor. She brought her knees up and wrapped her arms around her legs, resting her face.

Daniel quietly made his way over and sat next to her.

"Will you sit here with me?" she asked in a mute voice. "Daniel?"

"Yeah, Jenny. I will. I'll be with you. I won't—"

The bell rang.

Daniel snapped his eyes open and jerked in his seat. Everyone around him slammed their textbooks shut and gathered their backpacks. The crowded impatiently at the doors. Outside, cumulous clouds parted, revealing white spears of light that spilled onto the carpeted floor. The bell echoed loudly through the room and eventually faded.

"Be wise and start early on the packet!" Mr. Menfree hollered. He stood in front of class with his back turned erasing the whiteboard. "Doing so will only serve you for the better!"

Daniel watched as his peers noisily exited the room. He grabbed his notebook after a moment when they were all gone, and lazily made his way towards the door. He sighed. Eighth period IB Calculus was over. He'd finally made it through the day.

"Mr. Fischer."

He turned around. Mr. Menfree was at his desk packing his things in a leather satchel. He looked up from his things, and said: "Would you like it if I brought you a pillow next week to class, Mr. Fischer? I can provide plenty from home."

Daniel frowned. Mr. Menfree was usually the kindest of teachers, and his use of sarcasm was only very rare. He thought Mr. Menfree liked him.

"I'm sorry, Mr. Menfree," Daniel said. "I...I've been having a busy week. I didn't mean to doze off."

"Were it a simple matter about education and test scores, I would reprimand you, Daniel."

"I know."

"I also didn't stop you to give you a lecture about respect, either."

Daniel looked at him. "Um. Okay?"

Mr. Menfree snapped his satchel closed. He tapped his fingers for a moment, and then asked: "What do you value more, Mr. Fischer? Knowledge? Or life? Which will you choose later as a man?"

Daniel stared at him. He lowered his eyes for a minute, thinking. "I don't know," he said. "I don't think it's possible to exclude either."

"Ah. A very American answer."

Mr. Menfree gathered his satchel and brought the strap over his shoulder. He headed towards the doors.

"Listen, Mr. Fischer. Listen, *Daniel.* I know you are intelligent. I know you know yourself to be intelligent. And I know that your peers know you to be intelligent. They can only have the greatest respect for you while your teachers can only praise and hope the best for you."

"Mr. Menfree—"

"But the problem with you, Daniel, is that you *think too much,* and therefore, are unhappy. You sleep in my class not because it bores you, but because something great preoccupies your mind. Something that you cannot solve. You've become so accustomed to solving whatever it is your mind desires, that when you are faced with certain tribulations that have no true answers, your mind and heart are totally consumed, and you exhaust yourself. Is this what is happening right now, Mr. Fischer?"

Daniel said nothing. He thought back to Erika this morning in Mr. Domen's class and the way she'd turned away from him. He thought about the clothes she wore and the sour expression she gave when others noticed them. He thought about Kooper and his varsity jacket, his loud booming voice and his sad blue eyes, eyes that feared the world, eyes that were like a child's. He thought about Michael Lamb and his happy shrieking laugh when presented with the bag of M&Ms, the way Mrs. Stevens had laughed with him and ruffled his hair. And then he finally thought about Jenny and her hair, the way it wavered in the light like an ocean of black silk, the way her eyes looked like teardrops slanted on their sides, and of her face, the smooth, pale, porcelain shells that were her cheeks. He thought about her blood; he thought about her smell. He simply thought of how wonderful it had been to have encountered her last week in the parking lot, the parking lot where she'd awkwardly struck out her hand to shake his.

Jenny. Jenny Park. He wanted to see her. Ah, how he wanted to see her. It had been a week since the incident in the bathroom.

"Maybe," Daniel said quietly. "I don't know."

Mr. Menfree opened the door. He said, "Be happy with what you have, Daniel. You're still so young—don't waste it on trying to solve problems that only men and women are meant to solve. Enjoy your youth. Enjoy your friends. Find trouble, find love, but most importantly, find yourself. Don't think so much, Mr. Fischer. The world is already yours to command."

Daniel made no reply. He thought for a minute and felt warm afternoon sunlight on his neck. Outside in the flex area, students laughed.

"Mr. Menfree."

"Yes?"

"What if it's this intelligence that separates me from the world? What if the world I have to command turns away from me because it deems me too different and so won't listen to me? How do I compensate? Where do I find my friends?"

A smile went to Mr. Menfree's face. It was a sad smile. "Then find *love*, Mr. Fischer. It's that simple. Not knowledge, not truth, not friends, but love. Once you find love, you will realize that all knowledge comes secondary and easily. And then you simply realize that this is what life is about. This is the truth of humanity: love. With love, you need not command anything."

"What if I can't?" Daniel asked. "What if in life I'm always alone? What then?"

Mr. Menfree laughed. It was a sad and bitter laugh. "Good men like you are always alone at first, Daniel. I thought you understood this. What are we teaching you children these days? *Facts?*"

Daniel said nothing. He watched as Mr. Menfree exited the room and lowered his face from the sun.

# CHAPTER 7

A knock came at his door.

Daniel opened his eyes. He turned his head to the side and felt an old splintering sensation crack in his neck. He groaned. He squinted at his alarm clock and saw that it was 9:43 p.m.

"Daniel? Sweetie?"

"Hmm?"

"Awake?"

His mother's figure stood in the doorway. Light spilled past her shoulders and crept into his room. Slanted shadows trailed from her feet.

"Sure," Daniel muttered tiredly. "Awake."

"Someone's on the phone for you, honey. A girl from school."

"Tell Erika I'll call her back tomorrow," he said. "Maybe e-mail tonight or something."

"Not Erika," his mother said. "Says her name is Jenny, and it's an emergency."

His mind went blank. A jolt ran through his body and his limbs stiffened. "*Who?*"

"Jenny. She said you and her met last week and—"

Daniel threw off his blankets and sat on the edge of his bed. A tidal wave of sleep surged against him, and for a moment, the whole world seemed tilted crazily on its side. He carefully stood up and walked towards the door. "Is she still there?" he asked.

"On hold downstairs." Ellen Fischer frowned at her son. "Have you eaten yet, Daniel? At least a snack when you returned from school?"

"I'm fine," he said. He pushed past his mother and then stopped. He turned around. "I mean, I'll get something while I'm down there, mom. Sorry."

"Some casserole's left over if you want some."

He put on a tentative, sleepy smile. "Thanks."

Ellen Fischer smiled sadly at her son and walked away.

She knew about his habits and knew them like one does a sharp thorn placed in the heart. He was intelligent, he did well in school, and oh, how all his teachers praised him. But whenever looking at her son, there, always beneath his eyes, were dark spots of gloomy depression like clouds on a warm summer day, clouds that never went away, clouds that shadowed so much of his face. He was intelligent, and ah, how this hurt her. It hurt her so, so much. More than once Ellen had found herself staring silently at the ceiling in bed with Neil snoring loudly besides her, wondering, thinking to herself, unsure if she should cry for her son, or just sigh.

*Our son is so wonderful,* she'd sometimes think; *just so wonderful, and just so, so smart. And because of this, there's always just something so dark and pained in his face, something just so gloomy. I worry about the day when we will leave him alone in this world, worry so much about the day when he becomes a man. Daniel, my dear…your father and I love you. We love you just so much.*

He always missed dinner with his family these days because of school. And, because of school, he just slept so, so much.

Daniel waited until his mother was gone and raced down the stairs. A dull throb began in his ears as he went down the stairs. It beat there inside his skull like an angry drum.

He rushed into the kitchen and saw a girl dressed in pink pajamas rummaging through the fridge. When she looked up, the two stared at each other, and frowned.

"Move out of the way, Butt-face," Daniel said. "I need to use the phone."

Butt-face—a.k.a. Penelope "Penny" Fischer—pouted her fat fourteen-year-old lips, hollered, "MOM! Daniel called me Butt-face again!" and grabbed what she had been looking for from the fridge (a bag of baby carrots and apples. The Fischer children had been taught how to eat well at a young age). She hopped away, pigtails bouncing. Daniel briefly stared after her.

He found the phone on the kitchen counter and brought it to his ear. He licked his lips together and he breathed. He tried opening his mouth to say something, but then felt his throat close before any words could come out. Upstairs, he heard a door close, and knew that his sister was in her room happily munching away on her apples and carrots as she chatted away with her online friends. The house around him was empty; his parents had retired early upstairs to their room. His mother's casserole was on the dinner table nearby.

"Hello?"

There was a pause. "*Daniel?*"

A heavy sigh escaped his chest. It was a long exhale of breath, loud and relieved. He closed his eyes for a minute and felt that giddy beat in his chest calm to a tempered sound. He brought the phone up close to his cheek— *pressed* it even, pushed it hard against his face—and said: "Yeah. It's me, Jenny."

There was another long pause. Daniel brought another hand up to wipe his face. He'd been sweating profusely. He opened his eyes a second later and realized from somewhere in the back of his mind that he was holding the phone in a devastating death-grip, that the knuckles in his right hand hurt, that his *teeth* ached.

He gently loosened his hand.

"Daniel," she said. "Hey. I…I didn't think you'd ever…I mean—"

"Yeah," he said. "It's good…it's good to hear your voice too, Jenny."

"Yeah. Me too."

"How are you doing?"

"Okay."

"Sure?"

"Yeah. Yeah, I know, I sound out of it. But really…it's…it's fine. I'll be coming back to school this Monday. I had stuff that I had to take care of. My parents…they're getting a divorce, Daniel."

"Jesus, Jenny," he said. "I'm sorry. Is it bad?"

"Yeah. I guess you could say that." And then, in a voice so low that Daniel barely heard her: "Thank you for last week, Daniel. I couldn't have gotten through it without you."

"It's nothing, Jenny. Really."

They went silent.

"Jenny?" he said after a moment. "How did you get my number?"

"Oh." She sounded embarrassed. "I…well, remember the posters you put up for tutoring in chemistry and physics? Your number was on them, and so…so I kind of just took one and called you. You left your home phone number and cell number too."

"Ah," Daniel said. "I see."

"Yeah."

"Yeah."

"Daniel?"

"Hmm?"

"I need…I need to go now."

Disappointment filled him. It was raw and sudden, like a quick knife poke. "Oh," he said. "That's fine. Just glad to know that you're okay. Glad that you'll be coming to school again."

"Do you want to meet tomorrow?"

His eyes lit up. His heart kicked into overdrive and his mouth turned dry. "*What?* Tomorrow?"

"Yeah, I know it's out of the blue and all, but like…if you're not busy or anything…"

"No," he said quickly, "I'm not busy at all. I mean, I have the whole day free."

"Oh. Okay. Do you want to meet like by noon? Like, I don't know a place, but…"

"Do you know the ferry by the beach?" he asked. He stopped himself, taking a breath. He didn't want to sound desperate. "The one in Edmonds?"

"Yeah. It's right in downtown Edmonds, right?"

"Yeah," he said. "Brackett's Landing."

"Tomorrow at noon?"

"Yeah" he said. "That sounds good."

"Okay." There was a brief pause. "Bye, Daniel. I'll see you tomorrow."

"Bye, Jenny. See you."

She hung up. Daniel held the phone close to his ear for several more seconds, and then hung up as well.

*Jenny,* he thought distantly. *I'm finally going to meet Jenny tomorrow. And please God, don't let anything else get in the way of our time together.*

He trudged back up the stairs to retire to his room. Halfway up the stairs, he stopped, and suddenly turned around. He went back to the kitchen and got his mother's casserole.

# CHAPTER 8

Daniel sat at the beach the next morning overlooking the waves. He sat on a green metal bench at what was known as Brackett's Landing near a shallow field filled with sand dunes. A monochrome dark covered the skies while the waters below churned a dull murky gray; slow-trudging waves crashed against dirty dotted shores. Limbs of dead twisted hollow driftwood logs cluttered the area beneath his feet like old rotted bones belonging to a graveyard, and a dozen or so small dotted trails of creatures' feet littered random spots along the sand. Pebbles, snail shells, and muddy sand bubbles lay awkwardly exposed to the cold as the tide receded. Saltwater and ocean breeze filled the air—the wind blew. To his left was the Edmonds-Kingston ferry terminal, now derelict and quiet. On his right was the jetty, jutting out straight from the waterfront like a thrusting tongue stuck deep in the waters of Puget Sound. Far off into the horizon and across the waves, mountain ranges dominated the western sky, looking like bony knuckles surged forth from the ground. Kitsap County was there, and beyond that, the Olympic Mountains part of the Olympic Peninsula.

A rumbling sound came from behind him. It was her Mazda, making its way into the parking lot. Daniel watched patiently as she parked.

"Daniel?"

"Hey."

"Hey." They looked awkwardly at each other. "May I sit?"

He nodded. She gave him a faint smile, and sat down.

A small bulge came out beneath her sweater. It puffed out cutely from her stomach and looked like a small potbelly. She held on to it with one hand and used the other hand to trace back a lock of hair. Daniel frowned when seeing the potbelly, but said nothing, and watched curiously as her hand went to rub its swell.

*No,* a voice whispered to him, not *pregnant. She just has something underneath her sweater—she is* not *pregnant. God, how could you even think that?*

"Have you been waiting long?" she asked.

"No. I just got here and decided to sit down."

"Oh. Okay."

She hesitated. Daniel caught her biting her lip and realized she was cold. He could see the slight tremors her shoulders gave and noticed the way her fingers clenched together at the end of her sleeves. He wanted to offer his jacket, but knew already she'd refuse him.

She turned to him then and tried to smile. It was a solemn smile, false around the edges and dimmed in the eyes. She was trying to make him feel better, as if she knew his concern for her. "I'm sorry," she began. She reached under her sweater and brought out a newly bought white t-shirt wrapped in a plastic bag. The words *Fruit of the Loom* were written at the top. "I don't know your size. I went to Walgreens and decided on a large. I hope that's fine."

"Large is fine," he said, taking the shirt from her. It felt warm in his hand. He realized with a faint echo that it had been in close contact with her skin, her *bare* skin even, her bare midriff. Why had she put this inside her sweater instead of just carrying it with her? "Thank you, Jenny. You didn't have to."

"Oh. I know. But…still. I guess that's why I still did it anyway."

He placed the shirt aside. They sat for a while, and went silent.

Her eyes were tired; grim. They were a dull color that seemingly mirrored the leaden waves, not at all brown or calm like he remembered them. She'd tried hard to erase the dark spot beneath her eyes, he noticed, and had tried again to apply powder to her cheeks. Daniel saw through all of it.

"Do you want to talk about it?" he asked her.

She turned around. "Talk? About?"

"You know…" He gave her a shrug. "Whatever's bothering you. Your parents' divorce. Do you want to talk about it?"

"Oh. No, it's fine, Daniel, really, it's nothing. Just…" She squeezed her hands together. "It's just family stuff. Really. It's nothing I can't handle."

"Oh. Okay then."

"Yeah."

Daniel watched from the side again as her fingers began picking at the surface of her jeans. They went quiet.

"Do you—"

"How are—"

He stopped himself.

"Sorry," she said. She brought an embarrassed hand up. "I didn't mean to interrupt while you were talking. You go ahead."

"No, it's fine. What were you going to say?"

"Oh, I was just going to ask how your family was."

"They're fine." He thought for a second, and said, "My little sister won a math award at her school last week."

"Oh, you have a little sister? That's cute."

"Yeah. I guess it is."

"What's her name?"

"Penny."

She laughed. "That's cute too."

"Yeah. She's four years younger than us."

"What were you going to ask me, Daniel?"

He hesitated. He said, "I…I was going to ask if you'd like to walk with me or something. You know, just along the beach."

She thought for a minute, eyeing him thoughtfully. Daniel caught her gaze and felt himself grow small in size. *So this is it,* he thought dimly. *We're still a bit awkward with each other after all that's happened. I'm not surprised, but only taken slightly aback. After having her blood spilled on me, after having smelled her hair, after having gone into her car, gotten her shirt, watched as she slipped it on, carried her…we still have to obey social conventions of etiquette. That's fine; I understand. I just wish she'd stop smiling for me as if she were obligated to do so. I just wish she'd frown and let me see her for who she truly is.*

*I know you're lying to me about something, Jenny.*

"Walk? Sure. But, like, where can we walk to?"

"We can just follow the beach south," he said. "Towards Marina Park or the fishing pier. Less than a mile."

"Oh. Okay. Yeah, walking would be good."

She stood up, turned to him, and offered him another forlorn smile.

\*\*\*

They walked past the ferry terminal and made it to the small meadow area south of Brackett's Landing. Here the bricked sidewalk sinuously curved through tiny pastoral plots of green as they entered Olympic Beach.

Tall tuffs of brownish reed canary grass surrounded them to the sides and swayed pleasantly with the wind; loose Scotch broom drifted towards their thighs with slender-ribbed branches and brightly lit yellow petals. What looked like attractive pink Hardhacks gestured in their direction as they passed by. They gave the illusion of pink bulbous pyramid-heads bowing together before the wind, and looked, when swaying back and forth, like sadly bruised purple eyes covered in thin hooks of hair. Deep-green colored the grass beside them while white clover heads popped out randomly from the ground. Seagulls called out together in the distance as the Edmonds-Kingston ferry carefully arrived at its port. The ferry gave a loud bellow with its horn, interrupted the continuous and hypnotic rhythm of the breaking waves, and slowly merged with the long green glass walkway that attached to its upper deck from the terminal.

Jenny heard this noise behind her and instinctively brought her arms up to hold herself beneath the chest. She was being coy, she knew, but could think of no other way to handle the silence. There were multiple moments where she thought he'd walk alongside her and take her hand or something, brush it accidentally with her fingers and have it become one with their movements. But...no. He kept respectfully to himself and offered her space. He simply kept silent next to her.

*I'm scared,* Jenny thought distantly, *because I know that if I approach him today, I'm going to have to reveal myself to him. It's only fair that I answer his questions, but it scares me. I've never really trusted anyone else before, and we...we barely know each other. We've only known each other for a week.* The thought was bleak. It made her slow her footsteps and wrap her arms tighter around herself. *No. I shouldn't think like that. I shouldn't let that stupid fact get in the way of a possible friendship. So what if we came together out of disaster? He was there for me, and he...he's just very kind. I can sense it in him. He's just a kind person. But it's this very kindness I'm afraid of. More than anything else, more than being bullied or stigmatized by my Korean friends, it's this kindness that scares me the most.*

They traveled through the meadow together and made it down the steps leading to the first thin strip of beach. Waves crashed to their right as the beige Pinnacle Logistics building passed slowly on their left. They walked through the parking lot of the South County Senior Center together and emerged in a larger beach area filled with familiar up-heaved mini-sand dunes and broken log pieces. They were at the heart of Olympic Beach now. Rich moist sand filled their shoes and clung to the ankles of their socks. They went by the Ebb Tide Condominium, passed the Underwater Sports store, and walked past Beach Place Road. Here a small concrete walkway emerged alongside the Edmonds Bay Building and rose just a few feet above the sand.

Olympic Beach joined with Dayton Street along Admiral Way, and Jenny could soon see the fishing pier Daniel had been speaking of extending out in the distance. It stretched three hundred feet beyond the marina and raised high above the breakwater. Hundreds of boats floated moored next to their assigned docks.

They walked together along the walkway leading to the pier and eventually made it to the water. Here the pier took a sharp left turn and ran parallel with one side of the marina breakwater. Timid gusts of wind blew against them as they walked along; waves crashed beneath their feet, rocking the pier. Despite all this, a sliver of sunlight broke through the clouds and shone warmly on the water a few hundred meters away. It was just a slice of light, a small splash of gold against darkened blue, but Jenny noticed it, and quickly made her way to the edge of the pier. She placed one foot on the lowest railing and leaned herself over the water.

"It's pretty here," she said.

"Yeah," Daniel said. "It is."

They went silent. Daniel watched her admiringly from the back.

"Do you come here often?" she asked.

"Sometimes. But not always. I just come here to think when I have to, but it's always in my car."

"Think? You come to the beach to think?"

He nodded. "Yeah. It's kind of nice. Nice to just sit and look at the waves. Nice to look at the clouds and see the sunset."

"Oh," she said. "I've never tried that. Maybe I should."

"Yeah." He hesitated. "It helps with stress, especially with IB. You know?"

She laughed at him. "Yeah. I definitely know about *that*."

"What made you take IB in the first place?"

"Parents. And, er, this idea that I could do well in it."

"Full?"

"Ha. Yeah, right. I can barely maintain partial."

He smiled at her, but it was a rueful smile. Daniel wanted to offer it as a sympathetic smile, but knew that if she turned around and saw him, it would come out as a pitying smile.

"You seem like a smart girl to me, Jenny," he said kindly.

She smiled at him. "Ha. Well, it looks like you're thinking of some *other* Asian girl, Daniel." She leaned forward and stretched herself out toward the water. The long curve of her back and sudden tensing of her muscles stirred something raw and deep inside of Daniel. A slight pull of her sweater revealed a white patch of naked skin on her midriff.

"I'm not smart, Daniel. I'm really not. I know as an Asian girl I'm supposed to be, but I think God messed up when he made me, and just decided that I would be a girl. I can't seem to fulfill the stereotype. I'm a bit stupid in general."

Daniel said nothing. He watched quietly as a fresh burst of wind blew through her hair. She leaned herself into it and closed her eyes, exposing her neck. Hair fluttered past her shoulders.

Daniel, unable to take the silence any longer, stepped next to her and leaned in close so that their arms and shoulders brushed. "Please don't say that, Jenny," he muttered to the side. "Please don't ever say that about yourself."

She turned around and opened her eyes at him. "What?"

"That," he said. "Just…that. You don't have to say that about yourself."

She looked at him, confused, but then tried to smile. "I don't understand what you're saying, Daniel. Are you mad?"

"No," he said, a little too quickly, a little too harsh. He tried to look at her, but felt pathetic. "I mean…you know. You don't have to say those things about yourself, Jenny. Nobody does."

She just smiled at him, thoughtful and hurt, and turned to the side. "I used to imagine what it would be like to sail with my family on the ocean," she said. "I used to dream about it a lot when I was younger. When I was in middle school, I used to think I'd be the one to buy my parents a boat after I got married, and give that dream to them."

"I'm sorry. Is there something stopping you from that dream now?"

"Yeah. A few things."

She turned away just as another gust of wind swept through her hair. It swept across Daniel's face, but he made no comment. Strawberries filled his nose.

She moved away and Daniel silently followed. He watched her as she wrapped her arms around herself. It was a gesture not to just ward off the cold, but also to protect herself. A memory perhaps; a bad thought.

***

Last night Jenny had caught her father having sex with another woman—this was the reason for her solemn silence around Daniel. His questions, though well-meaning and kind, were akin to asking her to reveal a hideous scar on her body. With this feeling of self-disgust were feelings of permanent shame embedded deep in her heart. Her parents were getting a divorce. The finality of these words were just as cold when speaking them out loud. Though their decision to do so had little to do with her status as a daughter, Jenny still felt that she was responsible for their separation. The thought of her sex weighed on her mind like a permanent black cloud—she could no longer freely stare at herself in the mirror without the words "girl" and "daughter" marring her view.

Her mother was no longer with them. Where she was, Jenny didn't know, and hurt thinking about her. She was just…gone.

Last night she had caught her father having sex with another woman. She had caught him fucking…screwing. Doing. She'd come down stairs last night several hours after her call with Daniel and had spotted giant shadows dancing along the walls. They were disgustingly shaped, those shadows, awkwardly disjointed, looking like snakes on disfigured limbs. They were the shapes of her father holding the body of another woman on the couch with long legs lifted high in the air. The living room lights had been turned off and the TV muted; soft eerie blue had painted the walls.

Jenny crept her way down to the living room and curled into a ball at the foot of the stairs. She brought her knees up to her chin and wrapped her arms around her legs. Giggling came from the living room. Following it were quick bouts of hushed laughter. There were sounds of wet lips kissing, of zippers and sweaters unzipping, and of pants untangling. The couch they lay on was leather; skintight sounds of sliding flesh and taut muscles groaned out from the dark. There was panting too, quick and rushed.

It had been one o'clock in the morning.

"You look good tonight, Yongsook," a woman's voice whispered. It was followed by a chuckle, a soft inhale of breath, and then: "You seem in better spirits these days."

"The earth spins," Yongsook answered back. Jenny shuddered when hearing her father's voice. It sounded like a stranger's voice whispering in the dark. To hear her father speak so casually and informally was as frightening as being buried alive beneath the earth. They spoke in Korean. "People have a choice to be happy with each new day."

"Mmm. I see. And have you chosen to be happy with me, Yongsook?"

There was a ruffling of cloth, some rubbing noise of silk and thin fabric, and then more laughter. A suckling sound followed. More leather groans from the dark.

"What about your mistress?" the woman asked.

"Oh, don't call her that, Kyung-soon. You'll make me seem like the bad guy tonight."

They laughed again. Jenny swallowed a lump in her throat and took time to wipe her eyes. Her breathing became agitated and uneven. She brought both hands over her mouth and squeezed her eyes shut, feeling hot tears dripping down her face. Images of her father naked and lean filled her mind where his middle-aged body mounted the woman on the couch. His muscles were old, lathered with sweat, his feet, decorated with spider veins and wrinkles. His potbelly sagged like a tumor, and his pubic hair tingled with the cold living room air. *So this is the woman omma was talking about,* Jenny thought quietly. *This is the woman that drove my parents apart, the woman that made my mom hit me and that made my parents hate me. This is her voice; I'm hearing the voice that ruined my life. My appa is kissing her, and soon he'll be naked on top of her, and soon they'll fuck, they'll do it while I lay upstairs pretending to sleep, they'll do it right below me, and in the morning, when I wake up, my appa will pretend like nothing happened.*

*Fucking. My father is* fucking *her. My father is fucking another woman, and I'm here witnessing it.*

"How is your daughter, Yongsook?"

"Jenny? Same as always. I hardly ever know what goes on with her."

"You have a lovely daughter, Yongsook. I'm sure she'll find her way."

"Mmm, you're acting kind tonight. But I'm not sure about my Jenny. She's dim-witted and slow. And a bit stupid."

Jenny's ears grew hot. Something warm flashed through her cheeks, and more tears spilled down her face. She wiped them away and quietly retreated back up the stairs.

"Oh, such a mean man, my Yongsook. How can you say that about your own daughter? Don't you love her?"

"Of course," Yongsook whispered. "I love all my family just the same. Just that, I worry about my daughter the most. Sometimes I worry about her future, Kyung-soon. I worry about her a lot."

Jenny closed the door to her room.

\*\*\*

They were at Marina Park now.

Daniel stood near the water and watched as the wind took her hair and flung it across her shoulders. White light shone warmly on her face and illuminated her features, making her skin fuller, healthier in the wind. Mammoth white tusks of hollow logs decorated the beach behind them. Rotted branches and clumps of seaweed lay strewn all over the shoreline next to their shoes. The waves tugged at them playfully, menacingly, shredding eelgrass bodies and disturbing the tiny pebble-beds set deep in the sand. Beyond the water, hundreds of miles away, faint silhouettes of mountain peaks spread out beneath the horizon.

*Edge of the world*, Daniel thought as he stepped closer to the water. *It feels like the edge of the world where I'm standing. Some may tell me that I'm only standing along the shorelines of the Sound, that I'm merely at the end of Marina Park Beach before the waves and sky, but standing here, with her next to me…it feels like the edge of the world for some reason.*

She walked past him and tentatively dipped her foot in the water. Waves broke out and reached her ankle, soaking her sock. Daniel watched quietly from the side. She pulled her sneaker back and smiled, revealing faint dimples on the underside of her cheeks.

He stepped next to her.

"It's beautiful here," he said.

"Yes. It is." She smiled at him and turned around. She wrapped her arms around herself and began walking away, wanting him to follow. He did. "Do you know what Heaven is supposed to look like, Daniel?"

"No. Not really. I don't think anyone really know what Heaven looks like. Or Hell."

She nodded, revealing a longing look in her eyes that Daniel noticed. She kept her arms under her chest and walked through the sand.

"Are you Christian, Daniel?"

"No." The question surprised him. "I don't think…"

"Yeah?"

He shrugged. "I don't think religion offers any relevant answers to humanity's problems. I think it creates more problems than it does solutions."

She said, "I think that too," and jumped on a log. "What about Heaven? Or Hell?"

"I don't know. I think it's better to believe neither. That way you don't die and live with fear."

"Will you feel bad if you found out there's a Hell?"

"I think so. But then again, there have been so many hells in human history, who's to say which one is correct? Not all of them are eternal."

She smiled at that. It was a surprising smile. Daniel hadn't expected it. She continued on another log and picked her feet carefully along. Daniel walked alongside her. Overhead, more clouds parted, revealing soft light.

"Jenny."

"Hmm?"

"Can I ask you a question?"

"Sure."

"Do you remember Michael Lamb?"

"Michael? Yeah. Why?"

"A few weeks ago I saw you giving him a bag of candy. Do you remember that?"

She paused for a moment, balancing her feet and raising an eyebrow. "Candy? I…oh. Right. Like a month ago, right?"

"Yeah. Something like that. Why did you do it? Why did you go and buy him candy when you had no reason to?"

She bit her lip at him. A thoughtful look appeared in her eyes. She answered slowly: "I just thought it was the right thing to do at the time. My friends…or like, my church members…one girl said that it was God's will that Michael was born like that. She said that it was his purpose and destiny in life to inspire others with his disease, and was something he was meant to have to become stronger in life. I thought…I thought her reasoning was stupid, and wanted to see Michael myself one day. So I went to him a few times and became friends with him."

She looked at him. She pressed her lips together, thinking.

"He isn't a reason, and he isn't a means to an end for others," she said. "No human is an excuse to be an ends. He's just a boy, and he likes M&Ms. There is no reason for his condition that God can prove, because God has proven to be false. He is not an ends for any god because all gods have been proven to be false in all cultures in all of history; there's no reason to value one god over another. And so, when people tell me that certain things happen in the world because God says so, or because certain people are as they are because they're destined to be so, I get angry, asking them to show me the divine proof. We have scientific proof and medical reasons for why things happen as they do for people—we only have romantic rhetoric for justifying God's will. To say that Michael Lamb was a tool used by God for others is wrong. I'd rather see him as a person with some disease I can be friends with than a theme used at church."

"Sounds like you thought about this a lot," Daniel said.

"I guess. I don't know. People are afraid of a lot of things in life that I think they purposefully create things to make themselves feel better. They need to find meaning to live, even if it means creating meaningless means. I think it's better to accept life as it is. You become stronger that way; humbler."

"The Absurd," Daniel said.

"The what?"

"It's what we read in IB English last year. Mr. Kirk's class."

"Oh. Right. I have Mr. Kirk for seventh period." She hopped on another log. She said, "Also, I don't like it when people are bullied. I don't think Michael is ever bullied at our school, but the way my friends and church sometimes talk about him, like he was a means for our ends, it's like…like…"

"Patronizing and condescending," Daniel said.

"Yeah. Something like that. In church, we always talk about ourselves being better than everyone. Even if we say to ourselves we recognize other people, respect them, love them, it's always with undertones of us being better. We really don't respect others. We're in fact culturally insensitive. Our missionaries are a good example of this."

"You would never find the Koran or the Vedas in a church," Daniel said for her. "Or the Avesta from Zoroastrianism."

"Yeah. So when we always proclaim our god to be better without even taking into account other gods or other religions, it makes me embarrassed about my church. Millions of people before Christianity were as passionate about their gods as we are now about ours in church. Where can we find proof that their passion is wrong and ours correct? We only have absolute proof that their religions have become exhausted—Christianity should be no different."

"When you mentioned bullying just now," Daniel said, "what did you mean? Why did you use that analogy?"

She smiled at him, her eyes weary and sad appearing. It seemed as if she were recalling a bitter memory. A pained smile. "I used to be bullied at my church too," she said quietly. "It happened when I was fifteen. I was bullied by one of my pastors."

"A *pastor* bullied you?"

"Yeah. He was the head pastor of our church. To be fair though, I was a bit out of line."

Daniel stared at her. He'd never pictured her as a victim before. "What happened, if you don't mind me asking?"

She shrugged her shoulders, and said: "I stood up to him."

"And?"

"He left the church afterwards," she said softly. "He just completely went away and never came back."

"So you won then."

"No, Daniel. I just took whatever was given to me, and moved on in life. No one won."

She jumped forward on another log. Her arms wavered, she tilted to the side, and Daniel readied himself to catch her. She steadied herself, stuck her arms out, and finally found her balance.

"Maybe I was selfish," Jenny said. "Maybe I shouldn't have come to Michael and become friends with him the way I did. But I wanted to try and love him authentically instead out of duty, if that makes sense. I didn't want to see him as a Christian duty; I didn't want to see him as an obligation by God or anyone else. I didn't want to see him as a theme. I just wanted—"

"To see him as human," Daniel said for her. He thought of Erika then. He thought of Michael and Steven Kooper, and even of Mr. Menfree. "You just wanted to just see him as another person that is neither better nor lesser than you. An equal."

"Yeah," Jenny said. "Human. The creature better than all angels and gods."

Daniel watched again as she picked her feet along.

Perhaps it was the sun then, or the warming of the breeze, but the silence that fell around them was lovely and kind in Daniel's mind. Beautiful. He studied her, admiring her from the side, and thought: *This is a beautiful day, Jenny. This is a beautiful day because I have you with me as the skies slowly become clear. I wish I could thank you, Jenny; I wished you knew how lovely you were.*

"Jenny. Hold on for a minute. Look at me."

She stopped. She lowered her arms and looked at him. "Yeah?"

"Look, Jenny. I know I have no right to ask you to tell me what happened. I know your familial problems are your own and that you have every right to keep them from me. But I'd like you to know that I'm here for you as a friend. Whether it be for school or family, I'll always try to be here for you. As…as a friend."

She looked at him. "Daniel…"

"When this day ends," he said, "we'll return to our regular activities as students. You'll go back to your life at school, and I'll go back to mine. But I don't want this moment to become nothing. I don't want our time together today at the beach to be something that we just totally forget and let go to memory. I want…I want to be *friends*."

He brought a hand up and rubbed the back of his neck. Jenny bit her lip at him. She knew he was trying. "I don't want it so that last week was just an accident where you're repaying me out of obligation. I don't want to see you through eyes of pity and remorse. I want…I want to see you as a person. A friend. Someone that won't be afraid to rely on me, or me to you. I just don't want to see you as a girl anymore. You know?"

Jenny's cheeks bloomed hot. Her eyes slowly went to her shoes and one hand clutched tight the sleeves of her sweater. The other went to clutch her chest. "Yeah, Daniel," she said quietly. She raised her eyes at him. "Yeah, I know. Thank you. I…thank you for all that. I haven't heard anyone tell me that before. I guess I don't want to be strangers with you, either."

She jumped off the log and turned to face him. "I like this place," she whispered. "I really enjoyed everything you've shown me at this beach. If I were to say that I thought this place could be called Heaven, would you think I was being stupid?"

"No, Jenny. Of course not. I would never think you stupid for saying that."

They went quiet. Daniel felt her eyes on him and turned to stare at the shoreline. He stuffed his hands in his pockets and waited for the silence to pass.

"Sometimes I wonder what Heaven looks like," she said. "Sometimes I wonder, and sometimes I get scared."

"Why?"

"Because. Just because. I get scared thinking Heaven exists because it means we must someday leave this world."

She stepped next to him. She hesitated. She carefully locked her arm through his, and placed her head against his shoulder.

Daniel started. The muscles in his arm turned rigid and his breathing stopped. He relaxed when he smelled the top of her head, relaxed when he felt the familiar weight of her body against his arm, and let her lean on him, briefly closing his eyes. Her body against his was a light pressure that was barely there, a pillow of feathers against his arm—the hair that brushed against his cheek was soft.

"This world can be more beautiful than Heaven if we want it to be," she whispered. "I think you showed me that today, Daniel. Thank you."

He felt her weight shift. She was parting from him. He wanted to suddenly grab hold of her hand and interlock her fingers with his, to hold it, gently clutch it, grasp it, keep it within his reach, to show her that he understood and cared—but she was already too far away, already at an arm's length distance with her arms again wrapped beneath her chest.

"Heaven is a place filled with friends you can love," he said. He watched as a small smile broke out on her face. It was a genuine smile. Her gaze kept facing the water. "A place without friends to love is Hell."

"Yes," Jenny said. "I think that too."

They stood together and looked at the waves. Ahead, seagulls cried out in the distance.

# CHAPTER 9

Nothing had changed. This was the first thing Jenny noticed when reentering the doors of Evanston-Woods High School—absolutely nothing had changed. The second thing she noticed were the lights overhead: They were diffused and murky, aglow with a low luminescent hue that made traveling through the hallways a dreary experience filled with tired faces and sleepy morning eyes. Jenny had had it in her mind that the environment had irrevocably changed somehow with a solemn disappointment waiting for her through the doors. But the students were the same; the walls were the same, the posters taped on the walls were the same, and even the smell of cold morning air blowing through the doors was the same, the cool crisp scent of autumn air like fresh smells of freezing metal. The sky was dark outside and pregnant with clouds. Because of this, Jenny supposed, everyone around her was grumpy and tired-looking, acting like a bunch of bored cattle lumbering off to the butcher's shop.

Nostalgia tightened her chest as she made her way through the hallway. With it were other feelings difficult to describe: anxiousness; anticipation; thrill; exhaustion; sadness. The walls around her had remained the same, just exactly the same, but Jenny felt as if she could no longer see them as they once were. In her heart, a voice seemed to whisper: *If ever I left this place, I'd be so heartbroken. I'd be devastated, like having lost a group of people I loved. I'll miss this school once everything is over—I'll miss it so, so much, and want to remember nothing related to it because of the pain. It's a feeling of change, a feeling of moving on. Two weeks ago allowed me to truly see these walls as things temporary instead of things eternal, and I realized then just how short life is. When Daniel carried me, brought me into the bathroom, we broke certain social codes that always make us believe in the eternal world of high-school. A memory had been made then. It was made because it broke away from the tediousness of our existence as high-school students. I'm just so scared to see these walls fall away from me.*

It was Kyung-sung she thought of then as she neared the E-100 flex area. Kyung-sung was another student from her church that was part of her youth group. He in fact had been there when Pastor Hwang had assaulted her at the preschool. He'd recited something to her earlier this year that still greatly bothered her. It'd been a simple recitation, something said casually off to the side while at church in an effort to garner some attention from the other Korean girls that had been present. They'd been asked to write simple poems of praise to God, and what Kyung-sung had recited was simply this: *Monday is gone, and Tuesday is soon to come/ After all that has passed, what/ Can I say that I have done?*

Even now Jenny shuddered a bit as she recalled the whimsical voice from which the words came. The question in these lines was brutally honest and existentialistic: It simply asked the individual to reevaluate their actions to see if any meaning had been derived from their day of labor. But the implications were direr than that. Human life existed not as a single day, but as many, and these many days were finite. Thus the line simply asked this: What have I done in life now that my life is soon to part?

*Memory,* Jenny thought as she made her way through the halls. She wasn't even aware of the other students around her. *This is what these walls represent that now surround me—memory. When I look back at them, when I stare at their bare color, their bare sides, look at their naked structure, I'm left with fear of seeing either of two things: cracks and handprints where I made my existence once known; or simply nothing. A memory was made two weeks ago that disrupted this mundane cycle called life, and in remembering it, I realize now how to live life fully should I choose to live it. For in order for me to have remembered a memory, it meant that I had to live it as a moment in the past worthy of remembrance. But to live freely is so hard—just so hard. These hallways compel me to walk the way they want me to walk; these walls will me how far I can go and tell me where to stop. Culture will call me Korean and language will call me "female"; God will tell me whom I can praise and whom I can worship and how I can live. It's hard to go against these high-school walls.*

There was another thought that occurred to her then, something that slipped easily inside her mind like the teasing of feathers against the bottom of bare feet: *My blood's still on the floor in the hallway.*

Jenny shuddered. She shouldered her backpack and passed through the glass doors that led to Ms. Karens' IB American History class.

\*\*\*

School ended, and, just like always, and Jenny found herself once again making her way through the parking a few hours later. Cars zipped by and horns blared; brief shafts of sunlight broke through the clouds. It was a familiar scene, this journeying through the school parking lot, though to Jenny, there was something about this afternoon that was uniquely different and solemn. Where there'd been scattering leaves underfoot the days before, dry autumn colors now piled the sides of the parking lot looking like blankets of dried skin.

*Not going to be like this in a few more months*, Jenny thought quietly as she walked by. *In just a few more months, I'll be graduated, and this parking lot will have a new meaning for me.*

A group of students passed in front of her. Jenny jerked back with surprise when she saw them and let them pass, staring at them from behind. The group was a typical crowd of friends, three boys and two girls. Arms slipped comfortably around waists and hands firmly interlocked behind backs. Jenny watched with grim amusement as one of the boys reached down and grabbed a handful of denim ass on his girl. The grab was hard, gentle as an eagle's gasp on thick withering salmon, and Jenny frowned.

*Do I envy what I see before me*, she thought distantly, *or do I shame their vanity and just let them be? I'm not the one to judge and I'm not the one to know, but I know for a fact that life always changes, and in these changes, there are always losses in life. How does friendship play out in life as people grow older? Why do people fade away, and what consequences are there for friendship when people transition from high-school to college?*

*Daniel would never grab a girl like that.*

The last thought came out of nowhere, surprising Jenny. She took a minute to bite her lip and stared again at the ass-grabbing hand.

Daniel. She'd spotted him today in class. Their eyes had acknowledged each other when she'd sat down, but that was all. She'd smiled back, albeit timidly, and had turned around to open her textbook. Ms. Karens' IB History class was the only class they shared with one another.

*He would never just randomly grab someone like that,* Jenny thought again. *He'd never simply take advantage of a girl next to him. He's better and smarter than that. Monday may be gone, but at least for him, it'll always return.*

She sighed. She shouldered her backpack, picked up her pace, and made her way to the back of the parking lot.

A woman stood next to her car.

Jenny jerked to a stop so suddenly that her sneakers scraped against the asphalt. Strands of hair wavered past her shoulders and momentarily blinded her in the eyes. Her heart skipped a beat. Saliva dried in her mouth.

Dark sunglasses covered the woman's face. Thin bony shoulders stuck out haphazardly from her cotton blouse and gave her overall appearance a disfigured skeletal look. A thin green scarf covered her head and flapped gently with the wind, revealing wiry curls of black hair.

It was her hands that Jenny noticed the most. Her fingers were gnarled-like and cruel, covered in arthritic liver spots and lined with dark green veins. Tissue-thin skin stretch over bony knuckles and turned her hands into crooked claws. There was no fat on her hands, no meat of any kind, just simple wretched hooks ending in clutching fingers.

"Omma," Jenny whispered. "What...what are you doing here?"

Jaewha stared at her daughter. She sighed, and slowly removed her sunglasses. She squinted against the sunlight, and Jenny noticed as wrinkles traveled outward from the corner of her eyes. It seemed like her mother had aged ten years since they last saw each other.

"Jenny. How are you doing?"

Jenny made no reply. She searched her mother's face and felt another black sense of dread bloom in her stomach. She reached into the pocket of her jeans and found her car keys. She hesitated. "I'm fine, omma."

Jaewha lowered her eyes and saw the keys clutched in her daughter's hand. She sighed again, and said pleasantly: "Shall we have a cup of Starbucks, Jenny? It'll be my treat."

Warmth spread through Jenny's eyes. She recalled the scene where her mother had smacked her across the cheek; she recalled the pain that had raced through her forehead when her mother had pulled her hair, the pain that had occurred when she'd landed awkwardly on her left arm and cried out in agony. It had been claws that had dug into her scalp—sharp, bony, wretched claws. Jenny wondered if her mother knew the purse she had in her hands was the same purse she'd slapped her with.

*Oh, omma, I'm sorry. I'm so sorry, I really am, I'm so sorry to see you so frail like this, I'm so sorry to see your hands like this, but please—why can't you love me? Why can't you just love me as your daughter? You know I love you, but sometimes…sometimes I can't stand to love you, and just hate you. I hate you, mom. I just hate you sometimes. Why can't you just love me?*

Her mother had left her to cry alone on the living room floor once. The memory was still fresh and painful in Jenny's mind. Her cheeks had been stuffed fat with rice then, and sticky tears had burned down her face as she sat watching the TV. She'd wanted to watch cartoons with her mother then, and so, had prepared the living room table with two bowls of fresh rice and a plate of kimchi to share between them. She'd turned off the lights in the living room to create an atmosphere that was like at the theaters, and had sat eagerly on the floor waiting for her mother. Hours passed. Her favorite cartoons ended.

Jenny peeked over the living room couch and saw her mother still on the phone speaking with her friends. Laughter echoed from the kitchen. A sour hurt filled her, and Jenny's lips pouted. She tried calling out *Omma* several times to her mother, but her mother paid her no attention. Crying then, and with a painful lump in her throat, Jenny slowly took the bowl of rice she'd gathered for herself and stuffed some of it in her mouth. She thought that maybe by swallowing some rice she would help subdue the pain that was building inside her, but she ended up only feeling sorry for herself instead. Some part of her even wondered what would happen if she ended up choking—surely her mother would take more notice of her then, right? Her cheeks fattened and tears crept into her mouth; her sobs became muted like gloved fists against straining groans.

*Why isn't my mother playing with me?* she thought quietly. *How come she doesn't want to love me? She said she would come and watch cartoons with me.*

She'd been ten-years-old then.

"I thought…I thought you didn't like drinking coffee," Jenny replied. She took one tentative step towards her car. "I'm sorry, omma, but I don't want coffee right now. I have a lot of studying to do."

Jaewha rolled her eyes. She said abruptly, "Your father and I are getting a divorce now. You know this Jenny, yes?"

Jenny nodded. There wasn't anything else she could think of saying. "Yes, omma," she said quietly. "I know."

"I just finished seeing your father this morning. You'll be happy to know we left on mutual terms with one another. It seems like your father is just absolutely thrilled to have me out of his life."

Jaewha shrugged. The gesture was like collapsing bones to Jenny. "I just thought I'd see my daughter one last time before leaving. It was a vain thought, but I wanted to act on it anyway. I'm leaving, Jenny. Your mother is leaving for good."

She reached into her purse.

"Here." Jaewha handed her a thick manila envelope. Jenny, already knowing what it was, took it with a trembling hand. "A few thousand dollars," Jaewha said. "Let this be my last present to you, Jenny. Go and spend it on whatever it is you want. Boys, shopping, schoolwork, whatever. There's at least four thousand dollars for you to spend."

Jenny took the envelope and let it drop to her side. Numbness traveled through her arm. Holding onto the envelope was like grabbing onto an electrocuting power cord that just paralyzed everything in her body. She could feel the money between her fingers, and thought of, for whatever reason, a drowned baby's corpse being horrifically discovered.

*Please,* Jenny thought suddenly, *oh please, just let her say that she loves me. Let her say that at least before leaving, let her say that I was at least her daughter and that she loved me. Let her miss me, God. Please let my mom miss me when she goes away.*

"Well. That's all I have to give you, Jenny. Any last words before I leave you?"

Jenny shook her head. Her lips pressed together and her gaze lowered to her shoes.

"Yes, well...I thought as much. Goodbye, Jenny. Live a good life, and ignore these beasts we call men. Hearts are always broken when with men."

Jenny watched as her mother walked away. She saw her silver Acura parked down a few rows and noticed a pile of luggage stuffed in the backseat. There was a brief moment where Jenny thought her mother would hesitate before opening the driver's door, turn around, look her way, and express some emotion of sadness. But to her hurt disappointment (but oh, who had she been kidding?), her mother simply checked herself in the mirror, adjusted her sunglasses, and started the engine. Black exhaust spewed out from the tailpipe. After a few seconds, it was gone, and speeding through the exit gates.

A loud silence followed in her wake.

*Gone. My mother's really gone.*

Jenny stood where she was and wiped her nose. She walked over to her car and got into the driver's seat. She tossed her backpack to the side and stared at the manila envelope. A painful lump formed in her throat; warm salt spread through her eyes. She began opening the envelope to see if her mother had left a note for her, but then stopped herself. No. Her mother wasn't like that. Her mother had never left her a note for anything.

*Gone. My mother's really gone. I really no longer have a mother anymore.*

"Goodbye, mom," Jenny whispered. She laid the money on top of the dashboard and stared at the trees outside. She gripped the steering wheel with her hands and lay her head against it. "I love you. I'll miss you."

She cried.

***

She parked her vehicle in the driveway five minutes later and stared numbly at her father's Lincoln.

Her father wasn't supposed to be here. He was supposed to be at work still. He never came home early like this. Never.

*He's not supposed to be here,* Jenny thought thinly as she made her way towards the house. Her eyes were still red from crying. *He's not supposed to be home this early. Something's wrong. He only comes home these days when I'm asleep in bed, or at least, pretending to sleep, but he never comes home this early, he's not—*

The door was unlocked.

Jenny stepped inside and smelled a heavy aroma of freshly cooked rice. The smell was good and mixed with other fragrances of steamed vegetables and pork and chicken. The smell sent tremors to her knees, and Jenny's stomach grumbled. She hesitated at the doorway and then cautiously closed the door behind her. Her dad never cooked.

"Jenny-ah! Is that you?"

She took off her shoes at the doorway and pulled off her socks. She took three steps into the living room and saw her father appearing out of the kitchen. A smile was on his face.

"Jenny-ah," he began. "So good to finally see you. Come here, I want you to meet somebody."

A cold feeling went through her stomach. Her appetite disappeared, and, standing there barefoot on the living room carpet, Jenny suddenly noticed all the slight changes that had been made to the living room. The carpet had been newly vacuumed and was now filled with vertical streaks that cut through the entire floor; sunlight spilled through the recently scrubbed windows, and new drapes had been bought. The furniture had also been rearranged in the living room. The living room sofa had switched places with the larger and darker leather

*(fucking my father had been fucking)*

couch. New pottery plants adorned the shelves near the windows. It'd been Jenny's duty long ago to always water these plants whenever she arrived home from school, and now when she scanned the living room around her, she found only foreign species occupying the room.

*Come here. I want you to meet somebody.*

"Appa," she said quietly, "I...I need to go to the library and study. My friends are there waiting for me, and next week we have a test, so—"

"Oh? But you already have your shoes off, Jenny. Come quickly, I'd like you to meet a friend."

Jenny lowered her gaze and silently followed. Her breathing plunged up and down in her chest.

Yongsook entered the kitchen and opened his arms wide. His voice bellowed from his throat in a triumphant greeting, and a large grin filled his face. "Jenny! Meet daddy's friend from work. This is Katie Chung, daddy's good friend."

Jenny raised her eyes. A tall woman stood at the kitchen island with a knife in her hand chopping vegetables. Smooth black hair fell fully around her neck. She stood without socks in the kitchen, but when Jenny looked down at her feet, she noticed that they were covered with purple fuzzy slippers. Jenny realized with a sharp pang of disgust that the slippers belonged to her mother. Her face was small, her build, skinny yet healthy and lean—Jenny secretly envied the delicate shape of her neck.

147

She was pretty. Incredibly pretty. Jenny thought she was also still very, very young looking.

"Hello Jenny," the woman

(*katie*)

said. She spoke in English and her voice was sweet. "It's nice to meet you. My name's Katie, but you can call me Kate. Your father's told me wonderful things about you."

Jenny nodded. She gulped down a mouthful of saliva and timidly said: "I...um, nice to meet you too." She paused. She looked from her father and back to

(*oh don't call her that kyung-soon*)

Kate. She bowed her head. "It's...I mean, hello," she said in Korean. "It's nice to meet you." She raised her head. Her father beamed at her from the side, approving.

"Kate said she'd be joining us for dinner tonight, Jenny. She came over to help dad with cooking."

"Oh. Good." Jenny's eyes fell down to the woman's feet. She quickly raised her eyes and said: "I mean, thank you for preparing dinner. It smelled delicious when I entered. But I'm so sorry for tonight, because I already promised my friends we'd go and study at the library and—"

Her father raised a hand. "Cancel it. Eat with your family tonight, Jenny. Tell your friends you canceled."

"Yongsook."

Kate's hand slithered from her back and wrapped around his waist. Jenny watched as their fingers interlocked. She thought back to the ass-grab she saw earlier today, and shuddered at the thought of her father's middle-aged-man-hands on another woman.

"If Jenny needs to study tonight," Kate began in Korean, "let her, Yongsook. You know academics are more important than just eating for someone else's wishes."

"*Eating* is more valuable than studying in general," Yongsook replied. He

148

glared at his daughter. "Besides. This wasn't for you to go and taste what Kate made for us tonight, Jenny. This was for you to try and get to know dad's friends better. Do you understand?"

Jenny nodded. Her lips trembled, and she had to bite down to keep from crying. "Yes," she answered meekly, "I...I understand."

Yongsook nodded. He turned to move away from her, but then felt a tug on his arm.

"Yongsook, please. Let your daughter go out and study with her friends. Dinner won't be ready for another few hours at least—"

"She can study *upstairs*," he snapped. He pulled his hand from her. "She can study upstairs, Kyung-soon. She has no reason to go out with friends. She's so far behind on her studies that she needs to have *less* friends, *less* free time, *less* freedom..."

Jenny raised her head. Tears were in her eyes but she didn't cry. She'd been staring down at her feet as they spoke. She'd been staring, and remembering every little thing her father had said that one night when he'd

*(fucked)*

*(monday is gone)*

made love to Kate in the dark. She remembered his whisper; she remembered his husky tone, his sweat and strained laughter. She remembered the slight sounds of clothes being removed, the sounds of giggles and sighs. She remembered the devastating pain her chest had taken as she sat near the stairs listening as they made love together, as they kissed each other, as they caressed each other, as they *fucked* each other only a few meters away from her, as they tickled and held each other. She remembered their shadows; she remembered Kate's legs and arms twisting together against the blue flickering lights of the TV; she remembered her dad's heavy breathing and Kate's gasping. She remembered all of this, all this and more, all of this *fucking* and all of this *laughing*, but the one thing that she remembered the most was the guilt—she remembered the *guilt* that had erupted inside her and that had turned into violent hate, the *guilt* that finally made her feel worthless and pathetic and that had made her retreat back up the stairs crying. She remembered the guilt, she remembered feeling *guilty* for having felt hate, having felt *guilty* for having felt hate **FOR BEING CALLED** *STUPID.*

*No. Not like this. Just not like this. Please God, never again, not like this. I may not be smart, I may not be intelligent, but I am not so stupid to have to carry my parents' weight unfairly. I am not stupid. You're a liar, daddy. You're a lair, and I hate you like I hate mom. You're a liar.*

"No," Jenny whispered. She looked at her father. Tears sped down her cheeks. "No, appa. I'm not. I'm *not.*"

Yongsook turned to her. "What?"

*"You're a liar!"* she screamed. *"You're a liar to me, and you're mean like mom too!"*

Yongsook glared at her. His cheeks turned scarlet red and his jaw tightened. "Shut your mouth, Jenny," he warned. "Don't talk to me like that, don't you dare talk to me like that in front of—"

*"You're lying!"* she screamed. "You're just a stupid liar who betrays his family! You went off to leave mom and now leave me alone! You don't care about us, you never have! *You're a liar! You call me stupid and it's not true! You're nothing but a freaking liar—*"

"SHUT UP YOU LITTLE BRAT!"

He reached out to grab her. Jenny turned to run and felt one of his hands clutch her by the collar. He pulled her back. A loud *uck!* erupted from her throat and then her vision blurred. Her windpipe closed, and for one horrible second, the air cut from her throat. Her hands flailed wildly and thrashed through the air. Her right hand bumped something on the counter and she clawed at it desperately, blindingly, suddenly swinging it around and smashing it against her father's face.

It was a ceramic tea cup.

Yongsook screeched. White flares of pain burst through the corner of his left eye-socket and traveled through his temple. Water splashed on his face. The blow left him stunned and screaming with thick globs of saliva dripping from his mouth. He reached forward again and this time grabbed Jenny by the arm, grabbing her *hard*. His fingers clamped down on her sweater and burrowed deep into her skin, squeezing all the way to the bone. The grip was like iron, air-tight and crushing—Jenny let out a loud yelp and tried to pull away, feeling a horrible explosion of pain in her left shoulder as he yanked her back. Her father nearly dislocated her shoulder trying to pull her back.

"Let me go!"

*"You'd dare hit me!"* her father bellowed. "Huh, Jenny, is that it? You ungrateful little brat, I'll teach you a lesson so hard you'll never—"

Jenny spun around and brought the ceramic cup back up to her father's face. It smashed into his cheekbone. The blow before had brought his glasses halfway down his face; the second blow now crushed his glasses against his cheek. Specks of sharp glass lacerated his skin. Yongsook screamed. Jenny screamed with him, and felt a trembling jolt run through her wrist that made her lose hold of the teacup. It fell to the kitchen floor with a hollow rattling noise and rang loudly in Jenny's ears. She turned to run but then felt her father's fingers squeeze down. She snarled; tears blurred her vision and seeped into her mouth. She yanked forward and managed to loosen her father's fingers, but he kept hold, still clinging desperately to her sweater.

*Not my hair please God not my hair if he manages to grab hold of my hair then it's all over I can't escape if he manages to grab* my hair—

Kate, of course, throughout all of this, stood by screaming.

"Yongsook! What are you doing! Let her go, let her—"

"Shut up! Just shut UP!"

"Stop it Yongsook, stop what you're doing!"

"SHUT UP! SHE'S *MY* DAUGHTER! DON'T YOU TELL ME WHAT TO DO

*(monday is gone and tuesday)*

151

WITH MY OWN DAUGHT—"

A loud tearing noise erupted next to Jenny's side—the sound was like tendon and meat being pulled apart. An opening ripped down her woolen sweater and split vertically from her armpit to the left side of her ribcage. Pale flesh poked through. Jenny reached down with her free hand and brought the sweater above her head. It rubbed against her face as she brought it over and wiped aside her partial pangs. She was free.

*Run. Oh please, Jenny, just fucking run.*

She ran.

"**JENNY!**"

She ran through the living room.

"JENNY! YOU GET BACK HERE *RIGHT NOW*, OR I SWEAR—"

*My shoes, my shoes, oh God, I don't have enough time to put—*

*Forget the shoes! Run, Jenny!*

She slammed into the door and cried out in pain as the doorknob struck her in the side. She could hear Kate and her father screaming behind her. They were close, too close, she could already hear their feet chasing on the carpet, could already see their shapes popping out from the kitchen—

She struggled with the doorknob, cursed to herself, sobbed, and then finally managed to get it open.

"JENNY! YOU GET BACK HERE RIGHT NOW, DAMN IT!"

She ran barefooted across the lawn and made it out to the open street. Warm concrete and sharp gravel poked her soles, cutting her, biting her, scraping her. Her locket bounced lightly between her breasts and her hair fluttered wildly behind her shoulders. Sunlight warmed her bare arms and caused her to shudder. She had on a light white cotton camisole; one strap slid off her left shoulder and nestled in the crevice of her elbow.

"GODDAMN IT JENNY! DON'T MAKE ME COME AND GET YOU!"

Her feet hurt; pebbles poked at her. She continued running.

"Jenny!"

152

She could hear him falling away behind her, his voice becoming more and more distant.

Scattered sunlight spilled through the dry leaves from above and tattooed her skin with camouflaged-gray. Cold wind blew against her arms. Jenny pumped her legs faster and finally ran out of the cul-de-sac part of her neighborhood out onto 220th.

*Please, just a little more, just a few more blocks, please don't let me slow down, I'm sorry, I'm sorry, please, but my feet hurt, please, my feet—*

The road met 220th at a small T-intersection and soon gave way to the sidewalk. The sidewalk here was more painful than the asphalt road; it scrapped painfully beneath her feet like hardened lizard scales and caused her to wince. It was rougher, dirtier, filled with random tuffs of yellow dried weeds and uneven burst cracks. Decayed brown wooden fences surrounded her on the right as she ran while heavily dense pine trees stood by on her left across the street. Sharp rocks and broken beer bottle pieces threatened to cut her; dust, and other particulates like dirt and oil stains all made their way to the bottom of her soles, blackening her feet. Houses passed by her right and left.

*Please,* Jenny thought incoherently again as she ran, *please don't let me step on something sharp and get an infection. God, that would be the worst.*

Cars passed by on her left. They took the air around her and blew her hair, fluttering it around her shoulders. Jenny had a mental image of herself seen from the perspective of those passing her by, and suddenly laughed. *Half-naked barefoot Asian girl lost in Edmonds!* a voice screamed at her. *Jenny, look at you! Look at how you're running through the streets! Do you think people passing you by are looking at you, Jenny? Your hair's a mess* and *you have tears on your cheeks! Slow down, Jenny; laugh at yourself!*

She did laugh, only it was a bitter laugh, a hurt laugh, a laugh that came with winces and grimaces as her blackened feet encountered more and more sharp objects on the ground, and as her golden locket continued bouncing wildly between her small breasts. She gasped as she ran. She was getting tired,

153

and could feel the oily sting of tears on her cheeks eating through her skin. Phlegm collected in her throat and made her mad giggling sound like a grunting wolf.

She reached the four-way intersection between 220<sup>th</sup> and 76<sup>th</sup> and had to lean over on her knees to try and catch her breath. She bent over with her fingers digging into the denim of her knees and retched out dry vomiting sounds. The saliva in her mouth turned dry; swallowing hurt her throat. *Not only barefoot and half-naked with messy hair and tears on my cheeks,* the voice sighed at her, *but also, out of shape too. Nice, Jenny. Very nice.*

She picked herself up and wiped her mouth with her forearm. She gasped again. The bottom part of her neck was drenched with sweat and her hair smelled like sour yogurt. Moreover, her lunch from this afternoon shifted uneasily in her stomach with each aching breath, threatening to rise up.

A few traffickers at the four-way intersection turned their heads to stare. Jenny saw their eyes and quickly turned her head away, hiding her face beneath her hair. She became aware of a radio sounding somewhere in the distance and the impatient low grumbles of several dozen car engines. The sounds were discouraging to her ears, maddening, like the grunting cries of her father's spittle-filled voice. She stumbled backwards until her back hit the metal cross-light, and slid down to the ground.

How far had she run? Five blocks? Six, seven, *eight?* Maybe less than four? Had she really gotten tired just running four blocks in her bare feet while being chased down by her ballistic father?

The cars at the intersection drove away. Jenny felt them go and raised her eyes. A heavy weight filled her stomach and threatened to spew from her lips. She swallowed, forcing her lunch back down.

*What am I supposed to do now?* she asked soberly. *What am I supposed to do now without a mother or father?*

A sob built in her throat. It was a dry sob, just a few hiccups and sniffles, but it hurt. It hurt a lot.

*Please God, or whomever it is I'm supposed to pray to, let me stop crying, okay? I*

*already feel so bad, I already look like crap, I just really need to stop, please let me stop,*
*please let me find some shoes or a sweater or something, maybe let me get something to ea—*

Something hard poked her in the butt. Jenny reached for it, expecting her car keys.

It was her cell phone.

She bit down on her lip and stared at her reflection on the screen. Sweat covered the sides of her face while strands of black hair glued to her cheeks. Her forehead was glassy. Her lips were dry, and her eyes involuntarily winced as sweat dripped into them. She expected to see an oil blot or something on one of her cheeks, some grease stain to go with her overall appearance, but only faint scarlet covered her cheeks.

*Please don't let him think less of me if I call him. Please don't let him think I'm a girl that only needs him when I'm trouble. I lost my parents and my feet hurt, and everything's just so cold right now. Please Daniel—just be my friend right now.*

She dialed his number. She brought the cell phone to her ear and waited.

*Please, just talk with me, Daniel. Just talk with me.*

There was a piercing unresponsive beep on the other line. Then:

"Hello?"

Jenny's eyes closed. She let out a shuddering sigh and leaned her head back. *"Daniel?"* Her voice was high and shrill. "How...I mean, hi. How are you?"

There was a pause. In that pause, Jenny felt her tears flow, and did nothing to wipe them away.

"Jenny? Something wrong?"

# CHAPTER 10

They were at the beach again. Daniel saw her sitting on a bench near the sand dunes and slowly made his way over.

It was Friday today. He'd spent the entire week wondering about her since her call on Monday. She'd been extremely brief with her message and had just asked if she could see him at the beach again. He'd said sure. He knew something was wrong and had detected tears in her voice. He wanted to ask her what was happening, but knew that she would tell him when ready. That day was today, apparently. There was no need to further inveigle her with persuasive talk.

A fat purple bruise was on her cheek. It had dominated her face throughout the entire week at school and looked like an ugly nest of dead spider eggs. Daniel didn't know specifically what the bruise meant, but knew it had something to do with why she wanted to talk with him.

He made his way from his car and joined her near the bench.

"Hey," he said.

"Hey."

"Mind if I sit?"

She smiled at him. It was a sad smile. "Sit with me, Daniel," she said quietly. "I want you near me."

He sat next to her.

A string of black hair blew from her face and wavered in his direction. Her hair was in a ponytail today and held by a blue floral scrunchy. The sight was sublime to Daniel. He thought that seeing the white curves of her neck with black straying hair caressing her cheeks was the loveliest he'd ever seen her, lovelier still with the sound of waves crashing just a few meters away from them—it was made even lovelier still because of that ugly bruise on her cheek. Fresh saltwater breeze filled the air.

"I'm not taking up your day, am I?" she asked.

"No," Daniel answered. "You're not. It's fine. I don't do anything but sleep after school on Fridays anyway."

"The Losers' Club. Right? The term you used?"

"Maybe I should have called us winners instead."

A soft smile went to her lips. "Yeah," she said. "Maybe you should have."

"Are you going to tell me what's wrong, Jenny?"

She bit her lip at him. She said, "Before I do, can I ask you a question?"

"Sure."

"Why don't you ever bring a backpack to school?"

He laughed at her. The sound was soft and kind, more of a chuckle. He hadn't expected her to ask such a question. "It makes moving around a lot easier," he said. "Carrying a backpack around is a pain."

"What about your textbooks or your notes?"

"I don't take notes. I keep my textbooks at home and just read them in my room."

"You're smart then," Jenny said.

"Yeah," he replied. "I guess."

Jenny looked at him. She'd noticed a low drop in his voice. She asked: "How does it feel to be smart, Daniel?"

He paused for a moment. He said, "It hurts," and looked at her. "It just hurts to be smart sometimes."

"Why?"

He thought about the notebook he had on his desk at home, the notebook he always carried with him to school, the notebook his peers and teachers always noticed grasped tightly in his right hand. It was a simple one-subject wire-bound notebook with 150 sheets inside. The notebook contained no class notes, no complicated math formulae, no random pencil sketches. Instead, there in Daniel Fischer's elegant handwriting were neat paragraphs of written prose.

He wanted to be a writer. This was the most difficult truth to maintain with his peers and the rest of the world—he just wanted to be a writer. Disbelief, shock, jokes, and dismay always revealed to him the inconsistencies of these dreams. His parents were the only ones that provided him belief in his dreams, and it was to them, Daniel supposed, that he was indebted. His friends, however—or rather, peers—didn't want him to be a writer. Something about his dream to them was unseemly, and their reactions to his dreams were always unintentionally cruel. Why not a doctor, why not a scientist? Just last October, Thu Nguyen had come up to him with a similar snide remark about his dreams, stating rather cynically: "You're not gonna make much money by becoming a writer, Daniel. You're not going to get any girls either." She'd paused then, and said: "Unless, of course, you write shit and sell it in the market. People love shit these days, especially Americans. Write for young adults or teens, or for dumb women in loveless marriages, and you'll be fine. A lot of money comes from dumb people."

Daniel had frowned at her. He'd been hurt by the brutal truth of her words.

Smart. He was just so, so smart. He was just so smart that he could do what all of his peers expected of him but never what he wished to do as himself as an individual.

The notebook he carried to school every day contained fragments of a novel he wished to write someday.

"It hurts, because being intelligent means you have to always contrast yourself with others around you," he said. "When all you want is friends in this world, it's your intelligence that keeps you from speaking honestly with those closest to you. You are never seen as an equal but as a superior; you bring forth law with your words and are always alone. You moreover can never act as intelligent as you are as an individual because you risk the unwarranted chance of scorn from your peers. You become an elitist; you become pretentious. You are seen as someone always conceited, and are always mistrusted by the public."

"I'm sorry," Jenny said. "Have you gone through all this before?"

"Yes."

She looked at him. She bit her lower lip at him and felt a sense of hurt for him. His gaze lowered downward at the sand, and his eyes darkened with a deep thought. He said: "Earlier this year I had lunch with Kristina Nishimura. We were discussing the symbolic nature of rain. I told her I personally liked the rain because it offered the thinker the best sense of solace. She'd disagreed with me, saying that one had to interact with others to sharpen their minds. While I agreed, I told her the individual was best left to himself to think freely without the stained influence of others. She got angry at me, and said: 'Oh, so you think you're just *sooo* smart Daniel that you don't need to go out, is that it? That you don't need to speak with other people because you know everything already?' I tried to play it off as a joke. I said to her, 'Yeah, Kristina, I think I'm *sooo* smart. Duh,' and tried to change the subject." He shrugged at her. "I was told by her that when I speak with others, I should be less serious and loosen up a bit more. She said to me, 'You come off as a bit smart and rude, Daniel. People might get intimidated by you' and then she just sort of left it at that. She doesn't talk to me anymore."

Jenny said nothing for a moment. She studied him from the side and realized a deep look of hurt had appeared in his eyes.

"Maybe that dumb Kristina girl should have read more books before being so stupid to you," Jenny said. Her voice had been sharp. She hadn't meant it to be. "If anything, I think *she* was rude to have made an assertion against you when all you were doing was stating a preference. Just a random statement about the weather."

He smiled at her. He said, "Thanks. But even with this freedom that knowledge can sometimes bring, there are social expectations that hinder you from being free. Clichés, culture, Hollywood, stereotypes, prejudices—these all tell us how to live rather than promote us in our daily living. It's like wanting to be a write—" But he stopped then, eyeing her from the side, seeing her gaze thoughtful and sincere. She had leaned towards him with a slight pensive look in her eyes, curious.

"Are you going to tell me what happened to you, Jenny?" he asked kindly. He was staring at her bruise.

She pulled back with a sigh and looked down at her hands. She said without turning to him: "If I told you a few things about myself, would you still be my friend, Daniel?"

"Of course, Jenny. I'll always be your friend."

She sighed. She nodded.

She told him everything then. She began with the day when they first met in the parking lot (so long now. Just so, so long ago) and how she woke up to find her parents fighting downstairs in the living room. She told him about her mother; she told him about Kate. She told him of how she met Kate in the kitchen and of how she finally ran away.

"Jesus, Jenny. I'm sorry."

She nodded, wiping her eyes and allowing a brief sniffle. "Yeah," she said quietly. "I know. Thanks, Daniel."

"What happened after you ran away?"

She sighed. She said: "After I called you, I—

\*\*\*

—closed her conversation with Daniel and leaned her head back. She closed her eyes. Tears spread down her cheeks.

*Get up. I have to get up. I have to get up and move, get up and do something. I can't just sit here like a homeless person.*

Jenny opened her eyes. She brought the back of her hand up and wiped her mouth. The sweat on her neck had dried, but the sour-yogurt stench in her hair remained, forcing a foul reeking odor up her nose whenever the wind blew. Her face was oily, her lungs, a constant ache of pain with piles of iron laid against her chest. Her head throbbed. It felt like she'd sailed off the edge of the world somehow, splashed into a realm of dreams and illusory shapes. Every breath reminded her of the soreness in her calves; every face seen in each passing vehicle was like a ghost of fleeting milky color. And each blow of wind, though brief as it was light, was like a second afterthought to her skin, a caress of uneven leaves and autumn shadow.

It was cold again.

*My father,* Jenny thought quietly, *I went and hit my own father and ran away. I actually went and hit my own* father *and ran away while he went on screaming and chasing me. What the hell is wrong with me?*

She slowly picked herself up. She uttered a low grunt as she moved and heard her knees pop. She wiped her hands on her jeans and stood watching as cars drove by 76th Avenue. A queer feeling of self-awareness filled her. With it were the feelings of rape and nakedness.

*I'm standing here now barefoot and distressed,* she thought tiredly, *presented in such a way where when others see me, they must judge me with language and cultural misunderstanding. There is no way one can escape calling me 'girl' or 'Asian' because that's what I am. There's no escaping language and perception. No matter how much I try, people will see my feet dirty and bare. Just some Asian girl in a camisole and barefoot in jeans.*

The thought was barely bitter and sober. It instead was weightless and light as the air around her, stated with a casual coolness. Jenny sighed.

She pressed for the light on the crosswalk and waited. Four pink bands laced the area above her elbow on the meaty part of her bicep. When Jenny saw the marks, she frowned, and was only mildly surprised at her own disinterested reaction. They were her father's fingermarks when he'd brutally grabbed her by the arm.

*He gripped me so hard that I even felt it through my bones,* Jenny thought numbly. *He could have snapped my arm into two if he wanted to, or maybe even pulled out my shoulder when he yanked me back. Jesus.*

And again, like an echoing mantra: *I hit my own* father.

The light for the crosswalk changed, and Jenny quickly ran across. She headed east towards Highway 99 and heard the bustling breeze of afternoon cars to her right. To her left was the almost-built Eye Clinic of Edmonds and its widened parking lot. The Lynnwood Honda car dealership and Shell gas station were farther ahead on her right a few meters away.

It was the TOP Food & Drug that she was looking for. It was just past the eye clinic and massively set along the corner of 220th. Its parking lot stretched all the way to Highway 99 and was met with a smaller Starbucks coffee shop at the end. She was headed towards the store because she needed to buy shoes. She remembered seeing late summer items still for sale the last time she'd visited, and there'd been a rack showing off flip-flops and sandals.

She didn't know what else to do.

*I should have called Daniel and asked him to pick me up,* Jenny thought soberly as she made her way up 220th. The southern side of TOP Food & Drug loomed on her left. *But no. Asking him to pick me up like this would have been…been weak and desperate. I know I'm in distress but I don't want to burden him. I can handle this myself if I try. I refuse to be a damsel in distress. God, my feet hurt.*

A car honked her way, causing her to jump.

A person leaned out the passenger window of the Honda, cupped his hands around his mouth, and hollered, "YO, NICE BODY!" before finally disappearing down the street.

Gooseflesh tightened Jenny's arms. She heard goblin laughter in their wake and brought her arms up to hold herself. She shivered.

*So. this is the feeling of being a girl. This is me seeing myself against someone else for the first time, this is me finally seeing myself as a girl in public. My parents always made me see myself as a girl and daughter, and now when I'm out in public like this, I feel only disgust and nakedness. Is this who I am? As a girl, is this who I'll always be?*

She entered the store's parking lot. Cars bustled in and out of the lot as

162

Jenny made her way towards the entrance. Giant crates of yellow pumpkins lined the entrance and were placed alongside handpicked apples cluttered into shipping boxes; a table offering pumpkin pies with special savings greeted Jenny when she neared the entrance. Next to it was a long row of grocery carts lined together like tangled metal bones. A garden shop dominated the other side of the entrance where light perfumed fragrances of lilies and sweet roses filled her nose. Adjacent to the entranceway was a small corner dedicated to Tully's Coffee.

She hurried past checkout lanes and turned right past the personal hygiene aisle. She found a rack filled with summer clothes and quickly rushed over. There were beach sunglasses still for sale here, some tie-dye shorts, colored swimming trunks, inflatable swimming tubes, water-coolers, and, of course, a dozen pair of brightly colored flip-flops.

Jenny rushed over to the hanging flip-flops and grabbed a random pair off the rack. She tried them on. They were a happy yellow color. She rushed back to the checkout lane.

*Do I stand with them in line on my feet, or do I hold them while waiting?*

Jenny stopped. The question disturbed her, making her shudder. She stared down at her feet and felt gooseflesh on her back. She frowned.

*What the hell? Why*

*(nice body)*

*am I stopping? What the hell is wrong with me?*

"Find everything okay?" the cashier asked once she was next in line.

"Uh, yeah," Jenny said. The words TED was printed on his nametag.

Ted smiled. Jenny placed her flip-flops on the conveyer belt and noticed when an odd look of surprise went through his eyes. Black dirty imprints of heels and toes smeared the yellow skin of her flip-flops. Jenny was sure he thought something foul of her.

"Eight-seventy," Ted announced. She handed him a twenty-dollar bill. He returned her change and Jenny quickly smiled before walking away again. She clutched the flip-flops to her chest and then put them on when she was a short distance away. She realized that Ted hadn't asked her for a bag. He'd already assumed she was going to walk away with them on her feet and had said nothing more. Humiliation filled her.

Jenny hurried back the way she came, felt her new flip-flops slap the back of her heels, and jerked to a dead stop when she was outside the entrance.

Her mouth fell open. Her eyes grew wide and the saliva in her mouth disappeared.

Her father. He was making his way out from the middle of the parking lot. A flush of red rage filled his face, and Kate awkwardly walked alongside him.

Sweat collected on Jenny's brow. *Here?* Her father had decided to drive and find her *here?* Out of all the places to go and search for her, it had to be *here?*

Panic rose in her chest, sharp and sudden, and Jenny let out a quick gasp. Her father moved with a stiff stride in his walk, his shoulders hunched, his eyes directed ahead. He looked like a cunning predator stalking his prey, brisk but patient. Though he was still several dozen meters away, Jenny could see her father's determined expression, and felt another quiver of fear pass through her. His tie was loose and hung limp against his sweat-stained silk shirt. His glasses were off, probably still somewhere back on the kitchen floor as a billion shattered pieces—Jenny shuddered knowing that her father's face was still freshly lacerated with glass shards.

Jenny dodged back through the entranceway and ran through the fresh produce section. Her arms and legs weren't numb with coldness anymore; they in fact were flush with blood and hot adrenaline, the same hyper mode of fright that had occurred when her father had tried grabbing her. Old feelings of tired fatigue and oxygen-deprived muscles were simply gone now.

"Shit," Jenny hissed. "*Shit, shit, shit!*"

What if they split up? What if her father told Kate to wait at the entrance while he chased her like a cat in a maze? It wasn't difficult to find a dirty Asian girl with yellow flip-flops on her feet wearing nothing but jeans and a camisole—she might as well have painted a gigantic bull's eye on her back and screamed out loud for them to find her.

She ducked into an aisle and turned around, heaving. She bent herself forward and rested herself against her knees, panting heavily as strands of messy black hair slid from her shoulders. She carefully made her way to the end of the aisle and poked her head out to look in both directions. Her heart beat crazily in her chest. She glanced both ways again and saw an employee dressed in a red TOP Food & Drug apron scuttling past. A woman dressed in a business suit strode by, and another man with a shopping cart passed her aisle.

That was it—nothing more. Jenny sighed.

Just as she was about to turn around and walk away again, a heavy hand fell on her shoulder and made her yelp.

Her father twisted her around. He smacked her across the face and sent her flying into the shelves. Jenny shrieked. Her head snapped to the side and her feet tangled under her—blood gushed out between her teeth. Her hands clawed blindly at the air and pulled an entire row of packaged toilet paper off the shelves. She fell on her side, gasped, tasted the floor, and felt an avalanche of items fall on top of her. She swallowed, whimpered again, and managed to pick herself up midway before her father's fingers twisted into her hair and yanked her from the floor.

"Oh, *appa, don't please it hurts it*—"

He tossed her aside. Jenny's feet tangled again, and she collapsed once more to the floor where the air popped out of her lungs. Her flip-flops slid out from under her feet.

"Get up," her father said. His voice was dispassionate and cold. "Get up right now, Jenny."

Sobbing, Jenny obeyed, and slowly picked herself up with rickety arms. Bloody mucus spilled from her nose; tears ran down her face.

"Appa. Please—"

He grabbed her arm. Jenny winced and felt him pull her along. His fingers dug into the meat of her bicep and crushed the bone underneath. Jenny whimpered. She felt the end of her left arm going numb and tried again to scream.

"Appa, wait, my shoes, I need to get my shoes, I can't—"

Kate waited for them at the entranceway. She stood with her arms hugged beneath her chest and with her eyes darting in every direction at once. Her eyes widened when she saw Jenny. Sympathy and remorse filled her face when seeing the bloodied and barefoot girl.

"Take her," Yongsook ordered. "And follow me to the car."

Kate gingerly took Jenny's arm and gripped it with a light hand. Jenny sniffled.

"Yongsook—"

"I said follow me to the car! Don't argue, Kyung-soon. And keep hold of her. Don't you dare let her go."

They started walking. Hard asphalt once again scraped Jenny's feet. She suppressed another urge to cry and let out a strangled sniffle instead. Kate leaned in close to her side and whispered, "We're almost there, Jenny. Hold on." She placed a comforting hand on her back and led her to the car. Sweet lavish perfume filled Jenny's nose. It smelled like fresh grapes picked in the summer rain. Jenny hated the smell.

"Get inside the house, Jenny. Now."

Jenny heard the door close behind her. Her feet found the carpet of the living room, and then her father smacked her so hard on the back of her head that she fell down to her knees.

"Yongsook! Please, just stop!"

Fresh smells of vacuumed carpet filled her nose. Jenny stared stupidly down at the carpet and saw a drop of black blood in front of her. *Now look what you've done, appa,* she thought incoherently. *You vacuumed all for nothing.*

"Keep on your knees, Jenny," her father ordered. "Turn around. Look at me."

She turned around and faced her father. She kept on her knees and swallowed when another buildup of bloody mucus irritated her throat.

Kneeling before her parents was a familiar posture; Jenny had been a mischievous girl when she was younger. She talked back to her teachers and pastors, never listened to her parents, and always found ways to break things that weren't hers. Once, when visiting a prominent Korean family, she'd eaten an entire basket of raspberries without anyone knowing. The verbal abuse that occurred afterwards had lasted for more than an hour. She'd been nine-years-old then, and had cried bitterly in bed that night. Her father tended to do all the shouting while her mother did all the sighing—they rarely ever hit her. The last time she had knelt on the floor like this was when she'd defied Pastor Hwang. Then, her father had spanked her after forcing her on her knees. Her mother had just shaken her head. This had all occurred, of course, after her nose had partially healed.

"You think you can disrespect me in my *own household!*" her father screamed. Jenny raised her eyes. She realized he'd been shouting for some time now. The pain had barred his voice from her mind; the blow to the back of her head had left stars in her vision.

"You come home without even properly greeting me and suddenly embarrass me in front of my own guest! You little runt! You mischievous brat! How *dare* you! How *dare you* go on living in this household where all you do is…"

Her head felt heavy. She wanted to sleep. All the pain that had been administered to her body since this afternoon after meeting her mother in the parking lot now seemed far, far away. She wanted to shower; she wanted to collapse. She wanted someone to carry her upstairs and lay her down in bed, take off her clothes, and just let her dream. Since when did living suddenly becoming this hard?

*Tired,* Jenny thought distantly. *I'm just so tired right now. I don't even care about my shower. I just want to curl up in bed even if my feet are dirty. I just don't care.*

"…*listening* to me, Jenny?"

Jenny snapped her head around. She shook her head and saw her father glaring at her. An ugly green vein swelled beneath the skin of his forehead. Sweat drenched his skin. Jenny studied the damage she'd done to his face and was only mildly startled at what she saw. Sprinkles of blood dotted the left side of his face like disordered freckles; his left eye permanently stared at her with a half-wince. There were no great spots of blood, but only minuscule red dots that marked where his glasses had lacerated his skin. Surely his blows against her had done greater and more destructive damage than being smacked with a simple ceramic tea cup.

"I'm listening, appa," Jenny replied. Her voice came out in a slow draw. "I'm listening."

Yongsook glared at her. Jenny waited, thinly aware that the blood in her nose had stopped flowing but still collected somewhere in the back of her throat. From the side, she spotted Kate in the foyer near the door. An awkward yet frightened look of perplexity seemed to go through her eyes.

*Welcome to the family,* Jenny thought bitterly. *This is how I'm treated in this house. Sooner or later, you may grow tired of me too.*

"…want you to apologize, Jenny."

Jenny glanced at her father. She'd been drifting into a sea of her own thoughts when the word 'apology' entered his sentence. Now she stared at him, nonplussed.

"*What?*"

"I said *apologize!* Apologize to your father and your elders, Jenny! Apologize to me and Kyung-soon."

Kate moved towards her father.

"Yongsook, don't, please. I don't need an apology, your daughter did nothing wrong to—"

Yongsook pushed her off. He did it with one full swing of his arm, making Jenny believe he would slap her too. A cruel part of her secretly wished he would.

"Apologize, Jenny," her father said again. "Apologize now, and tell both of us you're sorry. Ask for forgiveness. *Now.*"

Jenny stared at him. Tears fell from her eyes.

"No."

The blow struck her in the face; it was the same side of her face where a fat bruise was already growing. Her head twisted sideways and tears exploded from her eyes. Tears soaked her cheek and burned her skin as her body crumpled on its side. A dull pain throbbed from her lower jaw. Fresh blood spilled from where her lip had cracked. She sobbed.

"Get up on your knees and apologize!" Yongsook roared. "Don't make this any harder than it is, Jenny!"

Jenny pathetically picked herself up and knelt before her father a second time. Visible tremors cascaded through her body. She closed her eyes and readied herself.

"No," she whispered. "I won't apolo—"

Her father struck her again. Hard calloused palms collided with her cheek and cut off her voice. Her teeth clashed together and bit down on her tongue; hints of blood filled her mouth. Jenny fell sideways and crumpled into a ball. She lay there, whimpering. The muscles on her face felt lopsided and numb. She let out an agonized moan.

"Yongsook, please! She's learned her lesson, can't you—"

Jenny quietly picked herself back up. She sat on her knees and faced her father a third time, her left eye barely opened. Swelling fattened the entire left side of her face.

"I'm not going to apologize to you, appa," Jenny said. She panted. "I'm not going to apologize for nothing I did wrong. It's *you* who should apologize to *me* for having sex in the dark last week while your daughter cried alone upstairs in her bedroom."

Yongsook stared at her. Blood faded from his cheeks.

"I know…I know that neither you nor mom like me, but that's no reason to excuse yourself as a father. Every day I come home waiting for a parent to meet me, but you're never there. I just do whatever I want, and because mom's not here anymore, there's nobody to love me. Last week when you had sex, you even called me stu—"

This time the blow knocked her completely unconscious. Her father's fist swung from the right and collided squarely with the untouched side of her face. Her father was left-handed; the wedding ring was on his right fist. The ring tore at Jenny's cheek and scraped away skin. Her jaw momentarily slid out of joint and an explosion of pain burst through her face. She blacked out just before she hit the ground, regained consciousness, and then momentarily blacked out again. She lay dazed on her side, hearing nothing but incoherent screams and shouts from far away. Kate was screeching; her father was raging. She drew her legs in against her chest and wrapped her arms around herself, curling into a fetal position. The world took on a blissfully dark color for her eyes to rest on. Her hair had covered her face as she collapsed, shielding her from the glaring lights of the outside world.

*Just like Pastor Hwang,* Jenny thought stilly. *This is just like Pastor Hwang three years ago. This is what happens when you stand up for yourself in this world. God's hands must just be massive to the person that refuses to worship Him on his knees. I just wished that we humans had come up with a gentler god to worship instead of a jealous god. Poor us.*

For a moment, there seemed nothing but peace and quiet, and then the pain suddenly returned with massive force. Jenny heard herself whimper and moan, and then felt something heavy fall on top of her. It smelled like sweet grapes plucked in the summer rain.

Kate.

*"Stop it, Yongsook! What are you doing! Do you want to put your daughter in the hospital! You're killing her! You're just killing her!"*

*Kate,* Jenny thought. *Why is she protecting me? Why is she here?*

Her mind slipped, and her entire world ceased to exist.

An untold time passed where Jenny later found herself lying in bed. It was her bed. The lights were off, and the shades to her room had been drawn. Footsteps came to her side, and soon there was a gentle stroking of fingers parting back her hair.

It was Kate again. In her semi-conscious, dazed awareness, Jenny recognized the sweet sugary perfume, and realized that someone—possibly Kate—had carried her to her room to lay her down. There was a damp rag placed against her face, some soft cooing in her ears, and then the occasional soft caress of fingers against her hair.

\*\*\*

She had to miss school on Tuesday, of course. That she should miss the second day of school just upon the eve of her arrival from an already week-long absence had been a verdict unchallenged by the residents of the Park household: Her face was badly beaten and the swelling wouldn't go down for a whole day. Her father refused to return home for two nights, and Jenny just bleakly did her readings for school.

Kate sat beside her all throughout this convalescence, of course. Kate was there. She was always just there with her.

\*\*\*

They stood now at the pier overlooking the waves.

Daniel watched as her ponytail draped smoothly over her shoulder. She brushed it back, involuntarily, and had him imagine for a moment a brief scene of naked skin accidentally glanced at between two pieces of garments. The parting of hair was so gentle that it seemed to Daniel no more than having her brush the smooth snowy-white shells of her cheeks with her hand. It allowed him to admire the bruise on her face without her notice.

"I'm sorry," Daniel began. "It must've been horrible."

"Yeah," Jenny answered quietly. "It was. It was really was."

Daniel watched her from the side. She had casually leaned against the railing of the pier to dangle her arms lazily above the water. A handful of fishermen were with them on the pier a dozen meters away, but they paid them no attention. A gentle push of waves rocked the pier beneath their feet.

"Did you miss school on Tuesday?"

"Yeah. I still had some recovering to do."

"Kate?"

She nodded. "She took care of me. I don't know why she did it, but she stayed home all day for me and cooked my meals. She also helped clean my face and bring icepacks. She cleaned my clothes too."

"She cares for you."

"I don't know. Maybe. I guess." She sighed. "It was just my face. She didn't need to stay and care for me so much. I just didn't want to get out of bed and move around the house. I wasn't paralyzed."

Daniel nodded, understanding how idiotic his vision of her had been. He'd envisioned her with bandages wrapped around her face, her body set in a cast or something, her time completely immobilized in bed. He'd imagined her physically encumbered and unable to move where Kate had to wipe her face every day and brush her hair, forever bedridden and in constant withering agony. In reality, she'd probably sat in bed all day with a miserable pout on her lips doing homework. She was right to tell him all these things; he was wrong to think her so weak.

"How were your feet?"

"Okay. Nothing bad. A few cuts and scrapes. When I showered later, a lot of black water went down the drain."

"Yeah," Daniel said sadly. "I imagine that would happen."

"Yeah."

They went silent. A loud *ooooorrrrnnngg* sounded behind them where the Edmonds-Kingston ferry announced its arrival at the terminal. Daniel sighed when hearing the sound, and took in a lungful of Puget Sound air. It was good today. With her beside him this afternoon again, it was good today.

"Do you miss your mother?" he asked.

"Yeah. I think I do. I think she was hard on me at times, but…she was my mom. I miss her a lot, Daniel."

"I'm sorry, Jenny."

"Yeah. Me too."

He waited patiently as she wiped her eyes. After she was done, he asked her, "Is it common for Korean families to hit their children?"

"I don't know. I don't feel like it is. It's a stereotype to think that all Asian families beat their children. No one at my church gets beaten. What my mother and father do…it's just a bit harsher than most. My dad's an angry man, and I think my mother was a depressed woman. I think it was only natural they took it out on me."

"Natural doesn't imply correct, Jenny."

"I know. But still."

"So you hold no grudges against them for beating you."

At this, she thought for a minute, and said: "No. Not really. Again, the beatings were rare, and when they occurred, it was just a spanking when I was a little girl. Most of the time they just shouted at me and told me to do better. I still have to kneel, though. That's part of it."

Again that nod, again that somber outward gaze towards the water. Jenny observed him from the side and wondered what was bothering him.

"Daniel?"

"Hmm?"

"What are you thinking?"

He paused. He said, "Truthfully I'm wondering why you didn't submit to your father when you had the chance to. You endured so much that day that it seems almost ridiculous for you to endure more than you had to. All you had to do was utter one simple apology and end everything. You simply could've apologized while still being untruthful. There was no need for him to beat the living crap out of you."

"Would you have submitted if you were me?"

He paused again. "No," he said. "I don't think so. I in fact would have risen three hundred more times if my body allowed it."

"Then what's wrong?"

"I don't know. Just something about this frightens me. I'm scared, Jenny."

"Scared?" She looked at him. "Scared of what?"

He shrugged at her. It was a modest display, a modest shrug, a gesture that indicated he in his mind (and perhaps *heart*), knew with words what he wished to say, but was for some reason unable. Jenny waited, giving him the necessary time to gather his thoughts.

"Should I voice it with words," he said finally, "it would be me stating simply that I was scared of our future. Your act of defiance against your father has made me think what it means to be an individual in life, and what it means for us when we enter college."

Jenny bit her lip at him. He had more to say. She let him continue.

"I want to be a writer in life. People hear this and they often laugh suspecting I'm humoring them or being contemptuous. They expect me to become a fulfillment of what they perceive, never an opportunity for myself. I know they wish for me to be a doctor or a scientist. Very rarely do their eyes regard me with a kind glance when I tell them my desire, and very rarely do they smile affably at me without patronizing. I can never speak openly with them because I'm always forced to repress my words lest I sound pretentious, and very rarely can I voice to them my dreams without incurring incredulous glances. It's simply so difficult to be an individual in life. Always, there is the culture of the Other that attempts to suppress us."

A picture of a girl standing half-naked in a glass case with her clothes torn and her hair a mess filled Jenny's mind. She is without shoes on her feet, this girl, and has bruises covering one side of her face. Strobe lights and camera flashes burst a few feet away from her and blind her eyes. A darkened crowd of faceless onlookers point at her, laugh at her, jeer and curse at her, throw insults at her, and mumble a few words of disgust at her. Tears cover her face, and she reaches up to cover her small naked breasts as she shudders into a ball in the corner of her cage.

"Yeah," Jenny said to the side. "I think I know what you mean."

"Entering college will dissolve the world we're so used to by granting us physical freedom as young adults. The dilemma that comes to us is as simple

174

as this: Will we conform? Or will we resist as individuals? The former offers comfort but with clichés, while the latter offers loneliness. You know the latter. Both you and I know the latter, Jenny."

"All our dreams we hold so dear are now going to be put to the test," Jenny said for him. "Now that we're adults, we're suddenly faced with whether or not we're still strong enough to uphold our dreams. The world is suddenly here, and we have to see if we can meet it without being distracted by culture."

"Yes," Daniel said.

She asked: "Why do you want to be a writer, Daniel?"

"Because I find in fiction a truth not offered by reality," he said. "And from this truth in fiction, I feel we can better our reality. To be emboldened with dreams of a writer is to become onerous with the structures of reality. I want to understand our reality through fiction."

Jenny smiled at him. It was a smile from the side hidden from his eyes, one that she offered with gladness. She knew then that he was passionate about his art, and she admired him deeply for it.

"Do you think when you die you'll be reborn again in Heaven, Daniel?" she asked quietly.

"I don't know," he said. "I don't think there's a need for Heaven, and so I don't think there's a need for rebirth."

"Once you die, won't you miss loving your friends?"

"I think missing my friends when dying means that I loved them enough."

She smiled at him. It once again was a sad and open smile. She turned away from him and made her way back across the pier. Old wooden floorboards creaked beneath her feet. She felt him follow.

"I think if I were to die," she began, "I'd like to be reborn here. Maybe as a human being again, or simply a plant or a tree. And during the sunset, I could watch as the sun faded behind the mountains. This is Heaven enough, I think."

"That sounds wonderful. Much better than eternal happiness."

He watched quietly as she wrapped her arms around herself and slowly ambled along the pier. He followed her as the wind blew against her hair. Black tendrils of silk wavered in his direction.

"Jenny."

"Hmm?"

"You called Kate Kyung-soon once. That's her Korean name."

"Yeah."

"May I to know your Korean name too then?"

She stopped then. She turned to him and smiled. In that moment, Daniel understood he had said something wrong and inwardly chided himself. Her eyes regarded him earnestly and kindly—but Daniel knew she was calculating something specific to say.

"My Korean name?" she said lightly. Her voice rose to an unnatural tone. "I actually don't have a Korean name, Daniel. My parents decided to just give me the name Jenny. I'm one of those rare cases where I simply have an American name."

"Oh," he said. "Okay."

She looked at him. He looked back, and they both quietly turned away.

"Daniel?"

"Hmm?"

"I really will need to go to Korea soon. I don't know when, but it'll most likely be after school. Just to...to sort out things with the family."

"Oh. Okay."

"But I'll be back after summer. It won't be permanent or anything."

They left the pier and rejoined Olympic Beach. They headed  back the way they came towards Brackett's Landing once again through the sand dunes.

"Daniel?"

"Yeah?"

She hesitated. "Thanks for taking time to be with me. I really appreciate it. And thanks for just…just letting me talk with you. Thank you for just hearing me and letting me be me. For being my friend. It means a lot."

He nodded, looking at her, admiring her, wishing he could say more to her. He said simply, "It's nothing, Jenny. It's nice being with you like this too," and stuffed his hands in his pockets.

She smiled at him. She slowed her footsteps and let him walk by her side. Their shadows briefly merged together as the sun drifted towards the mountains.

# CHAPTER 11

Nora Rhys understood that the reason why Red Moon operated successfully the way it did was because of its farcical demand for appropriate manners. What were appropriate manners? Something that only women knew and felt, and something that men could only intellectualize. She didn't know how deeply embedded this knowledge of appropriate manners was for some, but knew that it was a large subconscious part of the diner, so much so that it was something almost *natural* and essential.

These manners were a farce: They were masks to hide an even more dreadful truth kept hidden deep inside. Those who recognized this thin veil of quiet kept to themselves. Others, like Abigail and Ted in the back, were too stupid to recognize its presence (or merely just too naïve with their stupidity), and simply glossed over it. The parking lot outside wasn't empty tonight because they had no customers; it was empty because the world was dead and cold outside, sleeping in the dead of the night, sleeping like the dead, dreaming in a world of the dead. The black-and-white tiles that checkered endlessly along the floor were not so clean that they reflected the bright ceiling lights; they in fact were dirty, and required constant attention. And the music here was not a pleasant throwback to the 1950's or 1960's. The music here was a substitute for the piercing sounds of midnight silence that echoed in the air. Nora didn't know if anyone else realized these things as she did, but she suspected Jenny felt something similar. Yes, Jenny probably felt something similar. She was, after all, more 'there' than the rest of them at this pathetic diner, wasn't she?

They'd met about a year ago. Even then, Nora could tell something was different about her, something that was incredibly sad and immensely bitter. It was in the lack of emotion her face gave to the world when coming to work, in the way her eyes gazed out longingly at the rain and then peered down at nothing on the counter. Loneliness was the best noun to describe her, but Nora thought there was something severely *pained* about her too, something that sought but lacked, remembered but mourned.

These appropriate manners required a person to take on a role that was disproportionately conflicted with one's self, but that still, in some sense, portrayed some *part* of one's true self. In Nora's case, it had been taking on the bubblegum-chewing-magazine-reading hipster role that liked to "blond-talk" her way through the day (though she herself was a natural brunette).Why magazines? Because in general she liked to read everything, but in general she couldn't, and so, had to supply herself with an identity of celebrity gossip and the latest Hollywood scandals. In a world of men (poor *beastly* men), a woman compromised herself when she told the world she could read and dissect Faulkner; in a world of truckers and men, of wet yellowish snot wiped clean against dirty oil-stained handkerchiefs and obnoxious slaps to her ass whenever walking by—of having to smile obediently and submissively as the weaker sex to toothless grins, of having to provide herself as eye-candy in short skirts and black-heeled pumps, in having to doll herself up with earrings and makeup, lipstick and eyeliner, fishnet stockings and dresses—a woman became nothing when she revealed to the world that she once thought of being a scientist, a scholar, and was, on occasion, still a great fan of the History and Discovery Channel (when they didn't show those goddamn *awful* reality shows of truckers or stupid fishermen, at least). In a world that consisted of working two jobs to pay off student loans—one at the mall in the mornings as a Victoria Secret saleswoman standing out front of the doors handing out samples to wary customers, and one being a tired waitress at a diner—having to think beyond the boundaries of "what could have" versus "what *is*" was something

179

dangerously maddening. Because to think outside this box—this box now called life and social placement—was to think outside the appropriate manner, the same laws that governed the world at Red Moon's. And once you were outside the realm of appropriate manners, you were with the ultimate punishment: stigmatization.

Nora hadn't been able to locate Jenny's appropriate manner until only a few months ago. By then, she'd grown weary of the Asian woman that always worked with her, wondering if she knew any English at all. Her acquired role as that bubblegum-chewing figure had tried to probe and prod, probe and prod, but had found nothing. Then, finally, on one warm Idaho summer morning (before she, Abigail, and Jenny had all switched over to the graveyard shift), she'd noticed something remarkably strange: While all the girls came in to the diner dressed in casual clothes like shorts and blouses, Jenny always came to work wearing long-sleeved cardigans and sunglasses.

"Hey, Jenny!" Abigail had cried one day. "You look like Hollywood in those glasses of yours!"

And indeed she had. Nora hadn't been all too sure, but thought that the glasses Jenny sported on that day were Bvlgari taints, and that the purse she carried was an authentic Louis Vuitton Damier Azur Hampstead. No doubt these precious commodities had been gifts loaned from great King Tom, and Nora had felt a sense of unease course through her when she'd stared at Jenny's sunglasses. Thigh-high leather boots reached  past her calves over a skin covered in tight denim blue. It must've been in the high 80's that day, and she looked like she was dressed for early autumn.

"I try," Jenny said, smiling. "See you two in a bit after I get changed."

Nora watched as she went to the bathroom. She hadn't come back out until fifteen minutes later. And by then, Nora knew with the sudden application of red lipstick on her face, and the sudden blushing of powder on her cheeks (and the sudden wide smiling of her lips, and the darting apprehensiveness of her eyes), that not only were there problems in paradise, but also a beast in paradise called Man.

Jenny knew. Jenny knew about life and manners, and she knew what went on in Red Moon's. And because of this, Nora thought, there was a possible friend in her.

And so, that's why, standing there now behind the front counter of Red Moon's Diner, reading a paperback novel and blowing on a thick piece of pink bubblegum, Nora suddenly paused when she saw Jenny entering through the glass doors, and frowned. Her bubblegum stayed fat in front of her face like a bloated toad, and she placed the book she'd been reading beneath the counter before popping her gum. It made a loud *POP!* sound that echoed off the empty walls of the diner.

"Nora?" Jenny said. The bell on the door rang stupidly above her. "Good to see you! I thought you weren't going to be back for another two weeks or something. At least, that's what Abigail said."

"Oh, that girl Abigail's always getting her dates and places messed up," Nora replied. Once again her voice was that pretty-girl's voice. "I'm sure what she told you was way off from what actually happened, you know?"

She was smiling. Yes, that's what was so odd about this picture—Jenny Acworth was actually *smiling* as she walked through the doors of Red Moon's Diner. Actually *smiling*. It wasn't a cruel smile or even a pompous one, but something that looked happy and relieved. Reassured even. Nora had never seen a smile like that on her face before. Before she could ask what was so wonderful, Nora thought to herself: *Maybe things in paradise have gotten a little better after all.*

No. That wasn't likely. In fact, it was probably stupid to think that knowing the many times she'd seen her come walking in wearing long-sleeved shirts and cardigans. Not only that, but there'd also been times when she'd observed Jenny wearing scarves and gloves with those cardigans. This lasted for about three weeks maybe, sometime near the thawing of icy winter. Tom Acworth was no chivalrous knight in shining armor. He was tall, clean-cut, and handsome in the face, yes, but with gallant qualities he was not, and Nora supposed that Mr. Great King Tom was the type of man that believed himself to be audacious only because he imagined himself with a giant sword beneath his belt. On his first visit to the diner, Nora remembered his eyes snickering in disgust at the dinner menu. On his second visit, he'd visibly backed away from the kitchen, cupped his nose, and politely pulled Jenny away to kiss her goodbye. He'd given her a quick peck on the cheek and fled out the door, expensive leather shoes flying.

*Hey, if the place doesn't smell good to you, then smell your own ass, asshole,* Nora thought. *God, Jenny, why are you with him? If he can't even respect you, why are you with him?*

The question, of course, was irrelevant. Nora already knew the answer. In fact, right when her mind had asked the question, another had popped into her head, whispering coldly: *Why are you still here at this diner?*

"Oh," Jenny said, laughing. "Yeah. Abigail can be quite quirky at times. How's your foot? Abby said you weren't going to leave the hospital for another two weeks."

*Who the hell is Abby now?*

"That girl is really messed up now, isn't she?" Nora asked back, feigning a dubious smile. "No Jenny, my foot's fine. I said I'd be back to work in *two days*, not two weeks. Two weeks was a while ago, and two days just passed, so here I am. And I was just home all the time."

"Well it's glad to see you back. I'll see you in a bit, kay?"

"Kay."

Jenny smiled and went to change in the bathroom. Nora stared at her, tired and bleak.

She'd been in contact with Abigail, of course; the girl knew no one in the world that thought of her frivolous mannerisms as a quality loathed and despised—she was the exact model of happy irony. Abigail told her last night that Jenny had ousted her Tall, Dark, and Handsome. She told her how Jenny had picked a fight with him, how things had gotten out of hand, how the windows had shattered, how the roof had collapsed, how the police had come, and how they'd had to use K-9 units and pepper spray. She also said that her dog Spencer was doing well, that the vet continuously complimented her style of dress, and that new shoes were on sale at the mall, and that blah, blah, blah, blah, *blah*.

It was the man Nora was interested in. She wanted to know what happened between him and Jenny, wanted to know *why* she'd driven him away the way she had, and wanted to know where he'd come from. She'd seen him once or twice at the diner, and knew the gossip that surrounded him. What she wanted to know was the *before*. What was his relationship with Jenny, and *why* did she always want to push him away?

The novel she'd been reading before Jenny entered was a paperback titled *Heaven's Defiance*. It had been written nearly ten years ago. It was a novel written by a Daniel Fischer.

Nora had never heard of Fischer before. She stumbled upon his name only last week when she'd been granted a few days off to recover from her fall. The goddamn stairs at her apartment building were incredibly slippery when soaked with rain. Fractured her tibia, she did, and one could *bet* she'd screamed loud and piercing enough to wake all the tenants at her place. The few days she'd spent off from work and off her feet (*har-har-har*) had been compensated with an old joy of hers: reading. Names like Joyce, Faulkner, Woolf, Hemingway, Dostoevsky, and Nabokov soon filled her afternoons.

Her encounter with Fischer had come about as pure accident: Ms. Ferdinand, at the time, acting both as her constant caretaker and friend, was quick to understand her love of reading. So every day when she came to visit Nora with groceries and the mail, she'd surprise her with random novels and paperbacks from the old dusty bookstore up the street. One of these had been a thin paperback called *Heaven's Defiance*. Underneath the title were the words: Daniel Fischer.

At first Nora hadn't been interested. Judging from the cover (and yes, it was perfectly acceptable to judge a book by its cover. How else were you to pick one from the shelf if not by looking at its cover?), the book was a miserable thing, a retelling of lost innocence and life. The book was all-black and ominous appearing; the title *Heaven's Defiance* was smeared across the cover in what look like dark blood strokes. The words *New York Times #1 Bestseller* dominated the front.

Nora told Ms. Ferdinand to get rid of it.

"Oh? Are you sure, Nora? I hear he's a good writer."

"There's no such thing as a good writer these days, Mrs. Ferdinand," Nora replied. It was probably the only time she spoke with full authenticity in her voice. "You're either a popular writer or a non-popular writer. These days, Oscar Wilde's dream for art has come true, unfortunately."

Ms. Ferdinand, not bothering to say much else and merely shrugging her shoulders, replied, "Okay then," and walked away with a few groceries in her arms. She grabbed the book and waved farewell to Nora with her fingers.

"I'll see you later, dear," she called as she opened the door and let in a cold yawn of autumn air. "Take care, and I do hope that your foot gets better."

Nora bade her goodbye. Just as she was shutting the door behind her, Nora caught sight of the author's photograph on *Heaven's Defiance,* and quickly yelled out, "Wait, Ms. Ferdinand! Wait, sorry, I changed my mind. Could I see that book again?"

Ms. Ferdinand obliged with a cheery "Sure!" and came back inside with a smile.

It was him all right. Nora hadn't been too sure from the distance, but when finally holding the book in her hands, there could be no deny: It was the man. It was the exact man from the diner, the same man that always left two crisp fifty-dollar bills on the table with the initials *J.J.* written on them (and what did those double J's even *mean?).* He was a bit younger in the picture with more of a relaxed gaze and softer features around the cheeks, but the eyes were still the same. The chin was the same, and the brow, neck line, and even *nose* were all the same. The photograph had him leaning sideways in a chair staring directly at the camera with his left hand supporting one side of his face with fingers pressed delicately against his temple. It was a typical I-Am-a-Writer kind of gesture, one that Nora knew all authors felt ashamed of doing but still did so anyway. The little blurb beneath the picture stated that Mr. Daniel Fischer was a recent (Class of 2010) graduate from the University of Washington with a BA in English. According to the blurb, his current residency was in Seattle, Washington.

*Heaven's Defiance* was his first novel—it was written over a decade ago.

*Fischer,* Nora thought. *Daniel Fischer. Well I'll be damned. Who are you, Jenny, and where did you come from? What past did you have, and how hellish could it have been?*

Nora had shuddered when reading the book. She'd read it in one sitting and had sat in her chair thinking about it hours into the night.

The story had been about Kelly Robichaux, a seventeen-year-old girl who finds herself waking up naked and alone in the woods. She's just been raped. Her body is left for dead in the middle of cold January rain, and the first thing she realizes when she gains consciousness is that there is blood on her thighs. Throughout the story, the theme of rape takes on a mythological meaning where it eventually transforms into a commentary on cultural conformity and autonomous individuality.

Nora wanted to take the book and shove it in Jenny's face. She wanted to ask her to explain, to explain *now,* and tell her who Kelly Robichaux was. She wanted her to explain Daniel Fischer and tell her why she was so frightened all the time. Because that's what all this is about, isn't it? Fear. Trepidation. Simply being afraid of something that had no name, or sometimes, multiple names.

Was Jenny ever raped as a young girl?

*This is life at its most pitiful,* Nora thought with a kind of tired, inward sigh. She flipped through a page in her magazine without reading it. *Two women pretending to live life when life has already passed them by. Somewhere a long time ago in the past they both had friends to love, but now that dream is over, and reality becomes heavy. There is nothing here. There is nothing but façades and masks, makeup and long-sleeved cardigans, bubblegum and fucking gossip columns. This philosophical bullshit hurts, and it hurts because it's the truth. But it hurts more to know that everything in life has become numb now, now that we're so used to the hurt.*

He had a website. Nora checked it a few days ago and found his touring schedule. He'd just finished a lecture at Boise State University a week ago and was scheduled to return to Seattle. It also said he was *Doctor* Daniel Fischer now, someone who'd gotten a Ph.D. in the recent past. His *Existential Bondage*, a non-fictional work, had been translated into over 30 different languages. He wrote scholarly essays as well, apparently. *Bondage* was considered his magnum opus and was regarded as the next *Das Kapital* of the 21st century.

*So here's a young man, talented and bright, who quits this masquerade called life and finds himself early on. He gets lucky and writes something that allows him to have a name while everyone else around him becomes shadows with titles. He since then is able to keep that name and make a nice living as an adult. He goes on tour one day, does his thing, and eventually comes along and sees an old flame at this miserable diner. His tour has ended, but he decides to stay, decides to linger a bit to see if that old flame can rekindle. It doesn't, and instead burns him back for trying to find her. And apparently, according to Abigail, he's gone now, probably gone for good and back in Seattle.*

"Jenny Acworth," Nora muttered, sighing. She stared at her magazine. It was *Vogue* magazine. She frowned in disgust. "Jenny Acworth. Daniel Fischer. Just who are you two people? And how did you end up here in life, Jenny?"

As if to answer, the bathroom door opened, and Nora heard the high-heel clap of Jenny's approach.

\*\*\*

Jenny slid up next to Nora two minutes later and sighed contentedly at the rain. The rain was damp but light outside, no more than a thick drizzle that left chipped gems against the windows. Jenny thought the sight was beautiful. Cold…but beautiful.

She was content this night because she knew for a fact that the man—

Daniel—was no longer coming here. She'd confronted him last night, and he was gone. Just gone. The finality of the word grew cold in her bones like the gradual accepting of winter, and Jenny felt good when hearing the word. He was just *gone*. And good riddance.

She'd cried terribly that night after her episode with (*Daniel*) the man. After she'd vomited, she'd lain down for a while and had let John take her home. She'd taken a hot shower and immediately gone to bed afterwards, her mind blank and her eyes watery. There had been no dreams that night, thank God, and she'd slept naked again.

One could only imagine Tom's level of fury upon seeing her arrive home with pitiful trails of mascara dripping from her eyes—Jenny was just glad he wasn't back from his trip yet. In her heart, as painful as it was to admit, Jenny knew already what her husband would say to her should he find her shit-faced with tears and dripping makeup. He'd comfort her; he would hold her and pat her back. He would hold her for maybe twenty minutes and then tell her to go and take a shower to cool off. In Jenny's mind, the shower was for him, and the excuse to leave her alone and let her cool down was for him just another excuse to go back to bed. He would ask her if she was all right, and she would say yes. He would ask her if she needed anything, and she would say no. He would hold her then, cup tightly one of her breasts as they lay in bed together, and mutter something against the back of her neck, telling her to go to sleep. Nowhere in those few hours of returning home distraught to her husband would there be a grave sense of concern in his voice—not once would there be a look of understanding. In her heart, as much as Jenny hated admitting it, she knew that his eyes would only be half-awake when seeing her, and knew that any dialogue on her part would be received with a look of annoyance. *Can we talk about it later in the morning, babe?* his eyes would say. *I know you're troubled and all, and I'm here for you, really I am. But why don't you sleep it off first so that we can both talk about it later in the morning, okay? You're tired; I'm tired. We both can talk about this in the morning when both of us are thinking right, okay?*

Right, Jenny thought. Sure.

"Whatcha reading?"

Nora raised her eyes. Ten minutes had passed with nothing said between them. Outside, the rain had stopped, letting through a brief moon.

"Hmm? Oh this? Just some more gossip and people trying to dress pretty when they're all really ugly."

"Anybody kill anybody yet?" Jenny asked with a half-laugh and half-smile that made Nora frown inside. "Or like, get caught shoplifting?"

"Nah, just same ole, same ole. Society teaching young boys and girls the wrong values in life."

"Ah," Jenny said. "Okay."

Nora closed her magazine and raised her eyes. She suddenly thought of the book she had hidden under the counter. "A funny thing, this afternoon, when Abigail called me," she said. "She told me something big happened with you and that man that always comes here. You know?"

The smile on Jenny's lips died. It faded from her face and her eyes grew dark. She said nothing at first. Then: "Oh. Yeah. And?"

"You okay?"

"Yeah. Yeah, sure I am. Why wouldn't I be?"

"Just asking. Because what Abigail told me last night—"

"I'm fine. Thanks." She forced a smile.. "Let's not talk about it now, okay? I don't think that man's ever going to come back here again, so we can forget all about him. Okay?"

"You sure?"

"Yep. Positive."

"Okay."

Jenny watched as Nora turned away. She waited, expecting her next move. With a sigh, Nora placed her magazine down and said: "Jenny. Look. I need to ask you a question." She reached beneath the counter. "Have you ever read this boo—"

And that's when the doors to Red Moon's Diner opened, giving way to an extremely high chirpy-sounding Abigail.

"Oh hey, Nora!" she cried as the doors closed loudly behind her. She waved a hand in the air. "Good to see you! I didn't think you'd be back for another two weeks!"

***

Jenny stood in the women's bathroom and examined herself in the mirror. Tom's bruise was fading from her face. An odd sentence, that: *Tom's* bruise was fading from *her* face. Why had she thought of it that way instead of *her* bruise?

The bruise was almost gone now, nothing more than an odd lump of hurt muscle on the left side of her cheek. Jenny briefly ran two fingers across the bruise and felt a queer unsettling sensation pass through her. Her nipples hardened, and a shudder broke from her lips. The lump felt natural now, almost as complete as having two prominent cheekbones. Touching the bruise made Jenny think of high-school girls in the bathroom crowded in front of the mirror hastily applying makeup. The image was stupid.

She washed her hands and sprinkled a few droplets on her neck. After a few minutes, she dried her hands, changed out of her uniform, and stepped out of the bathroom.

Only a handful of customers had entered the diner tonight. Jenny was glad for their presence. She found them to be a relief from the dark tension that had occurred between her and Nora. She didn't understand what Nora wanted with her. She'd speak exclusively with Abigail and indulge her with anecdotes about her accident and the latest Hollywood gossip. And whenever they laughed, Nora always slyly glanced her way, as if clueing her in on a snide joke she didn't understand. In return, Jenny kept to herself and made conversation with the customers. It was an odd game to take part in; she didn't even understand the stakes to which they played.

She walked from the bathroom hallway and saw John at the front locking the doors. He pulled on the handles to test their sturdiness, turned off all the lights, and then went over to the security pad in the back.

"Got everything?"

Jenny nodded. "Yep. Go ahead and lock up."

John punched in the lockdown code on the security pad and briskly made his way over. They had thirty seconds before the thing went hot, and had to hurry out the kitchen back door before triggering the alarm.

"It's raining outside," Jenny said. "Better get on a coat."

John grunted (which was his way of saying "yes, ma'am"), and shrugged on a coat. They walked through the kitchen together and out the back.

"Oh," John muttered. He stopped and suddenly turned around. "Forgot something."

Jenny raised an eyebrow. "*What?* John—"

"Hold on, be right back."

He sped back inside.

"You have like, ten seconds!" Jenny called behind him as he dashed through the doors and disappeared. "John! What the *hell?*"

He was back outside eight seconds later, stuffing what looked like a book into his coat pocket and turning around to lock the door.

"The hell?" Jenny snapped as he appeared next to her. "What did you get?"

"A book."

"What *kind* of book?"

He shrugged. "Nora's book. She told me to give it to you when I dropped you off."

Jenny snorted. "I don't read the things she reads."

He shrugged again, leaving Jenny to sigh and grumble through cold lips.

John owned an old blue Honda Civic. It was a miserable thing, appearing to have suffered the worst of old-car years with foul scales of rust and decay on its doors. The engine was old, a hiccupping mechanical beast that that choked and stuttered whenever speeds pushed past fifty. Jenny was sure any slight speed bump or unfortunate pothole would dislodge the thing, and felt

190

unnerved whenever on the freeway. She accompanied John not for the love of his ride, obviously, but because he was a quiet mess with a contented demeanor. Jenny thought it a superb quality to have: The disorderly quality of his lifestyle belied his calm acceptance of the untidiness of life. What better way to live than with simplicity?

"Wake me when we're there, John."

"Kay."

John watched as she curled her arms inside her sweater. She lay her head against the window and closed her eyes. John said nothing as he watched her. He reached out and turned on the heater for her.

They drove for twenty minutes in the dark and chased yellow headlights. John kept the heater on throughout the ride and constantly checked to make sure the heat blew properly in her direction. She looked cold to him. Small. After a few more minutes of traveling, they reached her neighborhood, and John slowly put the Honda to crawl.

"Jenny."

"Hmm?"

"Ask you something?"

She opened her eyes and turned around. "Um. Sure?"

"Miss Seattle?"

The question surprised her. She hesitated. She frowned at him, and asked: "What? Like, do I miss it *often*, or like, do I *ever* miss it?"

He shrugged.

"Why do you ask?"

"Cause Nora told me to ask you. She said she was curious."

Jenny frowned. She thought about saying something mean but then decided against it. Instead, she asked: "How does Nora know I'm from Seattle?"

"Don't know." John slowed the car and stalled it next to the sidewalk. They were at her house now. He shifted to park and turned off the engine, looking at her house. It was a nice house; it was a big house. A low stone wall surrounded the manicured front lawn and was reinforced further by healthy green hedges from behind. John felt a sense of security from that house. "I thought you two were friends."

"Uh, no," Jenny replied. "I don't think so."

"You talk with Ted sometimes."

"Yeah, *sometimes.*"

"So you're Abigail's friend then."

Jenny stared at him. She tilted her head to the side to read his face, and found it impossible. "To answer your question, John," she replied sternly, "no, I don't miss Seattle. If your next question is do I *ever* miss Seattle, then no, I don't. There's nothing important back there."

John nodded, as if pleased by the answer, though Jenny could tell he didn't care. "Okay," John said. "Whatever you say."

Jenny's fists clenched together. Blood pulsated through her temples and sharp nails dug into her palms.

So, was this what Nora had wanted to ask back at the diner? Gossip-searching Nora had spoken with gossip-giving Abigail, and now everyone was just suddenly interested in her past? Now everyone just wanted to invade her *privacy* and get to know her like their best friend? What the *fuck?*

"...Northwest, too."

Jenny snapped her head around. "Huh? What?"

"I said, I grew up in the Northwest too."

Jenny stared at him. She wasn't expecting *that.*

"What? Where?"

"Portland."

"*Oh.* Um. That's...that's a coincidence." Jenny bit her lower lip and continued watching from the side. "What, um, do you miss back home in Oregon then?"

"Nothing much. I came over here after two years of college to be with my uncle and because it's more peaceful here. Stayed here since. Maybe it's changed back there."

"Yeah," Jenny replied. Her voice had lowered without her notice. "Maybe."

"Democrats."

"*Huh?*"

"I said, the mascot for my school was the Democrats."

"Are you serious?"

"Yeah. Jefferson High School."

"Oh. So like, a horse?"

"Donkey."

"Oh. Okay."

She looked out at the dark, biting her lip. Then she turned back, and asked tentatively: "Um…well, like, there must be something *you* miss back home. Or, er, do you consider Boise your home now?"

"I miss my first girlfriend," John said, his voice flat. "I lived in Seattle for a month."

"A month? Why?"

"Second girlfriend."

"Oh," Jenny said. "I see."

"I think both Boise and Portland can be called home for me. Also…"

"Yeah?"

He shrugged. Only instead of it being a nonchalant shrug, Jenny thought it was a sad one. "I miss the lights. Seattle's lights. Seattle's lights at night aren't like the lights in Portland or Boise. They're brighter. Deeper. It was a good month for me. Seattle was good to me."

An onrush of tears burned Jenny's eyes. She turned away, startled, and quickly wiped her face, using the dark to hide herself. The pain came out of nowhere, shooting straight to her heart with galvanizing fervor, causing sobs and dry gasps. Salt and tears burned her cheeks as she wiped them away, choking.

*The lights*, a voice whispered to her, *oh, I forgot about the* lights! *How could I have forgotten about the glow of the* lights, *of the yellow and diamonds, the streaks and*

193

*sparkles, the*

*(rape it's the sound the sound the rain)*

*way the Space Needle and Columbia Tower looked at night?*

"O-oh yeah," Jenny said unevenly. "Yeah. I...I used to remember Seattle's lights too. They were pretty once, you know?"

John nodded. He seemed to sigh again and then reached into his coat pocket. "Nora—

*(And Elliot Bay! Remember Elliot Bay? And then Lower Broadway, Queen Ann, Edmonds, Lynnwood, Mountlake Terrace, Mill Creek, the UW, the International District, Pike Place Market...and Puget Sound. Remember Puget Sound?)*

"—wanted me to give you this," he said, handing her the book. "Said I was just supposed to give it to you."

Jenny's heart dropped. She took the book without saying anything and stared at its cover. Though the lights were low, dim glows from neighboring houses painted a soft glare on the title.

"Yeah," she said distantly. Her voice was low. "Yeah. I...okay."

John watched with respectful silence as she traced her hands along the cover. He didn't know what was happening, but thought he'd done good in passing Nora's message along. And her message had been simple, really: Just tell her that there will always be people who will love and miss you in this world, and that, like they say, home is where the heart is.

*Provoke her a bit,* Nora had told him. *Let her realize where her life really should be instead of where it's now headed. I don't want her to be here anymore, John; she just doesn't deserve to be here. I'd rather have one of us escape than both of us drown in life.*

Nora had handed him the book and had prompted a few practice questions with him. He liked Nora, and thought she was a smart gal who knew more than what she let off. He watched her sometime from the back reading and blowing that bubblegum of hers, and suspected that maybe she did all of that just to put on a fake persona, like a costume or something. He liked her.

"Where did Nora get this?" Jenny asked.

"Don't know. But it's supposed to be yours."

Another frown went through her face, changing her look into something that looked both disgusted and angry. John couldn't tell which it was.

"Do you know how often Abigail and Nora talk, John?"

"No. I just work with Ted in the kitchen."

"Yeah. Okay."

She was about to say something else when John suddenly reached into his shirt pocket and produced a pack of Winston cigarettes.

Jenny's mouth turned dry. All inner voices in her head suddenly turned off, and her eyes simply stared. She watched hypnotically as he took a cigarette and placed it effortlessly in between his teeth. He did it by putting the pack close to his lips and then biting on a stick before pulling the pack away again. It was a natural move, easy and automatic, an old habit just reproducing itself—and still, Jenny kept staring, fascinated, and imagined the slight thin taste of paper clutched between teeth.

John must've noticed her, because he suddenly turned to her, offered her the pack, and asked, "Want one?"

Jenny's heart thundered in her chest. Sweat trickled down the back of her neck and her nipples turned hard again, rubbing uncomfortably against the inside of her bra. "Um. Yeah. Sure, yeah. Sure."

Her fingers trembled. She forgot all about the book and held the cigarette in her hands.

It felt oddly light in her hands. Like glass, almost. She was expecting it to be a bit heavier for some reason.

*These kill people,* an incoherent voice whispered behind her. *It's funny to think so, but these tiny small things can kill people where using one can take eleven minutes off your life.* Eleven minutes off your life! *Jenny! Can you believe that?*

*Shut up. Go away. Just…just go away.*

"Light?"

"Huh?"

John held something small and metal in his hand. Jenny realized it was a lighter, and felt her breath squeeze even tighter in her chest. "I…no. No, that's fine, Daniel. I mean *John!* Sorry, sorry! Sorry, *John*, I meant **John**, no, that's fine, that's fine, *John*. I, um…I'm fine. Thanks."

John stared at her. His eyebrows rose in slight curiosity.

"I think I should go now," Jenny said quickly, tossing the cigarette in her purse. "Thanks for the ride."

"Okay. Bye."

"Yeah. Bye."

She opened the door.

"Jenny."

She turned around. "Huh?"

"Don't forget your book."

She looked down; it was on the passenger seat. "Oh," she said (*You tried to forget it on* purpose, *you smart little girl!* a voice cackled to her). She laughed at herself. "Right. Ha-ha, forgetful me. Anyway, thanks John. Tell Nora…tell her I said thanks."

John nodded. She closed the door and left him in the dark. She turned away. She took five steps. Then, suddenly, she turned around again, and knocked on the passenger window.

"Yeah?"

"Um. About this." She took the cigarette out of her purse and held it between two fingers. "I…I'm supposed to light it and just suck, right? Or is it like, inhale?"

John stared at her. He blinked several times, and then said, "Huh?"

"To smoke. Like, I just inhale, right? Like a straw? And it's the brown end, right?"

He nodded. "Yes. Like a straw. Brown end."

"Oh. Oh, okay. Good. Thanks." She smiled at him. "Bye John. Thanks for the ride."

John said nothing, and watched as she walked away again. He watched as she entered the house and watched as the door closed behind her. The lights turned on, and then he could see her silhouette in the foyer, removing her shoes.

John thought for a minute, and then slowly pulled away from the house. He thought about Portland, the Rose City, and of his high-school years at Jefferson High, and the strange mascot representative that was supposed to be the Democrat. He thought about the Willamette River that cut smoothly through the center of town, and of how it often reflected the lights of the city at night with a surreal impressionistic glow. He thought of the unattractive truss Hawthorne Bridge and its ugly-green painted iron struts that held above the Willamette; he thought about the Washington Square mall located just on SW Hall Boulevard and Scholls Ferry Road and along Oregon Route 217. He thought of McCall park, and about Salmon Street Spring in the summer, and of the cherry blossoms that bloomed along the western bank of the river in early spring, and then of Jolin Horgan, his first lover and girlfriend, and of how wonderful it had been to hold her hand while in public together, to hug her from behind, to hold and kiss her when she laughed, and of how wonderful it had been when he first removed her red lace panties from her brown golden thighs, of how smoothly they had slipped off, like running oil, melting chocolate, peeling off red to reveal dark cream, as if they had been waiting for his prying fingers all day along.

He thought about all of this, all this and more as he drove away from Jenny's house, and slowly removed the cigarette from his mouth. He placed it in his front breast pocket and signaled again to turn right on an empty street.

He would smoke later.

***

Tom Acworth felt a burst of pain in his head and quickly bit down on his cheek.

His hands tightened over the taut leather of the steering wheel, and his knuckles popped out white through his skin. It was a method he learned to utilize long ago whenever those bitch migraines came up and invaded his brain. They hurt like hell, those goddamn migraines did, and were something similar to having the sharp edges of a giant sword slicing through one's skull. But the sudden biting of one's inner cheek was a sharper, more exquisite pain, something glassy and palpable; it helped bring down the galvanizing ache inside his head and helped numb down the pain to something almost manageable.

Pain to numb pain—what a great fucking way to go.

As Tom watched, John-whatever-the-fuck-his-name-was pulled away from the house and disappeared into the dark. He sat there for a minute and stared at the house, thinking not for the first time that day (or morning) of how dreadfully disappointing it was to be married to a woman that never cheated on him. He'd wanted that fat nigger to go inside with her and then catch them doing it in their bedroom together—to run upstairs, burst in, see them fucking, have their eyes widen in horror and shock, and then suddenly shriek at the both of them until his face bled red (no doubt his migraine would flare to high Heaven by then too). It would be an incredible way to make his return after just three days of absence, of literally just bursting in on a *fucking* party where everyone was caught with their pants down. *Here's Tommy!* a crazed, delirious voice would shriek; *here he is, here's Tommy the Breadwinner, here's Tom the Dude, Tom that brings in the green with the food. Oh, look! What's his pleasant pretty wife been doing while he's been away? She's been fucking around, that's what! She's been fucking around high-time, been fucking around just fine! Jenny dear, have you forgotten all the things that Teacher Tom once taught you? Have you suddenly relapsed into utter fucking-forgetfulness and suddenly just gone stupid? How unfortunate! It's detention for you now, young girl! Time for detention!*

But no—she wasn't the cheating type. And this, for some reason, righteously pissed Tom off even more.

He started the engine and pulled into the driveway. He'd parked across their place two houses away on the opposite side of the street; it was almost ridiculously absurd how they'd missed noticing him. Had she wanted to, she could have twisted her head to the side and noticed a suspicious (yet familiar-looking) black Audi lurking in wait for her.

*But no, my dear,* Tom thought wordlessly as he finally parked the vehicle and killed the engine. *You're not the suspicious type, and you never were. Nothing is dark about you at all, my sweet little Jenny gem, and sometimes I get pissed off inside how you always make me look to the world. Guess a man can't be anything but a monster in a woman's world, huh? Didn't even have to burn off your training bra for that one now, did you?*

She was in the shower. He could see the lights turned on in the bathroom window upstairs. She always showered hot. Tom knew this because there was always leftover moisture on the mirrors every time he entered the bathroom and because the hot water was never as potent as it was when it was his turn (although they had three-and-a-half bathrooms, the one across the hall was the largest, and, of course, the cleanest. There was also one adjacent to their bedroom that got used only in the middle of the night). He knew she showered hot because whenever she slid in bed next to him, all hot and quaking, she immediately rolled onto her side into a fetal position in order not to wake him. She always tried to sleep off those moments of entering the bed red as a boiled lobster, but Tom was no fool: He knew there was something going on. And lately, those nights where she'd come into bed with him all hot and curled into a ball were becoming more and more frequent.

Did he reprimand her for times like these? No. In fact, knowing that she showered with the water so hot was something that he brooded over, something that kept him in constant fascination for a day or two. In his mind, the water was some symbolic shit that was like having someone wash away all the wrongdoings of their past. She needed to *burn* off something that was a part of her, something that was beneath her skin, something that was *unclean*, and washing away the blemish while burning herself was a constant ritual her Id unconsciously always provoked her with. More than once in their five years of marriage had he heard her cry while in the shower, and in those moments of crying, more than once had he pictured her curled up on the shower marble floor, curled up in a fetal position, sprinkled hot and wet with torrents of rushing water (and, on some occasions where he'd eventually go up and comfort her, to see what was up and hold her, there'd be a wonderful pain in the seat of his crotch, an erection so hard that it was like swelling iron).

Sliding into her had been like sliding into smooth exquisite oil—there'd been no greater feeling in the world. Her scent had been exotically raw the first time he made love to her, sweltering with flushed nervous heat, delicious amongst the bed covers, fresh under the springtime midnight air. Blanketed layers of shivering skin had rippled with gooseflesh as she trembled. He had laid himself on top of her, slid himself inside, and had released a long hot sigh against her as she bit into his shoulder and muffled a scream. She had convulsed then, not from pleasure, but from a sudden onrush of unexpected pain, and Tom had felt the awkward and frightened movements of her body as she tried to reposition herself beneath him. Her arms cradled his neck from behind and her legs awkwardly wrapped around his waist. She had felt so frail to him—just so intensely frail, like a smooth shivering glass ornament about to break. And Tom had remembered, as he pulled back to enter her again, her whispering: "Go gently, Tom. Please, don't hurt me."

*Don't hurt me. Don't hurt me.* Yes—don't hurt me. Those were the first words she said to him as he first made love to her. They'd been good words in Tom's mind, *necessary words,* words that she sometimes whispered to him when he carried her hot and naked from the bathroom floor, still dripping, still wet with her eyes closed, words that seemed to be aimed at someone else. He liked those words. They meant that she'd be willing to give up everything for him so long as she was loaned a sense of security in life. He hadn't been her first, obviously, but the way she moved—the way she hesitated, became afraid at times—it was like she was still a young new virgin tasting life for the first time. She had asked him not to hurt her that night, and hurt her he did. But it had been a gentle hurt, a *necessary* hurt, a hurt that could only be understand and delivered from a man to a woman who was in need of desperate help.

Tom had felt her shame, had felt her fear and humiliation as he took charge of her in the dark, and knew that her cries—as well as tears and weak muffled protests—were all things necessary. She was a woman, but something about her mind was still young , still girly and childish. Thus it was this notion of purity—this notion of untouched innocence, undisturbed layer of skin-porcelain-snow ravaged by haunting dark—that Tom believed needed to be cultivated, brought up, and properly disciplined.

*Don't hurt me.* Please, *don't hurt me.* Those had been her words. And after those words—after an hour of love making, after an hour of panting and gasping, of hurt grunting and silent sobbing—there had been, "How many times did you come, Jenny?" And her face, hidden away by the half-shadows of the moon and the window blinds, turning away from the rough touch of his strong palms, had answered back softly: "Please don't ask me that Tom."

So he'd asked her again, more forcefully this time, this time plucking the lobe of her ear.

"Three times. Maybe four. I don't know."

He liked that answer. And after hearing that answer, he'd carefully laid himself on top of her again, wanting to see if he could do one or two more better.

Those were the things that came with the hot showers; those were the things that Tom thought of when feeling her waking beside him to use the bathroom on early mornings where he knew she thought he was asleep. Those showers helped break her down—and he always happily rebuilt her back to what was proper for a woman.

He got out of the car, locked it behind him, and stealthily made his way into the house. He left his travel suitcase in the car and carried only his briefcase with him; he laid this down on the dining room table and stood for a moment in the dark, listening to the heavy pounding of water upstairs (the wine stains where still there from three days ago, but Tom ignored them).

201

She'd kept the house clean, he saw, and that was good. He could make out the sharp scent of Lemon Fresh Pine-Sol from the kitchen passageway, and saw the surface of the dining room table cleanly swept. There were no loose crumbs on the table, no loose strands of hair on the carpet floor or odd foreign smells in the place. All there was, was the dull ticking of the living room clock in the dark, the light fizzle of the automated sprinklers outside, and the continuous beating of water upstairs.

He brought his briefcase into the house without his travel case for one simple reason: He wanted to show it to her. He wanted her to come down the stairs at the sound of his voice, walk hesitantly down the steps (he could always tell when she hesitated, even when she smiled), see him in the dining room area, and turn on the light. He wanted her to greet him. After that, he wanted her to open his briefcase and see what was inside. He wanted her— no, would *make* her—sift through his papers, look at all the names, and ask her in a cold, toneless voice: "Now Jenny. Where are the Whittingham documents I asked you to fax me?"

She would pause. Her breath would catch in her chest. Her eyes would grow wide, her mouth would drop open, and a hand would go up to her mouth in horrible realization. And before she could even say the words, "Oh Tom! I'm so sor—", there'd be a *WHAM!* right to side of her face, sending her to the ground.

Yes, ladies and gentlemen of the jury—he sometimes beat his wife. And *yes,* sometimes he let his anger get the better of him, and yes, this was what monsters sometimes were. But when a man (moreover, a *business*man) sometimes had to do things right for the family and for himself, and when he *needed* for his wife to provide for him, and when he in fact even specifically *told her* what was needed *of* her and of how and why and when—was there not a cause then for retribution when she failed? Or, say at least, some form of *punishment?* Because let's admit it, let's just say it as it was ladies and gentlemen: When you were meeting someone as reputable as Mr. Whittingham—when you were with your ol' pal Bradley Bunell from college with whom you once shared a dorm with for four straight years (as well as the same girlfriend with during a kinky threesome) and would later grow to become close business partners, and were promising each other that the next set of signed signatures would give you a nice fat commission bounce that was mighty dense with extra added zeros—when you understood that Mr. Whittingham was a certain man of class and style that liked his homes to reflect his prissy personality and were lucky enough to locate for him a fine estate just a mile up north of the newly-built Glacier Clubs golfing course…when you had all of that, when you *earned* all of that, when it was all right there in your palm to squeeze and hold, squeeze and hold, caress and grasp…was it not a bit natural to be somewhat fucking *pissed* that all of it slipped away just because your *goddamn* **WIFE** *forgot to fax over a few documents!?*

The shower raged overhead, and Tom bit down on his cheek again, closing his eyes. He could hear the clock *tick…tick…tick*ing away in the dark, and felt it rather sardonic that it matched with the blood-pulse of his heart.

Pain to numb pain—what a great fucking way to go.

*Come on Jenny, my sweet, what are you doing up there? Are you fingering yourself, babe? Is that what you're doing? You'd better get down here quick or I'll run out of patience, hon. I need to tell you something Jenny, I need to tell you something bad, and it's gonna be something that you'll never forget. Bradley's off taking a powder, he and his wife are probably screwing, but me? I've been screwed over by* my *wife, Jenny, and am nothing but rubble right now. So hurry up, babe. Hurry the fuck up, cause three days away seems like it's been too long for you, hon.*

He sighed. Time seemed frozen standing here in the dark. Just as he was about to grab his briefcase and head upstairs, Tom Acworth spotted something on the table, and felt his heart stop. He stared at it, feeling his blood grow cold, and quietly made his way over to the other side. All the voices and panicky memories of the past—all the pain and dull noises of the dark—faded into one distant whisper as he picked up a thin, white, unused cigarette stick.

*My wife. She's been smoking. Dear God in heaven, my wife has been smoking cigarettes.*

Dull rage filled him. After a few minutes of biting his cheek, Tom placed the cigarette in his pocket, grabbed his briefcase, and headed upstairs.

***

Jenny wasn't crying as she showered upstairs. She instead was standing motionless with her arms cupped beneath her breasts and had her eyes closed. Her head was lowered. Violent torrents of water splashed against her body and burned her skin. Steam blanketed the bathroom and made it difficult to breathe.

What she thought of then as Tom stealthily made his way up the stairs and into their bedroom was John. And what she thought of then when recalling her conversation with him was how she had lied when answering his questions.

*Lights. Seattle's lights. I told him that the lights of Seattle were beautiful, but didn't mention how I missed something else there. I didn't talk about how I missed Evanston-Wood and the smell and color of the hallways. I didn't tell him how I missed the UW campus in spring and summer, and how nice it had been to see the cherry blossoms in the middle of the Quad. But most of all, I forgot to tell him how I missed the beach. I forgot to tell him how I missed…missed the smell of the salty ocean and the cold blow of wind against my face. I miss the beach. I miss the color of water.*

She turned off the water and stood as the showerhead slowed to a dull ebb. Burning heat radiated off her body; she was cold now. She cupped herself tighter beneath her breasts and felt a sudden shiver come over her.

Jenny grabbed a towel. She wrapped it around herself without drying her hair and stood, letting the water soak from her skin to the towel. The steam began to thin and was taken up by the fan overhead, and soon she could see her feet again set against the dark onyx marble flooring of the shower stall. The memory of burning her foot while trying to make Tom's breakfast a month ago resurfaced in her mind, though she didn't understand why.

*Heaven's Defiance* was his first novel. Yes, that made sense; he'd first developed the idea to her when they were…what? Seniors in high-school? Had he been thinking about it then? It was his first novel, something that he first thought of while in high-school, and was something that he later flushed out during their college years. Just when did the final draft finally get finished? When had he truly become a writer? And when—

*Daniel,* Jenny thought silently. *Oh, Daniel. Daniel. I'm sorry. I…I miss you. I'll allow myself to say it now in thought, but when speaking…you know it hurts me so much to say your name. I miss you.*

This wasn't the first time she'd seen his book. She in fact, unbeknownst to either John or Nora, had purchased a copy of it years ago, right when it had come out as a new hardback. Intuition had overwhelmed curiosity then. She had no time to read books, had no patience to fully devour one, and had no eye or ear to the writing market. And yet still, on that warm, spring, sunny day before Tom or Red Moon's, she'd wandered into a Barnes and Noble bookstore and had spotted something that looked oddly familiar across the aisle. She'd walked over, unsure at first, and then was taken aback by the large black letters on the cover. She read his name across the cover and then gazed longingly at his photograph on the back. Her hands trembled, and though she didn't know it, a squirt of blood had gushed out from her lower lip from where her teeth had bit down.

She purchased it then. Quickly and without thinking, afraid that if she allowed her inner voice to speak up, it would tell her to put it down and walk away, Jenny had grabbed the book from the shelf, run over to the front cashier, and purchased it with sweaty palms and trembling fingers. Her hands continued shaking even as she walked back outside to greet Boise blue sky. She sat down on the bench near the door and collected her breath, squeezing her hands together in what looked like a tight prayer.

She'd felt jealous then. Was that the right word? Yes, she supposed it was. She'd felt *jealous* while reading the book that very same day, *jealous* that these were once his words, jealous and bitter, something that was like having a stupid high-school crush stolen away in a pathetic love triangle—she couldn't remember ever feeling so rotten with her anger.

He had published this without her; he'd written his first drafts without her, edited them, scrutinized them, published them, and then finally celebrated his achievement without her. Who had he confided in once she was gone? Who had replaced her as the person he shared his deepest thoughts with, who had he…

*Without you*, a voice whispered. *He did it all without you. He published his story without you, became famous without you, and you lied to yourself saying that you were happy for him. He cheated on you, Jenny. He cheated on you because you failed to admit your love to him. He cheated because you* failed to love him.

*Shut up*, Jenny whispered. *Shut up, leave me alone. I don't care. I just don't care. Liar. You're a liar, Jenny. You're nothing but a liar.*

And then, like a slight cold breeze to her ears: *You cried that night after reading the book, Jenny.*

Jenny slid open the glass door and stepped out of the shower. Her feet treaded gingerly across the floor, slapping lightly against cold, slick marble. Sudden tears came to her eyes. She wiped these quickly away and found it hard to breathe even with the steam now gone. She swallowed, and walked over to turn off the fan near the door.

She hadn't bought any more of his books after that. There were others, she knew, but fear and jealously had kept her from ever wandering through another bookstore again. She had read that one and only book before marrying Tom, and that was all.

She stepped out into the hallway and felt sweltering heat fade behind her. Wet footprints sank into the beige carpet as she walked. She reached the bedroom at the end of the hall, flicked on the light, and jumped when she saw Tom standing next to their bed. A hand went up to her throat. Her eyes widened, and for one brief horrible moment, she thought a burglar had entered their house.

He stood next to the bed with Daniel's book in his hands. He stood looking at it with a deep frown spread over his face.

"Tom!" she gasped. "I…I didn't think you'd be back yet!"

He didn't look at her. Instead, Tom Acworth continued staring at the book and brooded over the front cover, touching the corner edges with heavy fingers. He finally flipped it over and stared at the photograph on the back. His shoulders were turned at an angle that partially hid his profile. When he finally did look at her, it was with such a deep and distant gaze in his eyes, that Jenny suddenly became frightened, and knew that she had done something wrong.

*Oh God, what did I do, what did I do wrong this time, I tried hard to keep the house clean, I tried hard to make everything neat and tidy, what did I do, what—*

"Hey babe," he said. He threw the book on the bed and finally turned toward her. He smiled. "What's up?"

Jenny's heart picked up. Even though she was half-naked and out of the shower, she suddenly felt hot then, *too* hot, as if she were still standing under torrents of burning water. That grin on his face…he was going to hit her soon. Unless she figured out what she did wrong and found a way to apologize, he was going to hit her.

"I…I cleaned the kitchen for you this morning," she stammered, trying to smile. She stepped toward him, an old habit of hers whenever she became nervous and tried to charm him out of his anger. She went to him, smiling and almost dance-like, and would have hugged him if she hadn't suddenly remembered that she was still partially wet. She stopped midway in her advance with her arms open and beamed at him, showing all her teeth and forcing her smile to go as far as it could. "I…I'm glad you're back, Tom. What made you come home so early?"

The smile on his face darkened, faded, and returned again, scaring her badly. *Not the right hand then,* an incoherent voice blabbered, *please not the right hand, not the one with the college ring on it. If anything, if it has to be the right hand, let it be a slap, let it just be a slap on the cheek and not a fist, don't let his knuckle hit my cheekbone, it hurts the worst when it's against bone, it hurts the worst—*

The smile broadened. "Ah, babe," he said casually, "you're not really glad to have me back, are you?"

She mumbled a few sounds before pretending to giggle, and said: "Tom! Of course I'm glad you're back! You're…you're my husband, and I love you. Why would you say such a thing when I've been waiting for you to come back all this time? Look, I even vacuumed the carpet, and tomorrow I'll go and scrub the kitchen flo—"

It came out of nowhere, fast and strong, a packed fist with heavy knuckles. Pain exploded in her lower jaw like an M-80 firecracker, galvanizing and strong. Tears blinded her eyes and spilled down her face. A wet gasp escaped her, and then she was suddenly on the floor, gasping, a tangle of legs and wet hair, clutching the towel to her chest. She sniveled with pain.

"Please, Tom, please, don't, it hurts, it hurts, please, it—"

Tom turned around and reached for something on the bed. It was his briefcase. He snapped it open and threw it on the floor near her feet. Jenny stared at it, wide-eyed. She didn't understand.

"Tom—"

"LOOK THROUGH IT!"

She shrank against the floor. One hand clutched at the towel while the other balled into a tightened fist. Slowly, and without raising her eyes to his face, Jenny crawled forward and began sifting through the papers.

"I don't…I don't know what I'm supposed to look for, Tom."

He stomped his foot down. Jenny recoiled again and dropped the papers.

"You know, babe," he said, sighing and bringing a hand up to massage his temple. His eyes closed. "It's a really bad shitty place out there in the world. People get dirty all the time, and people always do dirty things. You know?"

Jenny nodded. She dared not say anything. Fresh tears spilled down her face. She wiped them away, quickly, afraid that they would offend him. Her jaw throbbed.

"It's a shitty world where crooks and assholes win over the simple guy who's just trying to make his way in this world. This place is so fucking shitty that even some of the good guys get shit and dirt on them, and *they* start doing shitty things too, you know?"

Jenny nodded a second time. She still said nothing.

"Sometimes though, when shit hits the fan, we gotta ask ourselves, *who* threw that shit against the fan in the first place, right? And in this world full of assholes and shitholes, sometimes we gotta ask ourselves *who* made these lost winners into assholes and shitholes in the first place. Right?"

"Tom—"

"In other words, Jenny babe, what I'm talking about is corruption, because corruption can come in many forms. We think of corruption in terms of politics and money and power, but ever rarely think about it in terms of *personhood*, you understand? And you know, ha, this is kind of funny, but you know, I was just thinking to myself while you were showering, babe…I was just thinking to myself, *who* corrupts the good guys and the guys just trying to do good? *Where* does all this shitty dirt and dirty shit come from that turns people into chumps?"

He was rambling now. Jenny curled herself into a tight defensive ball and held herself as he paced back and forth in the room. He was speaking to no one, looking across the opposite wall as if giving a lecture to an invisible audience. What fear she had inside her now bloomed to pure terror, something that seized deep inside her chest like a cold wretched hook through her heart. He was crazy.

"…comes from a place closest to that person, someone *familiar* with that someone. Corruption of the personhood, Jenny, comes from the ones closest to you, because they either can corrupt you in a shitty way through love or jealously, or they can corrupt you in a *fucking* shitty way, with betrayal and pissed-off hate. They turn you ugly or they turn you soft." He stopped then. He looked down at her and Jenny shrank away from his gaze. "*You*, Jenny, my darling," he said, pointing an accusing finger at her, "have *corrupted* me. Not *only* have you corrupted me as a person, but also as a *business*man who has lost reputation. Do you understand?"

Before she could say anything, Tom knelt down and picked up the briefcase. He began sifting through his papers and calling out the names of his clients, throwing them to the floor, showering her in a sheet of white. A dry sound, like reptiles sliding against each other, came from the tossing of papers.

"Murdock…King…Calderwood …the Johnsons…Price…"

He looked at her. He threw the briefcase aside and narrowed his eyes. He asked in a low voice: "But where, Jenny, throughout all of those, is the name Charles J. Whittingham?"

Tears cascaded down her face. "I'm sorry," Jenny whispered. "Tom…I'm so sorry. I know, I know I did wrong, I know I forgot, I know, I know, I'm sorry, I'm so *sorry*…"

He did something surprising then. Tom Acworth bent down, whispered "Shh" in a soft, low, steady voice to his wife, and suddenly hugged her. He actually wrapped his arms around her and *hugged* her, as if she were a little girl that had fallen and hurt herself. Jenny was so shocked that her sniffles actually halted to become choked hiccups, and her eyes stared wide-eyed past his shoulder. She stiffened as he held her, and for one brief second  suddenly had the urge to warn him that if he hugged her like this, he would get his clothes wet.

"Now, now, babe, it's okay, don't cry. Yeah, you probably lost me a few grand, and yeah, my reputation is probably so shitty that even my own shit would think it's disgusting—"

"Tom—"

"But hey! That's how you are, right, babe? Always messing up a bit and doing wrong once in a while, right? You *corrupt* me, Jenny, *corrupt* me bad at times, but that's how you are, right?"

Jenny nodded. She did so automatically, naturally, not letting herself hear his words so that they wouldn't hurt as badly as he made them to be.

"I forgive you for this, Jen, I really do. Just don't let it happen again, okay?"

"Okay, Tom. I...I won't."

He nuzzled his nose against her. She smelled good. "Your excuse was that you forget, right, babe? You were so tired working and cleaning that night that you just totally forgot, right?"

"Yes," she whispered back quietly. "I forgot, Tom. I'm sorry."

There was a soft caress on her back. Jenny shivered, and realized that Tom's fingers were stroking her. It felt like a fat spider was crawling on her.

"All right, babe, that's all done for now. Now then. Explain to me *this*."

He pulled back from her. Jenny watched as he reached into his pocket. She had a mad image of him pulling out Daniel's book again, of him handing her *Heaven's Defiance* and asking her to explain. But no, that was impossible. Tom didn't know who Daniel was.

What Tom pulled out instead was a cigarette, unused and still clean, and when Jenny saw it held there mere inches away from her face, her heart stopped. She gawked at him. Everything in her mouth went dry.

"What's wrong, babe?" he asked. "Cat got your tongue?"

"That...tha-that isn't mine," she stammered. "That...Tom, I know how it looks, I know, but—"

He slapped her. It was an open palm this time, no knuckles or ring, but it still hurt. A loud *SMACK!* echoed from where his hand hit her, producing a red blanket of needles that spread through her cheek. Jenny's head snapped to the side and she gasped an airless cry. Hair covered her face. Her cheek felt fat.

"Come on, Jen, don't do that to me. I've seen you with that nigger who drops you off sometimes when I'm not around. That fool smokes, doesn't he?"

"Y-yes."

"This is *his* cigarette, ain't it?"

211

"Yes. But Tom—"

He made a move to hit her. Jenny shrank away.

"See, Jen, it's like this. I don't give a fuck what you do with your body. It is, after all, *your* body, and if you want to pump it up with nicotine and lung cancer and mouth cancer and bad breath, then fine, do that. Just don't do it around me. *However*—" He waved the cigarette menacingly before her face. "—you have to sometimes consider those *around* you, Jenny babe; you need to think of others. And because wives represent husbands as well as husbands represent wives, *what*, my dear sweet Jen, type of statement do you think you make for *me* as a chain-smoking wife to a businessman, hmm?"

"I don't know, Tom," she whimpered. She couldn't bring her gaze to meet him. "I don't know. I'm sorry. I'm sorry, please, I'm sorry, I'm sorry…"

Tom snorted at her and flicked the cigarette in her face. He got up, sighed, and rolled his neck on his shoulders. Oh, how this morning was just getting started. It wasn't even 2:30 a.m. yet, and already, two sessions by Teacher Tom had been dispensed. He had only one pupil, sure, but she was a slow learner, and sometimes if certain lessons weren't taught well enough— or embedded deeply enough—well then, the teacher sometimes had to go all-out with discipline and punishment to ensure lessons were remembered.

*Cigarettes*, Tom thought in disgust as he stuffed his hands in his pockets and stared down at their bed. That spooky-ass book stared back at him from the pillow. *My wife smokes cigarettes when I'm just away for three days, forgets to fax me my docs, and starts a relationship with a cook at the very same place she works at. What a fucking shitty world it truly is, boys and girls. What a fucked-up world indeed. Now I really wish you* had *slept with that nigger, Jenny. Had it been just the Whittingham docs, I would've been cool as an icicle with marginal anger. But* cigarettes. *Oh, that just pisses me off like a squirting cock.*

"Did you two fuck while I was away, babe?"

Jenny was halfway up from the floor when she heard this. She froze, halfway up in a crouch position with both her knees bent and with one hand still gripped around her towel. She asked in a startled gasp so sharp that it

212

almost sounded like she had been slapped again, "*What?*", and involuntarily brought another hand up to nurse her throbbing jaw.

Tom bent down and picked up the book and turned his back toward her. Jenny's heart picked up. He was examining Daniel's picture again.

*Did you two fuck while I was away, babe?*

"Tom—"

"You and him were together just an hour ago. He gave you this book, and he gave you the cigarette. I'm wondering if whether or not he gave you something else, Jenny, something that he might have loaned you for a few hours while I was away."

"No, Tom, I…I would *never cheat on you!* I swear Tom, honest to God I swear, John and I, he just gives me rides because everyone else leaves early. You remember Nora? She leaves early 'cause she doesn't like anybody, and Abigail has her boyfriend to pick her up, and they live on the other side of town, while Ted—"

Tom held his hand up, silencing her. He peered at the book again and flipped through a few pages. He said, "All I know Jen is that this man loans you books to read and cigarettes to smoke. The cigarettes are fucking bad, but right now, I'm wondering if you two don't have a little reader's club going on that allows you two to have a little get together. You know?"

"No, Tom that's not it, it isn't like that at all! It—"

Again that hand, again that silence, and from it all, a deep horrible feeling of shame

*(did you two fuck)*

and hurt.

*Liar,* a voice whispered. *You're a liar, Jenny. You're nothing but a liar.*

Jenny shuddered. It was an internal shudder, something violent and sudden, having come from deep within. She clutched her towel against her body and felt a phantom draft blow against her shoulders.

He was talking with half his back to her to her again, going on and on about fidelity and cleanliness, and about the responsibilities that came with being married to a businessman. Daniel's picture was between his fingers.

*Daniel. Oh Daniel, I'm so sorry, I'm so sorry for everything.*

A sound of distant waves came to her mind—and with it, the familiar sounds of shy laughter. Yes, Seattle's lights…Seattle's lights had been beautiful. But the beach…the beach in Edmonds. Oh, how that was the most beautiful place of all.

*Not the writer as man, but man as boy,* Jenny thought sadly. *Daniel. Oh how I miss you, how I miss you so, so much, and how I miss you just as a boy. I miss you as the boy who once wanted to be a writer and who would always talk to me about love and life. You helped me so much once when we were younger. You…you allowed me to believe that Heaven could be a simple place filled with friends and love. Do you remember, my friend?*

The beach. The place with seaweed and unearthed sand pebbles during low tide, smells of wet morning salt and sea breeze. Olympic Mountains in the west; dirty sand beneath sneakered feet. She remembered all the things that had occurred during high-school, the things that had happened to her when she'd been younger and able to smile. Her parents' divorce; her nosebleed; the time she'd run away from home barefoot and cold. And then she remembered too the moments they'd shared together during Winter Ball and then Prom, and the way he had…had…

"…just fucking around and doing nothing—"

*(come back)*

you know, babe?"

*(Seattle)*

Tom turned around. He turned to see if she was listening, and saw that she wasn't. He snapped his fingers at her and felt his anger boil when she didn't respond. "Hey, Jenny! I'm talking to you!"

Jenny snapped her head around. She looked lost for a second. Then: "Huh? I…yeah. Sorry, Tom. Really."

He frowned at her. "Something on your mind, hon?" he asked suddenly. "You seem to be forgetting who's talking to you."

"No, I was listening Tom, really, I was. I was just…

*(with me)*

I was just thinking over the things you told me about corruption." She tried to smile at him, but the pain still hurt, so she offered a wince instead. "You know?"

Tom snorted at her, thought of something to say, then thought better of it. He threw the book back on the bed and sighed. He muttered, "Fine babe. Whatever the fuck you say. Just please don't ever let me catch you with that nigger fucking. And stop being so stupid sometimes."

He waited for her to respond. She didn't, and merely lowered her gaze, her lips in a sour pout. He scoffed at her and turned to leave.

"T-Tom?"

He stopped at the doorway. "What?"

"Don't...don't

*(stupid)*

call me that. That...that word. Please?"

He snapped his head around. "*What?*" he spat. His voice was sudden and sharp. The anger that had momentarily faded now suddenly reawakened. "*What* did you just tell me, Jenny? What did you just tell me I could or couldn't do?"

She bit her lip at him. She swallowed, and clutched her hand tight next to her side. Her other hand held her towel just above her chest. "Don't

*(fuck)*

call me that word, Tom. Please? It's...it's not right. Just...just don't call me stupid anymore. I...please just don't. It...it hurts my feelings."

Spears of pain shot through Tom's skull. The pain was maddening, like a jackhammer having gone full-blown berserk in his head. Blood pulsed through the veins in his forehead, sounding like a tired heartbeat about to collapse and explode. A sharpening pain filled the back of his eyes as he grinded his teeth together, and a sudden gush of warm blood spilled in his mouth as he bit down on his cheek. Oh, but this was it, this was it right here, wasn't it, ladies and gentlemen, this was it *right* here where his wife suddenly got all gusty and suddenly decided to talk back to him, wasn't it? This—

"I know…I know sometimes you think I'm low for working at Red Moon's, but I'm not stupid, and I—"

"Shut up! That's what you have to do, you fucking cooze, just SHUT UP!"

He brought a hand up to his temple and felt a series of heartbeats pound his face. He could see her standing there, afraid, docile, half-naked and frightened with one hand clutching the towel against the small shape of her breasts. Droplets dripped from the end of her hair and splashed against her feet. Two glittery golden chains ran down from her slim neckline to the hidden edge of her towel. Her locket. There was fear there, yes, fear in those almond-shaped eyes of hers, but when he tried to look further for the *terror* that usually came—the *terror* that seemingly always accompanied her submissiveness—Tom saw nothing, and was for one brief meteoric second, afraid.

*You bitch,* he thought suddenly. *Jenny, you sweet, utter, fucking* bitch. *You make me look like a fool to the people I need to most impress, smoke behind my back, and now suddenly start telling me* what to do? *Oh, baby, oh babe, this isn't going to end well, this isn't going to end well at* all *for you.*

"Please, Tom, don't yell at me," she said again. Her voice was calm, slow, soothing, as if she were talking to a child going through a tantrum. This pissed off Tom even more. "I know…I know you just got back, and I know I was wrong to have forgotten to fax your papers…and I'm sorry. But please—"

Tom Acworth started undoing his belt. He unhooked it at the front and pulled it from his waist—it slithered off like a thin, headless snake. He wrapped the buckle end around his right hand, looped it through once, twice, and then squeezed. It felt good in his hands; it felt like he was in control of something very dangerous and deadly. His hand squeezed and then relaxed, squeezed and then relaxed, squeezed…and then relaxed.

Jenny eyed the belt and felt her mouth go dry. Her eyes were wide, but her previous sense of panic was gone now, replaced with something that was cold and tense. The belt hung a few inches from the floor and dangled like a giant worm stripped of its skin. He rarely used the belt on her; it came out only when she did something bad, something that was absolutely *horrible* and that deserved extreme punishment. Once, when she and Tom had hosted the Lawrences, she had accidentally tripped and spilled a bowl of Caesar salad all over the dining room table. Some of it had gotten on Mr. Lawrence, but he had laughed and shrugged it off as a joke while Mrs. Lawrence had kindly offered to help clean up. Tom, however, didn't think any of it was funny, and had used the belt on her for the first time that night. What was she, fucking *stupid* or something? Couldn't she *walk?* Did she think her girly cutesy antics were charming *anyone?* Didn't she know how embarrassing it was to have a wife who couldn't even *serve salad?*

The second time he used it on her was when she accompanied him to a client's house wearing jeans and sneakers. He'd lost the sale.

"Here's what's going to happen, Jen." He searched her face for fear, saw none, gripped his right hand tight, and continued. "You're gonna get dressed. You're gonna clean up this mess, and then go sleep in the guest bedroom down the hall. I'm going to take a shower, go to bed, and in the morning when this will all be over, you're going to apologize, and tell me exactly *what* you're apologizing for. Do you understand?"

Still nothing. The slight fear bubbled up again, was pushed back, was gone.

"No."

"*What?*"

She swallowed. Tom could see the thin movements of her neck as she swallowed. "I…I said *no.* I already apologized for what I did wrong, and now it's *your* turn to apologize for calling John that dirty word and…and for hitting me when I told you I was already sorry. You—"

Tom had had enough bullshit for one night. His head hurt and his mouth was bleeding; his papers were scattered all over the floor, and his bitch-for-a-wife was talking back to him. Worse still was that unused cigarette lying menacingly at her feet, like some clever stick of dynamite grinning and about to explode (*Ha-ha!* that fucking white stick seemed to say; *ha-ha, Tom! Your wife was about to smoke me! She was about to smoke me for lung cancer!*).

Tom had had enough, all right—when teaching the stupid didn't work, sometimes whipping the shit out of them did.

He came at her fast, cocking his right arm up above his head and sending the leather belt down in a swift arc. It hissed through the air and slapped down on her shoulder. Jenny screamed and raised her arm up. It came down again and slashed across her back. Tom grabbed her arm and pulled her close, whipping her again, causing red welts across her arms. He hit her back, hit her neck, and when she managed to momentarily pull free and shield her face, he swept the belt sideways and slapped her thighs, producing a wet, meaty *slaaap!*

He whipped her again and managed to strike her straight across the face. Jenny wheeled, still with her hands in front of her, and uttered a shriek of pain. Her left eye warmed with tears and wouldn't fully open. Tom seized her by the wrist and swung the belt sideways. It hit her buttocks. *Slaaap! Slaaap!* Over and over again, hitting her, whipping her, slicing her skin red and making her cry. On the shoulder, on the forearms, on the head.

Jenny screamed, reached out to scratch him, begged for him to quit, and then spiked a devastating knee into his crotch.

Tom's eyes bulged. A loud *uck!* sound spilled from his throat. His right arm hung temporarily suspended in the air in one confused mid-swing arc, and finally went down to grab his balls. His mouth opened and cords stood out on his neck. His face blushed red. He collapsed awkwardly onto both knees with a high, wheezing sound, and stared dismayed at his wife.

"*Bitch,*" he gasped. "Fucking *bitch!*"

Jenny raced to the vanity on her side of the bed and picked up a large bottle of La Mer eye cream; her towel flapping  behind her as she ran. Her vanity was full of cosmetics Tom had bought for her in the past. La Mer, Avon, Bare Essentials, Coco Chanel, Sephora, Lancôme, and others. The bottles there—

Hands dug into her shoulder and whipped her around. Jenny screamed when she saw his face and felt his fingers wrap around her neck. Her scream cut off. She dropped the La Mer bottle she'd found and felt him pushing her until her buttocks and thighs pressed against the vanity's edge. A loud *ugh!* *ugh!* escaped her throat as her arms flayed helplessly against him. She clawed at his arms, scratched his face, feeling her strength slowly draining away from her as he tightened his grip around her, squeezing her, strangling her, digging the fat of his nails and thumbs *into* her. Red swam in her vision. Jenny gasped, feeling her airway close as his hands squeezed, crushing her windpipe.

Her hands sought desperately for something on the vanity, hit several glass perfume bottles to the floor, and heard them all shatter like seven different screams.

*Please, God, help me, I can't breathe, I can't—*

"Fucking bitch! You think you can kick me in the balls, Jenny? Huh, is that it, you cunt, you think—"

*Can't breathe, I can't...can't find anything, please, oh please, someone, anyone, help me—*

"—you can defy me in my own *fucking house!*"

Tom pushed himself against her. The vanity struck Jenny in the back and soon her feet lifted from the floor. She started kicking. Tom's hands squeezed harder, and her frantic thrashings began to slow. Her hands wrestled with his grip, failed, and then could only cling onto his forearms as her eyes rolled back to the top of her head. Tom, from somewhere far away, realized that he was getting a massive (and painful) erection.

*Please...can't...*

"That fucking *cigarette*, Jenny!" he shouted. "It could have stopped there! It could have all stopped there if you wanted, I would've just beaten the living crap out of you for it, but now you go and *talk back to me?* Now you fucking go and kick me in the b—"

White agony erupted in Tom's face.

He uttered a high piercing scream, stepped back, and felt another lightning bolt of pain pop in his mouth.

Tom's world blackened—stars seemed to swirl around his head. It was as though a grenade had exploded in his face. He staggered backwards a few feet, tripped over his own shoes, and crashed down on his ass *hard.*

Jenny brought a hand up to her throat and gasped. She leaned back against the vanity and coughed a series of high, retching dry sounds. Colors swam back in her vision and sweat dripped from her face. She gripped an Avon Anti-Aging night cream bottle so tight in her right hand that white knuckles ripped through. She'd smacked the bottle against Tom's face and had been rewarded with a hollow, dull, cracking noise when it connected with his skull. She'd struck it against his mouth next, and for one brief second, saw blood squirt from a horizontal cut along his gum line. She'd cracked his upper lip. She was sure she'd loosened a tooth too.

"You fucking yellow *cunt.*"

He was getting up again. Still with the belt around his hand, still with blood spilling down his teeth, Tom Acworth was slowly getting up from the floor again like a drunken man trying to find his feet.

He staggered, grunted like a large animal strained of breath, got halfway up with, "You chinky-eyed bitch. I swear to God once tonight's over you'll—" and fell back down again when a bottle of Sephora Total Truth Eye Crème struck him directly between the eyes.

Tom's head snapped back. The movement was so quick and sudden that the tendons in his neck cracked. Under severely different circumstances, it might have even looked comical. His head whipped backwards and he flopped down on his back. The Sephora bottle hit with a loud audible *crack!* that made Tom think his face had split open. Visions of blood and red swam to the corner of his eyes; a heavy blanket of black swept over him.

He didn't get back up this time.

Jenny stood with two more ceramic bottles clutched in her hands and felt the ache in her throat beginning to swell. Her breasts rose and fell in agitated movements, breathing heavily, up and down, up and down. She waited. She watched as he lay there still on the floor and watched anxiously as his fist loosened from around the belt. When she was sure he wasn't going to get up again, she dropped the bottles, quickly ran over to their large walk-in closet, and coughed.

She returned a second later with a black suitcase and a bundle of clothes in her arms. She dropped the suitcase onto the bed and began frantically stuffing it with clothes. She piled in random shirts and t-shirts, blouses and cardigans, jeans and shorts, everything, anything she could find. A shrill voice screamed at her

*(what are you doing what are you doing what)*

*(with me)*

but she ignored it, and ran back to the closet. She took out a pair of blue denim jeans and a long-sleeved black shirt. She slipped these on quickly, going as fast as her fingers would allow.

"Jenny."

She darted back into the walk-in and fumbled through the drawer that held the rest of her underwear. She rummaged around until she found a Ziploc bag holding folds of money. It was emergency money; it was money she'd been saving for the past year. Money she had saved just in case she had to…it was just emergency money she'd been saving. Tom didn't know about it.

"Jenny, you…you get undressed *right now*, or I swear to God, you stupid little slut—"

"Fuck you."

She closed the suitcase and pulled it off the bed. Tom was now in a sitting position; when Jenny spun the suitcase around, it whacked him directly in the head and sent him back to the ground. One of the wheels pegged him directly in the eye.

"JENNY!"

She stopped halfway down the hall and hesitated. She bit her lip, left her case in the hallway, and suddenly ran back into the bedroom.

"You think you'll get anywhere?" Tom panted as he saw her. He was on all fours now, struggling to get up. Blood dripped from his mouth. "You think you can just fucking walk away and think you can get rid of me? I *made* you Jenny! I fucking made and *built you!* You think—"

She ran past him and went to her side of the bed. She grabbed *Heaven's Defiance* and turned to leave again. Tom's hand shot out and caught her on her bare ankle.

"You won't get far without me," he gasped. "If it wasn't for me you'd *have no life, Jenny! YOU'D HAVE NO LIFE WITHOUT ME, NO LIFE—* "

She slammed her bare foot down against his face.

Tom screamed, felt blood spray from his nose, and let go.

*Gotta wash my feet afterwards,* Jenny thought incoherently as she raced down the stairs. *Always have to wash them after stepping on something dirty.*

"JENNY!"

She put her leather boots on in the foyer and opened the door. A crisp breeze filled her lungs, making her cold. It was going to rain soon. She grabbed a coat from the closet.

And then, after taking one last glance behind her—after glancing at the kitchen she so vigorously had to clean and make spotless, at the dining room table she always had to prepare, at the carpet she always had to vacuum and clean, at the two wine stains that looked like dried blood streaks left over from a wound created a hundred lifetimes ago—Jenny Acworth let out a sigh, closed her eyes, and finally stepped out. She dragged her suitcase with her and heard its rubber wheels following obediently behind.

She was leaving.

"JENNY! YOU GET BACK HERE RIGHT NOW, DAMN IT!"

Tom's voice. From somewhere in the background. She'd forgotten to close the door.

"YOU HEAR ME, YOU STUPID LITTLE CUNT! GET BACK HERE RIGHT NOW!"

*Make me, you bastard.*

She raised her head up to the sky. Something soft landed on her face. It was followed by a soft splash, and then another, and then another, and soon, Jenny was raising her head up toward the rain.

*This is nice,* she thought wearily, *this is how it should be. Have somebody else cry for me for once. Thank you, God. Hide my tears for a moment, won't you?*

"JENNY!"

She kept her shoulders lowered and kept walking, letting the rain pour over her body. Her fingers clutched her coat and her boots clanked calmly against the sidewalk. She was cold. She was shuddering like crazy while walking away into the night, and had she at least remembered to pack enough of her underwear?

*What a funny thought. Ha! To think of underwear at a time—*

"JENNY!"

*—like this. You must be going crazy, girl.*

"Yeah, maybe," Jenny muttered. She laughed at the sound of her voice and shivered again. Her voice scared her. "Maybe I am. Oh God, maybe I am."

There came another loud shout behind her, but Jenny ignored it, pretending it was just noise from a very bad dream.

# THE FIRST INTERLUDE

## The False World*

"The agent of the spectacle placed on stage as a star is the opposite of the individual, the enemy of the individual in himself as well as in others" (sec. 61).

--Guy Debord "Society of the Spectacle"

<u>May 10, 2010</u>

After watching Robert Downey Jr. don on his Iron Man costume (it is not a suit) for the second time to do battle with Mickey Rourke, diary, I realized that we Americans are cowards. We are cowards for one simple reason: We submit ourselves to a realm of fantasy rather than live a life of reality.

How many of us clapped, cheered, and laughed during the movie? How many of us ooooed and ahhhed at the special effects? For two hours at a time we as the audience were taken away by fantasy, persuaded by escapism, and dramatically swayed. But all for *what?* Once the credits had rolled—once the villain had been vanquished, once the heroine had been saved, and once the hero had reemerged—what did we as a people do? We got up; we removed ourselves from the theater. In that moment of leaving the theater, reality fell on us again, and we realized the brutal truth: Iron Man does not exist. He is not real, and no matter how troubling our plight or deep our despairs, he will *never* exist. He is false. Everything that Hollywood has ever produced in terms of these Men in Masks is <u>absolutely false</u>.

Remember: <u>Nothing is real on screen.</u> The dialogue spoken by the

---

* The *Interludes* are various journal entries and essays written by Daniel Fischer during his time as a student. They represent his thought process and offer scholarly critiques of the world.

typical chauvinistic hero and hopeless damsel-in-distress is a dialogue written by scriptwriters. Remember: The gazes and stances of these actors/actresses are not real, for they are guided by a team of directors who lead their every move. Remember: The faces we see on screen—the bodies we see on the Red Carpet, the images we see on fashion magazines, the faces we see on TV—<u>are false, for they are all decorated by makeup artists, stylists, and computer engineers who manufacture their bodies/faces as product.</u> This we know to be true. And yet, we Americans, fearful of the conditions of our lives (the *real* conditions of our lives, a world filled with death, poverty, disease and unhappiness), would willingly spend time, energy, and *money*, to allow these false heroes/heroines to live for us. This is an act of cowardice.

***

<u>May 11 2010</u>

Plato very much understood the dangers of *mimesis* ("imitation"), and warned of the possible implications magniloquent persuasion could have on the masses in *The Republic* and *Ion*. For the ancient Greeks, art was a form of representation that tried to imitate nature. Plato's concern was how such imitation removed the individual from the Truth, and how such imitation falsely enthused society into believing in falseness. Whereas philosophers were gifted with the ability to obtain Truth, those who attempted to represent the world through *mimesis* with persuasion were deemed discreditable and artless.

Plato begins this critique by investigating poetry. One must remember that for the ancient Athenians, poetry was not an act of solitary reading, but rather, a public <u>performance</u>. Poetry was a grand spectacle where the rhapsode stood before the mass audience reciting Homer's poetry (or any of the other great poets of the time). He stood accompanied by music and was "divinely inspired." This madness—this sense of *enthousiasmos*—was a state of possession where the rhapsode was controlled by the Muses. In producing this spectacle, the rhapsode suddenly speaks like his characters, *becomes* his characters, and moves audiences to endless states of passion. This mimicking of reality disturbs Plato for it instills a sense of falseness onto the masses. It moreover provokes our passions while disregarding our logic. Thus for Plato, the entire spectacle of poetry is a superficial spectacle where every member of the audience is falsely enthused. This enthusiastic state of mind veils Truth from the individual—or, rather, it at the very least moves them away from their *techne*, has them become what they are *not* along with the rhapsode, and has them forget who they are. The king weeps at tales of tragedy when he should lead; the farmer becomes embolden with rage when he should farm. Thus the audience becomes enthused with the rhapsode and temporarily forgets their reality. This chain (this "magnetic analogy") goes as follows:

Muses→poet→actor/[rhaspode]→audience

Once the poet and rhapsode become inspired, he is no longer *himself*. He is moved beyond himself, is enthused, "possessed," and so, is without any identity. He has lost his *techne*—or, rather, his *techne* is mere representation and <u>nothing more</u>. When he speaks, he speaks <u>falsely as someone else</u>. Yet we as the audience become *moved with him*, and we too are persuaded by this double falseness.

Hollywood follows the same format of falseness. Beginning with the actors, we understand their "inspiration" is not divine but technical: Actors speak what is written and given to them, act accordingly to what is pointed out to them, and follow whatever command it is given to them. <u>None of what they do is *real*.</u> It is the Director that leads them, the Scriptwriter that tells them how to speak. The actor/actress takes these commands and "becomes" their character. They thus are not themselves, but the simply characters they represent. They speak no "I" that is their own, and their actions do not represent their own Selves in reality—they thus only mimic fantasy. The scriptwriter gives Spider-Man words to speak; he does not speak himself. Computer engineers and graphic designers swing him through the city; <u>the actor does not do this himself</u>. The suit *itself* is not the actor's creation, but rather, the creation of the artist and costume designer. The actors/actresses we see on screen are<u> thus not real and do nothing.</u> But we as a culture praise them highly, become moved by "their" performances, loan them our money, give them our time, and submit to them our lives. We follow their fashions, wait for their latest scandals, take delight in the smallest gossip, and simply lose ourselves in our everyday activities.

Director/Scriptwriter→actor/actress→character→audience

Those who say actors are skilled are simply wrong; actors are perhaps the least skilled individuals of all of society. They simply know basic imitation and nothing more. And yet we, as a typical American society—so saturated with sensationalism and infantile tendencies towards a world of Hollywood and fashion—would rather pay these actors and actresses more than we would pay skilled individuals who specialize in a beneficial skill for society (doctors, scientists, scholars, historians, etc.).

\*\*\*

<u>May 12, 2010</u>

The makeup artist, visual-effects team, costume-designer, lighting director, editors, etc.—<u>these individuals are all more skilled than the actor</u> for they all specialize in a technical skill that can be utilized outside the production studio.

That the actor is nothing more than a mere imitator without any proper *techne* is a theme playfully investigated in Plato's *Ion*. Socrates finds Ion's position as a rhapsode a curious contradiction: He can recite all of Homer's poetry as the best rhapsode in all of the land, and yet, when it comes to reciting the poetry of Hesiod, the native Ephesian remains mute. As Socrates asks: Doesn't the sculptor with true skill have the ability to criticize other sculptors as well as their works? Cannot the art critic criticize the work of others in the same way he would criticize his own? What then is keeping Ion from being able to speak eloquently of other poets' works if in all their tales there are elements of commonality such as war and death? The answer, of course, is that Ion has no true *techne*, that he is <u>simply an imitator</u>, a *mimos*, an *actor*, and thus is unable to speak skillfully about other subject matters. His abilities as a rhapsode are not his own, but rather, abilities loaned to him from the Muses through an instance of divine possession, that is, *enthousiasmos*. He is "divinely possessed" when reciting Homer's poetry, a trait that is loaned to him through the poet from the Muses, and ultimately delivered in the end to the audience (the "magnet analogy"). He thus speaks as a madman when on stage.

Socrates recites various arts from Homer's poetry. In doing so, he asks Ion: Who has the greater *techne* when speaking about medicine? The physician? Or the rhapsode who recites passages about the physician? Who has greater skill at piloting a water vessel? The pilot? Or the rhapsode who pretends to be a pilot? Thus the rhapsode as actor has no skill, is without a *techne*, and <u>should not</u> be trusted to be a producer of knowledge, truth, or morality.

Shouldn't the same critique then be made to the actors and actresses that infest Hollywood? As said before, actors and actresses have no skill, and their presence on screen is nothing more than an illusion, an imitation. And yet, despite their lacking of skill, they become the embodiment of the ideal in American culture, the highest paid individuals in society, and become the highest worshipped figures of every generation. What of the graphic designers, what of the makeup artists? What of the computer engineers who make Superman fly through the city, who gives Spider-Man his graceful swing? And, moreover: <u>What of the scientist, what of the doctor?</u> What of the medical student who struggles every day to learn the secrets of medicine so that she may later in life find ways to cure disease? What of the construction worker, what of the historian? The young medical student that wishes to study cancer cells but that struggles every day to pay off her debt?

Will *they* ever walk the Red Carpet?

An actor who dons on the lab coat of a forensic scientist is not a forensic scientist; we foolishly pay money to see this illusion because we pretend we do not know better. The actor who speaks like a doctor is not a doctor outside the studio—yet they will receive a greater sum of money than the authentically trained doctor for simply looking like a doctor, whereas the real doctor—the one with actual *techne*—will save lives.

Hollywood is the greatest scheme America has ever concocted.

***

May 14, 2010

Why? Why do we Americans flee from reality the way we do, why do we cowardly turn away from life?

In speaking of life, one can only speak of weariness and labor, for this is the hidden mantra of all capitalist societies. Life is not a linear progression filled with obtainable wishes and wants, but rather, the paying of bills and mortgages. Because capitalism asks us to compete, one must wonder: Who are the losers? How do they survive? And in living under a capitalist system of winners and losers, how do the losers cope with their wretched existence?

Reality is harsh, but the world of Hollywood is warm and kind. To live briefly with the heroes on screen, to fetishize the newest fashion trends, to temporarily suspend all thoughts of labor, deadlines, paying of the bills, raising disobedient children, facing heartache of losing a loved one—this moment of fleeing soon becomes an unconscious habit where life suddenly *must* consist of celebrities and gossip. There *must* be a new viral internet video that we must all follow, there *must* be a new blockbuster from Hollywood that we must all talk about; there *must* be something to compensate the weariness in our lives. Without Optimus Prime to guide us, how would we live?

***

May 15, 2010

No matter how great the plot or wonderful the hero, <u>Hollywood will not benefit the individual after leaving the theater.</u> The reason is brutally simple: Once the movie has ended, life awaits the individual outside the theater doors. <u>He still must pay his bills;</u> he still must wake to go to work the next morning. Batman has done nothing for him.

***

May 15, 2010

We leave the theater and then <u>must exist as we are</u> once the movie has ended. We escape into fantasy because we are afraid of life. We are comforted by clichés in this country; we know the protagonist will triumph in the end; we know that the damsel-in-distress will be saved.

How wonderful it is to know that justice will triumph at the end! In a world so random, so confusing, with death and poverty surrounding us, how wonderful it is to see the Joker put in his place! When having to see the wrinkles on our faces every morning, how great is it to know that others are handsomer than us, prettier than us, and that they can wear fashionable clothes better than us! How great is it to see a man in a mask that can take on the weight of the world and do what we weak, pathetic, ugly, and wretched humans cannot! How great is it to be loved by a sparkling vampire that will never age and can forever nurture us!

*And yet.*

The sight of Iron Man flying through the city will not help address the gender wage-gap in this country; Captain America's presence on screen will not build shelters for the homeless. When Batman speaks his nearly inarticulate (and laughable) dialogue, no new conversation is made to help address racism in our culture—the word "nigger" does not exist in the world of *Twilight* or Peter Parker's life. Yet racism exists. <u>Disease, poverty, death, love, life, and friendships all exist.</u> Hollywood would only make us flee from

231

these things rather than address them.

Are all Hollywood actors and actress vilified in my view? No. I just simply dislike the spectacle that surrounds them. This is all that I dislike. I just wished that it we as a society placed greater emphasis on the sciences and humanities in the same way we do to celebrities. This is all.

***

<u>May 16, 2010</u>

Iron Man is not real and he cannot address racism. Batman is a hoax, and he will not prevent the next young girl from becoming a rape victim. The X-Men will not help end wars, and Captain America will not end poverty or provide relief for hunger on the streets. Why we cheer for these 'heroes,' I don't know, but I refuse them my praise.

I just absolutely refuse them.

*Vincit omnia veritas…homo sum.*

Daniel Fischer

Professor David Quinn

ENGL: 305 Critical Practice

16 April 2009

Weariness

The gods had condemned Sisyphus believing that his fate would bring eternal despair. On the contrary, Camus reminds us that Sisyphus is always happy despite his labor (123), and that his attitude towards the gods has made him the Absurd Hero. This attitude—this sense of recognizing the Absurdity in life—is an attitude lost to the common American. Whereas Sisyphus may find contentment in his labor and thus become the master of his fate, the mechanical procedures of everyday American life produce only weariness. In our modern American age, gridlocked in so many structures of capitalistic labor—the 40-hour work week, the paying of the bills, the gray walls of the eternal cubical, the longing of a paycheck at the end of the month—our sights of the Absurd have become lost, and so, in order to compensate our weariness, we create a culture of fantasy. The stars that we admire on the Red Carpet and the world of celebrities are images real insofar as the individual will believe them to be, for once the credits have rolled, this fantasy ends, and reality rushes back to the individual to accept again. The gossip, the scandals, the newest hottest fashion trends—Hollywood distracts from life because Hollywood is only a representation of reality. Yet the individual—so weary and afraid of life—will ultimately hope to flee into this unreality, wishing to cast aside her worries. In doing so, the true meaning of life—simply that life is meaningless and that it is often Absurd—soon becomes lost to mediocrity, and all hopes of authentic action in life for the *self* are exhausted. To recognize that the world is indifferent and that humankind will never find true clarity in the world—this is what is Absurd. Yet "the moment absurdity is recognized, it becomes a passion" (Camus 22) for only then can sincere action for the individual occur. To live without standards and stereotypes imposed by Hollywood, to define one's self as beautiful without having celebrities dictate definitions of beauty, and to think for one's self without speaking the language of cliché—these all would be to break free from the world of Hollywood and live as one's self in reality. Alas, weariness takes hold of the majority of Americans where a worshipping of Men in Masks and Women in Makeup constitute the bulk of our culture. Weariness prompts fantasy; in return, this fantasy prompts a fleeing from life into a world of falseness where the ability to recognize the Absurd becomes eliminated.

Camus suggests that suicide is a question already embedded in man's heart (5) and that it manifests itself when the individual begins to ponder. In asking "Why?" the individual undermines herself and is suddenly faced with a world filled with banal indifferences and uncertainties. Why Monday, why Tuesday, why Wednesday later? What meaning do these days have for me if in just seven more days I will return to the same day? In speaking of the Absurd, one must speak of life. In speaking of life, one must speak of habit (Camus 13). One learns to do out of habit in life than one does first think: Those who tiredly perform merger tasks everyday just to survive know this. The gestures that command the majority of our lives is this habit that keep us from realizing the Absurd—one cannot contemplate "why" when one is distracted by the paying of the bills. Yet habit has a chance to produce weariness, and weariness has a chance to produce a consciousness of habit. In recognizing this habit—in finally having the mind to ask *"why?"*—the individual is faced with a choice: to relive habit out of fear from understanding the meaningless of life; to commit suicide out of the meaningless of life; or to accept the Absurd out of the meaningless of life. And yet, a fourth choice arises, one not entirely discussed by Camus: to distract one's self with falseness out of the meaningless of life.

It is necessary then to examine the life of the typical American to understand the meaningless of life. She wakes in the morning; she leaves her home and braves the elements. She rides the metro bus through traffic, travels downtown, and goes to work. Once her labor is finished, she rides the metro bus again, endures traffic a second time, and finally arrives home wearier than before. She goes to bed fully exhausted. The process is repeated: Monday, Tuesday, Wednesday, Thursday, and Friday—the weekends now become spectacular. Throughout this process, bills are paid and taxes are collected, energy is exhausted only to be replenished again before being re-exhausted. She becomes weary; she becomes tired. No amount of labor she completes rids her the debt of life. Her body begins to show signs of aging and wrinkles dominate her face. Thoughts of love and friendship become secondary before the basic needs of common survival, and individual identity and self-worth become consumed by culture. Life is soon measured by deadlines and paychecks.

Where is her relief? Where in her moments of labor is authentic existence, and when will her labor end?

The spectacles found in Hollywood are those made to provide relief for those weary. Moreover, these spectacles are used to *conceal* the Absurd. In watching Thor wield his mighty hammer, or Edward Cullen seduce his weak and submissive beautiful swan, all thoughts of weariness are made naught. In return, the individual is offered a temporary relief from life through this false freedom. In this freedom loaned by the theater, the individual thinks: *I* am Bella Swan; *I* am Iron Man. Someday Edward Cullen will come and love *me* as a person. At this time in the theater, *I* am the characters I see on screen, and *I* am no longer weary. Every aspect of fantasy, idealism, and escapism is fulfilled in watching these characters on screen where, conversely, every notion of responsibility for one's self and others is *excused*. Thus this temporary relief loaned by Hollywood is not a thing to be celebrated, but rather, abhorred. The solutions offered by the unrealities of Hollywood are ultimately false, last only for several hours, and once the credits roll, offer nothing more to the individual that must leave the theater and reenter life. Hollywood has taken from her what she can never reclaim: Her two hours of life watching the Dark Knight are hours that now only death may own. Thus weariness was not eliminated, but merely postponed, where life—for two hours at a time—has fled her.

What reason does the individual have to flee into this falseness? Life, of course, is meaningless, and through this truth, one can develop their own reasons to live. This is the accepting of the Absurd. By understanding the brutal existence of life, one realizes one's freedoms in the face of finitude: "Man has to face the absurdity of his existence, that he is cast into the world merely to die there" (Coates 232). But in recognizing this absurdity, the individual is suddenly forced to recognize their freedom; in recognizing this freedom, the individual is suddenly forced to recognize their responsibilities. We are, as Sartre has declared, condemned to be free.

The meaningless of life should offer the individual an excuse to live life fully. Yet only the opposite has occurred, for the individual in life cannot bear the total responsibilities of her life authentically. She submits; she flees. She ignores her potential for freedom because to do so otherwise would be to accept all the consequences of her actions and inactions. She dons on the latest fashion trends culture has to offer her, listens with anticipation for the latest Hollywood gossip, awaits impatiently for the next commodity to arrive in society, looks for the latest new hit-song, and waits for the newest internet viral video—she becomes subsumed *into* culture, into the impersonal *das Man*, and suddenly conforms to all social norms and behaviors. Living is "so difficult that human beings have, during the course of history, developed a range of different ways to slough off responsibility for their actions" (Wartenberg 44).

These mechanisms that have been instilled in society to ward off responsibility have, in turn, produced a weariness that has ultimately led to escapism. The alarm clock, the paying of the bills, Sartre's awkward waiter at the restaurant—these are all modes of existence that we begrudgingly accept through acts of bad-faith to rid ourselves the responsibilities of life. To compensate, a world of celebrities has been created to rid us our feelings of weariness. We celebrate Batman's victory because to be the originators of our own victories in life would require work; we thus worship fiction as cowards.

Moreover, we praise Superman because we know victory in our lives may never occur, and thus take whatever simple pleasure we may have at worshipping the Red Carpet. One does all of this, again, through a hypocritical and cowardly lens of bad-faith. The fact that the individual *knows* her heroes to be false on screen is a case-in-point: She willingly abandons her world of harsh reality by paying money to briefly live in a world of fantasy while still saying she recognizes the real names of the actors/actress on screen; she is paying to purposefully be *fooled*. Moreover, once the movie has ended, a worshiping *from a distance* is still maintained where the individual worships her actor/actress as *celebrities*. To allow oneself to praise an actor as a character in a role and then worship him again as another character in a second role where a purposeful relinquishing of reality is made simply to maintain this illusion—this is an act of bad-faith. "Though I have seen the same actor a hundred times," writes Camus, "I shall not for that reason know him any better personally" (11). And yet, still, despite these strangers on screen, we as weary individuals in life would blindly throw away our money to them just to see their falseness. Why have we fled from reality?

The premise is repeated with an emphasis to be understood: Those who thrust themselves into a world of Hollywood become philosophical cowards for they do not wish to accept the brutal reality of life. Weariness, death, poverty, wars, disease, friends, love, and unfairness—these all exist in life. But safeguarded between the walls of the theater—protected by the triumphant chauvinistic hero, seduced by the salacious gaze of the heroine— these thoughts of life are eliminated, or at least, temporarily suspended. A falseness is created in this suspension where the individual renounces her identity to become one with the enthused crowd. She laughs with those around her, cheers with them, cries with them; she becomes subsumed into the hysteria of the spectacle that now suddenly *is* "Them." She becomes part of culture. The gazing at celebrities whose lives are perceived greater than ours, the tendency to follow a world of gossip made by superstars, to seek the facts of their world, admire them on the Red Carpet, wonder about their habits, gossip about their fashion—this is all meant for the philosophical coward that cannot authentically produce their own actions in life. Camus' praise for the actor and his revolt are misplaced: After the actor has finished his acting, he then must exist as himself. He is not his character.

Freedom produces anxiety, and from this anxiety, mechanisms are created to regulate freedom. But the maintaining of these mechanisms produces weariness, and so a secondary mechanism of fantasy is created to compensate. Social labor and work, trivial matters, chores, bills, social identity, fashion, culture, language—these all become mechanisms that lock us into cycles of capitalistic labor. Exhausted, we turn to Hollywood and its fantasies to escape ourselves. Throughout all of this, we maintain ourselves through a constant theme of bad-faith. But a change is possible; weariness can produce two alternatives for the individual to escape her plight. Like Sisyphus, forever damned to roll a boulder up his mountain, there in those moments of brief rest while watching his boulder fall back down are moments of triumph. For it is through weariness does the individual have the opportunity to seize upon the moment of realization at the meaningless of life and create authentic action—there is an ability, always, to realize the Absurd. Or, conversely, the individual can acknowledge the meaningless of life, fall back into the fatal mechanism of society, and continue worshipping what she knows is false.

The choice is, as any existentialist would say, up to her.

## Works Cited

Camus, Albert. *The Myth of Sisyphus, and Other Essays*. Trans. Justin O' Brian. New York: Knopf, 1955. Print.

Coates, J.B. "Existentialism." *Philosophy*. 28.106 (1953): 229-238. Print.

Wartenberg, Thomas E. *Existentialism: A Beginner's Guide*. Richmond: Oneworld, 2008. Print.

Daniel Fischer

Professor Joni Spears

ENGL: 358 Literary Theory

20 February 2009

## The Death of the Individual

Heidegger reminds us that authentic existence occurs only when coexisting with death. Because death is an individual's *ownmost* possibility, a full realization of death leads the individual into realms of sincere agency. Yet Hollywood distracts from death for it offers only inauthentic modes of existence through fantasy. Where reality is concerned, the individual exists in life and accepts his responsibilities as he is. Where fantasy occurs, however, the individual is relieved from responsibility and offered false escape. In choosing fantasy, the individual falls into *das Man*, the They, the One, and is subsumed by culture: Individual worth and sincere actions soon become integrated within ideological structures of clichés and stereotypes imposed by Hollywood. Hollywood is nothing but a false representation of reality, and as such, it can teach nothing about life. Moreover, because Hollywood is not reality—because it cannot produce truths like life or science, and because it cannot produce solutions to sickness or poverty—it consequently cannot teach about death. It is from this concealment of death—this suspension of an inevitable truth of life—does the individual lose their potential for authentic being and fall into the masses.

It is a fact: There is no death in Hollywood. What Hollywood portrays is an exaggeration of life and death where death itself becomes a parody. The hero dies, the heroine falls. And, on the very next day, society sees these heroes again as celebrities outside of their roles. What reasons did we have to believe in this falseness? The refusal to die—and thus the inability to live—is a symbolic sign of cowardice for it begs the question of several pertinent themes fictitious Hollywood characters have failed to answer: Where was Spider-Man when the homeless man asked for food? Why did Superman fail to prevent the latest shooting of schoolchildren? And why has Batman failed to prevent the latest rape victim?

Why have these heroes failed to save me when I have *paid* them?

Death becomes the individual's ultimate test of authenticity, of *Eigentlichkeit*, for it is the *ownmost* possibility of one's existence. No other body can experience death for the individual for death is always untranslatable. In recognizing that the individual as *Da-sein* will always die, a call for sincere action is thus made: "Da-sein can *authentically* be *itself* only when it makes that possible of its own accord" (Heidegger 243). Death therefore is the destiny of every living individual, a *Sein-zum-Tode*, and it should be with death that one considers their life. Every action however minute or grand will one day cease to exist when the individual reaches annihilation—the individual thus must live authentically because of his eventual demise. "Therefore let a man face his own death; in the resultant trauma it will be revealed to him what a special thing it is to be a man" (Killinger 307). Recognition of death does not necessitate a flirting with death; rather, recognizing death enables the individual to live fully when approaching death. Potentiality is unlocked when one understands their finite nature, for it is only then does life become meaningful. To understand that the beauty in this world will one day fade, to recognize the perishable smile of a loved one—these all in essence have a characteristic of death that enables the individual to cherish every moment of their existence.

Hollywood will distract from this understanding of death for Hollywood will insist on eternal life. Batman falls, but he again arises; we thus can safely believe in cliché. The heroine is in distressed but eventually saved; we thus can safely ignore the social plights and inequalities of women. The latest fashion trends and celebrity scandals, the newest Hollywood gossip, the next hottest television series—these all prevent a recognition of death in reality, for they all poison the individual with falseness and irrelevancy. A "tranquilization" of death is made where "the evasion of death…dominates everydayness so stubbornly that, in being-with-one-another, the 'neighbors' often try to convince the 'dying person' that he will escape death" (Heidegger 234).

Hollywood furthermore attempts to condition the individual to its current standards of social behavior. This thus eliminates all unique characteristics of the individual not only because death is no longer recognized, but because the individual's worldview and basic day-to-day behaviors become typical. Millions will bow before the mighty Avengers and pay them money—only very few will refuse them. Moreover, fewer still will ask whether or not their fictional deeds have helped console victims of war and poverty. Millions will fetishize and adore the Red Carpet when the Oscars appear—fewer still will love themselves enough to refuse the worshipping of celebrities. This public realm of celebrities and culture—this *das Man* without the ontological framework—persists in everyday American society as an imposing entity that wishes to consume individual identity.

The effects of *das Man* are not as obscure as they seem: Scholars have detected the sexist and racist tendencies Hollywood has had to offer and declared them many times through occasional discourses. Ethnocentrism is preserved in Tom Cruise's *The Last Samurai* simply because a hero of none white-European descent (as well as non-heterosexual orientations) would be unheard of. *Dancing with the Wolves*, Disney's *Pocahontas*, and the *Rush Hour* series all follow this format. In contrast, sexist ideology is celebrated when Rosie Huntington-Whiteley's body is compared to that of a 1939 Cabriolet 165 Delahaye and made into a sexual object by Patrick Dempsey in *Transformers 3*. Thus the effects of *das Man* in a casual sense is obvious when one learns to speak the language of scholars: Ideology, hegemony, and doxa all become consequences when believing in Hollywood heroes.

Such a relinquishing of identity—to the crowd, the audience, the masses—halts the authentic potential of the individual, for, if the individual "lives and dies only as one of the crowd, never aware of his special possibilities as a free agent and therefore never positing himself as an individual, he misses the chief glory of human existence. He never becomes authentic" (Killinger 307). Indeed, to adopt the hidden and unconscious racist and sexist ideological tendencies Hollywood has to offer is to not think for oneself, but rather, to think through a medium of cliché and infantile standards. Hollywood does not offer scientific discourse in offering the world tangible solutions. Rather, Hollywood attempts to imitate and persuade, and what it often persuades is a tired audience by imitating perfection. Yet despite all its grander, the actor as hero—however spectacularly dressed in his spider suit and donned with makeup—has done nothing for the world, and, indeed, has prevented change for the world by having us believe in fantasy. Stereotypes, clichés, and childish wonder all become prepackaged themes for us to consume in the theater; any thought outside the world of Hollywood becomes a thought too great to bear.

What reason do we as a culture have to flee into *das Man* and falseness? The masses, so often times made weary under the heavy hammer-blows of capitalism, flee into the theater to relieve themselves of their plight. In this refuge of the immortal masked hero and heroine, death becomes "an indeterminate something which first has to show up from somewhere, but which right now is *not yet objectively present* for oneself, and is thus no threat" (Heidegger 234). Continuing, "*The they does not permit the courage to have* Angst *about death*," where such indifferences eliminates Da-sein's potentiality-of-being (235). It is a relief from capitalism, this journey to the theater, for capitalism demands competition and subsequent losers. And, in being losers, American mass culture must continuously look to fictitious 'winners' to provide for them.

Death is a frightening thought for it connotes the inevitable end of existence. Moreover, because death is ubiquitous, it is often treated with fleeing and escapism where a more perfectly crafted world awaits the individual. But such a retreat is cowardly, and one often forgets: no matter how great the hero or fantastical the world of Hollywood, death spares no one, and reality inevitably must resume itself when the individual returns from fantasy. Thus the actors and actresses one sees on the theater screen are not impervious to death—morality governs all human laws. In avoiding

242

death and fleeing into Hollywood and the They, the individual becomes inauthentic, an *Uneigentlichkeit des Da-seins*. Yet to be able to accept one's life as finite and fallible—to recognize the eventual end of all things, and thus, to live life authentically—means to stand higher than the artless gathering of Men in Masks, and to live for one's self. Only those who are fearful of life and who are cowards will flee from life; only those who cannot accept life will wear masks and makeup.

A true hero will not wear a mask to face death.

## Works Cited

Heidegger, Martin. *Being and Time: A Translation of Sein Und Zeit.* Trans. Joan Stambaugh. New York: State University of New York Press, 1996. Print.

Killinger, John. "Existentialism and Human Freedom." *The English Journal.* 50.5 (1961): 303-313. Print.

# PART II

Out in the sky the great dark clouds are massing;
I look far out into the pregnant night,
Where I can hear a solemn booming gun
And catch the gleaming of a random light,
That tells me that the ship I seek is passing, passing.

My tearful eyes my soul's deep hurt are glassing;
For I would hail and check that ship of ships.
I stretch my hands imploring, cry aloud,
My voice falls dead a foot from mine own lips,
And but its ghost doth reach that vessel, passing, passing.

O Earth, O Sky, O Ocean, both surpassing,
O heart of mine, O soul that dreads the dark!
Is there no hope for me? Is there no way
That I may sight and check that speeding bark
Which out of sight and sound is passing, passing?

--Paul Laurence Dunbar
"Ships that Pass in the Night"

# CHAPTER 12

*Heaven passed by outside her window.*

*Jenny opened her eyes. She closed them again when feeling a soft weight of light fall against her, and turned her head away. The light was gentle, drying the last strands of her hair and soothing the dark bruises on her cheek. She opened her eyes again after another moment and stared quietly outside.*

So, *she thought slowly,* this is Heaven. This is what Heaven looks like outside my window, and this is what it means to be in a place of paradise. There is nothing but loneliness here.

*The world outside was dominated by bulging dirt hills and vast stretches of nothingness. Sagebrush dappled the hills. Sparse patches of dead grass and other shriveled shrubbery littered the ground next to the blacktop of Interstate 84 while bare earth colored the world a dead brown. Overhead, thin cirrus clouds stretched across the horizon, spreading outward like white feathers.*

*She was on a Greyhound bus now. She was headed west. She was headed home.*

In a place called Heaven and Hell, *Jenny thought quietly, closing her eyes again,* it's Heaven now outside my window, and it's Heaven now that I wish to scorn. Heaven right now is beautiful, but because Heaven is eternal, I find nothing great in Heaven. There is no ugliness here that makes me appreciate what is beautiful; there is no eventuality that makes me cherish my present.

*How grim and liberating these thoughts were. Jenny shuddered when she heard them and pushed her jacket across her chest up to her chin. She was cold in spite of the light, and heard behind her the dry, rushing sounds of the A/C blasting in the background. There were a few intermittent coughs, the loud wails of a waking child, and the low, steady drone of the bus's tires beneath her. The slow, subtle shaking of the Greyhound bus had an almost hypnotic rhythm to it, making her sleepy.*

*Several hours had passed since her flight from Boise. She'd passed the Idaho border only a few hours before, and now was making her way towards La Grande, Oregon. It was just 11.00 a.m.*

In a place called Heaven and Hell, *she thought again,* I would rather be sent to Hell than live in a place as beautiful as this. In a place of Heaven where everything is just so endless, love and life become false, and I am left feeling free of any responsibility for life. What reason would I have to love?

Dear God, if you are real and you grant me the opportunity to live in your paradise, know that I will turn away from you, and would instead allow myself to enter Hell. For I will not bow to you simply to love; I will not cherish this world simply out of fear. I will love this world on my own terms and will never bow to you. You will envy me for having an eventual end to life where I can understand the need to cherish and adore. Allow me to love and be loved, and I will love any hell you damn me to. I would rather yearn with pain for love than have love be exhausted by your eternal paradise; I would rather hurt knowing I loved and once loved than having you allow me to love only once.

*Tears filled her eyes. Jenny wiped them away, slowly, gently, not understanding where her thoughts were coming from, not really caring. She heard an echo of Daniel's voice in her head, but pushed it away, too tired to hear.*

*Outside, the Greyhound bus sped on and on, cruising through the empty hills and dead landscape like a sliver bullet beneath the sun.*

*Seattle. She was headed towards Seattle now. She was headed* home.

*Images of her working as a checkout girl at the local grocery store after having moved to Boise filled her mind then, followed by images of her wearing a tight purple kimono and itchy tabi socks waiting tables at Boise's one and only authentic Japanese steakhouse, of her exhaustingly vacuuming up after loud rambunctious teenagers every Friday night at the local theater, of her losing her virginity to a horrible one night-stand under the influence of alcohol, of coming home tired from work every night, exhausted, breathless, tired, her eyes* red, her feet sore—and then there were images of her crying, crying just so, so hard at the news of her father's death, just absolutely petrified of life now, lost, confused, a young woman barely twenty-six-years-old now suddenly fatherless and without a family. And then Tom. Tom and his handsome smile. Tom and his attractive good looks. Tom and his wonderfully pale blue eyes. Tom had come for her; he'd come to her with a sense of security and at a perfect time. The beatings had been light at first and always justified. Jenny had let them go on as naturally as one does when seeing their tired selves in the morning mirror. He had been rough, he had been good, but always, he had at least been a presence near her. There'd been their marriage; there'd been their honeymoon. And, somewhere in between, there'd been Red Moon's Diner and a fading of life.

Seattle. The word had no weight to it until finally thought of and properly heard, and once then, it took on the full weight of a distant planet. She was going home soon; she was going home. Home to the iconic Space Needle; home to the great Jimi Hendrix. It was home to Benaroya Hall and Pike Place Market, home to the great and black towering Columbia Tower and the wonderful Seattle Center. It was the birthplace of Starbucks, Amazon, Microsoft, and Boeing. There were the awesome Seahawks, the struggling Mariners, the Sounders, the great University of Washington and their Huskies, Sakura-con, and the delightful Seattle International Film Festival.

Seattle. It served as the backdrop for things like Grey's Anatomy and that god-awful thing called Twilight and 50 Shades of Grey. It was home to the Seattle Youth Symphony Orchestra and the Pacific Northwest Ballet, Safeco Field, the University District, the "Ave," the International District, the Quad, Belltown, Capitol Hill, Queen Anne, the Seattle Science Center, Elliot Bay—everything.

Home. She was headed home.

The time on her Greyhound bus ticket stated that departure began from Boise, Idaho at 7:25 a.m. and moved swiftly to Nampa, ID at 7:55 a.m. From there, Interstate 84 heading west crossed the Idaho border and went to Ontario, Oregon. From Ontario, I-84 continued to Baker City, OR, where there was a forty-minute layover. I-84 continued westward, and soon ran through La Grande, OR (10:30 a.m.); Pendleton, OR (11:35 a.m.); and Stanfield, OR (12:05 p.m.). I-84 diverged into I-82 and ran through Pasco, Washington (2:00 p.m.); Sunnyside, WA (2:55 p.m.); Yakima, WA (3:35 p.m.);

*Ellensburg, WA (4:25 p.m.). And then, finally, after an estimated five hundred miles of travel—of almost five years of lies and self-pitying, of hurt and bad dreams, of boiling hot showers and burned red skin, of vigorously cleaning the carpet and windows, wiping the kitchen countertops, making his specialized food, of painstakingly washing her hair for two hours in an effort to clean away That Shit Stink and Clogged Arteries Shit, of endless nights of mere existence in a place with black-and-white checkered tiled floors filled with heavy smells of black midnight coffee, grilled chopped up hashbrowns, cheese-smothered omelets and crisp sizzling bacon, frozen T-bone steaks done medium rare, of hot fluffy morning pancakes spilled with jam and runny syrup, and a goddamn horrible golden bell that rang whenever someone opened the door—the final destination printed on Jenny's schedule read: Seattle, WA. 6:40 p.m.*

Home, *Jenny thought again*, I'm going home. I'm going there, and once I get there, I'll cry. And once I cry, maybe those that are there can accept me for who I am. And maybe this is what home is; maybe this is what the true meaning of home is. Maybe it's a place not only where your heart is, but also a place where your tears belong. Home.

*Sleep threatened. Jenny turned her face to the side and let the light warm her face. She swallowed.*

I'll be home soon. And Edmonds will be there. Brackett's Landing will be there. And Olympic Beach will be there too. The pier will be there, and so will the ferry, the train tracks, the high school, and the waves. Edmonds will be there. It'll always be there.

Edmonds will be there. It will be.

Edmonds. It—

# CHAPTER 13

—was dark this morning, but as Daniel raised his head to look up at the sky, he saw a few spots of light spilling through, cutting the gray. He stared at the light with an innocent kind of wonder, and thought that perhaps it would be clear today. It would be good if today was clear; it would be good.

He stood at the Edmonds Park-and-Ride facing 72$^{nd}$ Ave waiting for the 871 transit bus to come. He stood there because school was about to begin. It was a new year again: Summer had gone while autumn had reappeared. It was the first day of college.

*Two minutes late,* Daniel thought, checking his watch. *Already late, but so easily expected. Two minutes.*

There were twelve lined up behind him. In his mind, Daniel pictured those behind him as ghosts waiting on the sidewalk. They stood poor and shoeless, these ghosts, most in torn clothing and dirty faces. They stood transparent, and while they all saw and participated in the world around them as casual observers, none in return observed them. Some coughed and sneezed into clenched fists; others yawned and produced airless sounds. Some texted messages on their cell phones, while others—these being girls—checked their reflection on their cell phones and fixed their hair.

*This is my first day at college,* Daniel thought coldly from the side. *This is the feeling I take with me when first entering the UW campus. These are the people I have to see every morning and the people I may have to work with. I feel tired just looking at them.*

*Three minutes. The bus is three minutes late. If my first day of college is having me arrive late to class, then—*

But there it was, the blue-white Community Transit bus making its wide turn onto 72nd from 212th, rolling forward like a giant mechanical caterpillar that had only six feet as wheels instead of a dozen little pads. Black smog poured from its top. Daniel heard a woman sigh with relief behind him and saw as everyone straightened their shoulders. They all reached into various pockets and purses, and pulled out their UW Bus Pass.

"Eight-seven-one Edmonds to the U-Dub campus!" the driver announced as the bus doors swung open. Wind blew in Daniel's face, forcing him to step back. Dead pine needles and old leaves fluttered around the giant wheels next to the curb. "Come on up."

Daniel showed his UW card and climbed on. When one spoke of the University of Washington here—whether it was about the main campus in Seattle, or the sister campuses in Bothell or Tacoma—one always pronounced UW as U-Dub.

The 871 turned away from Edmonds and made its way to Mountlake Terrace. It traveled south on 99 and then east down 220th, passing a familiar TOP Food & Drug store. When it eventually reached the Mountlake Terrace Park-and-Ride, Daniel let out a weary sigh.

A whole long line of morning passengers stood next to the Mountlake Terrace Park-and-Ride sidewalk. There were probably fifty bodies, all of them students, all overburdened with heavy fat backpacks and with seasonal coughs stuffed into fists. They were UW students, and they all stood tired and gloomy with runny noses.

*Stuffed lobsters in a gray aquarium tank,* Daniel thought randomly as the bus doors opened. *That's what we are, just lobsters with rubber bands around our pincers stuffed together in a corner. It's going to be so crowded this morning.*

Shuffling bodies and swinging backpacks squeezed through the aisles and hurriedly looked for empty seats. There were grunts and murmurs, "Excuse me's" and "Sorry's", slight smiles of plastic politeness and weary-eyed agitation. Everyone sought to sit in the back seats, and those who had to stand in the middle enviously looked around their shoulders to see if they'd missed a spot while reaching up to grab the metal bars overhead. The line moved back, always back, forcing the crowd of newly arrivals into a crammed mess of tangled limbs. Daniel smelled morning-showered hair and cheaply bought shampoo, newly washed clothes with lingering soapy detergent, heavy deodorant, Old Spice, perfume, cologne, and a distant whiff of body odor. He could hear key-chains inside denim pockets, the mechanical munching of tireless jaws chewing on pieces of Trident, hear the thin crinkling of a *Seattle Times* newspaper being folded and re-crumpled, and could hear the *tit-tit-tit* sound of tireless texting fingers. There were those that coughed and those that sneezed, those that blew their noses into handkerchiefs and hastily stuffed them back into pockets. It was a klutzy claustrophobic rendition of fitting a dozen clowns into a car, only instead of it being anything comical, it was sad, and became a jumbled showing of what one could expect when sending animals to the slaughter.

"Mind if I sit?"

Daniel raised his head. It was a girl. "Not at all," he said. He tried to smile. He grabbed his notebook and placed it in his lap. With some annoyance he realized the girl had a violin case in her hands and that her backpack was overstuffed with textbooks. She looked at him, almost apologetically, muttered, "Thanks," and gave him a waning smile before taking off her backpack. She placed the violin case on the compartment shelf above them and sat with the backpack in her lap. It took up leg and arm space.

She smiled again, apologetic and timid with a brief brushing of hair from her face, and that's when Daniel spotted Jenny up front.

She was the last person to get on. And by the looks of it, she had run far to get on before the doors closed, her hands rapidly rummaging through her backpack trying to find her UW pass.

Daniel stared ahead. The girl noticed his blank face, withdrew her smile, and looked bleakly down at her lap.

She'd dyed her hair, he saw; it was russet red. She had grown bangs, gotten a new backpack, and had on a new pair of jeans that looked just freshly bought and hardly worn. From where he sat, Daniel could see new brown sheepskin boots on her feet. Ugg boots they were called. *Ugg* boots. Diamond earrings dimpled the spots on her earlobes and thin mascara outlined her eyes. Her face looked thinner and whiter now, not pale or unhealthy, but lightly powdered, smoothed and clear. A silver bracelet hung on one skinny wrist.

Her hair. It was the *hair* that he noticed the most. It was red, dark red, a russet red, an old autumn burn that brought to mind September embers. From far away it looked like she'd hardly dyed her hair at all, but had instead just added tints to accent her already dark appearance. But when the sun fell against it—when it dazzled that dark crimson wave, made it burn like a black flame—Daniel felt his chest sigh, and became hurt with one brutal realization. She was beautiful. She was absolutely beautiful, and now more than ever did he feel a strong physical attraction toward her, something that was nearly primitive and powerful as simple lust. She was beautiful. For a moment he imagined what it would be like to run his hand through that hair, that soft smooth flame of fire and autumn, and thought it would be softer than gold, sweet and wonderful for the fingers. He glanced at her legs and imagined the denim-tightness that must have come with, the dark blue that wrapped around her calves, her thighs, her waist. Tight. Taut. Skintight. He wondered what she would smell like, and recalled that one moment where they'd stood at the beach together staring out at the waves, her head leaned against his shoulder, her arm locked around his, both their shoes wet, their socks dirty. Had it been strawberries that day? Maybe. Possibly. He recalled all of this, all this and more, and suddenly felt an explosion of sadness fill him, one that took away his fleeting fantasies of lust and desire. Because what he saw then less than ten meters away from him was something false, something that was untrue and unfair, hidden away under a layer of dark flame. What he felt then was pity. He pitied her and was disgusted by her. He felt hate for his disgust, and hated that she would evoke his disgust. What he saw then was a girl who had purposely lined her eyes with mascara to make her eyes look larger, different, more noticeable, prettier, a girl that had gone and changed her *hair* for onlookers to see. She had done something for onlookers to *see*, had transformed her hair, and this, for some reason, saddened Daniel all the more.

This brief feeling of lust and desire—Daniel threw it away now, disgusted. He felt angered too, and in that anger, felt an unfair sense of bitter betrayal.

*Just now,* Daniel thought suddenly, *I had a sudden impulse to want you, Jenny. I wanted to feel your hair and smell your scent, to have you with me and feel you. Just now, you reduced me to instinct, and I thought it was good, but I realized that it wasn't. Because to believe I must be nothing more than mere instinct to lo…to adore you, means to say you don't believe I can be beyond simple appreciation of you in every great sense. You dyed your hair and evoked in me lust, Jenny, not love, and I hate the way you tricked me.*

*Oh, Jenny. What happened? What happened in one year? What did you do in Korea while you were away and I was here all summer?*

The bus lurched forward. Daniel watched as she clumsily slid between two bodies and reached up to hold onto the rail.

*Her hair,* he thought again. *It isn't the color, isn't the slight physical attraction I feel, but the falseness by which she tempts me. Jenny, I liked you so much more when you had no makeup and no dyed color in your hair…when you were simply naked. This is false to me. Just so false. I like it only because it's pretty, never because it's real.*

The 871 merged onto the freeway and sped down south I-5 towards the UW campus.

***

Jenny got off the 871 at 45th NE and University Way. The bus doors closed behind her and blew a brief wave of warmth against her calves. It pulled away with a slow rushing roar that sounded like an automatic hand-dryer in an empty bathroom.

She was on the Ave now. And yes—the Ave had no period. She was on

254

the Ave now, something that was properly called University Way by those who wanted political correctness, and stood in what was perhaps Seattle's finest cultural melting pot part of the UW district. Over 70,000 UW students roamed here in an area stretching eight blocks long before the campus. The Ave ran south cutting through NE 50th St. to 41st St. Overhanging awnings and old-fashioned decorated marquees advertised a vibrant international community on both sides of the street; brightly colored sandwich boards strategically placed on the sidewalks announced exotic foods and homey places to dine. From 50th to 47th, one could choose between Indian cuisine at the Jewel of India or Mexican food at Memo's Mexican. Rudy's Barber Shop was one of three salons that competed in this short section of the Ave. Shear Madness stood alongside Citra Frozen Yogurt across the street from Hair Masters; Hair Masters stood directly across the street and was adjoined with Shinka Tea and Bánh Mì. Tully's Coffee and Bank of America ended the corner of 47th, and from 47th onward to 45th, restaurants such as Costas, Starbucks, WOW Bubble Tea, Continental Greek, Thai Tom, Pagliacci Pizza, Lounjin, Ruzhea Mongolian Grill, and Yunni's Bubble Tea dominated the right side of the road. Parallel to them were clothing shops, shops like the ever-hip, elegant, and very retro Red Light (which had a wonderful proactive feel to it upon hearing the name) that sold not only the hip and retro, but also, pure vintage Victorian and '80s accessories. The Buffalo Exchange (which was, according to their slogan, "Not the usual thrift store!" among such urban sprawl) was a bit farther down past the crosswalk from Pagliacci's; Urban Outfitters (which was just *huge* with its glass display windows and dozen mannequins staring out at the street) was next; and Pitaya (not the fruit, but the little chic boutique that sold the hottest fashion trends for women) was last in line huddled in a white block corner. Where Jenny stood on 45th next to American Apparel and across Bartell's Drugs, the Ave continued southward, and included things like Mee Sum Pastry, Goorin Bros. Hat Shop, Big 5 Sporting Goods, Bombay Jewelers, Sindhu, the University Book Store, Shiga's Import Shop, Nasi's Teriyaki, Crossroads

Trading Co., and Häagen-Dazs ice-cream. A store just a few yards down called the Pink Gorilla sold gaming consoles both new and old for the cheapest prices, and a newly added store just right next to it, Piece of Mind, boasted itself unique and radical with its fluorescent neon sign above the doors. The sign showed off an orange grinning skull with the peace symbol drawn in its gigantic bulbous forehead—as Jenny passed by, she noticed that the shelves were filled with newly ordered bongs.

Indeed this was the Ave: Alive and vibrant, cluttered and messy, always congested with traffickers with passing feet never missing a beat—this was the Ave known to the world. Students roamed, worked, and ate here. Scholars, teachers, philosophers, poets, scientists, researchers, and musicians all did the same while local "Ave Rats" gathered on random street corners in heavily shredded winter coats and dirty woolen beanie caps asking for spare change (most were, according to their wet cardboard signs written in scrawled handwriting, VETERANS of some recent war). Yes, it was true—the Ave had rats. And while Jenny disliked the term, the truth couldn't be denied: The Ave had rats. Even when she'd gotten on the 871 this morning and turned onto the exit ramp from I-5 to 45th, there'd been a man standing on the corner with a Styrofoam cup in his hands wearing a green windbreaker. His face had been red and his cheeks had been cracked; tuffs of yellow hair swayed into his eyes while his hands badly trembled as he desperately held them out towards the street. So, yes, this was the Ave—both its young inhabitants, *and* its rats. And as always, whenever seeing these homeless people, a bitter spike of disgust and pity filled Jenny.

This morning at this moment was not her own, and Jenny supposed this was the reason her footsteps slowed to a dull trudge as she made her way through the Ave. She had denied herself the opportunity to disembark from the 871 near her class this morning because she needed time to think. This moment was not her own and its time not unique, for the celebrated concept of "The Frist Day of School" was realized by millions of other children around the world. And yet—this moment *was* hers and hers alone, for the possibility of life as simply *being* as it is as a linear progression of time with a finite number of hours was solely *hers*. This moment was shared by millions of individuals around her, and yet, they could not share the same feelings with her that weighed against her heart, not physically *be* or *become* her. Those that she encountered in this world were forever separated from her and were only experienced in a parallel fashion: There was no need to offer sympathy for the cold autumn morning when sympathy itself was insincere.

*This is it,* Jenny thought as she made her way past Häagen-Dazs and across 43rd. *This is life now unfolding before me with limitless possibilities. In life, I am abandoned from hope because of my finite nature—but in life, I am left with limitless possibilities by my freedom. No one can share with me their stories or charge me with orders to follow. I am simply one step closer to death today and have all possibilities laid out before me of whom I want to become. These high-school walls have fallen; I am left afraid before the world. I've become one day older.*

It was the dyeing of her hair that evoked these thoughts. She'd traveled with Kate this summer to Korea by the order of her father. It had been an order given stringently and carried out acquiescingly. Jenny understood his intentions were a way of permanently severing familial ties made foul last year by the divorce. Kate had acted as delegate for her father and had regulated the proper procedures for declaring the divorce to her family. Kate had been chosen for a specific reason: Her family was stationed in America. Because of this, she'd been privileged with a sense of immunity from the curses and scorns that came about as a consequence when revealing the divorce papers—her family received no death threats from the Park or Shin family (Jenny's mother's maiden name). There was, of course, no talk of the new mistress that had divided Jenny's family: Kate, always dressed in her professional slacks and blazers, presented herself to each family as a professional lawyer with a superior and dominating quality. To argue against her was to argue against her J.D. in Law and her MBA. It also meant arguing against her green card. She was not the woman who had once had sex with her father on the living room couch when dressed in her business suit—she simply was Katie Chung, a.k.a Chung Kyung-soon.

Her father's plan had involved another ulterior motive: The hopeful reconciliation of daughter and new mistress. Jenny knew about the plan, but did nothing to deter his efforts. When Kate was idle and without work, she'd often take the time to speak with her at their hotel room. Sometimes she even invited her out to expensive places to dine. Jenny was indifferent to her tactics. She cared less about what they ate than did she yearn for a good night's sleep in their room. It was only until their journeying together into a beauty shop did Jenny finally allow her defenses to finally yield.

"What do you think, Jenny?" Kate had asked her. "I think you look beautiful. Really."

Jenny stared at the mirror in front of her. She sat partially leaned back in a chair with the ends of her hair still wet and matted. The hairdresser over her shoulder ooh-ed loudly how beautiful she looked and clapped her hands together. Kate beamed beside her.

*Why don't I like this?*

The thought was faint and cold. To Jenny's ears, it was a voice unlike her own.

*Who is this in the mirror looking at me? Who is she? And why don't I know if I'm beautiful?*

She cried that night. With such heavy thoughts weighed on her mind, Jenny had gotten up from their hotel room bed, gone to the bathroom, and had wept silently on the toilet with her face held in her hands. She'd wept bitterly with a tight feeling of self-hate built in her chest, and had let her tears sear her cheeks. Kate had found her twenty minutes later. She immediately cradled her to her chest and sat there with her on the bathroom floor, comforting her, cooing her, just holding her there and soothing her.

*I don't know if I'm pretty,* Jenny had cried. *I just don't know if I'm pretty or not.*

*Oh Jenny, don't say that. Of course you're pretty, of course you—*

*I don't know who I am. I just don't know what I'm supposed* to be. *I just miss my mom so much.*

Kate held her. Jenny pressed her face against her breasts and moaned something terrible and hurt.

Her hair. It was her hair that Jenny thought of as she made her way from the Ave and to the UW campus. Her hair like this moment was hers and hers alone, and it forced her to recognize this moment no matter how much she tried to deny it. Her hair was representative of the passing of time; it inexorably declared to her that she had grown one day older. And now that Monday had passed and Tuesday was to come, what could she say she had done?

***

Daniel spotted her two hours later on campus walking from Suzzallo Library to Odegaard. She was walking through Red Square where he himself was headed. He spotted her because of her hair. The clouds had disappeared and the sun had prevailed—the light shone on her shoulders like a red liquid flame that was almost like blood.

"Jenny."

She didn't hear him. He quickened his pace and called out again, passing through a crowd of bodies.

"Jenny."

She turned around, sending a flare of red around her shoulders. Daniel raised his hand and then stopped. He thought he'd called out to the wrong girl. A person suddenly rushed up behind her and grabbed her by the waist. He lifted her off her feet and twirled her around, sending another cloud of red around her face. He put her down, twisted her around, and kissed her on her forehead.

Ice water filled Daniel's chest. He stopped for a moment and drew a blank. He began walking again, his mind a jumble of falling words.

*So that's it*, he thought darkly, *that's why she left me, that's why she left me with such a long period of absence. It was because of him, because of him, her new boyfriend, her new lover, her new...friend. Her hair, her makeup, her mascara, her shoes, even the way she walks now—it was all because of* him.

Jenny stared as he made his way over. Her eyes widened and her mouth dropped into a large O. The word *Daniel* crossed her mind, but before she could think any further, strong hands fell on her shoulders again, jarring her from her thoughts.

"Hey!" Another light kiss fell against her forehead. Junghee—the boy that had spun her—gave her a large goofy grin and asked, "What's wrong, sleepyhead? Still asleep this morning?"

"I—"

"Jenny. Hey."

*Crap! Not now Daniel, not now, hi, I'm sorry, I'm sorry, but not now, not when there's two guys in the same place with just one girl, please not now.*

"Daniel," she said, turning to him. "Hey. I mean, h-hi."

He scanned her; Jenny felt it. His eyes dropped down to her legs, and for one absurd moment, she thought he was checking her out, weighing the size of her thighs and judging her bust. But no—he was glancing down at her feet and looking at her Ugg boots. His glanced at her hair.

"Um, Jon, this…this is Daniel. Daniel, this is Jon—" *My boyfriend*, a voice supplemented for her, *this is Jon my* boy*friend.*

Daniel turned his head. He smiled. "Hey," he said pleasantly. "Nice to meet you."

Junghee stuck his hand out. Daniel automatically took it and widened his smile. He squeezed. "Likewise!" Junghee cried happily. "Nice to meet you too."

Junghee pulled his hand back. Daniel held onto it a second longer, squeezed as hard as he could, and let go.

*Tits guy*, Daniel thought suddenly, *I can tell what type of guy he is just by looking at him. He's a tits guy, God Jenny, why are you with him, he's not good for you, he's too shallow for you, he's so beneath you, you—*

Daniel's smile brightened. He gritted his teeth together and balled his fist in his pocket. He turned towards her

260

*(and does he speak in Korean to you too, Jenny? Does he speak with you, flirt with you, joke with you in Korean, and do you laugh with him, do you two have moments together, do you—)*

and asked in a steady voice: "Jenny. Hey. Haven't seen you for a while. How are things?"

"Fine. Yeah, things are fine." She tried to smile for him and found herself running a hand through her hair. "I mean, yeah, it's great to see you again too. Just, you know…first day of college and all."

He nodded. Jenny bit her lip at him. She looked down at his hands and saw longingly as he gripped his notebook against his thigh. The other hand was stuffed in the pocket of his jeans. The image brought a nostalgic ache to her heart.

*Daniel, let me explain, please. It's not what you think, it's—*

"So, you two getting lunch soon?" he asked.

"Yep," Junghee replied, still smiling. He stepped back, reached out from his pocket, and took hold of Jenny's hand. It had been an unconscious gesture, barely deliberate. Daniel noticed. "We were thinking of getting something on campus like at By George, or something down on the Ave. Chipotle or Teriyaki."

"Nice," Daniel said.

"Yep," Junghee replied. He paused. He said, "Hey, it's Daniel, right? I heard from Jenny that you're a pretty good writer."

Daniel laughed. It was a sudden sound. It was loud and hilarious, deep and full, like he'd been kicked in the stomach and was forced to chuckle. "Me? *Good?*" He shook his head at them and said, "I wish. Anyone these days can call themselves writers. The way the writing market is set up in America, you can write about crap and still call yourself great. I just like to read and study literature, that's all."

"Ah. Well…"

They chuckled awkwardly at each other.

"How about you?" Daniel asked, his voice higher than normal. "What are you majoring in? History? Poli-Sci?"

"Business," Junghee answered. "Maybe with a minor psychology, but we'll see. It depends how things get going."

"Ah. Neat." Again that glance, again that distant look. Then: "And you, Jenny? Business too?"

Jenny dropped Junghee's hand and reached to rub the back of her neck. "No," she replied nervously, "I think I'm just going to major in psychology, and that's it."

He nodded. There was the briefest of silences between them, and Daniel quickly turned back to look at Junghee. They smiled.

"Well, it was nice meeting you, Daniel. Jenny's told me a few good things about you. Later in the quarter when we get our schedules finalized, let's get lunch, okay?"

"Sure, no problem. It was cool running into you guys. I'll see you two around. Bye, Jenny."

She'd been staring down at her feet. Now she looked up, surprised, and said, "Oh. Yeah, bye, Daniel. I'll call you up sometime, okay?"

"Sure. No problem."

Junghee took Jenny's hand again and bade him one last smile. They walked cheerfully away.

Daniel, with one hand still stuffed in his pocket and the other one still clutching his notebook, watched quietly as they disappeared off the Square, and turned away.

# CHAPTER 14

Daniel sat in the very back row of the lecture hall. The room before him spread out wide and far like the descending slopes of a dark valley. Professor Vorbieva stood near center stage blocked from view by the lecture podium and spoke with a soft voice that boomed out heavily from the loudspeakers. Behind her was a series of slides that flashed against the large projection screen. Massive gothic windows opened the walls to the southwest—leaden light spilled through. It was a brief light, nothing more than a few splinters of sun that vaguely cut through the dark and splashed onto the floor, but when Daniel saw it, he let out a heavy sigh.

*Why am I here?*

A loud mechanical click echoed from the floor. The projection screen switched to a new slide, and Daniel raised his eyes. Professor Vorbieva's voice boomed again from the speakers. Daniel could hear her but not understand her. She spoke a foreign language that he had no interest in learning, something that had no meaning, and was just a monotone drone part of the background. Laptop monitors reflected the faces of his classmates; *tak-tak-tak-tak* keyboard noises sounded from the dark. Intermittent whispers broke out to the side while seasonal coughs punctured the air.

Daniel no longer brought his notebook to school.

*What am I doing here?*

The student next to him shifted in his seat. Daniel jerked around, sharply, anxiously, waiting for something great to happen. There was nothing. The student simply shifted in his seat, ruffled the seat of his jeans, rubbed the cotton and polyester fabric of his jacket unintentionally together, and bent forward again to scrutinize his handwriting. Daniel peered at him from the side, hoping, wanting, expecting him to raise his eyes at him and frown—to make *contact*.

*I woke up this morning just to bore myself,* Daniel thought dismally. *I woke up this morning in the present with an anticipated vision of the future and of what I wanted to achieve, and now everything has suddenly halted. There is no present now because boredom fills me. My presence and present at this moment have no meaning because I am making nothing of my life at this instant where, paradoxically, I am totally free to choose what I want to do.*

*Look at me, damn you. Show me that you at least are real enough to be spontaneous and random.* Look at me. *Show me you can think for yourself while excluding the will of Hollywood and language. Just* look at me. *Show me you can think without someone speaking for you.*

He deliberated. He thought for a minute, and then raised his arms. He stretched as wide as he could and feigned a massive yawn. His hand rudely nudged his table partner and jolted him from his writing. He turned his head.

"Sorry," Daniel whispered. "Bored."

The student stared at him, blanked several times, and then smirked. "I know," he said quietly. "Right? Boring as fuck."

He went back to his notes. Daniel, sullen, frowned from the side.

*Why do you exist?* Daniel thought coldly. *Now that you are here, now that you are conscious of your being, why do you exist? Do you hunch your shoulders the way you do because everyone else does so also, laugh at what everyone else laughs at because you fear stigmatization? Do you look up the latest gossip in Hollywood because you're so appalled over your own wretched existence, watch the latest Hollywood movies to escape cowardly from your own reality, follow the latest fashion trends because you're so disgusted with yourself, dye your hair because you're afraid of—*

But he stopped himself, unable to go on, not wanting to think of her, hurting that he refused to think of her, *wishing* that he could think of her. Overhead, Vorbeiva's voice droned on and on.

*I don't need to be here. I can choose not to do this.*

He stood up. The unfolding of his jeans when standing caused a loud cascade of noise that drew the brief attention of his classmates. He quietly made his way through a row of seats and eventually found the central aisle leading away from the lecture floor. From the corner of her eye, Vorbeiva took notice of his movements, but said nothing. To her, he was just a shadow in the dark.

***

He walked for an hour through campus. His feet ached by that time, and his ankles throbbed painfully against the sides of his sneakers. He traveled from Gowen Hall and walked across the brick pathways of the Quad. He traveled southeast along Stevens Way where he eventually passed by Paldeford Hall, and then looped back again to the Quad past the Communications Building. He wandered towards Red Square.

This wasn't the first time Daniel had chosen to wander aimlessly through the campus; his trips had become more and more frequent as the school year progressed. Always, whenever strolling across the countless walkways that crisscrossed the grounds, Daniel's hands went deep inside his pockets, and his shoulders depressingly hunched. And always, whenever conscious of his posture—whether meandering through the Quad, drifting through Red Square, or ambling through Memorial Way—he'd think to himself: *My God, look at me. Inundated with feelings of anger and anguish, I've become the thing I most ridiculed and loathed when I was in high-school. I've become a Romantic; I've become a vessel filled with senseless passion whose back is constantly turned away from the world out of bitterness and hate. Just look at me, just look at what I have become. I even have enough sense to rationalize my own self-hate.*

Two months had passed since the beginning of the school year. In that time, Daniel had observed the world around him with a cold lens of anguish and despair. It was the limitless unfolding of everyday as a student that prompted this first mood of anguish. Against the vast backdrop of the university campus, filled with autumnal trees lining the pathways leading to and fro to almost senselessly nowhere and everywhere, there in those moments of gazing at the dark skies overhead seemed to be no limits to freedom. To be a musician, a painter, a writer, a scientist—all these nouns were left for him to define. But each day was limited despite this perpetual freedom; more and more hours piled uselessly together with each senseless morning being spent in lecture halls doing nothing, where an eventual death awaited him at the end of each hour. This burden of freedom was lessened by the nonsensical *prattle* of everyday life—this was the reason for the constant bitterness and anger in his heart.

*We've all changed now*, Daniel sometimes thought when eyeing the leaves near the ground; *we've all become a day older without realizing the passing of these days that constitute our being. We are filled with routine chores of everyday life that prevent us from realizing this change, and only with dismay and startling despair do we ever find it too late in life that this change is always occurring in* us. *These leaves near my feet—I see them with gratitude and despair for I know what they represent; I know their withered surfaces are the wrinkles that eventually become my face. Every day is an irrevocable change that separates us further and further from the past; we all do childish things to prevent us from realizing we are becoming adults. Why have we changed with such cowardice?*

It was his cousin's wedding he thought of then as he quietly made his way back towards Red Square. His cousin had wed this year just one month before school began. The ceremony had been held at Ann Wright School in Tacoma and then later celebrated at the Tacoma Yacht Club. Daniel barely knew his cousin. His cousin was only ten years older than him.

The ceremony had been brief and had lasted less than an hour. It'd taken place in the open courtyard of the school beneath a hot summer sun where Daniel had sat through the entire program wincing against the light and fanning himself with the wedding program. He wasn't the only one suffering from the heat; others too had languished under the sun with sweat dripping from their faces. The reception that followed had been with less travail. The yacht club they had attended afterwards had offered music, dance, drinking, food, and a private cocktail party for singles upstairs. White cloth-covered tables had been set up to accommodate guests and families, while music and flashing lights surrounded the dance floor in the center of the room.

Daniel had sat with his family throughout the evening reticent and calm. His only move towards the dance floor had been to collect whatever was offered at the buffet table and slowly walk back. Even his father with his new deluxe Nikon digital camera seemed bored with a wary eye cast toward the guests, and his mother and little sister had only dutifully gone out on the dance floor when invited.

*All of us here are participating in a farce,* Daniel thought quietly as he stared at the dance floor. His sister and mother were dancing in the corner. Ear-splitting booms exploded from the speakers. *This ceremony is no greater than involving one's self in a particular spectacle where masks and costumes are used to adorn the occasion. A sporting event; a movie theater. So many of us here would have never gotten together were it not for this wedding, and so, no one here can say that they actually authentically love one another without providing an excuse for their absence. We all laugh together, drink together, dance together, maybe even hug and kiss each other, but all of this is just for an occasion and for a moment—never for a sincerity that transcends time. You are all my cousins, but I barely know you. How then can you say you love me? Why then do you laugh for my sake?*

Daniel stared at his cousin. With some dismay, he realized he'd forgotten his name.

*My congratulations to you are not void, cousin. Truly I am happy for you, and truly I am envious of you. But I don't need this elaborate showcase; I don't need this parody of love, this moment of the spectacle. My congratulations to you are the same congratulations I would offer a stranger where I would give them my kindhearted handshake and a warm smile; you thus are no better than a stranger to me. You need not this excess from me, need not the lights or this elaborate ceremony.*

Daniel paused. He watched somberly as his cousin leaned over and kissed

267

his new bride on the lips. Cheers and laughs followed. A frown went across Daniel's face.

*You don't need me to dress in a suit to tell you how lucky you are. You don't need me drunk to tell you how much I admire you, how envious I am of your happiness. Cousin…you don't need my name, and I don't need yours. It's possible to love all strangers like you if the heart is strong enough. Everything in this moment is just a farce. Why should the heart be so biased to cheer?*

These leaves cluttering the walkway of the UW campus…they were akin to what Daniel felt when observing his cousin's wedding. They represented a theme of concealment: Dancing and wine helped disguise an outcome that was to befall every individual attending the wedding. And that outcome was this: weariness. That every member of his family had cordially greeted each other simply for the occasion rather than sincerity helped justify this thought. The wedding had marked a joyous occasion for memory to recall simply because thoughts in the present were overburdened with existences made to be endured—the wedding had become an excuse to sigh and a moment to breathe; it had been an opportunity to turn away momentarily from life.

Daniel knew with his heart that those who attended the wedding with gay cheer would later wake in life groggery and miserable before going to work; he knew that those who danced that night would curse and scorn, hate and hurt, and find unhappiness with something trivial in their lives. Bills would be paid with disgust; children would be raised with sighs; work would be approached with loathing. In order to combat this brutal existence of unhappiness and forlornness, they threw themselves into falsehood and lies. One looked to Batman to compensate the troubles of reality; one went to the theater to escape the world. One watched television and saw faces that were handsomer than them, prettier than them, heard stories filled with greater misfortune than them, and looked to models and fashion to compensate for the perceived ugliness in them. One went to weddings out of obligation and farce.

He hurt not being able to shake his cousin's hand.

The second theme—the theme relating to his sense of despair—came from an understanding that a moment had passed. It was a moment not casually defined as *passed* or of the *past*, but a moment that had marked the passing of *being*. The wedding had represented a physical unfolding of time. A day had passed; he'd become one day older and was now one step closer toward death. A day in passing was a thing neglected by most individuals through instilled notions of culture and language, but Daniel had seen these social codes momentarily broken at the wedding. How was he supposed to life live now?

*There is a third aspect to all of this,* Daniel thought as he made his way through the Square. *It's because of Jenny; it's because of her. It simply declares to me that the past has passed, and that no amount of yearning can ever reconcile my feelings for what I once adored. Everyone around me has changed. We are no longer in high-school; old friendships have simply diminished. And it hurts. It hurts so much.*

*Why did you dye your hair, Jenny?*

The last thought came out of nowhere, causing Daniel's arms to break into gooseflesh. He sucked in his breath and raised his head, realizing that he'd been pacing at a quick rate that had excited his heart. Cold layers of sweat formed on the back of his neck. He recalled all the things they'd done together in the past, the moments they'd shared, the brief episodes of love they'd expressed. And had it been love? If not love, then what else? He remembered how she held him over the news of Kooper's death. He remembered how she smiled during Winter Ball and Prom. He—

—tripped over a dislodged brick on the ground and jerked his hands out of his pocket for balance.

His feet tangled together; he tittered. The world skewed on its side for a heart-pounding second, and Daniel finally found his balance again, his face flush, his cheeks hot. Adrenaline rushed through his veins.

"Nice trip, Fischer!"

Daniel spun around. A large student in brown khaki shorts made his way over and smirked. Daniel frowned. An inward sigh escaped him.

Bill. Bill Bukowski. *Fat* Bill Bukowski. It was Fat Bill that had called out behind him. Fat Bill and his overweight protruding gut hanging sloppily over the waist of his khakis, Fat Bill and his contemptuous manner, Fat Bill and his faded dark blue t-shirt and his lolling rolls of fat under his arms, sagging breasts on his chest, inflated double-chins on his neck. It was Fat Bill that had spoken, Fat Bill and his reddish peppered dimples, his cowlick brown hair, his unshaven sideburns, his small, beady eyes, eyes that constantly regarded Daniel with a hated leer and a wanton smirk on his face.

Fat Bill.

Bill was enrolled in his ENG HONORS 282: Short-Story Writing class. The class was taught by Clara Inwood. The class was, Daniel thought balefully, a typical writing class built on liberal grounds of spectacular stupidity and typical infantile escapist tendencies. Inwood's class operated like this: There for fifteen minutes or so every morning was an exercise placed on the board related to last night's readings. Students would complete the exercise in the given time and be allowed an opportunity to share what they'd written. Because everyone seemed "so very funny" and "was so very clever," according to Inwood, morning exercises were always accompanied by morning giggles (Daniel never giggled). A summarization of last night's readings would then commence where any slight observations, questions, or surprises were dutifully noted and observed (Daniel never asked questions). Afterwards, Inwood would order them to open their course packet (a packet Daniel had refused to buy at the Ave Copy Center) and briefly read to them the two or three short stories provided for the day. The class finally concluded with Inwood writing to them on the board which pages to read for tonight's homework, and wishing them all a wonderful morning (Daniel's mornings were never wonderful).

*An exercise in snobbery and a showcase of typical infantilism,* Daniel once thought as he stared at his instructor writing on the blackboard. *Our efforts made here are used only to pamper our professor's egotism by apathetically agreeing to her shallow standards where we inadvertently compliment her as a capable instructor so that we may find basic joy in ourselves when receiving high marks on our assignments. We do nothing to*

*raise the standard of intellectual caliber in this class.*

His peers did not share his discouragement. There instead seemed only to be a high level of revelry in which they enjoyed, and of which Daniel simply thought was a celebration of mediocrity—hate swirled through him like black surging whirlpools whenever in their company. Workshop Wednesdays were not used to properly critique each other's writing, but instead used to promote idiotic moments of banter and idle wit.

"Why did the pilot leave work today?" his peers would ask; "Oh, because he had the flew." And, "Why are celebrities always so cool? Because they have a lot of fans." And, "What do you call an obese alien from another world? An extra-cholesterol."

*I came here to learn, goddamn it,* Daniel sometimes thought when hearing the high-laughing squeals of his classmates, *not to be with a bunch of children. Has our culture fallen that much since entering the twenty-first century? Can anyone around me read or write intelligently without referring to Wikipedia or typing L-O-L on their cellphones anymore? Christ. This is a culture of vampires and transforming robots.*

His clash with Bill had occurred during Workshop Wednesday. ENG HONORS 282 required that four students every week were to submit their works on Blackboard online to be later downloaded and critiqued by the class. Each student then printed out a copy to bring to class. Submitted manuscripts were meant to be simple short stories of no more than fifteen to twenty pages.

One student had asked if the pages needed to be numbered—Daniel had sighed. Another student had asked if they needed a cover page, and Daniel had brought his hand up to rub his face, massaging the ache in his temple. His story had been about a young Marxist radical who becomes deluded at the corruption of American culture and the governmental system. The student attempts to incite a riot at his university and is soon killed by the police. His diary is later found with an entry predicting his death. It is finally revealed at the end of the story that the student is/was actually a second-generation Muslim-American girl having suffered religious, cultural, and familial prejudices. The story ends abruptly with the protagonist's ethnicity never being discussed and left open to interpretation.

A girl in his class had written about breaking up with her boyfriend; another student had written about his pet hamster named Max. Bill had written about a boy who wakes up in bed and becomes a rat.

"Such a funny and clever story, Bill," Inwood had commented. They sat together in a circle with their desks pushed together. It was the common formation required for Workshop Wednesdays. "It's quite radically different from what most people might expect when reading."

"Thank you, Professor Inwood," Bill said. He beamed at her, his lips split wide and fat across his face. "I take great care of my work. I'm very interested in literature, and try my best to produce the highest quality of writing."

A girl near Daniel's side rolled her eyes. "Suckass," she muttered. Daniel agreed.

"Ah, well yes, this story is quite fascinating," Inwood continued. "I think the philosophical depth of it is quite amazing. Don't you all agree?"

Obedient heads nodded. Daniel frowned at his peers and glanced at the girl to his side. She too had nodded, and now peered down at the papers in front of her.

Daniel frowned. He turned back to Bill's story and thought: *Come on. You've got to be kidding me. Is everyone* serious?

"I like how the family completely ignores George in the end and just leaves him there while they go on their vacation," Inwood said in a high, airy voice. Daniel always thought of a dentist's drill whenever hearing her voice. "How cruel of them! It's a commentary on child neglect, isn't it?"

"Why, sure!" Bill cried. "I was thinking about that too, Professor Inwood. I wanted to show how some parents actually neglect their children instead of loving them, and used George's condition as a way to…"

Daniel flipped through Bill's story. He again thought, *Is everyone serious?*

and felt a steady pulse of dismay and anger quicken his heartbeat. *Why is no one saying anything?*

He waited. He raised his hand.

"…the commentary on the parents, and—oh? Yes, Daniel? Do you have something to say?"

Daniel licked his lips together. He said: "I think Bill's story is reminiscent of Kafka's *The Metamorphosis*. The basic premises are the same where the main protagonist wakes up to find himself transformed into a large creature. The protagonist is unable to change his situation in life, and later just dies. Kafka called his main character Gregor Samsa while Bill calls his character George Suma. The two stories are comparable."

Silence filled the room. Daniel saw astonished eyes widen in his direction. Those that had idly stared at nothing now gave him their venerable—if not frightened—attention.

A livid expression filled Bill's face across the room. His lips pressed together and a threatening glare cut through his eyes. Daniel frowned. He said: "I mean, the character in Kafka's work is a traveling salesman; the character in Bill's story is said to be a newspaper boy. This just suggests to me a great simil—"

"I DIDN'T PLAGIARIZE!"

The two girls next to Bill jerked in their seats. Inwood's head snapped to the side and a burst of red flushed through her face. Every head in the room turned in Bill's direction and then quickly turned away again, embarrassed, some with skepticism, others, with revolted looks. Girls turned away in wary disgust and managed to find something under their nails to ponder.

Daniel's heart picked up in his chest. He frowned at Bill.

"If you're accusing me of plagiarizing, Fischer, then prove it! I wrote this story Saturday late at night, so if you're—"

"Bill, please calm down," Inwood said. A tremble of fear escaped her voice. "I'm sure Daniel didn't mean—"

"Even your opening sentence is reminiscent of Kafka," Daniel said. He picked up Bill's paper and read: "'George Suma one morning woke from uneasy dreams and found himself transformed in bed into a giant vermin.' This is one of the most legendary opening lines in all of Western literature, and it is derived from *The Metamorphosis.*"

Bill's lips sucked back into his mouth. Apple-red flared across his cheeks and his hands clasped together on the table. He seemed to be painfully digesting his tongue and holding back an agonized moan. To Daniel, the man looked horribly constipated.

*Jesus, Bill, calm the fuck down. I'm making an assertion against you that you have every right of refuting while still saving face. You can explain yourself if you'd stop fucking shouting.*

"There are *innumerable* translations of Kafka's work, Fischer," Bill spat. "And not all of them are written the same."

"Yes, you're right," Daniel replied. "They're not. Willa and Edwin Muir use 'gigantic insect' to describe Gregor's transformation, whereas J.A. Underwood uses the term 'giant bug.' Stanely Appelbaum uses 'enormous bug,' Joachim Neugroschel uses 'monstrous vermin,' and M.A. Roberts uses 'gargantuan pest.' The reason they do this is because the original German word *ungeheuren* carries no equivalent connotation in the English language that can mean 'large' and 'horrifying' simultaneously. In that regard, Roberts is most inaccurate in his translation, because 'pest' in English connotes—"

He stopped himself. He glanced at his peers. Blank, dull, and empty faces gawked his way. Even Inwood had her head cocked to the side with an intrigued expression on her face.

"What I mean," Daniel said, "is that you're right to say Kafka has numerous translations. But you're also wrong to accuse me for saying that you plagiarized. I never used that word. I just said that your story was uniquely similar to Kafka's—that's all. The opening line is very similar, and the plot, ending, and symbolic themes are just reminiscent of Kafka."

"Yeah, well, you were *trying* to accuse me, weren't you?" Bill snapped.

Daniel stared at him. His eyes narrowed in disbelief towards Bill.

*Jesus Christ Bill, come on. I'm trying to save you face here, all right? Christ.*

The confrontation had ended with Inwood calling a timid truce. She had announced rather joyously (and briskly) that Bill was an "intelligent, and smart writer," that Daniel was "well-versed and smart himself," and that, "we should move along now."

The occasion since then had provided Bill an unnecessary excuse for hate and rage. The stories that followed the next several weeks had been ones very familiar: Always, Bill had a character in his stories that was named either Daniel or Dan, and had him always suffer a horrible and depressing death. The protagonist was always with brown hair and eyes, a tall build, a stoic gaze, and a distinctive habit of always sitting slouched backwards in his chair whenever bored.

Daniel had sighed when reading the stories. Clara Inwood had only nodded and given praise.

Bill made his way over. As he walked, uneven globs of fat rolled through his body. Sandals peeled from the back of his feet and clapped his heels. He wore his trademark blue t-shirt and brown khaki pants despite the autumn cold, and carried with him a spiral notebook against the meaty part of his thigh. Daniel frowned when seeing the notebook. Something about it was familiar and old. Nostalgic.

"Bill," Daniel said dully. "Hey."

"Getting a bit clumsy these days," Bill said derisively. "You all right, Fischer?"

"Fine."

"Of course you are. You're Daniel Fischer, the invincible writer from Seattle! Nothing fazes you, does it?"

Daniel relaxed his fists in his pockets. He stared at him, and thought: *Is that it, Bill? Jealousy? It's jealousy causing you to act like an unwarranted prick toward me? If you want, I can loan you all the books I've read, recommend to you the teachers I had, and tell you openly what knowledge I still lack in certain areas. But it won't ever get me a friend, Bill. It just won't ever get me a friend.*

"What do you want, Bill?" Daniel asked, tiredly.

"Want? Nothing! Jeez, Fischer, can't a fellow colleague just say hello anymore? You act as if I were out to get you!"

Daniel said nothing. He glanced down at his thighs again and thought of Jenny when seeing the notebook. Thinking of her hurt. He thought of her during Prom last year when they were still in IB. He thought back to when they were still speaking to each another, when Kooper was still alive, and—

—oh, but it hurt to think about Kooper.

"Written anything brilliant lately, Fischer?" Bill asked with a tight smile. "Come up yet with the greatest American novel?"

"No, Bill," Daniel said dully. "I was just making my way to By George for lunch."

"Hey, that's cool! I was making my way there too."

Daniel stared at him. Bill leered back.

With a sigh, Daniel said, "Fine, Bill. Whatever. I'll see you in class tomorrow," and walked away. He headed east towards the stairs between Kane Hall and Odegaard Library, *away* from By George Café and off Red Square.

"Fischer, where are you going! I thought we were going to have lunch together!"

Daniel ignored him. Bill's voice rang dull and empty in his ears, reminding him of ghosts on the sidewalk.

"Let's have lunch, *Daniel!* What do you say? You're not too smart to have lunch with another human being, are you? Do you think you're too good to have lunch with me!"

Daniel raised his hand over his head, signaling an apathetic wave of goodbye. He climbed the stairs out of Red Square and traveled through Memorial Way until he was in front of the half-completed façade of Paccar Hall. He boarded the 871 when it arrived and sat down with a tired grunt. He was still hungry.

# CHAPTER 15

*Jenny stared at the computer screen in front of her. Her eyes widened.*

No, *she thought.* This can't be right. This just can't be right.

*She tapped out of the screen and retyped his name. She typed in* Daniel Fischer *and the words* current address Seattle *in the search engine. She hit* ENTER, *and waited.*

It's true, *she thought after a moment.* It's really true. He still lives in Seattle. After all these years, he still lives in Seattle.

*The webpage she opened was an article retrieved from* The Seattle Times. *The article was brief, and was titled:* "Daniel Fischer Finds Luxury Nest in Seattle." *The article read:*

Local Seattle writer and intellectual Daniel Fischer buys the last condominium unit at the famed Empyrean Tower for a hefty 1.5 million dollars. The condo, actually marketed as a 'luxury penthouse,' is one of four condo units at the E.T. that has private roof terrace access. Not only that, but the unit also offers a personal viewing balcony that encompasses all of Elliott Bay to the west, as well as all of the wonderful sights and sounds of downtown Seattle to the east and south. It's enough to make any Seattleite green with envy.

*Jenny scrolled to the bottom of the article. The article was written in 2016. That was only three years ago.*

Maybe, *Jenny thought thinly.* Just maybe. If all of this information is correct, then…just maybe.

*She did a search for the* Empyrean Tower. *The tower was located on 2ⁿᵈ Avenue between Pine and Pike. It was built like a giant glass skyscraper and acted as a high-rise condominium that dominated the skyline of downtown Seattle. Elliott Bay bordered it to the west, Pike Place Market was just at its feet, and the Seattle Art Museum and Benaroya Hall were just at its doorstep. The tower was over seventy stories tall.*

Pike and Pine, *Jenny thought.* God, that sounds so familiar. Could he be that close? Could he really just be a few blocks away?

*She did another search and this time pinpointed the E.T.'s location.*

*She was in The Deadbeat Gecko Lounge now; she was in Seattle. The Greyhound had dropped her off two hours ago, and now the sky was dark with rain outside. She'd found the Gecko after a few minutes of wandering.*

*The Empyrean Tower was just eight blocks away.*

If he's really here, *Jenny thought, studying the web map in front of her,* if he's really just on Pine and Pike, then I can skip the thought of finding a hotel for the night. I can just find him. I can just walk from Stewart, find Olive Way, and find him. I can see him tonight.

*The thought brought butterflies to her stomach. She touched the screen, logged off, and gathered her jacket. Her stomach rumbled as she stood. She hadn't eaten anything yet. She hadn't eaten for the entire day.*

Later, *Jenny thought.* When I find him, when I know he's here. I'll sleep and eat later. Just…later.

*She shrugged on her jacket and walked back into the rain.*

# CHAPTER 16

Jenny stepped off the 871 and stared upward at the sky. Snowflakes clung to her hair like nuclear ash adrift with the wind. She listened somberly as the 871 sped away, and felt a brief pocket of air hit her from behind.

She moved from Paccar Hall and ambled through Memorial Way. Tall naked sycamores dominated the sides of the road as frozen leaves piled the walkway. She shivered as she walked past. The ground beneath her feet was frozen. It felt like walking barefoot over a graveyard of bones.

Junghee waited for her at Thomson Hall. He was in the process of completing his finals for the quarter and had requested that she be there with him as he finished. Jenny, on the other hand, didn't want to be here. She in fact had *no reason* to be here. She'd finished all her finals a day early and was already on her winter break. Junghee's call last night asking her to meet him had just pissed her off even more, where his eventual high, shrilly voice had forced her to cringe with embarrassment and exhausted hate.

"Aw, come *on*, Jenny! It'll be fun! We're just gonna go to Shultzy's and have a few burgers with friends. Besides, we need to celebrate the end of the quarter!"

She'd sighed. She'd grudgingly acquiesced and had grumbled "Fine, Junghee" before closing her cellphone. It was that high whiny voice that had finally forced her to yield; she couldn't stand it when his voice took on that high, girly quality. She just felt so embarrassed for him whenever he used it.

Jungee. Park "Jon" Junghee. In thinking of his name, Jenny realized just how much had changed in the past year. The thought of these changes

279

weighed heavily against her like a giant boulder whenever she allowed them to take hold in her mind. Things had changed; life had transitioned. These irrevocable changes to life were apparent whenever Jenny found herself staring at the reddish-brown tint that was her hair, whenever she noticed the blood-red sheets that were her bangs, and whenever she recognized the newly applied eyeliner that shaped her gaze. The limitless possibilities of life were now open before her, and this, Jenny supposed, was what frightened her the most—she had made these changes to her appearance and hair, and now she had to live with the consequences. Who then could she blame for her freewill?

It was the nature of two individuals *being* together that fascinated her the most, perhaps, even, saddened her. With dismay, Jenny realized that those in love (or, at least, those considering love) could never fully recognize each other, for the past was always a concept foreign and other-worldly to both partners in love. No lover could ever appreciate their partner fully when the past was always reiterated with just words. To recall facts, to explain past events, to detail moments of personal history—these were nothing but sounds to be accepted as facts through blind faith.

Last week, Jenny had asked Junghee what his most memorable game had been when he'd played basketball for his high-school team. He said it was when he broke his leg during a badly timed layup.

"You broke your *leg?*" Jenny gasped. "*How?*"

"Got a bit too aggressive with what I was doing," Junghee said, shrugging his shoulders. "I ran up and crashed into the other team. I stuck my leg out as I fell, heard it crack, and then felt three other players stomp on it as they landed on top of me. It hurt big time."

Jenny winced. She looked down at his leg and tried to picture the bone inside suddenly cracking. She shuddered.

She realized later that night that she'd accepted his story with full authenticity. It wasn't the quality of his character or the trustworthiness of his words that had bothered her, but rather, the inarguable fact that she could never *physically verify* the event. It was possible to speak with friends and other witnesses to confirm the account, to seek medical records, to observe if whether or not his left leg moved with an uneven gait whenever he walked—but none of these could ever authentically verify the actual *happening* of the event as a moment to be witnessed as *in-being* as a person to herself. She could not fully realize him as a person, a body, an entity. Like the friend who could only *offer* feelings of sympathy upon hearing the words "My father has just passed away," so too was there always a void between two new lovers when speaking of the past. Empathy did not bridge this void. Just as it was not *her* leg that had broken, so too was it not the *friend's* father that had passed away. Empathy and sympathy were just empty words; each individual had moments in life that could never be experienced with another. Death was one of these experiences.

*And who*, her mind said to her, *has been there for you in the past that has created good memories for you? Who was once your friend, the person that had been closest to you in sharing your past?*

Jenny shuddered. She ignored the voice and wrapped her arms around herself. She quickened her footsteps and lowered her face from the snow.

She made it to Thomson and strolled up the small flight of steps that led to the doors. She opened the doors, felt warm air hit her in the face, and entered. Warm blood returned to her cheeks.

Daniel. He would be home at this moment. He would be home at this moment sleeping in bed, or perhaps he was just now waking up. A painful ache came to her chest when thinking about him, and Jenny released a sudden, unexpected sigh. She took an empty seat in the hallway and waited, cupping her face in her hands.

Daniel. It had been so long since she last spoke with him. Just so, so long. In realizing this, the ache in her chest tightened, and Jenny brought another hand up to wipe her nose. There was no excuse for the silence that had occurred between them; she was the one who had alienated herself from him. She had made it so that communication between them was nothing but an awkward moment, a farce, something to be cautious of and continuously avoided. Jenny hated it with all her heart, and wished there was some way to reconcile all that had happened. The way he'd spoken with her that one afternoon last month, the way he'd spoken about Kooper's death and turned away from her silent and hurt…these were all things Jenny just now yearned for.

*You dyed your hair,* he had said to her; *you dyed your hair.*

The doors to the lecture hall opened.

"Jenny! Hey!"

She raised her head. "Hey," she said. Her voice rose to a girly chirp. "How'd it go?"

"Perfect," Junghee said. He beamed at her. "I knew this gender-studies class was going to be an easy elective. Four hour study-session my butt!"

Jenny smiled at him (tried to, at least), and took his arm. She waited until the rest of the hall was empty of students, and asked: "Ready to go?"

"Sure, sure. In a minute. We're gonna head over to Benson and meet Eugene and Andrew. Okay?"

She frowned at him. She waited for him to say more, and then said: "*What?* We're not all going to meet at Shultzy's?"

"Oh, we will be. We just have to wait a bit before they finish. You know how it is. It should just be another hour."

Jenny stared at him. A hot flash of red rose to her cheeks. "What are we supposed to do in the next *hour?*" she cried. "I thought we were all just going to meet on the Ave!"

"We are. They should be done soon. Besides, Eugene is smart." He gave her a kiss on the forehead. "Don't think too much about it, okay?"

"Fine," Jenny said. She pulled her arm away. "That's just fine."

Junghee blinked at her. He watched as she took several steps and then reached out to take her by the sleeve. "Whoa," he said suddenly, "hold on. Why are you angry right now?"

*I am NOT ang—*

"I'm *not angry*," Jenny said. She brushed his hand off. "I just woke up this morning tired and looking like crap, all right? It's cold this morning, I haven't eaten yet, and I almost missed the bus. *Okay?*"

"Okay," Junghee mumbled. His voice had grown timid. Scared. "Okay. Sure. Whatever you say." He cautiously drew back. He hesitated, studied her face, and moved in to give her a kiss on the forehead. "Well," he said again, "you look pretty now. In fact, you're the prettiest girl on this campus, Jenny. You know that, right?"

Jenny sighed. She let his arm slither around her neck and obediently leaned in against him. She kept her face turned.

"We can go to Shultzy's first if you want," Junghee said slowly. "We don't need to wait for them."

"No, it's fine. Let's just go to Benson. Let's just *go*."

Junghee kissed her on the forehead again and opened the doors.

***

It was death that Jenny supposed was the most foreign concept of all human things. In death, Jenny thought, individuals truly faced themselves as they were before their final moment of obliteration. Death was a personal experience that could never be related, never retold, and never relieved. And yet, paradoxically, death was a theme every individual had to live with. Death was inescapable, but through everyday activities was a theme that was avoidable. Death was absolutely final for the individual, and no one else.

These thoughts passed swiftly through her mind as she walked with Junghee through the snow. She thought these things because she thought of Daniel. In thinking of him, she recalled their time together a few months ago in autumn quarter. It had been the first and only time they'd met since college began—the thought of their infrequency hurt her.

Steven Kooper had been killed in a car accident. This Daniel had told her with redness in his eyes and a break in his voice. The accident had involved a drunk driver and an incomplete text message on a mobile phone. The drunk driver had been identified as Robert Jones. The mobile phone had belonged to Timothy Rochester, the driver of Kooper's vehicle.

"Timothy was driving and texting when Jones crashed into them," Daniel told her. His gaze avoided hers as he spoke. They sat at The 8 lounge, a dining area beneath McMahon Hall that had windows opened towards the east overlooking Lake Washington. Gray clouds filled the sky that day. Light rain fell against the windows. "Jones was drunk; Timothy was distracted. Kooper was on the passenger side with his seatbelt on."

Jenny observed him somberly from across the table. His Adam's apple bobbed up and down whenever he spoke, and he constantly swallowed. Jenny knew his throat (and heart) hurt.

"Was Kooper drunk too?" she asked.

"No. He was clean. He was just there for the ride. He was just…just there in Timothy's car in the passenger seat when Jones came alone and crashed into them. There was no alcohol in his blood."

The last part was said with quiet ambivalence. Jenny waited, knowing that he had more to say.

"Where you two close?" she asked quietly. Rainwater beat the windows next to them.

"No. I don't…no." He swallowed. "Every time I think of him, I think back to the moment in high-school when he approached me for the first time in the library asking help on physics. When I saw him, I thought…I felt sorry for him, Jenny. I looked at his height, looked at his varsity jacket, the way he wore his jeans, the way he looked at me, and just felt *sorry* for him."

His voice cracked. "Daniel…"

"I saw the way he looked at me, and knew that he was scared. Of *me*. In that moment of fear, I realized that he had nothing, and knew that he knew this too. His strength, his reputation, his ability to command those around him in the hallways, his status as a jock, his ability to get any girl he wanted…all of this meant nothing to him when he looked to me for help. *He* realized this; *I* realized this. In those few seconds where he hesitated asking for my name, he became subordinate to me, and he knew that this would be his lifelong status. He—"

Another sharp hitch interrupted his voice. Jenny watched, pained, and noticed as he turned away again with another effort to swallow. His Adam's apple vigorously bounced up and down. A warm sensation began in her eyes.

"He always used to say to me I would go far in life while he'd just burn out," Daniel said. "He used to hug me every time he got an A or B on his tests, and always used to call me his lifesaver. He…he gave me the name Captain and spread it all over school. One time he even called me at night after a football game, and I could barely hear him, just that he was thankful, just so *thankful*, that he was *so happy* he hadn't gotten cut from the team, that everyone else on his team had just been so *happy* that they won that night…"

Jenny turned away, her throat hurting, her eyes burning. She brought a hand up to wipe her eyes and released a low sniffle. She didn't know who she was crying for. She didn't care. Tears collected in Daniel's eyes.

"He introduced me to his mother at graduation," Daniel said. "He took me over to meet her after everyone had gotten their diplomas and just…just introduced me to her, like a boy introducing a girl to his family. And she hugged me, she just kissed me on the cheek, and just cried against my neck. She hugged me so tight that I couldn't breathe, and she started crying so loud that I was almost embarrassed for her, but she didn't care, she just kept on saying to me 'Thank you, thank you, thank you so much for saving my Steven, thank you so much for letting him be the first Kooper ever to get into college.'

"I just held her back as best as I could and told her it was nothing, that Kooper did it all by himself, and then over her shoulder I saw Kooper crying, I saw *Steven* crying, and I told myself, 'Please, God, no matter what, at least let him succeed, if there's anyone here that deserves to succeed and be happy, please let it be him. Don't let him upset his mom, don't let him hurt her, let me do right in life and let him *succeed*.'"

"Daniel—"

"His mom wanted him to be a doctor. When I heard this I felt so hurt, and when Kooper heard this, I knew he felt hurt too, but I told her I would help him. With everything I could afford to do, I would help. But I didn't; I just didn't. And after we entered college, he just faded away, and I never heard from him again. I just…I just remember thinking to myself how pathetic he was with his varsity jacket in school, and thinking to myself how much I pitied him. That's all. That's all I ever think when I think about him."

Daniel swallowed again. He reached into his pocket and placed something on the table. It was the front page of *The Seattle Times*. A murky photo showing vehicles and police cruisers on a street corner dominated the page. Orange flares surrounded two heavily damaged vehicles. The vehicles had smashed into each other so hard that their twisted, wrecked metal bodies were pushed onto the sidewalk with a long trail of broken glass in their wake. One of the vehicles—a red Mazda, Jenny thought—had its passenger door folded inward and its sides thrust outward. A brown Nissan sedan sat a few meters away with its front crushed. Its windshield had collapsed.

"Oh, Daniel. I'm sorry. I'm so sorry."

"This is him now," Daniel said, taking the page away from her. He coughed again and briefly turned to the side.

*This is how men like him cry,* Jenny thought quietly. *This is how they try so hard to act so brave when all they want is comfort. Oh, Daniel.*

"This is Kooper. This is who he is. This is how we have to accept him. With fact; with reality. He isn't someone we can talk to now, and is just someone permanently part of our past. He has no future with us; he's just dead."

His hand squeezed into a fist on the table, and Jenny stared at it, unsure, hesitating. She gently reached out and took it. She squeezed.

"I'm so sorry, Daniel," she said again. "Please don't cry. Just…don't. There…there was nothing you could do. Just please don't be sad anymore."

He regarded her with a somber look; he withdrew his hand. Jenny let him, feeling his retreat from her like the withdrawing of a son from his mother. Cold hurt filled her.

"I've been thinking about the changes that occur in people as time progresses," he began. "I've been thinking about how so many of us change when we enter the world of college, how time just seemingly transforms everyone so easily and casually that it almost seems invisible. I think about the past and of our previous selves; I fall into despair knowing how easily things change and are taken for granted. The friendships we once had, the friends we once knew, the gossips, the rumors, the jokes—all of these were for nothing, and all that we tried to achieve in the past was for nothing. Time and culture changes us into things we are not. They mold us into clichés; they make us follow rules."

Jenny bit her lip. She watched as his eyes traced her, and realized with horror that he was scanning the dark tints of her hair. She looked away, ashamed, and tried to think of something to say. She found nothing.

"So many of us have dreams and wants when we're growing up," he said. "So many of us try to pursue these dreams, but when we become older, when we are grown, we become afraid, turn away from our freedoms, and instead take easy delight in the casual and idle. What happened to the loves and friendships we once fostered and sheltered during our youth? We talk; we prattle. We listen to gossip and let gossip overtake us. We become sensationalist; we live for the spectacle. We sleep around, *fuck* around, fuck with teachers, fuck with students, watch Batman and Spider-Man save the world—but all for what? Once idle talk is gone, what have we done? Once we strip naked, once we remove our clothes, wash off our makeup, once we die, what value do we have for designer clothes? Batman saves the world, but once we leave the theater, where is he in the real world? Why did we pay money to watch him, why did we flee from reality and for two hours to become cowards? How does entertainment benefit us if it's not real?" He paused. "Why didn't Batman save Kooper?"

Tears filled Jenny's eyes. His words were heavy hammer blows to her heart, pounding and relentless, merciless. She wanted to face him but could not, wanted to speak to him, but could not. She could only lower her face from him and feel his eyes on top of her, eyes that peered deep into her heart. *I have nothing to say and nothing to offer,* Jenny thought. *Ah, God, I have nothing to say, nothing to comment on. Have things really gotten this way? There's just so much hurt in his voice, so much anger, and the way he stares at me…please God, I'm sorry, but please let him be my friend again. I can't stand seeing him so hurt; I just can't stand not being able to comfort him.*

"Daniel."

"Yes."

"Stand with me."

He stared at her. "What?"

"Just…just please. Stand with me."

She got up. Daniel eyed her, questioning, and watched as she stood before him.

"Jenny—"

"*Please,*" she said. A sniffle broke through her voice. "Just stand with me. I don't know what else to do."

He got up and slowly stood next to her. "What—"

She held him.

Daniel stiffened. Jenny felt him pull away, but held him tighter, refusing to let go. His body tensed and his arms tried to pry her off—she resisted. He relented. He wrapped his arms around her and took her gently from behind. A sob broke from his mouth.

"I'm so sorry, Daniel," Jenny whispered. "I'm just so sorry for everything. Just…everything."

He squeezed her. His arms hugged her waist and he immersed himself deep into her hair.

"You dyed your hair, Jenny," he whispered.

"Yes."

"Do you like it?"

She said nothing. She simply held him and cried against his shoulder.

Daniel held her and felt the soft touch of her tiny breasts. Against his body, Jenny felt something hard and strong nudge against her lower stomach.

They held each other.

*\*\**

Shultzy's (also known as Shultzy's Sausage) was an Irish pub. Or at least, that's what Jenny supposed it was, but she wasn't certain. Perhaps it was German. They also said they were a bar and grill, but she wasn't certain about that either. All she knew was that they served sausage, beer, hamburgers, and more sausage. Or perhaps it was bratwurst. The place smelled like grilled meat and freshly brewed beer. Wooden booths helped create an atmosphere that was, in Jenny's mind, calm and very German-y (or was it Irish-like?). Though the place was still largely empty due to Winter break, there were still a few tables occupied by students on the other side of the wall. Three TVs above the bar area showed three separate sporting events going on (football, soccer, and NASCAR racing, if indeed the third one could be considered a sport and not a hazard to the environment), and a mellow country guitar mix blasted somewhere high above from unseen speakers in the ceiling.

It was all very college-y.

There were twelve in her group. Junghee had invited his friends and insisting they invite *their* friends, and, much to Jenny's chagrin, they had all complied. She sat cramped between the bustling armpits of two Korean men she didn't know, occasionally gagging and recoiling at the acidic pungent body odor both gave off. Their table was a mess, a landfill of half-eaten sandwiches and sausages. Eugene's Swiss Mushroom Burger glared at her half-eaten from the side like a retarded mouth drooling with cheese. Half-bitten bratwursts and half-devoured chili cheese fries disgustingly decorated her end of the table. Balled-up napkins smeared with cheese and grease lay scattered all over the floor. There was Junghee's half-eaten Spicy Bacon

Cheesesteak slowly growing cold with no one eating it, Nick's Baja Veggie Burger's romaine lettuce and tomatoes splattered like guts all over the table, someone else's BBQ Bacon Cheddar Steak melting with thick yellow goop, and Brent across from her, Brent across from her always trying to get her attention, Brent saying to her, "Want to taste my bratwurst, Jenny?" and laughing, always laughing, everyone around him just always laughing as if it were the funniest joke in the world (she was one of only two girls at the table. The other girl was a Vietnamese girl named Thao). They were on their third round of drinks then; a colorless jungle of beer bottles jutted up from the table like glass stalactites. Jenny herself held a bottle of Guinness Stout in her hands, something that, despite her not wanting him to, Junghee had ordered for her.

She hated beer.

"And then like, I was suddenly *locked out* of my lab room, *naked* except for my boxer shorts, *screaming* and hollering for them to open the door—"

A bursting crescendo of laughs followed this, forcing Jenny to grip her Stout bottle tight with both of her hands. She placed it between her thighs and felt the two male students around her laugh and holler, rudely bumping her shoulders. She muttered a dry curse.

*A group of twelve Asian people sitting together in a German bar laughing and speaking in English,* she thought dryly. *That's something you don't see every day. Brent and Rick are white, Nick is Chinese, Thao is Viet, but everyone else around me is Korean, and that somehow makes it so that everyone around me knows each other. It's kind of sad how the world works.*

She placed her beer bottle on the table and stood up. Her space was too cramped; she had to squirm and wiggle her way out. "Excuse me," she said. "I said *excuse me.*"

The two men next to her looked at her. She offered a polite smile and said: "Um, I have to use the restroom. Please excuse me."

They smiled. One even said, "Sure, no problem!" and stood up for her. Jenny mentally thanked him and got up from the table.

"Jenny?"

"Just going to the bathroom," she said lightly, smiling at Junghee when she saw his frown. "Just, you know. The beer and sausages and all."

"They're called *bratwursts*, Jenny!" Brent yelled. He laughed, popping his head back and revealing a large gaping mouth full of pink. "There's a difference between bratwursts and sausages! One is bigger than the other, and size *does* matter!"

They laughed. Jenny managed a tight smile and caught Thao's eye. *They're all yours*, she thought dryly.

She waited until Junghee was turned around and headed towards the rest rooms. She passed them, continued past the bar, and neared the rear of the room. There was a door there with an EXIT sign hanging above it. Jenny checked over her shoulder, made sure there were no signs of ALARM WILL SOUND IF OPENED, and pushed the door open.

Afternoon snowflakes greeted her. She raised her head up to the darkened skies and breathed a sigh of relief. She gripped the sides of her flimsy jacket, and set off.

Out. She was just finally *out*.

*I'll just text him I got sick in the bathroom and had to leave*, she thought casually as she walked out from the alleyway and emerged onto the Ave. The Ave was abysmally empty this afternoon. Thin carpets of snow covered a frozen derelict road. *He'll understand if I tell him I didn't want to embarrass him in front of his friends. He'll understand if I tell him I was so sick I had to go home. Sure. Right?*

"Anything to s-s-spare?"

Jenny yelped. She jumped two feet into the air and felt her heart explode in her chest. She spun around, red hair flying, adrenaline flushing hot through her veins.

The man was dressed in a tattered green poncho with splotches of red on his cheeks. Naked veins bloomed across his cheeks, his skin cracked, the veins like bloody spider-webs. Dark-blue mittens with the fingers cut off covered his hands; several fingernails were missing. Dense, shaggy bristles of blackish gray covered his chin in a rough blanket, and old haggard lines ran vertically across his cheeks and alongside his nose. He held a Styrofoam cup in his hands. Egg-yellow colored his teeth.

"Didn't muh-muh-mean to s-s-scare you, muh-muh-ma'am." Canned tuna stained his breath. "Ja-ja-just wuh-wuh-wanted to know i-i-if yous h-h-had any s-s-pare ch-ch-change."

Jenny backed away. Her eyes widened and the saliva in her mouth turned dry. Her heart panicked in her ears.

"*Do* you h-h-have anything t-t-to s-s-pare?"

"No," Jenny replied. "I…I'm sorry. I…I don't."

He held his hands to her. "A-a-anything wuh-wuh-would h-h-help."

"I said no! Get *away!*"

She slapped his hands away. The Styrofoam cup flew out of his hands and change scattered across the pavement. The sound was like metal teeth clicking together. Gooseflesh burst through Jenny's skin.

"I didn't…I didn't meant to. Oh God, I'm so sorry, I didn't mean—"

The man began humming. Jenny watched, horrified, as he bent down and began collecting his change.

*Oh my God, oh God, I'm so sorry, I didn't mean to, I just didn't* mean to!

"Please, let me help you. Let me…"

She bent down. Her breathing caught in her chest and became ragged. Warmth flushed through her cheeks and tears suddenly collected in her eyes. Her knees popped as she bent down, the skintight layers of her jeans frozen and cold, and Jenny realized with horror that there were no coins to collect, there simply *were* none, they were all gone, there was nothing on the sidewalk, they were—

"Here!" Jenny gasped. She found a nickel. "Here, I found one, here it is, here's—"

A hand shot out and closed around her wrist. Jenny shrieked.

"That's mah-mah-mine," the man said. He looked at her, somberly, and said: "*Give it* to m-m-me."

Jenny stared at him, wide-eyed. "I…but I'm helping you. Please, here, take it, it's yours, take—"

"It's mine. Just *m-m-mine*."

Jenny pulled her hand back, terrified. She watched as he crawled on the sidewalk and picked up the nickel. His fingers wouldn't hold it. He tried again and again, picking with his nail-less fingers, muttering incoherently to himself, unable to pick the object from the ground. He looked like a starved dog pathetically eating the last bits of meat on a piece of bone.

*Oh please God please God let me help him please just let* me help.

"Sir, please, I…I can help you, I can get that for—"

He pushed her away. "Y-y-you're a la-la-liar," he said. His hands kept picking at the nickel. "You're just a la-la-liar. Go away."

Jenny stared at him. Her nose started running. She wiped it with a loud sniffle and stood up. She watched as he crawled around the sidewalk and collected several more pieces of his change.

"I'm sorry," Jenny whispered. "Oh God, I'm so sorry. Please forgive me."

She bowed her head toward him. She turned around. She ran away.

She broke out into a run and passed the Ichiro Teriyaki restaurant and Lutheran Center. Wind tore at her face and tears blinded her eyes. Her hair flew out behind her and drifting snowflakes caressed her face. Eventually she reached 42nd next to the Rams Copy Center and paused at the street corner. She gasped. She leaned forward and panted unevenly with her hands against her knees. Tears slid down her face and froze her cheeks. Jenny wiped them away, bitterly, and felt her gorge rise. She swallowed it and felt a sickening pain in her stomach.

"Oh, God," she gasped. She wiped her face and felt more tears stick to the back of her hand. "I didn't mean to God, I didn't *mean to!*"

She turned her head and saw the man still on the ground crawling around the sidewalk. His shape reminded her of a scuttling beetle desperately searching for food. He crawled on his hands and knees, picked randomly at the ground, and then placed his change back into his Styrofoam cup.

*God, how come nobody just* helps *him?*

She turned away. More tears sped down her cheeks. Jenny did nothing to wipe them away and let them freeze her face. She sucked in her lower lip and crossed 42nd, her arms wrapped around her, her face lowered. She shuddered violently as she walked through the empty sidewalks of the Ave and uttered another loud snivel.

*What have I done*, she thought as she made her way through the snow, *just what did I do? Oh, God, Daniel, I'm so sorry. I'm so sorry for not understanding, so sorry for having abandoned you.*

She passed by the University Book Store. She was headed towards NE 45th St. across the Neptune Theater near the Key Bank building. The 871 stopped there.

*I understand everything now. I just understand everything, and understand why this world just hurts so much. I sneered at him; I snarled and lashed out at him. When I tried to take back the moment, I was denied, was called a liar, and in turn was pushed away. I was called a liar because in that moment of wanting to help him, the man knew all I wanted to do was preserve my frightened Self, and no one else. I understand half of the world now; I see what Hollywood has missed. Daniel…I wish you were here right now.*

She thought of Michael Lamb and then shuddered, feeling more waxy tears on her face. She remembered how Daniel had asked about Michael that one day at the beach, and how she had explained to him her reasons for kindness. She thought about the man back on the Ave, of the way he crawled on his hands and knees, and suddenly thought back to when she'd run away from home barefoot and scared. And then she suddenly thought of Winter Ball where she and Daniel had spent the entire evening together sitting in his car at Edmonds Beach listening to the waves, their voices gay, their faces bright, the space in his mother's car filling with fresh smells of French fries and burgers, the moon in the sky bright, the stars around it, dimmed.

She would call him. Yes, while on the bus, she would call him, and they would talk. They would talk and catch up on things, hear each other's voices, comfort each other, heal each other, laugh and cry with each other, and just…just *talk*.

Jenny turned onto NE 45th Street and pulled out her cell phone. She found his number in her contact list and stared dumbly at his name.

*Daniel. Oh, Daniel my friend…what happened to us?*

She pushed the call button. As she waited—and as more light snow drifted towards her—she thought back to high-school and Winter Ball, and how wonderful it had been (*just so wonderful*) to have been loved by a friend.

***

"Mr. Park. Good evening. I'm Daniel Fischer. I'm here to pick up your daughter for Winter Ball?"

Daniel's heart swelled in his throat. Sweat collected on his brow and popped out on the back of his neck. His shirt collar became drenched with sweat, and his mouth instantly dried. He waited, aware of the thunderous beat in his chest, and tried to smile.

It was his first time wearing a tuxedo like this. He felt absolutely ridiculous. He wore a black bowtie just below his neck, had his hair gelled into an Ivy League haircut, and wore polished leather patent shoes. Learning all the parts of a tux was like learning quantum mechanics: there was the notch lapel, the peak lapel, and the shawl lapel to understand, the single-breasted and double-breasted shirts to memorize, wing-tip formal versus lay-down formal, two- or three-buttoned single-breasted jackets to comprehend, the "black tie" versus the "white tie" concept, donning on the cummerbund (which was *not* a sash, his sister, Penny, had been quick to tell him with her tongue stuck out. She thought he was a complete doofus for not being able to dress himself like a man), and the horrible episode of finding just the right pair of socks to match (Daniel owned no black socks. He had to borrow his father's). It was his mother who had forced him to gel his hair. Daniel *hated* the gel. It had taken him a full hour to get his hair to what he *thought* was appropriate, and by then, Ellen Fischer had just shaken her head and quietly loaned her son the car keys.

He had expected Jenny's father to speak in broken English. He had expected something like, *Yes, Jenny upstair now. She come down soon in fibe minute*, but what came out instead was: "Yes, I see. Jenny will be down shortly. Come in then."

Daniel nodded. He tried to offer Mr. Park a smile, but was presented with the turning of his back instead. He nervously stepped into the Parks' residence and gently closed the door behind him.

"Go ahead and keep your shoes on," Yongsook called from the living room. He moved towards the kitchen. "There's no need to be so polite."

Daniel, in a half-crouching position about to untie his shoes near the door, started, and quickly rose to a standing position. He had read it was custom to remove one's shoes in Asian households. He watched anxiously as Mr. Park disappeared into the kitchen and came back out a minute later with a drink in his hand. He went to the foot of the stairs.

"JENNY-AH!"

Daniel jumped. His voice boomed like a trumpet.

"JENNY-AH! Your friend is here!"

There was the quick sound of muffled feet upstairs, a door opening, and then Jenny's voice was speaking rapidly from the top of the stairs. She spoke in Korean with a few mixed words of English in her voice. Daniel heard the words "Kate," and "Daniel" and "I-5 accident." She sounded near tears.

Yongsook let out a heavy sigh and took a sip from his glass. Daniel watched from the side. He wondered if it was water.

"You can go up and meet her if you want," Yongsook said. His voice was heavy. "She's anxious right now. She doesn't know what to wear, although I told her to get prepared two hours ago. That girl never listens to anybody."

Daniel nodded. He said nothing as he slowly made his way past, and politely lowered his head. As he passed, a rancid odor filled his nose, making him grimace. It smelled like sharp needles dipped in poison, something that smelled sharp and hot. He had never tasted or smelled Scotch before, but imagined this poisonous plastic smell to be reminiscent of the drink.

*That's not my concern. My concern now is Jenny and whether or not she's okay. I don't need to worry about Mr. Park's drink.*

As he reached the hallway and saw Jenny's room with the light beneath the door, a thought emerged in his mind, stopping him cold.

*Does he get drunk and then* beat *her?*

"Jenny?"

He tried the knob and found that it was unlocked. He hesitated, unsure.

"Jenny?"

There was a sob. It was followed by a hiccup, and then a wet sniffle.

"Daniel?"

"Yeah. It's me. You okay?"

Another sob, another sniffle. Then: "Daniel. I don't think…I don't think I can go with you anymore."

He frowned. Before disappointment could fully settle in, he asked, "Are you okay, Jenny?" and before she could answer with a lie: "I'm coming in."

He pushed the door open.

She sat sobbing on her bed with her hands covering her face. Jeans, shorts, sweatpants, tank-tops, sweaters, and shoes spilled all over the floor. Makeup kits littered her dresser. An unused curling iron lay awkward and out of place on top of the dresser. Her closet door was open, revealing more mayhem and tossed sweaters and jeans. It looked like a tornado had gone through here.

"Hey." He went to her and sat next to her. He wrapped an arm around her shoulders. "*Hey.* Come on Jenny, it's okay, don't cry. It's okay."

She planted her face against his chest. "*I'm so sorry,*" she sobbed. "I'm just so sorry, Daniel. I *know* you wanted this night to be special, I *know* you wanted to do things, but…but…I have *nothing to wear*, I just don't have *any* of the right clothes anymore, and Kate was supposed to help me find something today, she was supposed to get me something while she was downtown, like a dress or something, and I tried calling her, I tried calling her *ten times* already, but she got caught up at work, and now she told me that there's an accident on I-5 and that everything's backed up, she won't be here *for another hour—*"

Daniel held her and felt her body curl deep against him. He felt her tears through his shirt and was not at all surprised to feel them burn.

She smelled good. Daniel couldn't help but smell the faint scents that radiated off her skin. He realized that he was in the room of a girl he deeply cared for and, at that moment, loved, that he was holding her while she wore nothing but white shorts and a green t-shirt, that they were on the bed together, that they were close, so physically close, and that the lights to her room were low…

She smelled good.

"It's fine, Jenny." He hugged her, and carefully drew away. "Shh, don't cry, it's all right. Don't say sorry, I'm not mad."

She wiped her eyes. "I'm just not that type of girl, you know? I don't buy a lot of clothes for myself, I don't dress up a lot, I don't know how to do makeup or whatever, I don't buy a lot of shoes, don't like keep extra dresses in my closet for parties and stuff. I don't even know how to put on *makeup*, Daniel, I don't even know how to use my *curling iron*, I just don't know *anything…*"

Her voice trailed off. She sniffled again.

Daniel, hurt more than he had been in a long time, rewrapped his arms around her and folded her in a quiet embrace. She leaned her face against him and sobbed hoarsely against his shoulder.

"If there's one thing I hate about you," he whispered softly, "it's that you apologize too much, Jenny. And then you in turn hurt me for thinking you wrong me when all I ever want from you is just to be happy with me."

"Are you mad?"

"No, Jenny. I'm not. You know I'm not."

"What are we going to do then?" she sobbed. "I can't go to Winter Ball without a dress, Daniel. It's part of the rules."

He nodded. He thought for a minute (breathing in her scent, breathing in her hair, breathing in that forest of black silk), and said: "Let's not go to the dance then."

"What?"

She pulled away, her eyes watery and dark. Once again Daniel noticed that they were the deepest of brown, a slow swirl of molasses. Something that was sweet and wonderful.

"Let's not go to the dance," he repeated with a shrug. "It'll be boring anyway. All the lights, the loud music, the people we know from school…it'll just be like school again only without the work and teachers. Let's skip out on seeing everybody we hate."

"But you really wanted…I mean, you got dressed up and everything."

"Jenny, it's fi—"

"No, you did! Daniel, you…you got dressed up and everything. You came to my house to pick me up, brought your car, and even went to reserve a place for us at a restaurant."

"Here." He reached toward her dresser and picked up a stick of lipstick. He opened it.

"What are…*Daniel!*"

He took the lipstick and began scribbling it across his chest. He drew it on his arms and scribbled it across his thighs. He finished by making a large red circle across his vest, and then made a few more zigzags across his left arm

"Daniel! What are you *doing!*"

"Here," he said, handing her the lipstick. He sighed. "God, that feels good. I hate wearing this thing."

"But…didn't you *pay* for that?"

He looked down at himself, frowned, and said: "Huh. I guess I did. But oh well. I can always take it to the cleaners. Besides, the rent came out of my allowance money, not my parents'. They won't ever know."

"Daniel."

He turned to her, smiling. "Now you can't complain about not having anything to wear," he said. "I look like I was just drawn on by a bunch of kids. Now we both look bad. Who are you to compare and complain, Jenny?"

"But—"

He took her hands. It was, Jenny would realize a year later while walking down the Ave, the first time he'd ever taken her hands like that. "Let's go someplace," he said calmly. "Let's just *go* someplace tonight Jenny, and let's forget what we're wearing. We'll look good either way. No matter what Jenny, we'll still look good."

"Is it okay if I just wear jeans with you?" she asked, biting her lip. "Like, you don't mind going to a fancy restaurant with a girl in jeans?"

"I don't mind. In fact, we don't even *need* to go to a fancy restaurant. In fact, I kind of *don't* want to go to a fancy restaurant with candles and an expensive menu and a waiter waiting on us. We're seniors in high-school, Jenny. I don't know why we need to act like adults."

"Where?"

"Anywhere. Just…anywhere."

She wiped her face. There was phlegm at the back of her throat, but Jenny gingerly swallowed it, nodding. "Yeah," she said softly. "Yeah, okay. Thanks, Daniel. Like…really. Thanks."

He smiled. He got up from the bed. As he moved, the fabrics of his trousers slid together, Jenny noticed for the first time then how handsome he looked. He looked awkward and out of place wearing that tux, but something about that, something about the way he seemed so uncomfortable and yet still trying to be balanced, as if he were doing all his best to make everything all better, a young boy trying to be an adult…it was all just very handsome. Funny, but handsome.

"I suppose I should leave you to change now," he said as he walked to the door. "Unless, of course, you *want* me to watch you undress."

She snorted a chuckle and brought a hand up to her mouth. She shook her head. "No, that's fine, Daniel. I think I'll be down in a few minutes."

"Okay. See you soon."

She nodded, watching as he turned away.

\*\*\*

They went to the beach, of course. Where else were they to go?

They went to the beach, and there, parked at Brackett's Landing above the sand dunes, Jenny sat beside him in the passenger seat gazing out at the evening dark, her neck turned, her features smooth, her shape silhouetted by the bright moon. Daniel noticed the way her neck curved fully down from one side of her ear to the hidden depths of her collar, and thought of the firm swells of a ripened peach frozen in winter when seeing her. He wanted to taste that piece of skin…to bite it, suck it, bring his mouth to it, and kiss it. He wanted to taste her.

She looked lovely in the darkness.

Black waves crashed against an unseen shoreline and produced a roar that was like distant thunder; silver moonlight peeked through indigo cotton-candy clouds. The jetty was there somewhere in the dark, lost and shapeless against the black.

Jenny knew he was watching her. She felt him studying her, observing her, *wanting* her, and made no gesture for him to stop, letting his eyes instead gaze freely at her as she contentedly stared out at the waves. She knew he was watching her.

They'd gotten dinner at Burger King. Jenny knew that if any of her peers had been there to see what they'd done, they'd all gasp at her in disgust, roll their eyes at her, and scoff. *Burger King,* they'd all sneer; *really Jenny?* Burger King *for Winter Ball? What are you, cheap?*

And so? So *what?* She had *wanted* Burger King, and Daniel had been more than willing to go along with her request. He had, in fact, paid for both of them despite her protests at the drive-through. And how wonderful it had all been; how wonderfully *simplistic* had it all been, their evening together, just two good friends enjoying each other's time, eating burgers together, and chatting in the dark. Daniel had unquestioningly driven towards the direction of the beach, and Jenny hadn't stopped him. They parked the car right when the sky was becoming a dying horizon enflamed with bright orange, and had watched as violet streaks turned to dampening black. They ate heartily, and had laughed everywhere in between. Daniel had spilled ketchup on himself once, and Jenny had laughed, saying that it matched perfectly with his newly self-designed tux. He rolled his eyes at her, and had quickly smeared ketchup across her face with a handful of fries when she hadn't been looking. She'd slapped him in return.

It was good. No high-heels, no dresses, no over-the-top fancy displays of glitter and limousines. Just casual jeans and sneakers. Just...good.

Now though, with the moon in the sky, full, save for when passing random clouds eclipsed its swelling shape, Jenny felt his eyes on her in the darkness a second time, and briefly turned toward his direction. He averted his eyes to the front when he realized she was looking, and feigned interest at something in the dark. She smiled at him from the side.

*Still a boy but wanting to become a gentleman*, Jenny thought quietly. *I wonder what omma would have thought seeing him like this. What would she say knowing that not all men were beasts?*

"Have you written anything more about your story, Daniel?"

"My story? No. Not really."

"Writer's block?"

"No. Just busy with homework and stuff. IB testing is about to come up, and everyone is scrambling to finish their work early so that they can study."

"Nervous?"

"I don't know," he said. "I guess. Fail or pass, it's no longer important to me, Jenny."

"What is then?"

She had an absurd moment where she thought he would turn to her and say *you*, and chastised herself for thinking so. That wasn't his style. Had he said that, she would have frowned at him, and possibly rethought him just as another guy who knew how to sweet-talk his way to a girl's heart when really caring only about one other organ. But…no. He wasn't like that. He wasn't.

"Life," he answered. "I've just been thinking about what happens when school ends. About starting college and everything. Where I'm supposed to go, how I'm supposed to handle myself, which friends will stay near, and everything else in between."

"And does it scare you?"

"Life?"

She nodded.

"Yeah. I guess. More than I know how to admit, Jenny. It really scares me."

He went silent. Jenny waited, knowing that he had more to say. He said: "I was at the U-Dub last week. I was at the HUB. There was a man there, and he approached me in distress. He said his car had broken down and that he needed money to buy parts or make a phone call, or whatever. He said he needed twenty dollars."

"Did you give it to him?"

"Yes. I did. And in doing so, he went up and hugged me, thanking me *deeply* for what I did. He wasn't a homeless person on the Ave or anything, wasn't an Ave Rat, wasn't some street person wandering the sidewalks with dirty clothes; he was just a big black guy in a red shirt and blue overalls wandering through the HUB looking for help. We were inside, we were safe, and there were other people around us.

"After I gave him the money, I walked to Padelford and stood waiting for the bus. All I could think about then was whether or not I did the right thing, whether or not I was cheated, or whether or not I even made a difference. It was just twenty dollars, but I spent three days thinking about what I did. I asked this kid named Amir at school if he thought I did the right thing, and he said no. He said I shouldn't have loaned him anything, and should have just lied about it. I asked this girl named Libby, and she said that I was right to help the needy. Some others told me I should have asked other questions to ensure the authenticity of his story, like maybe loaned him my phone or something, given him someone to call, or asked if I could see his car and fix it. Whatever. But none of them really helped me with this one thing that's been bothering me since then, this one thing I can't get out of my mind."

"What thing?"

"Disgust," he said. "I was disgusted when I saw him, Jenny, and I was disgusted at my feelings toward him when I realized my disgust. I saw him, judged him, and gave him my money just so he could simply leave me alone. I was *disgusted* at this idiotic human being who had happened to waste my time. I gave him that twenty just so he could go away. He reminded me of—

"*Of you*, a voice suddenly whispered to him; *he reminded me of you, Jenny, reminded me of you when you ran away from home in your bare feet and without a jacket on your shoulders, when you were in distraught and had your hair in a mess, when your tears were dirtying your cheeks. He reminded me of you, Jenny, and I suddenly hated myself for comparing him to you, and hated you that you would let me compare him to you. But what's more, I became moved to a level of self-hate for myself when I realized my own weakness and prejudices, and realized I was not perfect. I became then those motorists and drivers that perceived you as an "Asian girl" Jenny, those that saw you dirty and unclean for what you would wear, and I just absolutely hated that I was like them. I became disgusted, Jenny. In that moment, I suddenly became disgusted at you.* "—of all those homeless people we sometimes see in Seattle," he went on. "He made me think of them, and I became disgusted at how easily I let my mind generalize everyone who asks for money in a certain way. I thought of homeless people, lower-income families, uneducated persons, and just associated his neediness with this stereotype. I hated myself at that moment. I hated projecting my will and privilege onto others I didn't know."

Jenny said nothing. She peered at him from the dark, wondering if he could feel her gaze, knowing already that he could. His face was turned toward the unseen waves outside, his brow furrowed, his eyes dark. "Do you care that you lost twenty dollars?" she asked.

"No. Money will come and go; this I know already to be the secret of life. What I care about instead was how I saw him. I shouldn't have hated him for unjustifiable reasons, shouldn't have vilified him. I shouldn't have *hated* him for any reason, and shouldn't have objectified him as a category for my hate. I'm better than that. *Humans* are better than that. I just hated how I judged him prematurely with a language that I know is biased. I didn't allow him to be himself."

"Kind of like how I ran away," Jenny muttered quietly.

Daniel turned to her, surprised. She was looking down at her hands with half the moonlight revealing her face. "Yeah," Daniel said. "Kind of like how you ran away."

She looked up at him. She asked: "Is it possible to have equality in this world, Daniel?"

"No. Those who say so are idealistic and idiotic, and without proper training in philosophical, historical, or theoretical thought. Inequality will always exist because language will always exist; diversity will always lead to difference. Scholars in the humanities know this; scientists in the sciences readily accept this. Egalitarianism is a sham."

"If there can never be a utopia for humans, why do you despair?"

"Because no one else will."

"But your despair is meaningless."

He nodded. "I know."

Jenny opened her mouth to say something, but stopped when he went on.

"Every religion, society, and philosophical form of thought regarding ethics has addressed this notion of altruism, but all with one fault: difference. In helping others, though we maintain altruistic conduct, altruism by default will always lead to an Other that sees itself as Superior. Altruism thus is not an act of selflessness, but of superiority. In order for one to help another, one must recognize the *difference* in the Other that is not the same in *the them* that is the Other-Being-Viewed. In order for the welfare of others to be

305

satisfied, an unsatisfactory quality of those others must first be identified; this identification is made only through evaluating eyes of those already satisfied as superior Others, thus leading to difference.

"I walk through Seattle's streets and see a beggar. He asks for a penny. I give it to him, expect nothing in return, and thus fulfill my altruistic duty. But in giving him the penny, I see this: I was the giver; he was the receiver. He was the receiver because *I* was privileged as the Giver, and he was disadvantaged as the Receiver. In order for him to exist as a 'beggar,' or a 'homeless person,' or a 'needy person,' I, by default, with the laws of language, must see myself *first* as the *opposite* of what it means to be a 'beggar.' Whether or not I expected reciprocity in return is unimportant, and whether or not there can be true altruism in this world without selfish gratification is a useless question. What matters is that in kindness and charity, there will always be an Other as superior."

"This sounds like something you've thought about a long time," Jenny said.

"Yeah," he said. "I suppose."

She asked: "Do you think all altruistic acts are unfair, Daniel?"

"Yes. I think I do."

"Why does this bother you?"

He paused. Jenny felt him pause, knowing that what he had next to say was something carefully considered. In her heart and mind, she heard herself think: *It's because of me. All of this has something to do with me.*

Daniel stared at the dark, thinking: *Never has there been someone yet I can call my equal, Jenny. No matter what I do or how much I try, I always find myself standing above others. I have no friends to equally love, no friends to share totally my mind and heart. But you're the closest person I know that has stood beside me, Jenny; you're the closest person I know. And for me to hurt for you when helping others where I find myself always imagining you always in distress makes me hate you. I hate that I hate you, hate that you would even evoke this hate in me. I hate that I hate you because I adore you, Jenny; this is how much I care for you. When you cried for me, when you let me hold you*

306

*on your bed, I hated that you would hate yourself, and hated that you would degrade*
*yourself with tears for my sake.*

*I simply hate that you would hate yourself for me.*

"It bothers me because I don't know what it means to love in this world," Daniel finally said. "I hate knowing that no matter what I do, I can never love and give love sincerely. I don't know if it's possible at all. And because of this, I'm always in some form of despair."

Jenny reached over and took his hand. Daniel looked at her, surprised.

"You're a good person, Daniel," Jenny said softly. "And you care about others. You really care about them, not just with words, but with thoughts too. This is good. This is always good to have."

She squeezed his hand. She said: "I can only say what I think, and not what I know. Is this okay?"

"It's more than enough, Jenny."

"It's impossible to change the world," she said, "but not impossible to care for it. And if there are those who *are* the world to you where they mean just absolutely everything, then caring for them should be enough in caring for the world—this is what I think. If everyone simply cared for the well-being of those closest to them, their families and loved ones, friends and comrades, then they wouldn't need to worry so heedlessly about strangers around them. And the strangers themselves would already be loved by those closest to them. It's impossible to love or change the world; I know this is true. But it's not impossible to love one or two people in this world with all your heart. This I think is the full capacity of a human heart: to love simply those you love; not the strangers you wish to love."

"Can there be love without objectifying those closest to you?" Daniel asked, already knowing the answer.

"No. As you said it yourself, Daniel—we're all in language. Language will always objectify us. But at least with those we love and are loved by, this objectifying is made willingly rather than forcefully. We *let* ourselves become objectified by the gazing view of the Other that loves us. We do so willingly because we know they will love us and never hurt us. This is the required submission in love."

They sat in silence. Jenny looked at him, worried that she'd said something to upset him. His gaze was far off, directed toward the stars. Then: "Thanks, Ms. Park. Thank you for the lesson. I think I just learned a thing or two from you."

Jenny smiled at him, incredulous. She thought to herself, Me? *Teach* you? *Daniel, please*, but said nothing as he started the engine.

She sat back as he drove out of the lot. Her heart warm, and a warm gladness filled her. She watched as he drove from the beach and felt a quiet sleepiness overtake her, glad he was with her. She smiled.

# CHAPTER 17

Daniel stood on the tenth floor of McMahon Hall with his hands in his pockets. His cellphone was in his pocket, but what he heard then when Jenny tried calling him while on the 871 bus was silence. His cell phone was off. He'd turned it off this morning when about to take a final, and had left it off since.

He took one hand out and knocked on the door. The door was decorated with cute paper cutouts and other girly designs. Random scribbles and messages cluttered the front. Beneath them was a list of names:

*Seeun Kim*
*Gianna Souza*
*Olga Vilkotaska*
*Elizabeth "Lizzy" Wallace*
*Nicole Gufalus*
*Emma Evans*

He frowned when reading the names. He had expected the dorm rooms at McMahon Hall to be single units, not dorm clusters. The thought was strange for some reason.

At the sound of his knock, a shuffling of feet sounded behind the door, and Daniel immediately straightened his shoulders. The *thud-thud…thud-thud* in his chest grew louder.

"Daniel, hey," Emma greeted as she opened the door. She smiled when she saw him. "Glad that you decided to come by. Finished?"

"Just got done with CHID," he answered. He tried to return her smile.

"Still want to grab lunch?"

"Of course. Mind if I get dressed?"

He looked at her, confused, and then suddenly noticed what she was wearing. She wore a pair of white shorts and a tight pink tank-top with her hair spilled past her naked shoulders. Her thighs and feet were bare, her shorts, just below her waist in a snug fit over the swells of her hips. When Daniel noticed all of this, he swallowed, and felt a burst of heat flow from behind her.

*Of course*, he thought suddenly. *This is her first time in Seattle, her first time experiencing the cold. This is the first time she's ever been out of Arizona. She probably has a portable heater turned up behind her, probably has it blasted to the max, probably—*

*Nice thighs, Emma*, he thought quietly. *Really nice thighs. Milky swells.*

Emma, noticing his slight unconscious gaze, chuckled, and took one discreet step back behind the door. She wiped a lock of golden hair out of her eyes, and waited.

"Sure," Daniel answered. "I'll wait for you right here."

She smiled at him. "Great. Be ready in a few seconds."

He nodded. Emma chuckled when seeing his face, and gently closed the door.

***

"How was your final?" Emma asked once they were at the Thaiger Room on the Ave. Two plates of Phad Thai sat in front of them. "Easy?"

"Very," Daniel answered. "Not at all what everyone was making it out to be."

"Big fish in a small pond."

"More like a sperm whale about to blow."

She laughed at him. Daniel smiled at her, liking the sound of her laugh. He said, "The CHID program is absolutely wonderful, but those in my class just make it so pathetic."

"And what did one of your magnificent peers say to you that so upset

310

you?" Emma asked, cupping her hands together to support her chin. She looked at him, smiling warmly, her eyes, a sea of bright lapis that reflected the light. Daniel thought her eyes were lovely, and imagined naked winter skies because of them.

It had been like this since their first meeting together in autumn. Always, whenever dining together like this, he would begin with an engaging topic, and she would lean forward with captivating interest. They would discuss everything together, things like history, ethics, morality, philosophy, literature, art, music, poetry, the decay of American culture, and science. She adored it when he talked; just absolutely adored it. So too did she love it that he was a man of letters, and knew names such as Ezra Pound, William Carlos Williams, Octavio Paz, Robert Haas, and Heather McHugh. He spoke of fiction while she recited poetry. He referred to 20<sup>th-</sup> century existentialism while she recited *Howl*. He spoke of post-modernism while she talked of romanticism. Where he mentioned Hemingway, she quoted Eliot; when he spoke of Joyce, she offered Yeats and Pound. And somewhere always in between, there was talk of Marx and Gramsci, Freud and Lacan, Barthes and Saussure, Butler and Said, Sartre and his lovely *castor*, Spivak and Derrida.

*A cliché couple*, Emma sometimes thought as she sat gazing at him across the table. *Were I in a book, my life as a young woman would seem cliché sitting with a man like this, drawing on every word he says, listening to him speak his mind and being moved to a point of euphoria by what so passionately fuels his heart. God, it feels so good to be intellectually fulfilled. Why aren't there more intelligent handsome men like this in the world anymore?*

The Ugly Mug Cafe, Starbucks, Tully's, Trabant, Café on the Ave— they'd hit all of these places and more, always after class, always when autumn was still colorful and simply falling, always with their books in hand. How wonderful was it to be taken on a journey of a thousand pages? They traded essays and wrote to each other, critiqued each other's writings, and sometimes texted each other in childish Latin (which more or less were just phrases and quotes they'd picked up from their classes together). He had essays where he hoped to expand existential thought and post-structuralism to the world; she shared drafts of poetry reminiscent of the modernists. He displayed a male arrogance about him that was subtly attractive, and always, whenever presenting his ideas to her, he'd thump the table in front of them, gesture with emphasis, and wave off her speculations like annoying flies in his face. And always, whenever it was his turn to listen, he would sit back in his chair with a lazy slouch and with one of his legs crossed, frown intently as she spoke, and closely observe the movement of her lips and eyes, his temple supported with one hand, his eyes darkened. It was, whenever Emma noticed it, an endearing gesture, one that she found attractive and intimidating.

"One girl in a class a few weeks ago," he began, "just absolutely disheartened me when she asked a question."

"What question?"

"Our professor was giving us the historical background of what helped constitute Augustine's writings after having read *The Republic*. From Plato, we traced our way through the Peloponnesian War, the founding and fall of Rome, Alexander, Constantine, the Edict of Milan, and so forth. Afterwards, a girl behind me suddenly raised her hand and asked, 'Didn't the Enlightenment happen right after Plato's *The Republic* then?' I literally face-palmed myself so hard it sounded like a slap."

Emma's eyes widened. "*Wow*," she said. She stretched it to sound like *woo-ow*. "You have *got* to be kidding me."

"I wish. I turned around to see if she was joking, but you could tell by her face that she was serious."

Emma shook her head. "That's just sad. I can't believe they don't actually *teach* something as vital as that in our high-school curriculum anymore and assume it can just go unnoticed in life. How can you *not* teach about the Enlightenment and the French Revolution when it comes to talking about American politics or history?"

"Another girl in my class asked why Socrates was hanged."

Emma burst out laughing. Her voice came out loud and cheerful, covered up by two small hands, hands that Daniel enjoyed looking at as she covered up two rosy cheeks.

"And what is the French Revolution supposed to be?" she asked mockingly, still grinning. "'Oh, some revolution in France.'"

"And where is Paris supposed to be?" he asked, returning her smile. "'Oh, somewhere in her Malibu mansion.'"

They laughed, and Emma tilted her head to the side.

"And so?" Emma began again, smiling. "How are you and your large friend, Bill Bukowski?"

Daniel rolled his eyes. "Don't get me started," he said. "It's enough I'm slowly becoming the scorn of all my teachers; it's another thing having a pompous ass on my back all the time."

"Most asses are on the bottoms of people, Mr. Fischer."

"Ha-ha, listen to you, Ms. Evans, sounding clever when talking about other people's butts." They stared at each other. They burst out laughing. "My teachers all just loathe me," Daniel said. "And it's even worse with Bill always up in my face."

"Still coming up to you every day after class acting like a prick?"

"Every day."

"What an ass."

"More like a gigantic ass*hole*, Emma."

She laughed at him. "That's right. Our friend Fat Bill *is* an extremely large fellow, isn't he?"

"Large enough to break my bones whenever he gets on my nerves," Daniel said. "There's always just something pitiful about the way he—"

Something passed outside their window. Daniel stopped himself and turned around.

It was a man in a plastic poncho. The poncho was green. Shredded holes ran the length of the poncho and down the sides. Cracked cheeks covered his face with exposed red veins, and dense messy stubble covered his chin. Daniel watched as he made his way past and noticed a slight limp in his walk.

He held a Styrofoam cup in his hands, and, much to Daniel's dismay, the man's fingernails were missing. He limped his way past, breathed out something harsh that seemed to hurt his chest, and had his breath escape his lips as a white plume that fogged his face.

"Daniel."

He turned around. Emma was gazing thoughtfully at him across the table.

"Yeah?"

"You were saying?"

"Oh. Right." He paused. "I seem to have forgotten what I had to say."

Emma frowned at him. She bit her lip and raised an incredulous eyebrow. The gesture surprised Daniel. He was briefly reminded of Jenny.

"Thinking of the man that walked by just now?" Emma asked, somewhat kindly.

"No. I just…I just had a momentary relapse of something. Something else."

He reached out and took a drink of his water. Emma studied him, carefully, silently, and watched as he placed his glass back down. She said nothing for a moment.

"You know," she began, "it's not bad to feel for the needy, Daniel. It's always good to care for them. What's wrong is to care for them excessively and *ob*sessively. One can only change so much in this world, and with this world, one change made by the heart of one person is ever rarely good."

Daniel looked at her. His gaze was darkened now, his eyes, serious and pensive. It was a look Emma knew well. It was a look she had come to admire, a look she thought was darkly handsome, and one that sometimes frightened her.

"Don't think so heavily about the man," Emma said, trying to make him feel better. "It's not your responsibility to think of him more than your emotions allow. Your thoughts are not obligated to him. You know this."

"Just now," he said, "you explained a thought to me expressed in dichotomies. You explained him to me as a 'they,' and regarded 'me' as part

314

of your 'you' separated from 'them.'"

Emma nodded. They'd had this conversation before. "Based on what you described to me, Daniel," she said, "it's impossible to express ourselves without this dichotomy in language. We are all racists, sexists, and dominating conscious agents in the realm of consciousness. *Langue* and *parole.*"

"But you're wrong to assume that this is what is going through my mind," he told her. "On seeing him, I've already accepted the fact that I stand different from him."

"Then what's bothering you?"

He thought for a minute. He leaned forward, placing his hands on the table. "You've read the first draft of my essays."

She nodded. He'd loaned her five essays, while she'd loaned him several of her poems. He was a man obsessed with freedom and identity: The entirety of his essays consisted of existential freedoms expressed through structural and post-structural systems of meaning (a paradoxical mixture, surely). In this regard, he was heavily indebted to Saussure and Barthes. He also shared bloodlines with Western Marxism.

"Let me set up a hypothetical scenario," he began. "You see a homeless man; he asks you for two dollars. You know he is in distress and is not lying. You give it to him. Have you done the right thing?"

"Yes," Emma replied.

"Is it morally and ethically right to help others less fortunate than you?"

"Yes, I believe so. It's always morally and ethically correct to help others less fortunate than you if you have the ability to do so."

"You watch movies also."

"Yes."

"The price for a movie ticket is ten dollars."

"I…yes."

"If you tell me it's the right thing to do, both ethically and morally to help others, then why do you benefit your*self* more with five times the amount of money to watch a movie when you could have helped someone else?"

Emma hesitated. "Because…because I like watching movies," she said. "I like to be entertained."

"You *choose* to watch movies."

"Yes."

"Just now, you told me that it is ethically and morally proper to help others if *one has the ability to do so*. In having the freedom to *choose* to watch a movie, doesn't this assume that the individual has the ability to help those less privileged than they as well?"

"Yes."

"By your premise just now established, in *choosing* to pay ten dollars to watch a movie instead of *choosing* to donate more to charity, you have done an immoral and unethical act."

"I…yes."

"Would you ever give ten dollars to a homeless man and two dollars to watch a movie?"

Emma shook her head.

"Why do you choose to give ten dollars to Hollywood and only two dollars to the homeless man?"

"Because I become entertained by what I watch," Emma said slowly. "And because I like the movies. I would rather pay more to watch movies than pay more to help those less unfor…I'd rather just pay for movies."

"So you admit then that watching movies is much more satisfying than performing acts of charity?"

At this, Emma turned her head to the side, biting her lip. She hated it when he cornered her like this; just absolutely hated it. But always, after they finished speaking, she'd feel so alive and relieved, if not a bit solemn with enlightenment. No one else caused her to pause or stumble the way he did; no one else caused her to hesitate.

"I guess so," she said. "I guess I like Hollywood more than I do altruism."

"Just now you said that helping others—altruism—is a moral and ethical act. But just now you said that you enjoy Hollywood more than altruism. Does this mean that moral and ethical acts are not as pleasurable as Hollywood?"

Emma nodded.

"Hollywood is false."

"Yes."

"You find pleasure and happiness in it."

"Yes."

"You find happiness and pleasure in falseness."

Emma said nothing.

"Hollywood is false; you acknowledge this. You also say you derive pleasure from it. Thus you derive pleasure from falseness. The homeless man who asks you for money on the streets—is he Hollywood?"

"No."

"Is homelessness and poverty real in life?"

"Yes."

"Can a man like I propose in this hypothetical scenario exist?"

"Yes. Homelessness exists in reality."

"Can a man like Batman, Captain America, Iron Man, or Spider-Man exist?"

"No."

"So the man is real because homelessness in this world is real. And yet you say there is less pleasure in helping what is real than there is in watching what is false. You would rather pay to watch what is false to derive pleasure than to help what is real."

"Yes. I guess so."

"You flee from what is real by paying to watch what is false, and do so by your own freewill with full knowledge of what is false."

"Yes."

"You're fleeing, Emma."

Emma lifted her head. "Daniel…"

"You asked me at the beginning of all this why that man that just passed by disturbed me. I'm getting to that. Okay?"

"Yes. Okay. Fine." She ran a hand through her hair. "But after this, it's my turn to lead this dialogue, okay?"

"Fine."

He placed his hands back on the table.

"In choosing Hollywood, you choose what is false. In choosing what is false, you deny what is real. In this falseness, you gain pleasure. This pleasure from this falseness is not the same type of pleasure you gain in reality. You are, as I have defined it, a philosophical coward derived from Camus, for you are unable to accept the harsh realities of life, and throw yourself willingly into a world you *know* doesn't exist."

"Yes."

"The homeless man that passed us just now…before, I would have despaired knowing that I was different from him. I would have hated myself knowing that I was more privileged than him, that I was warmer, better fed, smarter, healthier, richer, and so forth. For the longest time I tried to find ways to reconcile differences in my life, and have finally just accepted the fact that differences are what this world necessitates. But I'm on to a new phase of life where I only see weariness and exhaustion around me. This exhaustion—whether it be from poverty, disease, labor, or emotional torment—is not an ethical dilemma, but a philosophical one. For I realize now that it is indeed impossible to change the world and love everyone in it. Instead, it is far better to accept and love one's Self as an individual, and accept life *as it is* than to foolishly hope for something different.. Do you understand?"

Emma nodded. "Rather than force love or equality, it's better to admit there is hate and inequality in this world."

"Yes."

"Hollywood for you produces only ideals and romantic versions of life, thus perverting life."

He nodded. Emma was glad. "This is the same thing with fashion," he said, "and everything else that is a spectacle and that later becomes a commodity. Sports, fashion, magazines, technology, whatever. I don't care anymore that I feel disgust at the homeless man. Or, rather, I've accepted my disgust. I feel disgusted instead that no one else will see the homeless man, and will have their sights turned up upward at the sky waiting for Superman to save him. Superman isn't real."

Emma nodded, watching again as he reached to take a drink of his water. She waited as he set his glass down, and took a deep breath before speaking.

\*\*\*

Emma said, "Man is not a sacrificial animal. You admit this."

"Yes."

"Yet some parts of altruism are detrimental to an individual's well-being."

"Yes."

"In being an altruist, one sacrifices oneself for those unworthy of sacrifice. Those less fortunate than us are privileged with ethical and moral charities when such charities should be reserved for the individual."

"Yes."

"Just now," she said, "you criticized me for saying that I fled away from my ethical and moral obligation of giving charity to the homeless man."

"Yes, but my critique had nothing to do with moral obligation, although that is a part of it. It instead has to do with what is real versus unreal."

"And what things are 'real'?"

"Those who act as individuals who contribute positively to society in order to progress it further into the future are 'real.' Scientists and scholars are the ones I think of when I say this. Specifically, biologists, chemists, physicists, and every other branch that extends outward from themselves. Doctors, teachers, engineers, whatever. All these individuals are 'real' in that they produce something beneficial to society with their minds.

"Moreover, that homeless man just now was 'real' in that his poverty is felt all over the world, whereas the Autobots are only felt in the world of fiction. There is a universal trait with 'real' as well as a civil service. Those that are 'false' produce only commodity and spectacle with their face and body. The face has done nothing to advance the world—but it was the mind that determined its size."

"In declaring all this, you do a great disservice to the individuals in this world who are *not* scientists and scholars."

"I know. But this isn't a commentary on my thoughts; it should instead be a commentary on our society as a whole, and what we as a nation prioritize."

"So you say that your critique of Hollywood is not ethical or moral, but philosophical, though you admit that both ethics and morality play a part."

"Yes."

"You admit that man must choose himself to live in life, that he must obey no one in order to be free. This is derived from the last school of the existentialists."

"Be wary. When I say freedom, I don't mean an anarchic state of being, both personal and political. Freedom requires responsibility, both moral and civil. Yet the individual should never subordinate themselves to a trend, or a popularity contest."

"In choosing himself, man recognizes his own freewill."

"Yes."

"But with his own freewill, cannot he *choose* to become a sacrificial animal for others? Cannot he choose to follow the latest cultural trends?"

"Yes. He can."

"And with his freewill, can't he *choose* to become a coward and live in fiction?"

"Yes. But he'll be living insincerely, blindly, and without authenticity."

"But you yourself say that every man is responsible for his own actions, and that they have freewill. With their freewill then, why should they believe you when you call them cowards?"

"Because they submit themselves to the unrealities of Hollywood."

"This doesn't make them cowards; this just means that they like Hollywood."

"Then they are hypocrites. To choose to pay money to watch what one knows is false, to *believe* in it when they *know* it is not real, to waste two hours of *life* when knowing life is finite…they are hypocrites for saying they are living life. They believe heroes will save them; they don't trust in their own abilities as individuals. To live life is to live life as *one's self*, and yet, you would pay money to watch a man wear a stupid spider suit and cheer at his triumphs and despair at his demise. Aren't you brave enough as a human being to cheer for your own triumphs? Must you wear the fashion of culture and be 'part' of what everyone else has so fetishized? Must you be a man that wears a mask to show strength, a woman that wears makeup to be called *'beautiful'*?

"There's always a misunderstanding of what I mean by 'real' and 'belief.' When I say people believe in Spider-Man, I don't mean they believe in a man who swings around New York City. What I means is that they believe in Spider-Man *ideologically*, and will have these ideological thoughts preserved through *hegemony*. We will not believe in Spider-Man, but we *will* believe in the White Messiah complex in which we Americans believe that *only* white, male, heterosexual men can save this world, thus relegating all other types of 'men' to the margins of society. We try not to believe in stereotypes, but nearly *all* Asian actors and actresses we see in Hollywood will be exoticized by their 'Asian-ness', made to be 'foreign', and know some form of mysticism or martial arts, speak bad English, and so forth.

"Those who find Captain America noble and attractive forget wearing a blue costume does not end poverty or cure illness in this world. TV and everything from it is just an escapist medium for cowards to turn away from life; there is no burden of responsibility for life when you know Batman will save you. Our heroes are cowards."

321

Emma looked at him, saying nothing, her golden hair behind her shoulders, the sides of her neck and cheeks revealed. Daniel thought she looked beautiful then, and realized that he wanted her—physically, passionately, lustfully. He wanted to take her; he wanted to hold her, *break* her, suddenly see her on her back with her golden hair spread out behind her naked shoulders.

From across the table, a warm flaring heat filled Emma, making her pause.

"Despite all this," he said, breaking the silence, "there's another reason for this conversation. It's a personal reason, and it's something that runs deeper than the philosophical or ethical."

"Yes?"

"I want to know how to love, Emma. I just want to know how to love authentically and sincerely without culture, and without superiority. How do I do this? How do I love my friends?"

She looked at him. She didn't understand what he was asking.

"Love those closest to you, Daniel," she said kindly. "Always love those closest to you. It's impossible to love the world. You've stated this before."

He put his glass down and stared at her, watching as she bit her lower lip again. *No, Emma,* he thought quietly. *Even that strategy won't work. Even when loving those closest to you, love won't ensure love. For friends leave you, Emma; friends leave your life, and love diminishes. The friends you grew up with, loved and laughed with…loving them does nothing in the face of life.*

*Don't bite your lip like that, Emma. You remind me of a girl I once knew.*

They stared longingly at each other, saying nothing.

# CHAPTER 18

*"Excuse me, ma'am? Ma'am?"*

*Jenny ignored the voice. Rainwater spilled down her face and soaked her neck.*

*"Ma'am? I could really use some change right now. Ma'am?"*

*She continued walking. Her boots clacked against the wet pavement and her suitcase squeaked behind her. She shuddered.*

*"I'm awfully hungry, ma'am."*

*Jenny stopped herself. The stop was sudden, scraping her boots against the sidewalk. An old jab of pain grew in her chest, and she turned around, sighing.*

*The man next to her was bulky and wore a blue woolen cap and gray windbreaker. Heavy wrinkles crisscrossed the area beneath his eyes and detailed his face. His large brown nose was broken, skewed awkwardly to one side where a prominent bump seemed to jut out. He was shorter than her, and had dark olive skin stained with dirt. Black stubble covered his chin.*

*"I'm sorry," Jenny replied. Her breath spilled out cold and white from her lips. She shuddered. "I don't…I can't offer—"*

*"Just some spare change would be good," he said. He held his hands out to her. Jenny carefully drew back. "Anything, ma'am. A dollar or two. Even fifty cents."*

*Jenny stared at him, eyeing the cuts and scrapes along his face. His face was wide, and his lips were thick and pink on the inside. She didn't know what to say.*

How is this possible? *she thought.* How is it possible that we are both in need like this while he still asks me for help? Doesn't he see the bruises on my face?

*Pictures of war and starvation flashed through her mind, briefly, incoherent, images*

323

*bleeding into each other and fading. There were images of bodies, hundreds and hundreds of naked bodies piled on top of each other on the ground, waiting to be burnt, their limbs cold, their eye-sockets blank, their mouths hung slack and ajar. There were pictures of malnourished children walking barefoot and naked through the streets looking for food, their bellies distended, their faces black, their eyes wide. Ribs jutted outward from their thin brown torsos, and calm flies landed on their bodies to dine on their snot and tears, crawling into their mouths, sleeping in their ears.*

*And then there was an image of a homeless man in a green poncho, his teeth yellow, his fingernails missing, a white Styrofoam cup in his hands.*

*Hard asphalt scraping bare feet; the feeling of bony fists against her jaw. And then a sound behind her, a sound that had tightened her skin and filled her with self-loathing and realization:* YO! NICE BODY!

*Who was Michael Lamb?*

*"Ma'am?"*

*"I…I can loan you a few dollars," Jenny said. She shuddered a second time. She reached into her coat pocket and pulled out a Ziploc bag filled with bills. "I can't offer a lot, but like…"*

*Her hands fumbled. They shook uncontrollably in the cold and looked like tangled spider legs.*

*Around them, heavy rainwater dripped from an overhanging awning and splashed nearby in a steady stream. They stood beneath a covered canopy near Taylor's, a midnight bar with neon signs set in the windows. Laughter echoed from behind the doors.*

*Jenny unzipped the bag and pulled out forty dollars. It was the same bag from her underwear drawer back in Boise. She'd begun collecting her own secret income since the beginning of this year, and had done so without Tom's notice. She hadn't even remembered taking the bag with her when she ran away yesterday. There was almost three hundred dollars in the bag, most in twenties.*

*Jenny held the bills to the man. Water dripped from her chin and her hands quivered. The man stared at her, breathless, and his wide lips suddenly pursed together.*

*"Take it," Jenny said. Her voice came out as a tremble. "Please, just take it. It isn't a lot, but you can get—"*

*The man snatched the bills from her, grabbed the Ziploc bag, and shoved her aside.*

*"Hey!"*

*The push sent her tumbling backwards. The heels of her boots stumbled, lost their footing, and suddenly tripped over her own suitcase. Jenny yelled out loud and threw her hands out. She landed on her ass* hard, *and felt rainwater soak into the seat of her jeans.*

"HEY!"

*The man ran away. His bulky shape jounced up and down in the darkness like the uneven shape of bulldog shoulders. He disappeared into the night.*

*Jenny stared after him. Rainwater trickled down her face and her breathing came in uneven pants. Water soaked her ass.*

*She picked herself up and felt cold rainwater on the back of her coat. A damp touch rubbed against her lower back as she stood and made her shiver. She stared at where the man had run off.*

*What the* hell?

*She stared down at her hands.*

Who

*(I like your rice buns, girl)*

was Michael

*(chinky-eyed bitch)*

Lamb?

*She frowned. She wiped her hands against her jeans and quickly grabbed her suitcase. She walked away from where she stood sheltered beneath the awning, and*

*(rice with that ass)*

*sighed. White breath spilled from her mouth.*

So much for starving children, *Jenny thought coldly.* Christ.

*She walked back into the rain.*

# CHAPTER 19

"Have you decided where to eat yet?"

There was no answer.

"Jenny?"

She turned her head. "Hmm?" she asked.

"Eat," Junghee repeated. "Like, where do you want to eat?"

"Oh. Um…" She scanned the area around them. "Let's keep walking."

Junghee frowned. But before he could say anything, she was off again, walking with her head down and with her arms wrapped around her chest. Junghee followed beside her with an exasperated sigh. He lifted the umbrella he'd brought with them as high as he could, and felt his arm ache. It was a small umbrella. It was an umbrella meant to shelter only one person. Junghee walked next to her soaked in the rain.

They were on the Ave now. Rainwater drenched the sidewalks around them and turned the ground a black bruising color. Cars to the side moved in a sluggish line down the Ave while students cluttered the walkways. Jenny felt the sidewalk beneath her feet and wondered, randomly, if walking down the Ave without the rain pelting was the same as walking with it. Slick concrete scraped the bottom of her shoes. She no longer wore her Ugg boots to campus.

Junghee kept pace with her at her side, his feet tripping, his arm aching. He'd been carrying this stupid umbrella for almost three blocks now, and he was getting tired. He was getting a bit irritated too, but this he kept to himself. His hair was wet and his stomach was growling; it was already 3:30, and he hadn't had lunch yet.

She'd been like this for the past couple of weeks now. Junghee didn't get *what* was wrong with her. He thought maybe it had something to do with her period or whatever it was women regularly went through, and that she was just being a "girl" again, constantly hostile and moody. The way she kept from him, the way she wrapped her arms around herself, the way she flinched whenever he tried to touch her…weren't women supposed to get *cramps* instead of acting all cold and distant? Weren't they supposed to, like, eat ice cream or whatever when going through their periods and watch lame romantic movies with their boyfriends?

And then, just a few months ago, in December during winter break, there'd been that stunt she'd pulled at Shultzy's…

"Want some pizza?"

Junghee looked up. They were at Pagliacci's Pizza.

"Sure," Junghee said. "This is fine."

Jenny smiled at him, said "Cool," and left a puzzled frown on Junghee's face. She turned away before seeing his frown, and went to open the door. Junghee sighed.

*I don't get girls,* he thought vaguely. *I just don't get them at* all. *Why they go shopping all the time, why they like makeup, and why they like buying shoes. I just don't get any of it.*

Her hair…it was black now. Junghee didn't know why, but she had re-dyed it this weekend. It looked a bit unnatural since he had never seen her with black hair before, but he supposed he could get used to it.

Her hair was just black now.

\*\*\*

Jenny pulled out a chair and sat down, observing with mild interest as Junghee closed his umbrella. His hair was wet and his face was soaked; a wet slippery slithering sound came from his shoulders as he peeled off his jacket, reminding Jenny of an eel.

*I had a hood,* Jenny thought tiredly, *and I could have worn it while we walked from campus to the Ave together. I don't understand why he insisted on protecting me with an umbrella when he didn't even do a good job.*

"What do you want?" Junghee asked.

"A slice of Hawaiian would be nice."

She smiled at him. Junghee looked at her, dubious, and then managed a small smile in return.

*Look at me,* Jenny thought as he walked away. *Look at what I'm doing, look how I'm manipulating my boyfriend like a dog. I'm a horrible person.*

She was planning to meet Daniel today. She was going to meet him in less than an hour. They had plans to meet on the Ave at Shultzy's. The reason she was with Junghee at Pagliacci's Pizza was because Pagliacci's was in the exact opposite direction of Shultzy's. Junghee knew nothing about the meeting.

*This is wrong, this is all wrong. I shouldn't be like this, I shouldn't be lying to a person who just wants to take care of me. But I am. Somehow, I've put myself here, and now I'm just hurting him. Maybe it was through my own cowardice I put myself here.*

*Junghee…Oppa. I'm sorry. You need to find a girl better than me.*

She sighed. She ran a hand through her hair and felt cold raindrops brush her fingers. She closed her eyes.

Her hair. It was black now. She'd re-dyed it this weekend on Sunday. She had re-dyed it this weekend while crying in the bathroom and had ended up sobbing quietly on the floor with her legs curled up against her chest. She'd been naked as she cried. Splotches of black solution had stained parts of her naked body, and latex gloves had covered her hands. The bathroom tiles had been cold, and she had shuddered violently for almost an hour on the floor before getting up again.

Her hair. Oh, her lovely, lovely hair. Perhaps it had looked beautiful once, and perhaps it had even looked sexy. But when she had stared at it this weekend—when she had scrutinized the almond-shaped eyes beneath its feathery thick bangs, traced the soft red liquid flow that covered her shoulders—all she saw then was the homeless man on the Ave with his ugly red cheeks and an image from long ago in high-school where she'd helped a young boy named Michael Lamb buy a blue bag of M&Ms.

*Ugly*, Jenny thought to herself as she stared at the mirror. *I'm just so goddamn ugly. How is it that people think I'm pretty?*

But oh, how horribly unsatisfying it was to be a girl! To be seen as an object both lusted after and patronized, to always be constantly reminded of her rights, to be pressured and twisted by fashion and cosmetics, to be seen always as the weaker noun that had a face instead of its own definition! Why had she pushed Daniel away? Why had she done something *so stupid?*

*This is not a mental breakdown or an identity crisis,* Jenny thought as she cried on the floor. *It's not an identity crisis because I know who I am, and this is the reason why I'm crying. I'm crying because I know who I am.*

Last month Junghee had asked her why she never called him *oppa*. In asking the question, his brow had furrowed and his voice had tightened. Jenny had been surprised by the look. They'd been having lunch at Mee Sum on the Ave then.

"Er, like, why?" Jenny asked.

"Yeah. Like…why? Why don't you ever call me oppa?"

Jenny frowned at him, nonplussed. She thought he was being conversational, but then saw his frown.

*Oppa* meant "older brother" in English. The term was used with familial settings as well as social settings. It was a term used by younger females to address older males. *Oppa* thus indicated a "closeness" between younger girls and older males, and could be, when in a relationship, used affectionately.

Junghee was one year older than her, so technically (or rather, culturally) he was her *oppa*.

Jenny refused to call him *oppa* because she saw no need for it. The innumerable degrees of formalities, the many layers of speaking, and the continuous efforts needed for respectful indirect-addressing of those older than her—these were rules that applied to the Korean language only, and nowhere else. She was confused by his question because they both spoke in English and Korean; she didn't understand the need to submit to one rule.

"We speak in English," Jenny said casually, eyeing him. "We don't speak in Korean that much."

"Yeah. I know. But still." Junghee shrugged, unwilling to drop the subject. "Why don't you, though? That's all I'm asking. Every other Korean girl says it to their boyfriend."

Jenny glared at him. She asked sharply: "Would you *like* it if I started calling you oppa when we spoke Korean? Would you like it so your Korean friends heard it?"

"Yeah, that would be great," Junghee said. "At least, call me it in front of other Koreans. You don't have to say it in front of anyone else."

Jenny stared at him, dumbfounded, and watched as he went back to eating his fried rice.

Since then, Jenny found herself staring more and more at her reflection when passing by mirrors, wondering about her bangs, scrutinizing the shape of her eyes. It wasn't necessarily which language she had to *speak* in that bothered her (which *culture*), but that she could not speak *freely* in general that angered her.

And now, her hair. Her lovely, horrible, cowardly hair. It was now a licorice black that was reminiscent of a natural Asian shine, but was still too light to be called her old self. She had gone through two bottles of Garnier Nutrisse to get her hair the color it was now. She supposed she would have to go through two more before she could make it onyx black again.

Her hair. Her ugly hair. She had cried because of her hair. She had cried because of everything it entailed.

*Daniel,* Jenny thought as she watched Junghee walk back with their plates of pizza, *please wait for me, my friend. Oh please, just wait for me. Be my friend again. I'm so sorry how things turned out, I'm so sorry for abandoning you. But please just wait for me, and please just be my friend again. You helped me so much as a young girl, and I...I just miss you. I miss you so, so much.*

"Not hungry?"

She raised her head. A slice of Hawaiian pizza was in front of her.

"Oh," she said, feigning a smile. "Thanks, oppa. I appreciate it."

Junghee raised an eyebrow at her. When she took a gigantic bite out of her pizza, he relaxed, and gave her a smile.

.

# CHAPTER 20

Daniel smelled her lotion in the air.

The smell was like peaches…creamy. Soft. It had a sugary fragrance to it, was heavily feminine, and was with hints of morning milk. It brought to his mind images of naked breasts lying beneath a summer sun, of smooth curving swells budded and ripe with morning dew, and of rippling gooseflesh that tightened the skin. Peach-breasts. Emma's peach-breasts. The smell reminded him of Emma's peach-breasts. And beneath it—beneath the heavy aromas of milk and cream, beneath the aromas of summer sweetness—was another smell, thin and meaty, almost with a raw malodorous reek. It was the wet smell of meat dripping with honey, of hot, gushing sweat from pores, and of lovely, lovely pale thighs parting wide to enable a hungry mouth a suckling of fruit.

Peach-breasts. Emma's peach-breasts. Daniel remembered her breasts being succulent and sweet. She had smelled lovely that day.

He stood in her room and stared at her things. He scanned her unmade bed and felt a quiet solemnity grow inside him. The rain had stopped. Around him, through the walls, voices carried over into the room while passing feet sounded from the hallway.

A stack of papers lay on her pillow. His essays. Daniel made his way over, collected the essays, and felt again something dark inside of him. Several strands of hair lay on top of her pillow, their shapes like thin, long, random pencil marks. They were golden colored, but in the darkness of the room, her hair looked black and dull, just random strings of hair left on the bed.

*She doesn't have black hair anymore*, Daniel thought quietly. *It's red now. Let it go.*

A message had been written on his essays. It read: *If God is eliminated from this world, does this ensure Evil? And if Superheroes are unmasked, who will protect us?* There was a P.S. at the bottom. It read: *Thank you for your critiques on my poems. They were lovely to read. Leave the spare key under my pillow, and be careful when you sneak out!*

The message was followed by a smiley face and three x's.

*Jenny*, Daniel thought suddenly. *Am I supposed to show this to you when we meet? Or am I supposed to lie to you?*

He grabbed Emma's spare key from his pocket and did what he was told, placing it under her pillow. It was a key she had given him in January after their first physical time together. Smells of cream and peaches lifted from her pillow. With it were feelings of nostalgia, excitement, lust…and sadness.

*She sleeps in this bed*, Daniel thought sadly. *Her scent, her hair, the traces of her body—all these things are in this bed. I became part of her last month, and now this bed is no longer a foreign object to me. I know everything in this bed.*

*Emma. I'm using you and I'm sorry. You're such a kind person. I loved how your body was mine last month.*

Daniel closed his eyes. He lowered himself to her pillow and took in a lungful of her scent. He breathed it out slowly, releasing his breath as a heavy sigh.

He turned around and headed towards the door.

\*\*\*

Bill Bukowski.

It was Bill who waited for him on the eleventh floor of McMahon Hall, and this was why Daniel took the elevator upward instead of down. Bill lived one floor directly above Emma in a single unit. Daniel knew this because he had visited Bill several times in the past since the beginning of the new quarter. Bill was his partner for two writing projects; they were required to meet at least once a week and report their time together. He was going to get their project today before going to meet Jenny.

Working with Bill was like working with a stubborn ox. He had a pompous attitude about him and had an egotistic edge with everything he said. He argued with Daniel about everything: MLA formatting, in-text citations, annotated bibliographies, theses statements, proper semicolon usage, and even word count. He lectured him about his views of life, belittled him on his work habits, and constantly praised himself in front of him. Daniel sighed whenever in his presence.

"What a pompous and pretentious *douche*," Emma had said to him one afternoon at lunch. "I can't believe he made you do the entire annotated bibliography just so he could tell you how wrong you were when summarizing your sources. He's such an asshole, Daniel. I can't believe he lives one floor above me at the dorms."

"Thanks," he said soberly. "At least someone cares."

Despite the support, Daniel was too tired to care, and was only incredibly weary whenever near Bill. He thought that working with Bill would spark an untapped latent anger in his mind, but it seemed only that the opposite was true. There was no real hate or loathing for Bill, and Daniel's sense of pity for him just grew more and more indifferent. This all changed, however, when Emma approached him one afternoon with a video. The video had been shot by Charley Neesler. If there was anyone who deserved this world's spite, Daniel thought, it was Neesler.

Charley Neesler was in his ENG HONORS 310 class. How Neesler had gotten into the class, Daniel didn't know. He was lazy and arrogant, more hateful than Bill, and stupid and wrathful. He was in a fraternity, and wore all the classical signs of a high-school jock having evolved into a party-going frat-boy: the shorts, the cap, the Polo shirts, the swagger, the jutted chest and stretched-out shoulders, the loud, rambunctious roars of stupidity and glee.

Daniel was wary of Neesler whenever they were in class, and knew something was cruel about him. His lips turned crooked whenever he grinned, his fingers tapped rhythmically on his desk, and a slight, lascivious predatory gaze came across his face whenever he stared at a female student. Daniel was sure Neesler had once been a high-school bully. He was also sure Neesler was a sadist.

He was not like Steven Kooper.

Neesler needed help perfecting his writing skills, and the Writing Center offered at Odegaard Library failed to meet his requirements. He thus went to Bill. Bill provided him with the basic understandings of writing essays, crafting theses, and citing sources. Because of this, Daniel discovered, Bill was finally privileged with a friend he'd never had. He got together with Neesler after class, had lunch with him, spoke with him in the hallways, and sometimes even went out and partied with him. Because of this, Daniel knew, Bill had also been privileged with a small group of friends that included girls.

Daniel felt sorry for him.

"Yeah, Fischer," Bill always said when they were in his room together (Daniel, always forced to stand, Bill, in his chair never offering him a seat), "Neesler and I are going to be hitting up this party in Broadway this weekend with a few friends. It's a shame *you* can't join us. I suppose you'll just be staying home all weekend reading and stuff."

"Yeah, Bill," Daniel said dully. "I suppose."

Other times, Bill scoffed at him, and said, "Have *you* ever been with a girl before, Fischer? Neesler and I went to this one place down in Belltown, and you know, we met a few girls there. Sweetest sets of tits *I'd* ever seen. You know what I'm saying, Fischer? Ever been with a girl like that?"

"No, Bill," Daniel said with a sigh. "I've never been with a girl like that."

"Ha! Looks like you need to get out more, Fischer!"

Despite the lies—and the sneers, the scoffs, the lectures, and the self-praise—Daniel remained patient near Bill, and calmly just carried out his tasks. And then, last week, Emma and the video.

"Daniel, look at this. Tell me what you see."

She brought out her laptop and opened a Facebook video. The video showed a large orange bonfire raging in the center foreground. Groups of shirtless men paraded in the back while groups of female students drunkenly laughed and danced nearby. The video randomly panned to the fire and then to the men, jerking violently around. Daniel realized he was viewing a homemade video of some late night party. A frat party, maybe. Or just some random event in the woods. Crushed beer bottles and other junk littered the grass. Wild screams filled the air.

"What—"

"Keep watching."

The video switched over to one of the shirtless men. Patches of brown curly hair covered his chest and purple paint smeared his face. He screamed "*Hoo-raa!*" when the camera focused on him and threw his hands up in the air. He downed a can of Budweiser, let it foam over his mouth and chest, and then screamed again, crushing the can against his forehead. The owner of the camcorder—Neesler, Daniel thought, from the sound of his voice—laughed.

"Having a good time, Punkie?" Neesler shouted. His voice was consumed by the other screams in the background. "Tell me you want more, man! Tell me you want more!"

Punkie—or whatever his name was—grabbed another Budweiser from the cooler on the ground, shook it in his hand, screamed, "*Yeah, baby! I want more! Hoo-raa!*" and opened the can of Budweiser, letting it explode in his face. White foam gushed out and spilled down his chest. Punkie lifted his drink and let it stream down into his mouth, splashing it all over his body. Neesler cackled with laughter.

The video switched around, wobbling toward the bonfire.

"It's Bill," Emma said grimly. "I didn't think it was at first, but it's him."

Bill stood next to the fire like a giant shadow. The fire gave his backside an orange eerie glow while the other half of his body stayed concealed in darkness. He wore a gray hooded sweatshirt and held a can of beer in his hands. He stood alone.

"Hey, Big Bill! What's up, Big Bill! Eat anything good lately?"

Bill turned around. The camcorder zoomed in on his face. A quick look of surprise and fear passed through Bill's eyes, and Daniel felt himself frown. He'd never seen Bill afraid before.

"Neesler," Bill said quietly. "Hey."

"Hey, *Pig* Bill!" Neesler screamed. "What's up, *Pig* Bill? How you doing?"

Bill looked at him, still smiling. He said calmly, "Not much, man. Just you know…enjoying the party and stuff."

Neesler laughed. "Yo, Bill! Bill Bukowski! Do you like 'Big Bill' more, or like, 'Pig Bill'?"

Giggles followed. Bill kept smiling.

"Whatever you want, man," Bill replied. He lifted his can of beer. "Some party, right?"

"Fuck *yeah*, some party! You think we could get this running in Seattle? *Shit no!*"

Mad giggles spilled behind the camera. Bill laughed with him, his laughter, hollow and forced. In the dim lights caught by the camera, Daniel saw another flash of fear in Bill's eyes.

"Yeah. Some party. Like, when does it end?"

A hand shot out from the right side of the screen, punching Bill in the shoulder. "This party ends when *I say it ends!*" hollered Neesler. "This party goes on all night long, Bukowski! *You hear me! All fucking night!*"

Emma paused the video. Daniel raised his eyes.

"This weekend they went out to this place called Woodinville or whatever and did this dumb elaborate party for like the football team. I guess Neesler is Bill's new friend now, because Bill decided to come along." She paused. Daniel watched her, noting the changes in her breathing. He thought she was going to cry. "This is part two," she said.

The next video showed an ugly pink mass of flesh dancing in the dark. It was Bill. He was shirtless. He hopped up and down in the grass and howled wildly into the night. He was in his boxer shorts, and meaty globs of fat rolled evenly down his enormous body, quivering like massive mounds of pudding. Sweat drenched his backside and gleamed in the firelight. Daniel thought he was dancing out of a drunken frenzy and making a scene. Now he realized he was struggling to run away.

Several loud popping sounds came from the video—the sound was like exploding wood galvanized by fire. Bill yelped in surprise. He jumped into the air and stumbled back to the earth, mounds of fat sliding. His gut, like a bulging tumor, swung up and down over the waist of his boxers. Neesler shrieked with laughter. The camera wobbled, and another series of loud pops occurred, forcing Bill to scream. He hobbled up and down, blabbered something incoherent, and yelped again as something hit him from behind. Around him, surrounding shadows laughed and cheered.

"Do you see it?" Emma asked quietly. "They're throwing firecrackers at him. Those mini kinds that pop when you throw it at hard surfaces. Only these are the big kind. The *illegal kind*. The kind that you aren't supposed to throw at *anyone*." She paused, biting her lip. "They got him surrounded by a group of people, and are just throwing *firecrackers* at him."

Bill danced and screamed. He waved his arms up to protect himself, shrieked "*Hey, stop it, that hurts, that hurts!*", and jerked again as more firecrackers popped against his body. His chest sagged like a deflated balloon, and his buttocks quivered; flaps of fat under his arms shook violently like wind-battered sails. He shrieked. His feet slipped in the grass, his arms randomly jutted out, and his body crashed face-down to the ground.

"*Run pig, run!*" Neesler screamed. "*Come on and squeal, Bill! Come on and let me hear you squeal!*"

Bill's body trembled. He tried rolling on his side but then remained flat in the grass. Slaps of fat quaked on his body; shouts and delirious screams filled the air. He brought his hands up and covered his head, shuddering as more popping noises filled the air. The video zoomed in on Bill's half-naked body, and Neesler laughed again.

Emma stopped the video.

"There was another video that was taken down," she explained quietly. "In it, it shows a bunch of guys forcing Bill to take off his sweatshirt. They have him surrounded in a circle and are kind of pushing him around. He's going along with it, trying to laugh with them, but you can see it's cruel, Daniel—you can see that it's fucking *mean*. And then, eventually, they just rip it off his body. Neesler's laughing in the background, that fucking asshole is just fucking *laughing* and recording everything, and he's screaming shit like, 'Tits pudding! Tits pudding! Who wants a bowl of tits pudding?'"

Daniel stared at her. Tears formed in the corner of her eyes. Emma turned away, sniffling, and brought a hand up to wipe her cheeks. Daniel reached over and took her hand.

"I know I called him an asshole before," Emma said, "and I know we make fun of him sometimes. But not like *this*, Daniel, God, not like *this*! I would never degrade him like this, I would never throw *firecrackers* at him, never have my friends *humiliate him*! I would never do that!"

"Shh, Emma. I know. I know."

"Will you go see if he's okay?" she asked. "You see him every week. And you...you kind of talk with him. Can you make sure he's okay, Daniel? Please?"

"I'll see what I can do, Emma."

"Thank you."

He took her hand. He kissed it.

He kept Emma's promise and traveled to McMahon Hall to speak with Bill two days later. He found Bill's door, but when he knocked, there was silence. Sighing—and somewhat relieved—Daniel stuffed his hands in his pockets and turned away. He made his way back toward the elevators and then stopped when he heard something echoing from the bathroom. It sounded like a cat's meow. He made his way over, curious, and realized it was someone sobbing. He carefully opened the door.

"Bill?"

There was a gasp. Daniel waited. He could see Bill's shoes under the stalls.

"Bill, I know you're in here."

"Who is that? What are you doing here? What do you want?"

Daniel closed the door. "It's me, Bill. Daniel."

There was a pause. Then: "GO AWAY, FISCHER! Just get out of here! I'm...I'm in the bathroom! You're not supposed to be here yet! You—"

"Bill, I came to talk to you."

"Fuck off! If you want to talk about the project, then give me five more minutes! Can't you see I'm on the fucking *toilet?*"

As if to prove himself, a loud flushing noise erupted from Bill's stall, drowning out Daniel's sigh. Daniel stood near the doors, his temples hurting, his mouth dry. A heavy feeling of sadness and nostalgia filled him. *I've been here before*, he thought quietly. *Long ago, when I was younger, I was here before with someone else who needed me to comfort her and wipe her tears. I've been here before.*

*Jenny. What happened to us?*

"If you want me to leave, Bill" Daniel began, "I will."

"*Yes!* Get the fuck outta here, Fischer! Just get out and leave me alone! You—"

"Neesler is a joke," Daniel said. There was a brief pause, sharp and sudden like a knife stroke. He went on. "He isn't worth your time, and he isn't your friend. You're better than him, Bill. Don't spend time with him."

Silence filled the bathroom. Then: "I DON'T KNOW WHAT YOU'RE TALKING ABOUT, FISCHER! Do you hear me? I don't know what you're talking about! *I don't know who you mean!*"

Daniel clenched his fists together. He sighed in disgust and turned to leave, pushing the door open.

*"You're just talking shit, Fischer! I don't know who you're talking about! I don't know..."*

The door closed behind him, muting Bill's voice. Daniel stuffed his hands in his pockets and moved through the hallway. Heat reached his face and burned his ears. He thought of Emma then, and wondered whether or not if he'd failed her, wishing that he hadn't kissed her hand that day, suddenly yearning for her touch. He also thought of Jenny, and felt hurt remembering her voice. He realized he wanted to see her then. He just wanted to see her so, so much.

***

The elevator came to a gradual stop. Daniel opened his eyes.

He stepped out when the doors opened and traveled down the long length of the hallway. He made it to the dimmed area of the hall and came to a door that was set apart from the rest of the dorm units. It was Bill's door. Daniel brought his hand up and knocked. He waited.

"Fischer," Bill said once at the door. "What do you want?"

Daniel stared at him. He scanned his face and noticed a red cloud in his eyes. His cheeks were pale and deflated, his lower lip, almost puckered and sad. He'd been crying again. He wore his trademark blue t-shirt and had on his brown mid-length khakis. Reading glasses filled his face.

"I'm here to collect our project, Bill," Daniel said. "I e-mailed you about it."

"This isn't a good time."

Daniel stared at him. Bill stared back and lowered his eyes. Daniel waited. He gently pushed Bill aside, and stepped through.

Bill's room was dark inside. Cold. Soft red light passed through the thin membrane-skins of drawn curtains and cast shadows along the floor. Late afternoon light illuminated undecorated drywalls and yellow ceilings.

A bright stack of *Marvel* comic books sat on his desk. Daniel frowned when seeing the comics. He had seen those comics before, and had felt something miserable and sad inside of him when he first spotted them. X-Men, Iron Man, Spider-Man, the Avengers.

Bill's laptop sat open on his desk.

*Have you been crying in your room all day by yourself, Bill?* Daniel thought quietly. His eyes went to the laptop. The screen was blank, but Daniel could hear it running. *Were you masturbating just now, Bill?*

"Bill."

Bill went to his desk and slammed his laptop closed. He turned to Daniel. "What do you want, Fischer?"

Daniel gazed at him. He noticed his reading glasses again, and realized he donned them on to hide his tears.

"Is Neesler still bullying you?"

Bill's eyes widened. His mouth momentarily dropped and then closed. He said: "I don't know what the fuck you're talking about, Fischer."

"Bill."

Bill stepped towards him, straightening his shoulders, puffing out his chest. Daniel watched, wary, but made no move to step back.

"Do you think because you're intelligent you think you're better than most people, Fischer?"

"No."

"You're a fucking liar. I see how you look at people, and I see how you compare yourself to me. All because you think you're smart and clever, you feel entitled to every privilege in this world. Is that it? Huh? You think you're better than me? You think you're *smarter* and better looking than me?"

His voice had risen a full octave. Daniel, still calm, glanced to the side and noted again the pile of *Marvel* comic books. A feeling of hurt and bitterness filled him.

"You can talk to a counselor," Daniel said. "They can help you, Bill. You don't need to suffer from Neesler anymore. They have centers for bullying."

Bill glared at him. His eyes widened and then narrowed into daggered slits. A hot puff of air blew through his nose and red surged through his cheeks. His meaty throat quivered. His hands balled into fists, and then he suddenly shot his hands out and pushed Daniel in the chest, sending him backward. The blow was mild, sending Daniel back two steps.

342

"Bill—"

"You're not better than me! Stop talking to me like you know me!"

Daniel's back legs hit the side of the bed, nearly knocking him over. Bill's hands shot out again and grabbed him by the collar. Daniel snarled, pried his hands off, and shoved Bill back. His hands touched the meaty portion of his chest and briefly reminded him of Emma. Bill staggered backwards, his eyes wide, an inarticulate croak spilling from his mouth. A look of pain and surprise twisted on his face and his hands went up to where Daniel shoved him.

"You think all because you hate yourself you need to hate others as well!" Daniel shrieked. His voice tore out from his throat like a bone-saw cutting wood, hurting his ears. Bill visibly shrank back. "All because you feel miserable in life, you suddenly have the right to make everyone *else* miserable? You accuse me of dominating when you yourself are *subjugating?*"

"*Fuck you!*" Bill screamed. He straightened himself again, puffing out his chest, his hands balled into fists. "*Fuck* you and everyone else like you, Daniel! *Fuck you!* Just get out of my room and leave me alone!"

"I came here trying to *help you, goddamn it!* Are you so dense you can't even tell when someone wants to be you friend, Bill?"

"I *have* friends, Fischer! More than you! I—"

"Neesler isn't a friend! Him calling you Fat Bill isn't being a friend! That's him being an *asshole!* And him inviting you out to a party where you're suddenly naked in front of a hundred people isn't what friends do to each other. That's what *sadists* do. You're hanging around a sadist because you're a fucking coward and a *masochist*, Bill!"

Tears formed in Bill's eyes, sudden and clear. They sparkled on his face and then slipped down his large cheeks, dripping like dew.

"Fucking leave me alone, Daniel," Bill whimpered. "Just fucking go. I don't need you here. You're not my friend."

"Fine," Daniel spat. "That's just fine. It was a mistake coming here."

He turned to leave. Just as he was about to walk out the door, Daniel

343

stopped himself, and turned around.

"You can beat me up, Bill," he said coldly, "but it won't change your situation in life. And if at the end of the day you can't come to terms with you being *you*—if you can't manage to look at yourself in the mirror, acknowledge your shortcomings and be happy with your strengths, anticipate with delight the future—then you're just a victim of your own cowardice and self-pity. You've done nothing; you've *lived* for nothing. You're just a waste to this world unless you accept everything this world has given you."

Bill's throat throbbed up and down. The teardrops near his eyes smeared the inner side of his glasses and gave his gaze a distant, surreal look.

"Not every one of us is as privileged in speaking so eloquently like you, Fischer," Bill sniveled. "Not everyone can be like you."

Daniel slammed his hand against the wall, bruising his knuckles. A red flaring pain shot up his wrist.

"You want to transcend your self-pity, Bill? *Then stop fucking around in life!* You want to make some friends? Stop thinking that Spider-Man will save you! Get your fucking head out of those stupid comic books of yours and live in reality! You think Captain America is going to help lower obesity rates in this country by throwing his fucking shield around?"

Daniel threw his fist against the wall a second time, rattling the doorframe. Heat flushed through his face and his temples throbbed. His hand ached, and sweat gushed down his forehead.

"Heroes aren't *real*, Bill. *Nothing* in the theaters is real. The only thing real in this world is what we see in the mirror every morning. *Humanity* is real. Batman doesn't exist and he won't help you lose weight. Batman won't help you find a *friend*."

A sound escaped Bill's throat. It was low and broken, almost like a croaking toad. Bill turned his face away and brought his hands up, shielding his eyes. His glasses fell off and clattered loudly to the floor.

"Leave me alone, Daniel," Bill sobbed. "Just…leave me alone. Fucking go away and leave me alone."

Daniel stared at him. He said nothing. He clenched his hurt hand into a fist and turned away.

***

She was at Shultzy's now.

Jenny lifted her eyes from her menu and let out a contented sigh. She glanced out the windows at the Ave and noted how shadows cut across the sidewalks in steady slants that grew longer and fuller beneath the sun. More and more students walked by with umbrellas tucked under their arms; less congested traffic passed through the streets.

*Five minutes*, Jenny thought. She glanced at her cellphone. She'd placed it on the table to make sure she wouldn't miss any calls or text messages. *Just five minutes. Soon, I'll be reunited with a close friend I once knew, and soon, things will be okay again. Things will just be...okay.*

She swept a hand through her hair.

*Soon. He'll be here soon.*

Jenny placed her menu aside and cupped her face in her hands. She stared patiently at the door.

***

Daniel made it halfway through Red Square and stopped dead in his tracks. His breath caught in his chest and his eyes widened. He stared at nothing for a minute, and heard a loud dismaying heartbeat pound in the back of his head.

His essays. The essays he had let Emma read. He'd forgotten them in Bill's room. He'd forgotten them at McMahon Hall. He also forgot to get their final project.

*Jesus. Fucking Jesus Christ. Fuck me.*

He spun around and bolted back the way he came. Wind tore at his face and dried his eyes; the sun behind him turned orange and disappeared behind a stray cloud.

345

*Fuck, fuck,* fuck! *Jesus Christ, Bill. Come on! Wait for me, Jenny. Just wait for me.*

Gasps tore at his lungs. Daniel pumped his legs felt his muscles tighten. Wet bricks slid beneath his shoes and then turned into uneven cobblestones as he dashed through the Quad. Around him, naked Yoshino cherry trees with their thin needlelike branches and thickly moss-covered trunks passed by in a rushing blur. Broken gasps spilled from his lips as his feet stomped through the Quad—the noise was like an offbeat rhythm of a reverberating drum.

He raced through the campus and traveled along Stevens Way. He found the glass doors to McMahon Hall after a minute of running, swung them open, and dashed through the lobby. Red dots filled his vision and sweat drenched his neck. He darted towards the elevators.

*Jesus, hurry up. Come on, just hurry up and* get down here!

The elevator doors opened.

"Bill!"

Daniel slammed his fist against the door.

"Bill! Open up!"

There was nothing.

"*Bill?*"

Daniel drew his hand back, wincing. He panted for several seconds and knocked on Bill's door again, rattling the doorframe.

"Bill! I left something in your room!"

No answer.

*Fuck you,* Daniel gasped. *Jesus, Bill. Fuck you. Go ahead and cry in your room. Jesus.*

Blood rushed to his face. Daniel brought his hand up and clenched it into a tight fist, wincing again as a dull pain flared through his knuckles. He stared at Bill's door.

*Now what?*

He turned around. There was a dull stillness in the hallway, punctured by a hissing sound. The sound was coming from him—he was panting.

346

Daniel made his was back towards the elevators and then stopped when noticing something from the side. A door was opened. It was just past the bathrooms and at the other end of the dorm units, farther down the hallway. A brief rectangle of light had spilled from the open doorway and oddly crawled onto the opposite wall. It was the only door opened on the floor.

*What the hell?*

Daniel flexed his hurt hand and made his way over. The doorway opened to a small common area. Beyond the common area was a small balcony separated by sliding glass doors. The doors were opened, and there, sitting on the railing along the balcony deck with his bare feet dangling casually 120 feet in the air, was Bill Bukowski.

Daniel's heart stopped. The sweat on his neck turned cold and his tongue slipped back into his throat. He hesitated at the doorway and stared.

Bill sat on the railing with his back toward him and had his shoulders hunched. His bulk made it seem like he was an old man slumped down with depression. As Daniel watched, a quiet wind blew, ruffling his hair. Orange sunlight silhouetted his shape and cast his shadow across the common area floor. He sat motionless, observing the sun, teetering on the edge.

"Bill."

Bill turned his head. He regarded Daniel with a tired sigh and turned his gaze back to the sun. "Daniel."

"It's not safe there, Bill," Daniel said, stepping into the common area. "Get back from the ledge. You could fall."

Bill glanced down at his feet. Daniel stopped and remained where he was. He swallowed.

"You're asking a lot by doing this," Daniel said calmly. "Get back inside and think this through, Bill."

Bill scoffed at him. He asked cruelly: "Why do you want to be my friend, Daniel? Tell me why, and don't say it's out of pity."

Daniel stared at him. He had nothing to say.

"Has the great Daniel Fischer lost his *words?*" Bill snapped. "I thought

347

you were a *master* of words, Fischer."

"Come back inside with me, and we'll discuss writing together," Daniel said. Bill laughed at him.

"So it *is* pity. You really are an asshole, Fischer. Despite your intentions and your intelligence, you're no better than Neesler. You're exactly just like him."

"Bill. Please."

"I know how you think, Daniel. Despite how you may see me with that arrogance of yours, I know how you think. You're a bully just like everyone else, only you hide your bullying with your intellect and words. But you're an elitist; you could care less about the people around you. So long as people suffer in this world, you keep your business of being their intellectual caretaker and bully. Am I right, *Daniel?*"

Daniel said nothing. He took another step towards Bill and stopped when he reached the doorway leading to the balcony. His arms felt cold.

"Pity. It's what you intellectuals use to justify your elitist tendencies. Without us poor, dumb, fat, and ugly people, you intellectuals wouldn't exist. How else would you define yourselves if not without us to contrast against?"

"Not all pity is a game for the ego," Daniel said. He scanned the length of the balcony. "Sometimes kindness for one another comes from pity."

"What kindness, Fischer? Weren't you the one that stated that there is always an Other before the venerating eyes of the Inferior in acts of kindness? Weren't you the one that stated that a Superior will always be the one to grant acts of altruism? And weren't you the one that called all of us philosophical cowards for believing in Superman?"

Daniel stared at him.

"*Oh,*" Bill said mockingly, "you don't think I pay attention in class, Fischer? You don't think I read your essays too? I saw the ones you left in my room, and saw the love note left by your friend Emma. Is she the blonde one in our class? The poet? Is her ass as good as it looks, Daniel, or is it better? How's her pussy? Wet and nice?"

"Bill. Stop it. Now."

Bill turned his gaze toward the east and let a cool wind blow against him. Daniel's heart raced in his chest. Just as he was about to move, Bill turned around again.

"You've failed to become my friend because I now know you'll only be my friend out of pity; there is nothing else you can offer me that isn't authentic. The way you'll praise me, think kindly of me, compliment me—these will all be acts done out of pity. No matter how much you attempt to intellectualize it, Daniel, you'll always put me beneath your feet as someone inferior. You just use words to excuse yourself from this truth. I am, after all, a coward in your eyes."

"This world isn't built with absolutes and equality," Daniel said. "Even if communism were achieved for a perfect utopia, there would be a need of dichotomies for our existence. Pity and privilege are just one of those dichotomies."

"So for me in order to exist before you, I must subordinate myself to you and in your eyes remain pitiful."

"In order for you to *exist*," Daniel said, slowly, "you have to *choose*, Bill. Either submit before me, transcend above me, or just negate yourself. These are the three choices."

Bill turned on him, eyes ablaze. "You just don't get it, do you? You with words can offer philosophy and sympathy, but empathy will away just be a noun for you. Unless you're my body, Daniel, unless you've been made *fun of* like me, *hurt* like me, and felt as fucking *fat* and *ugly* as me, you just distance yourself with words. The closest you can ever get to me is pity, and even then, it's not enough for friendship. Even if I were to transcend and dominate you, even if I were to negate myself and have you forget me, I'd still be with this *other-world* looking *at* me. You said in my room that me hurting you would do nothing unless I could accept my Self as I am, and here now you hypocritically tell me I must transcend to exist. What's wrong with you, Fischer?"

"You're confusing two terms with two schools of thought. You—"

"Take off your jacket, Fischer."

Daniel paused. "What?"

"I said, take off your jacket. Take it off *now*, or I jump."

Daniel stared at him, wondering if he was serious. He was.

Daniel unzipped his jacket and threw it to the side. Immediately, a cold chill came cooled his neck, stirring the hairs on his back.

"Now kneel to me."

Daniel stared at him.

"I said *kneel*, Fischer."

"You're crazy."

"Is this your act of *defiance?*" Bill shouted. "Is there where you assert your individuality against the subjugating forms of another? Where you retaliate to make your voice heard?"

"I will not bow to you, Bill."

Bill scoffed at him. "It's no longer a question of pride, but of principle, isn't? For you, individuality is the apotheosis of everything, and when it's suddenly put on the line, you choose to defend it. But what happens when principle is in conflict with human life, Daniel? What happens when life and principle are suddenly pitted against each other? You say as an intellectual and hypocrite that human life is what concerns you, and that human life is your principle through discovery of the individual—but what happens if that search for individual identity comes at the cost of life? Of the cost of love and friendship?"

Daniel said nothing. He simply stared at Bill and remained mute, his hands, still by his sides, the jacket he'd thrown now crumpled on the ground and in a pool of fresh rainwater. He was cold. Bill eyed him, waiting. "One last time, Daniel. Kneel before me. Get on your knees and *bow*."

Daniel clutched his hands together. He stared at Bill, grinding his teeth, and felt a dry gust of wind blow in his face. He stood in Bill's shadow and saw the slight way his body quivered in the cold. Bands of fat stretched the fabric of his shirt and caused wrinkles to spread across his back; winter wind ruffled his brown hair.

"If I kneel," Daniel said slowly, "will you come back inside?"

"Maybe."

Daniel stared at him. He took in a steady breath. He closed his eyes and slowly sank to the ground.

*Do it for Jenny,* a voice whispered. *Just do it for her. Think of no one else but her. Not Bill, not yourself, not your mind or heart. Just…Jenny.*

Daniel's knees touched the ground. Rainwater soaked through the knees of his jeans and chilled him. He opened his eyes. A look of wretched disgust filled Bill's face.

"You really are pathetic, Fischer," Bill sneered. "Look how easily you submit principle simply for pity. You would sacrifice yourself just to enable yourself to dominate others with your intelligence. No wonder you want me to live. You don't want to help people, but just want to find an excuse to keep your intelligence—you just want to help people to not deal with them. What hubris."

Bill turned around. He sighed. "I was bullied a lot when I was a kid because I was fat," he muttered quietly. "But you're the worst bully of all, Daniel. You're worse than Neesler."

"Bill. I—"

He went off the edge.

**"BILL!!!"**

Daniel scrambled over, heart pounding, adrenaline flushed through his veins. He reached the railing and saw Bill's body plummeting towards the earth. It sailed almost serenely through the air for what seemed like several long seconds, and then smashed headfirst with the concrete court below.

His skull erupted—blood burst from one side of his face and exploded in a jetting stream of thick red. His body jostled momentarily from impact, and then laid still. A dark pool of blood began gathering near his head. His legs stuck out vertically from his body like two neat parallel sticks. Daniel saw the bottom of his feet from where he stood and noticed how absurdly pink and clean they were, how incredibly polished.

*(the worst the worst daniel you're the worst)*

He felt…nothing.

Daniel drew back from the railing and felt his legs buckle. From somewhere down below, a loud scream erupted, building into a mad crescendo of shrieks and wails. He made his way back to the common area and found the couch. He sat down.

*(worst worst daniel you're)*

*(told you batman wasn't)*

*(what hubris)*

*(real)*

Daniel stared at his hands. They trembled uncontrollably, but were clean.

*Bill. I killed Bill Bukowski. I just killed him.*

A gasp spilled from his lips. Without knowing what else to do, Daniel brought his hands up and covered his face.

# CHAPTER 21

Jenny stepped through the doors of Shultzy's Sausage with her eyes red and her throat aching. She managed to take five steps away from the restaurant before tears finally gushed out and spilled down her face. They seared her cheeks and clung to her chin. Mucus built in the back of her throat and snot dripped down to her lips. She brought a hand up to wipe her eyes, uttered a loud sniffle, and tasted stinging salt in the back of her mouth. She let out another quiet wail and walked through the dark.

He hadn't come. He hadn't shown up, hadn't called or left a text message or anything. He'd just…he'd just *stood her up* and made her wait for three hours. *He just stood her up.*

*Don't think about it, don't cry, just let it go. Maybe there was an emergency ,maybe something urgent came up, maybe—*

*But he didn't call. He didn't even text, he didn't even…even…*

*Stop crying! You're being such a baby! So what? You waited three hours for him, so what?*

"Why didn't he just *call* me?" Jenny wailed. She brought her hands up and covered her face. "Why didn't he just text, why didn't he…he just *tell* me he wasn't going to show up? *Why did I have to wait three hours for him?*"

A couple holding hands next to her jerked away. Jenny barely noticed. She managed another loud sniffle, and cried again.

It was dark now. Thin twilight purple cloaked the sky above while down below thick shadows stretched through the streets. Neon lights from stores and restaurants warded off shadows along the sidewalk, but for the most part, the Ave was dark, becoming darker still with the swift retreat of the sun.

*I even re-dyed my hair for him. I even went out to show him that I'm still the person he once knew, even went and cried on the floor for him in trying to get my hair black again. Oh Daniel. I hate you, I hate that I hate you, and I hurt so much being this mad at you. Why did you* stand me up?

Jenny wiped her face again, smearing warm tears across her cheeks. She let out another loud gasp. It was cold, and her breath came out foggy and white in front of her eyes. She continued walking blindly down the Ave past 42$^{nd}$.

*I tried calling him. I tried texting him. I even left three voice messages for him, and he still didn't even bother picking up.*

*So it* was *an emergency! There, you see? He would have surely called back after seeing all your calls! Stop crying, stop acting like such a girl, and calm down!*

"If it was an emergency," Jenny sobbed to herself, "I hope it means he's in the hospital. I...I hope it means he was unable to get to me because he was so hurt. I hope...I hope..."

Jenny stomped her feet on the ground and screamed again. She uttered a low howl that was both furious and pained, gripping her hands into fists. She brought her hands up to her temples and placed them there, hearing the enraged sound of her heart against her skull. She could smell the warm sugary fragrance of her strawberry shampoo, and cried again when she realized why she even used this particular bottle of shampoo in the first place. It was the same strawberry-shampoo smell she'd worn during their first visit to the beach together. She'd gone off to the mall to find the brand again and paid thirty dollars for it.

*It doesn't matter,* Jenny moaned. *It doesn't matter anymore, it just doesn't matter. I lied to Junghee; I lied to myself. I even lied to Daniel. And now look at me—I've been lied to as well.*

She continued walking, not really caring where she was going, unaware that some on the sidewalk had stopped to look at her. Her cheeks were red and her face was smeared with tears; her breathing came in and out as sharp haggard gasps. Her feet continued mechanically along wherever the sidewalk took them, brisk and unaltered. Her stomach grumbled. She hadn't eaten anything yet, thinking that she'd share a meal with him when he arrived.

*Stupid. Just so fucking stupid. Everything I've done up to this point has just been so fucking stupid. I'm just so cold.*

She kept walking, unaware that she was slowly moving away from the Ave and out of the major part of the University District. From far away, a police siren blared in the darkness, a horn honked in the distance, and more and more tears just surged down her face, stinging her eyes.

She passed by American Appeal and Bartell Drugs near 45th. Soon she was moving past Pagliacci's Pizza and the adjoining stores surrounding it.

*I don't care,* Jenny thought again. *Daniel, Junghee, just everyone around me…I just don't care anymore. I know I'm overreacting, I know I'm being stupid crying like this, but…I just don't* care. *I won't ever care again. Just…I just don't care.*

She wrapped her arms around herself and increased her pace, not realizing that the lights of the Ave were slowly falling behind her. Jenny wiped her nose, shouldered her backpack, and traveled along the sidewalk through the darkness.

***

She was lost.

Jenny stopped herself and raised her head. The saliva in her mouth turned dry and warm tears stopped on her cheeks. She breathed, felt thick mucus in her throat, and coughed. She turned back to look over her shoulder and felt the first prickly fingers of fear touch her.

*Where am I? Oh God, where the hell am I?*

She was in a derelict section outside of the U District, some dark industrial region with low lights and no stars. An abandoned Texaco station dominated the area to her right, its forsaken state reminding Jenny of an unearthed graveyard relinquishing old rotten bones. The lot was empty, filled with widening cracks, glass beer bottles, and trash. Graffiti stains decorated one side of the storefront while large wooden boards took the place of broken windows. Shattered glass littered the ground.

Next to her on the other side of the street were ramshackle store outlets with empty windows and threadbare façades. What once was perhaps a 7-Eleven store was now nothing more than just a vacant building with blank windows and worn colors. Next to it was an empty plot of bedraggled land sectioned off with a rickety chain-link fence. The lot there was in dilapidated ruin, its concrete surface in uneven upheavals of fragmented sections and broken earth. Ankle-high weeds broke forth from cracks that spread through the lot. Beer bottles littered the ground.

*Jesus, where am I? How did I get here?*

Jenny turned her head. She saw a black road behind her and shuddered when realizing she'd walked an unimaginable distance by herself in the dark. If she hadn't taken several random turns during her walk, she could have just retraced her steps and followed the road back to the Ave. But she didn't know where she was anymore. She didn't even know what *street* she was on.

"Okay," Jenny breathed. She brought her arms up and hugged herself. "Okay. Just…okay. Just head back the direction you came. At least that way you'll be heading in the right direction again. Maybe."

She turned around and headed back through the dark.

Several long minutes passed. Another bubble of panic built in her chest. She panted for a few minutes and realized that she was cold. Sweat had dampened the collar of her shirt. She looked around, hoping to find a street lamp, a sign, something, *anything*, and saw in the distance a single traffic light eerily suspended on wires in the darkness.

*A crossroad,* Jenny thought suddenly. *There are signs at every crossroads telling the name of each street. Sure, yeah. Okay.*

Towering brick buildings now made up the world around her, and with them, a familiar stench of warm food somewhere in the far-off distance. Sirens sounded in the distance. Jenny neared the crossway and squinted her eyes in the darkness. Relief filled her. She was at crossway between Chester and 63$^{rd}$, maybe just a mile or two from the Ave. She could—

"Hey. Where you going?"

Jenny started. Her heart exploded in her chest and fresh sweat poured down her face. Her breath caught in her throat and blood rushed through her veins. A cold feeling of crawling spiders passed through her.

"Looking for a date tonight?"

Jenny turned the corner. She hadn't seen who was behind her, but didn't care. The skin on her arms prickled and her nipples turned hard. She increased her pace and gripped the shoulder straps of her backpack.

"Hey, where you going, girl? Where you going!"

Another rush of adrenaline spread through her heart. The voice…it was different than before. Two people maybe. Maybe three.

"Do you speak English, girl? You speak any good *Engerlish?*"

Laughs exploded behind her. Yes, it was more than just one now—there were at least three behind her. Jenny quickened her pace and felt her chest ache.

*Please, oh please, please God, help me God, please, just let me get out, just let me go, just let me—*

"*I like your ass!* Hey, come back, I want to tell you I like your ass! Where you going!"

"Me love you long time!"

Giggles sounded behind her. Jenny's calves hurt, and the weight of her backpack strained her shoulders. A sickening panic just loomed beneath her subconscious, ready to burst, ready to cry. She took a blind turn left and heard another loud shout behind her. Her keys jingled loudly to the side and her backpack jounced up and down.

She was in a narrow alleyway now, made narrower still by the mounds of garbage piled to the sides. Wet cobblestones made up the ground beneath her feet and gleamed in the moonlight like giant beetles. An inhumane stench filled the air, causing her to gag. The alleyway belonged to Packer's Meat and Packaging, Stars Beef Warehousing, Alfred's Pure and Sausage, and Chang's

Fresh n' Cut. Malodorous smells of old meat and wet garbage came into her lungs as she gasped. Clouds of dark flies zigzagged in the moonlight. There were smells tinted with blood, sharp fetid stenches of raw processed food, and the overwhelming odor of fresh slaughter from warehouses. Black overstuffed dumpsters surrounded the sides.

Jenny gasped as she walked and felt the muscles in her legs cramp. She wasn't running, but the quick pace of her feet tired her lungs and caused her to breathe in and out with sharp pants. Her jeans were too tight and frozen by the winter air; she could only pump her legs so much without being restricted by the frozen denim on her legs. She passed by a pile of garbage, saw a filthy mess of what looked like yellowish vomit on the ground, and held her breath, her heart pounding, the sweat on her brow heavy and hot.

"Can I get some *rice* with that ass, girl?"

White terror seized her. Jenny clutched herself tighter and picked up her pace. She was lost again. She'd twisted and turned randomly without thinking in the dark, now finding herself caught in a labyrinth of cold bricks and darkness. Crumpling stone buildings and chimney tops filled the sky; angular shapes eclipsed the moon and discouraged the sight of stars. Trickling water dripped from rain gutters and bubbled on the cobbled pathways while a metallic crash came from somewhere in the dark as a stray cat jumped out of a nearby dumpster. Jenny screamed in surprise.

*Please oh please don't let them find me don't let them*

*(rape)*

*me don't let them please God don't—*

"We're gonna get you!"

The voice was louder, closer, coming from everywhere in the dark.

"Shake that ass, girl! Shake that thang!"

*Oh God please please don't let them touch me don't let them touch*

*(rape)*

*me I don't want them to touch me here I don't want them to—*

Their footsteps were closer now, gaining, maybe less than ten meters behind her. Even if she could run she'd have to deal with her backpack. Their shoes scraped along the uneven cobblestone pathway and made her skin crawl, closer than ever now.

"I like your rice buns, girl! I like them a lot!"

They were gaining. It was obvious now. She—

—a sound of feet came behind her, rushing forward.

Jenny let out a sobbing gasp, threw out her arms, and ran. A howl of laughter rang out behind her.

"Hey, where you going! Where you *going!*"

*Please God please God oh PLEASE don't let them touch me don't let TOUCH ME—*

Jenny let out a feral scream and felt strong arms suddenly grab her. The hands snatched her backpack and pulled her back so fast that her feet shot out from under her.

"*DON'T TOUCH ME! DON'T!*"

Her hair smothered her face and tears blinded her eyes. She screamed and felt her backpack rip painfully against her shoulders as she was jerked backwards. She twisted, slid out of her backpack, and felt one massive hand grab her wrist.

"NO! PLEASE NO!"

"I *knew* you spoke English!" he screamed. "*I knew it!*"

"LET ME GO!"

She brought her hands up and felt his other hand take her wrist. He spun her around, twisting her shoulders.

"*Please,*" Jenny sobbed. "Please don't, please just don't! I'll do anything, please, oh God, *don't*—"

His hands touched her breasts. He cupped them, squeezed them, massaged them and let his fingers pick them.

*Oh, help me, please, somebody, just anybody, oh God, just please HELP ME—*

He smacked her ass.

Jenny yelped. His other hand grabbed her ass again and squeezed. He smacked her again, harder this time, and shoved her forward.

Jenny's feet slipped. Her ankles tangled together and her sneakers lost their footing. She crashed down to the ground and bit her tongue as hard cobblestones caught her fall. A bone-shattering sensation exploded through her kneecaps as she landed, forcing her to cry out. She stared numbly at her hands, realized she was on the ground, and uttered a low, pathetic sob. Tears ran into her mouth.

"Like that, girl?" the voice asked. He giggled, almost with a girly sound, and said: "You gotta be careful out here. Lots of them weirdos in this place, you know?"

The voices giggled again. Jenny stared from where she was on the ground and saw a pair of sneakers making their way over. She sobbed, curled herself into a ball, and listened quietly as they approached. They laughed at her. They high-fived each other and chortled, sounding like a bunch of happy hyenas over a fresh kill.

"Get some sushi next time, aite, girl?"

"…nice tight-ass bitch. See you later next time!"

"…some Japs and Japanese food."

"…get some *rice* with that ass, girl!"

"Suck my American eggroll, hon."

Jenny lowered her face. She waited, shuddering, feeling tears on her face and tasting rainwater in her mouth. After a while, the footsteps faded, and their voices became nothing but echoes in the dark. Jenny opened her eyes.

*My body,* she thought numbly. *They…they just wanted to come to me and touch my body. Grope me. Feel me. They just…just wanted to touch* my body.

Tears exploded from her eyes. Jenny brought her dirty hands up and used them to cover her face. She cried against the blackened surfaces of her palms and let tears trickle down to her lips. She moaned as she cried, tasting dirt and grit in her mouth.

"My body," Jenny gasped again. "They just wanted *my body!* They just wanted me. They just…they just wanted everything that *was* me."

Sharp particles of salt stung her eyes. Jenny convulsed again, swallowing. She wiped her eyes with the back of her hands and stared ahead. Slime, and other sticky, wet, and disgusting filth, soaked the skin of her jeans. Black hair clung to her cheeks matted by tears.

A puddle of rainwater lay undisturbed beside her. She had stepped in it when falling. Jenny stared at the puddle and saw her dirty snot-filled face. Her face looked like crap, and her eyes were red and puffy. Two white cheeks were heinously stained with dirt and hair.

*My ass. He just wanted to touch my ass. He just took away everything from me, and just...just left me on the ground.*

*Why didn't you protect me, Daniel?*

A sniffle broke from her lips. She hadn't meant to allow the last thought, but it came unexpectedly, forcing an ache in her throat. Jenny stared at herself one last time in the puddle, and sobbed.

# CHAPTER 22

*She was falling apart.*

*"Is it with a K, or a C, Ma'am?"*

*"C," Jenny replied. She let out a shuddering breath. "It's spelled with a C. Acworth. A-C-W. Worth."*

*The receptionist nodded, seemingly pleased with her ability to use the English alphabet, and dialed the phone. Jenny waited behind the desk and shuddered a second time, feeling an involuntarily gasp escape her.*

*She was at the Empyrean Tower now; she stood soaked in the center lobby with her hair wet and with puddles of water near her feet. Her hair hung limp on her shoulders and her clothes wrapped tight around her body. She felt like she had donned on an extra layer of cold skin and now carried it with her like a cumbersome weight that ached her legs. Water soaked her skin and made her face a thin pale-white, seemingly delicate enough to break. She'd gotten a glimpse of herself as she passed through the glass lobby doors and had sighed with fatigue. She looked dead and anorexic.*

Falling apart, *Jenny thought to herself.* Dear God, I'm just falling apart. I can't even feel my hands and feet anymore. I'm so cold.

*Vast atrium ceilings opened the lobby area above her. Below, slick polished floors spread out wide with dark green marble stone. Gigantic crystal chandeliers dangled from the ceiling like hung ghosts and shone on the marble floor as yellow glares. Behind her, a common area opened to a grand fireplace that was accompanied by several reading chairs and a large sofa. A massive stone fountain trickled water behind her while elevators to her left opened and closed with a charming* ding.

I don't belong here, *Jenny thought.* I don't belong in this world. Not with my bruises. Not with my face.

*"Please tell him it's Jenny," she said. She took a moment to breathe, swallowing. "I'm his friend Jenny, and I'm here to see him. Please tell him that—"*

*The receptionist—J. Bennett, according to his nametag—stopped her with a white-gloved hand, and politely averted his eyes. Jenny sighed, hearing the pained grumble of her stomach. Around her, somewhere from unseen speakers, a nice soothing piano melody filled the air.*

*"Your party doesn't answer, Ma'am."*

*Jenny stared at him. "Can you try again?"*

*"I'm sorry, Ma'am, but it is quite late, and I believe your party—"*

*"Please," Jenny breathed. "Just…just one more time. Please. I just really have to see him."*

*Bennett stared at her, letting his eyes pass through her soaked face and wet hair. He sighed, "Very well then," and re-dialed the number.*

It's fine, *Jenny thought faintly.* Let him see my bruises, let him see my face. I know how I look with my wet clothes and with my single suitcase. Damsel-in-distress, anyone?

*"Ma'am. I'm sorry, but Mr. Fischer isn't an—"*

*He stopped. Jenny waited, her heart pounding.*

*"Mr. Fischer? Mr. Fischer, this is Jeff Bennett from the reception desk downstairs, and I have a visitor here who says she must see you. She says it's urgent. She…"*

*There was a pause. Jenny waited, desperately searching his face. A horrible black thought grew in her mind. What if he rejected her? What if he suddenly decided to turn her away after all this time?*

*"Yes. I understand. Yes, of course, Mr. Fischer." He turned toward her. "Mr. Fischer says he isn't accepting any guests at the moment. I'm sorry, but you'll have to leave. I believe he—"*

*"No!" Jenny screamed. "Tell him it's Jenny! Jenny!"*

*She slammed her hand down on the reception desk. Bennett recoiled, a slight grimace of disgust and shock twisted on his face. He frowned at her, wary. He said nothing.*

*"Please," Jenny gasped. She withdrew her hand. She clutched it to her side and winced*

with pain. "Just mention my name. He'll know who it is if you say my name. Tell him it's Jenny. Jenny Acworth. Just tell him—"

No, *a voice whispered to her*, that's wrong. Park. It's Jenny *Park*. You're Jenny Park to him. You've always been Jenny Park to him.

"Park," Jenny said. "My name is Jenny Park. Not Acworth. Please just say that to him. He'll remember if you say that. Please, just say my name."

Bennett eyed her. He again said nothing as he scanned her face, and again said nothing when noticing the bruises. The way the raindrops dripped from her hair, the way her clothes clung tight to her body, matted and wet…Jenny felt his gaze on her, and quietly lowered her eyes.

Bennett brought the receiver back to his ear.

"Mr. Fischer. The woman that wishes to see you says her name is Jenny. Jenny Park. I do believe she says you know her. She…"

There was another momentary pause, this time longer. Jenny waited. Her heart quickened in the background of her ears and more raindrops dripped from her face. She waited.

"Yes. All right, Mr. Fischer. Thank you."

Bennett placed the receiver down. He stared at her.

"Mr. Fischer will accept you upstairs now."

She sighed. Her knees buckled, and Jenny had to bite down on her tongue to keep from collapsing. Blood squirted in her mouth.

"Place take the elevators to your left," Bennett said, indicating with his hand. "When you are in the elevators, press TF. This will lead you to our top floors reserved for our exclusive residents. After pressing TF, the computer will prompt you for a passcode. The passcode for Mr. Fischer's floor is five-one-eight-eight-two-eight. Any questions?"

"No," Jenny said. "Thank you."

"Mr. Fischer's suite will be to your right."

Jenny nodded, thanked him again, and moved to the elevators.

There was a blank screen on the control pad of the elevator. Jenny did as she was told and pressed the button marked TF with a thin, white, trembling finger. The words PLEASE ENTER RESIDENT CODE flashed at her from the control screen. She *punched in the number, hit ACCEPT, and waited. The elevator hummed to life.*

The bruises, *Jenny thought again.* It was the bruises that he saw on my face. It was the bruises that finally convinced him to allow me to enter the elevators. That, and pity, I guess.

*The elevator ride was smooth and silent, reaching the floor in just under ten seconds. When the doors parted, Jenny swallowed again, and felt a slight pain in her throat. She was getting a cold.*

*She stepped out of the elevator and entered a darkened hallway with purple carpet and undecorated walls. Tall leaning plants cluttered the sides along the walls with overhanging ropy green leaves. Jenny, for whatever reason when seeing them, shuddered, and quickly made her way by.*

This is it, *Jenny thought silently as she approached his door.* This is finally it. I'm actually going to see him after all this time. This is finally it.

*She knocked on the door.*

*There was nothing. Jenny waited, swallowing, feeling more raindrops dripping from her hair. She knocked again.*

*A slow buildup of faint panic rose in her chest.*

"Please," *she muttered.* "Please, oh please. Don't let me get stopped by just some fucking door."

*She knocked again.*

*Feet sounded behind the door. Jenny stood back and waited, hands clutched in front of her. Her heart beat wildly in her chest and her stomach grumbled a second time. She was starving.*

*The door opened.*

"Jenny?"

*He stood in a dark robe. A deep frown came across his face as he saw her. His eyes were dark; tired. Maybe even angry. When Jenny saw his face, a sickening feeling of hurt filled her. She had expected him to be wide-eyed with shock and delight, not...disgusted.*

"Daniel," *she said faintly. She stepped towards him.* "I...hi. I...I just..."

*He stared at her. As he studied her face, his dark look softened.*

Not disappointment, *Jenny thought quietly.* Just suspicion. He was just suspicious to see me, just cautious and unsure. Daniel. Oh, Daniel. I've wanted to see you for so long, I've wanted to finally just see you, I just—

*"Daniel?"*

*Jenny jerked at the sound. Her blood turned cold and the hairs on her arms stiffened beneath her coat. Her skin tightened.*

*Female. The voice was female. The high-pitch soprano tone was obvious. Jenny stared at Daniel, confused, and saw something sad and familiar fill his face. It was a look of shame. Guilt.*

*"Daniel," Jenny said, "I just…I just wanted to stop by. I just…I thought that—"*

*A woman appeared behind his shoulder. Jenny stared. Everything inside her turned to ice in that moment and her tongue slipped back down her throat.*

Like me, *Jenny thought dismally.* She looks like me. Ah, God, she looks like me.

*Jenny turned towards him. "Daniel…"*

*Daniel reached aside and gently grabbed hold of the woman's hand. "Jenny," he said quietly. "I'm glad to see you. This…this is Irene. My wife."*

*Jenny stared at them. Her lips trembled. She felt a ridiculous smile rip through her face and felt something propel her legs forward. "Oh!" she gasped. The horrible smile spread itself larger across her face. "I didn't think…I mean…how…you're…you…"*

*Her knees buckled. All the strength in her legs gave out, and Jenny collapsed forward.*

Wife, *she thought distantly as her world blackened.* Daniel has a wife now. Why didn't I think about that before?

*The floor rushed up and banged her knees, causing a bolt of pain. Jenny heard herself cry out, but wasn't sure. The last thing she heard—felt—before her eyes rolled back to the top of her head was Daniel's voice, calling her, and his two strong arms reaching out to catch her.*

*After a while, there was only darkness.*

# THE SECOND INTERLUDE

Daniel Fischer

Professor Kathy Ludgate

C Lit: 700 Literary Theory and Critical Practice

15 April 2010

Enslavement*

"Celebrities exist to act out various styles of living…they embody the inaccessible result of social *labor* by dramatizing its byproducts" (sec. 60).

--Guy Debord "Society of the Spectacle"

…Sartre's famous dictum *existence precedence essence* does not exist in America. America has become too distracted by material to worry about its existence and finds no reason to exercise its individual freedoms. The existence of man exists only as an extension of his materialistic surroundings—freedom for the individual thus is manufactured. Moreover, commodity has conditioned man's nature and has enslaved him to the necessities of material where he must masochistically want and have each day. This need for survival—this need for *commodity*—displaces thoughts of existential revolt from the individual's mind and has him instead desire irrelevant cultural trends. The need for the newest gadget, the need for the next spectacle—these all distract from life where life now under the shadow of capitalism comes prepackaged with price-tags. It is the material of culture and capitalism that enslaves the individual from freedom…

…Those who declare living as a mode of existence as never easy fall trap to capitalist ideology. Living, for the capitalist, will always be about material. But because society always produces more material—and because

---

* The following is a master essay written by Daniel Fischer during his senior year at the University of Washington. Due to the size of the essay, only certain excerpts have been presented with ellipses designating section breaks. The contents of the essay are used later in his highly-acclaimed work and magnum opus, *Existential Bondage* written during his adult years.

commodities continually persist, and because Hollywood continually influences—the individual is never satisfied. Thus material enslaves the individual materialistically just as Hollywood enslaves the mind ideologically. I want, I must have, this is the newest commodity, the newest celebrity trend—despite Americans being the unhealthiest and heaviest in the world, our appetites are never satisfied.

Capitalism is derived on the basis of natural competition, and, in natural competition, there inadvertently always occurs a loser and a winner. Marx and Engels systematically understood this and abhorred the effects capitalism had on the industrial slave worker. "The worker at the machine, concentrating upon immediate aims, has no time or inclination left for the contemplation of life as a whole" (Japsers 51, quoted in *Existentialism and Human Freedom*). Commodity, in turn, does not attempt to hide the inequalities of capitalism, but instead hopes to romanticize it. In this romance, the weary individual—or groups of individuals—are offered 'freedom' from their labors through moments of 'leisure.' These moments of leisure are meant to reward the individual for her hard work while simultaneously disguising the fact that these very same properties of 'leisure' in fact enslave her further:

As humanity is required to devote fewer and fewer resources to socially necessary labor, it has greater time away from the workplace. However, this separation of work and leisure is largely illusory, as the kinds of activities people practice in their free time secretly reproduce the conditions of work…On the other hand, bored by the endless repetition of the assembly line, people want novelty in their leisure time; on the other hand, the exhaustion of the labor process means that most are either unwilling or unable to devote the concentration that would be required to truly break from the patterns of thought and experience to which they have become accustomed at work…While leisure masquerades as free time, it is an open secret that its true purpose is the replenishment of one's working energies. (Gunster 45)

There indeed is nothing free in America regardless how luxurious the activity. In going to the theater, shopping at the mall, watching television, or simply reading a book, there is something, always, that must be paid to have this 'leisure' time. And in paying for this moment, the individual becomes replenished, believes herself to be properly rewarded, and embraces the new work week with renewed vigor, unaware that her weariness will eventually remerge a second time just as it did in the beginning: "As we become more and more dependent upon modern scientific inventions (do not luxuries always tend to become necessities?), we become more and more dependent upon the civilization that produces them" (Killinger 308). Moreover, in order to prevent discontent in the individual and keep her from thinking, the culture industry produces more commodities to fulfill her 'needs.' These commodities are nothing new, but are instead repeats to appease what is familiar to the weary-prone individual. As Adorno states when analyzing television:

Every spectator of a television mystery knows with absolute certainty how it is going to end. Tension is but superficially maintained and is unlikely to have serious effect any more. On the contrary, the spectator feels on safe ground all the time. This longing for "feeling on safe ground"—reflecting an infantile need for protection, rather than his desire for a thrill—is catered to. (216)


...Marx sought to understand how the commodity form objectifies the worker. In his analysis of commodity fetishism, it is not the value of the worker's labor that is sold, but rather, the exchange-value of the product in the market environment. Whether or not the product holds any *useful* value for society is irrelevant under capitalism: What is important is its abstract 'value' to potential consumers. Thus its 'use-value' no longer exists. Moreover, the 'humanness' of the product becomes eliminated by this abstract value system where "the social nature of the good—the fact that it was made by human beings for others—is ultimately lost" (Gunster 49). Once again, it is not the hero in the suit we as an American culture should worship, but rather, the designer of the suit itself. Moreover, our praises are misguided when we solely worship Hollywood celebrities, for we often forget the amount of script-writing, set-designing, and graphic-engineering that comes with the glorifying of these masked characters. We have, unfortunately, succumbed to worshipping the "face" of a celebrity instead of the "bodies" that constitute him. Like our gluttonous appetite for commodity, rarely do we as a culture ever question the human labor behind the newest generation of, say, flat-screen cellphones. "We come to believe that it is the autonomous movie, song, or book that so profoundly movies us, not the process by which these things were made" (Gunster 50).

…The mass consumption of culture can only lead to mass assimilation. As a consequence, individual identity becomes subordinated before the structures of conformity. Those who insist on individuality insist on becoming pathologies to society, for it is their very uniqueness that resists culture. Culture—in its commoditized form produced for consumption—comes prepackaged with stereotypes and clichés for the typical American to devour (Gunster 58). Those who wish to revolt against stereotype—those who bravely say that heroes can exist outside of America, or that women can be individuals, or that men can be strong without masks—are often met with hateful backlash, for culture can have "Nothing at all remain outside, because the mere idea of outsideness is the very source of fear" (Horkheimer and Adorno 16, quoted in *Mass Culture*). Moreover, the They—the false Hollywood heroes who wear masks asking to be worshipped by countless millions—expect man to conform to "established usages and opinions, of being assimilated to the general forms of human existence. By this means he becomes 'one among the many,' he achieves anonymity, he becomes buried in the impersonal *das Man*" (Coates 231-232). Indeed, if the masses as a whole continuously worship repeating archetypes in society as a spectacle, how is it then that individuality is preserved?

The consumption of mass culture in commodity form is as detrimental to the consumer as it is to the rebelling individual. The consumer, ever so ready to partake in this system of wide-eyed anticipation for the newest fashion trends—the newest television series, the newest gadgets, the newest Hollywood blockbusters, the newest celebrity gossip and scandals—awaits nothing innovative or grand, but rather, things typical and cliché. In watching the Avengers perform their grand and mighty feats, we may cheer at the work of the special-effect artists, but, truly, when examining the movie and the rest of Hollywood itself, "The accents on inwardness, inner conflicts, and psychological ambivalence…have given way to complete externalization and consequently to an entirely unproblematic, cliché-like characterization" (Adorno 217). The culture industry thus operates to not move audiences to new intellectual heights, but to restrict them and appease infantile desires. In fact, in order for the general mass in America to consume material, culture has to be *dumbed down*, where "the more *inarticulate* and diffuse the audience of modern mass media seems to be," (emphasis added), the more successful "mass media tend to achieve their *'integration'*" (220). Those who produce culture—those who are capitalists—understand the flaws of a democratic society, and know very well the intellectual disparities that exist in America. And so, to profit from this knowledge, culture is packaged in such a way that it is effortlessly bought while bypassing intellectual scrutiny: "Middle-class requirements bound up with internalization such as concentration, intellectual effort, and erudition have to be *continuously lowered*" (218, emphasis mine). Remember: It is not the scholar or intellectual that Iron Man saves; it instead is the archetype, the middle person, the everyman and damsel-in-distress.

Like 'high' fashion, everything in culture is the same while parading beneath a false guise of 'new' and 'innovative.' This sameness is hardly unintentional, but is, again, made with effort to please the general public. What is familiar becomes comfortable; stereotypes are safe. Moreover, "*Banalization* dominates modern society the world over" (Debord, sec. 59). Like the existentialists who first discovered the true reasons for human anxiety, freedom—the freedom to think for one's self, the freedom to think against stereotype, against culture—becomes a burden too heavy, and so,

372

"the more stereotypes become reified and rigid in the present setup of cultural industry, the less people are likely to change their preconceived ideas with the progress of their experience" (Adorno 229). And so:

The cognitive dimension of cultural experience is limited to the mere sorting of sensations into a crude schematic according to labels…and thus, the capacity to have new experiences, to critically reflect upon things that do not fit into a predetermined cognitive schematic, is fatally damaged…In other words, the products of the cultural industry do not allow people to reflexively secure the intellectual distance that is necessary to think critically about…the world around them. (Gunster 53, 55)

… Thus the greatest threat facing the individual is not death, but wearing the masks of Hollywood.

## Works Cited

Adorno, T.W. "How to Look at Television." *Quarterly of Film Radio and Television*. 8.3 (1954): 213-235. Print.

Debord, Guy. *Society of the Spectacle*. Detroit: Black & Red, 1983. Print.

Coates, J.B. "Existentialism." *Philosophy*. 28.106 (1953): 229-238. Print.

Gunster, Shane. "Revisiting the Culture Industry Thesis: Mass Culture and the Commodity Form." *Cultural Critique*. 45. (2000): 40-70. Print.

Horkheimer, Max, and Theodor W. Adorno. *Dialectic of Enlightenment: Max Horkheimer and Theodor W. Adorono*. Trans. John Cumming. New York:Continuum, 1972. Print.

Karl, Jaspers. *Man in the Modern Age*. Trans. Eden and Cedar Paul. New York: Doubleday, 1957. Print.

Killinger, John. "Existentialism and Human Freedom." *The English Journal*. 50.5 (1961): 303-313. Print.

Reflections on Friendship

June 5, 2010

I've set about writing in this journal as a way address a seemingly irreconcilable pain. This pain is not philosophical, but rather, personal: No great method of the past, school of thought, or great philosophical framework can cure what so violently ails the heart. The mind can only write and rationalize while the heart simply wonders: *whither?*

I am about to graduate soon. Yet on the eve of this new day, I can only wonder: Where are my friends? Why have they all abandoned me? In asking these questions, I reflect on my own life, and realize a bitter truth: Friends are nothing more than environmental consequences; love is a false transcendental value. There is only weariness in life, and it is from this weariness do friends and lovers fall away. Those that we once loved in life when once young, those that we once adored—these faces become meaningless to the adult. A noun, a signifier, a word with significance—all these once meant something to me and were more than just signs written on the page. I use the past-tense now to declare their value to me; I reveal to the world my relationship to them. 'I once was', 'she was before', 'we were once happy', and 'we were once friends…' This is how I talk now.

Friends are nothing more than environmental consequences, and there is no other truth in life that is more devastating. Once one enters college, love and friendship suddenly deteriorate. Life soon becomes replaced with conformity, culture, cliché, fear, and exploitation. In order to exist in the world, the young girl chooses to conform, leaving behind her ideals of love and friendship. She submits; she conforms. She has fear persuade her into becoming something typical. <u>In doing so, she throws away the one and only friend she once had to love and nurture her</u>. She speaks the language of celebrities, laughs at clichés, and dons on the fashion of culture—she simply submits to the world.

What reason would she have to remain friends with the boy that she once knew? The boy that once adored her? That once cared for her? The boy that once grew up with her during high-school, that she attended college with, that took her out to movies, dined with her, went and sat at the beach with her?

That once drank bubble-tea with her?

*\*\**

<u>June 6, 2010</u>

Life as an adult produces no new thought of love or friendship; <u>these instead are supplemented through Hollywood and TV.</u> What exist now for the individual as an adult is weariness, labor, and habit. One must labor in order to live—how can idyllically loving friends put food on the table? One must submit to capitalistic slavery in order to survive—how can speaking about love with friends pay off the mortgage? Love does not change the world; it is the need to survive that ultimately causes for tomorrow to occur.

*\*\**

<u>June 11, 2010</u>

I wonder what my friends are thinking now, now that they're adults and weary (did you note the irony in that sentence, diary?). Sometimes I wonder if they at all regret their mistakes in life, and <u>sadistically feel happy at their unhappiness.</u>

It was *you* that made yourself weary, I shout to myself; *you* fucked up in college, *you* messed up your life by conforming, by believing in Men in Masks! You brought this onto yourself! You had a chance to love me, but you went and *fucked everything up* by sleeping with that slut you knew was

375

manipulating you, by getting *raped* at that party you knew you was trouble, by sleeping with your TA and teachers you knew would blemish your reputation, by *going to the theater* when you should have lived your life! You looked to Iron Man to save you when your friend was right by your side! You…you…

…You fucked around in life and got pregnant, are now struggling to raise two kids and finish school, are juggling two jobs trying to feed three mouths…and I laugh at you. I fucking laugh at you with bitter tears in my eyes wishing that you'd let me help you.

…You joined the wrong crowds of friends in life and started drinking and partying. You threw your friends away, gave up on your goals, and ended up dead in a car accident. I laugh at you. I laugh at you, and ask wretchedly inside: *Why did you leave me?*

…You come to college bruised with childhood neglect, come to college humiliated, and soon commit suicide because no one is there to love you. I laugh at you. I laugh at you with tears in my eyes, and cry out to you, wondering why you refused my words of friendship.

Smart. I'm just so fucking smart. Compared to everyone else, I'm on a pathway straighter than an arrow…

Fuck you, I say to my peers who praise me; fuck you for believing in my intelligence, fuck you for thinking I'm not lonely. I fucking *laugh* at you when you fail, fucking *holler* when I see you lost and poor in life, so FUCK YOU!!! *I'm* the one that's going to graduate from college with high honors, *I'm* the one that has a novel published just fresh out of college, *I'm* the one that's going to graduate school, and *I'm* the one that has a full scholarship. What the fuck do you have? Stories of how great he was in bed? A nice hot ride that girls want to jump on? Some nice clothes you bought? What? *What?*

…I hate myself. In being the pride of my teachers, the son of my family, and the envy of my peers…I just hate myself.

I have my first novel published. Who here gives a fuck?

*(I would trade in all my scholarship money just to have a friend by my side).*

***

<u>June 13, 2010</u>

Graduated today. Received an e-mail from my agent the bidding price for my first novel. Got just under six figures.

Great. Just fucking <u>great.</u>

# PART III

Nil ego contulerim iucundo sanus amico.

--Horace

# CHAPTER 23

*Seattle / 11:38 p.m.*
*2019*

Daniel gazed at the city before him and felt something cold fill his heart. He thought of suicide then, and his gaze shifted melancholically at the lolling waves of Elliott Bay to the west, and then downward to the darkened streets below. Images of lost children filled his mind when seeing the streets. The lights there were the fleeting colors of Seattle's nightlife drifting across Western Avenue. Even here, elevated so high with the skyline and city lights, he could hear the soft murmurs of life and energy below him, and felt another cold feeling of uncertainty cross his mind.

*Suicide*, he thought as his hands tightened over the balcony's railing. *Certain disquiet has settled over my life, and I now see in the city a reason for suicide. This city—it envelops me in a halo of spectacular light, but when I stand here on the balcony gazing out to where the sun has fallen, toward where the sky is blackest and the most quiet, I forget the world below me, and hear not the subterranean shuffling feet of urban youth, but the beckoning calm of suicide.*

He sighed. His shoulders momentarily sagged, and his breath spilled out long and soundless. Seattle. Seattle was a city of desire, and what it desired was suicide. It was not suicide of the Self as Body that Daniel pondered, but the city *it*self, symbolic and imaginary. He could hear the distant rush of midnight traffic, hear the sounds of black languid waves. He could feel the gentle rush of rustling wind against him, and hear in the far-off distance blaring police sirens cutting the dark. All these sounds fell on him as gently as listening to a crow take flight on hastened wings. This was Seattle at its most cacophonic and suicidal state; this was it at its loudest: the offbeat ground-shuffling feet of modern-day traffickers making their way through the day; the hustle and bustle of shifting pedestrians in flooding numbers carelessly traversing the crosswalks; the clanks of heels, the lofty sprints of Italian leather soles, the scoffs and coughs of waking-day life. Roads patiently crumbled while sidewalks filled randomly with cracks. Graffiti stains, like faded tattoo marks etched on derelict buildings with shattered window frames and boarded doors, diminished with the weather. Trash, and other scattered pieces of garbage like old Styrofoam cups and abandoned shopping carts—empty grocery bags and candy wrappers, old yellow newspapers and outdated flapping flyers—littered derelict streets of the International District while rain beat hard the uneven and hilly avenues that constituted Seattle's metropolitan frown. And at this moment here, when stepping off the Metro Transit to fulfill complicated deadlines clad in tailor made suits and expensively bought stainless steel Swiss Legend watches—when sighing in morning-day breaths and receiving only diesel smog in return, when suppressed from joy at spotting heavily blanketed clouds overhead, when impatiently unnerved at the gentleman chit-chattering on his cellphone at the back of the 19 metro, when exasperated at the lack of prompt and proper service while waiting in line for a Starbuck's Caffè Latte espresso, dipped, but ever so lightly, in delicious white foam—and when hearing suddenly the cold howl of a western wind blowing through the modern steel maze that was Seattle's skyline—the Emerald State no longer became green, but industrial gray. Capitol Hill had its eccentric gay nightlife to the east; Queen Ann had its rustic hills to the north. Belltown housed homes for the homeless. Everything here was an urban maze of toiling labor and uselessness.

Seattle. This city wanted to die.

*There is no postcard in the world that truly captures a city's decay more graphically than one's mind,* Daniel thought. The surrounding skyscrapers around him— with their dazzling lights and luminescent glow—produced a shadow at his heels. *What words attempt, experience and knowledge surpass, for metaphor can only relate to us the true dying nature of a city. I am here witnessing its destruction, and I myself want to be a part of it, for I too desire it like it desires its annihilation. I desire this city in the same way it desires me. It tempts me, persuades me, gives me wonderful lights to see and music to enjoy. I desire this city like one does sin, viewing it with a glancing eye regularly accustomed to lust. But what befalls me is death and meaningless as consequence, for after I have indulged my senses with its gluttony—its wonderful nightlife and music, its operas and plays, its parks and gardens, its museums and Indie concerts, its taverns, its bars, its restaurants, its clubs—I am left unfulfilled again, for I must afterwards live my life according to what I want. And if I have wasted my time with only lust and desire, my life becomes a life full of naught.*

*Seattle. Your desiring of youth has us desire you, and while we help constitute you as a modernizing metropolis, you give nothing in return but lies and capitalistic slavery. And in doing so you degrade yourself, for we as your youth are your future, but you poison us with your presence. You bitch. You lovely, voluptuous, bitch. I cannot have learned love without ever having tasted your hate. What will you be to me at the very last hour of my life?*

*Why have you come back to me, Jenny?*

Footsteps sounded behind him. Daniel took one last gaze at Elliott Bay's black shape, and turned around.

***

Irene laid the back of her hand against the woman's forehead and felt another cold chill pass through her.

She'd spotted the marks on her body minutes before and had thought them to be belt marks. They crisscrossed her back like bleeding tongues tattooed to her body. The marks cut across her shoulders and went across her buttocks; they layered her entire backside with pink lacerations. When Irene had turned her over, she'd noticed small breasts covered with bruises. They were fingermarks, and they matched the reddish pattern around her neck.

It was the yellowish bruise on her face that sickened (and even

382

frightened) Irene the most, for it seemed to her the most obvious, the most casual, the one wound that was not afraid to hide itself. All these other marks—the bruises, the scars, the belt marks—were placed on her body in hidden areas the eyes couldn't see. But the bruise there, the one on her face—it seemed to declare to the world it was fearless and unafraid.

*A calculating monster did this to you,* Irene thought coldly as she took a rag and began drying her hair. *The wounds he left on you—they're there for him to see and no one else. When he holds you at night and when you're naked, he sees what he has done to you, and as a sick bastard, takes delight in his work. You can't even see them. You can't even see what he has done to you, can't even see the marks he's left on your body because you cover them up. You cover them up with clothes, with guilt, with makeup; you cover up what's on your back and put makeup on your face. How much money does he spend on you to look pretty?*

Her hand was shaking. Irene stilled it and forced herself to gaze at her face. Her hair was still wet. Irene gently wiped it dry and then dried her shoulders, being careful not to touch the bruises. Hate filled her. Sadness and fear taunted her. As she worked, she could only think of one thing, and what she thought of was: *She looks like me. Dear God, she looks like me. I'm wiping a face filled with bruises that looks like me. I feel like I'm tending my own dead body.*

Daniel had been quick to catch her as she fainted, and had carried her swiftly to their living room. He placed her on the sofa and began loosening her clothes. An unsettling noise had sounded beneath her body as he laid her out: it had been the sound of dried leather rubbing against damp clothes, a taut sound, a tight noise…a skintight sound. It'd reminded Irene of a dozen naked corpses huddled together trying to break free from the earth. She'd watched bewildered and stunned as he carried her from the foyer to their living room, and had cried out once "Daniel" behind his back. He ignored her, and she silently (but quickly) followed, noticing the water that trailed from the woman's body, the wet tendrils of black that almost reached the wooden floor. Her arms hung slack, her feet and legs, awkward with a stiff jounce. He laid her on the sofa and began ripping off her jacket. He pulled it off her shoulders and threw it to the floor where it made a wet, heavy, rumpled *SPLAT* sound next to the chair. He began undoing her shirt next, aggressively ripping it down the middle and tearing off the buttons.

"Get some towels, Irene," he ordered briskly. "The bathroom. Now."

Irene, understanding, quickly dashed away and came back several seconds later with a bundle of towels in her arms. When she came back, she saw that he was undoing her boots. She placed the towels down and went to him, gently grabbing him by the hands.

"Daniel," she whispered, "stop it. You're shaking." She brought his hands up and pressed them to her lips. "I can do this for you. Look away."

He stared at her, surprised, but then slowly nodded. "Take her into our room," he said. "Take off her clothes, get her dried, make sure she isn't freezing. Use extra blankets if you have to."

She nodded. She kissed his hands again and began removing the woman's jeans. She wrapped her body with the towels.

"Help me carry her, Daniel. I can't do it myself."

He carried her to their bedroom and placed her in their bed.

"You need to leave," Irene ordered him. "I can take it from here."

"Are you—"

"It's fine, Daniel. Just trust me, please. Turn away."

He nodded. Before he made his way out, he turned to her and said quietly, "Thank you, Irene." He looked hurt as he said those words, but Irene knew it was only because he was afraid. She didn't want him to see the marks.

She stripped her naked and threw the rest of her clothes in the hamper in the bathroom. Now she dried the last strands of her hair and quietly placed the towels aside.

Her face. Were it not for the fact that she was Korean and she Chinese, almost anybody (especially Westerners) would have mistaken them as sisters. The lips, the ears, the chin and the shape of the eyes—she was tending to her dead-self in the dark.

*There is a deep, dark, psychological ramification for all this,* Irene thought coldly as she parted back one loose strand of Asian hair, *and it fills me with dread as I think of it. But I am not this face. No, I am not this face, and thank God I'm not. I'm sorry, whoever you are, but I'm not your face, and I will never be with a yellow bruise on my cheek or with belt marks along my back. I'm sorry; I'm not you. You'll never be me.*

A cold voice at the back of her mind whispered what her heart was too afraid to say: *He won't take you back. I'm sorry, whoever you are, but he won't. He has me now.*

Shame filled her, hot and revolting, and Irene quickly pushed the voice away, disgusted. She grabbed extra blankets from their closet and gently laid them across her body. She paused at the doorway and turned around.

*Whoever you are,* Irene thought mutely again, *get better. Though I don't know you, I know you enough as a woman to want you to get better. I hope whoever did this to you burns in Hell. But I'm sorry—he won't take you back again.*

She turned away. She flicked off the lights and prepared to confront Daniel in the living room.

***

"Her name is Jenny," he said quietly, "and I knew her once as a young girl. We met in high-school and attended college together. We parted ways at the end of our freshman year in two-thousand-seven, and we haven't spoken to each other since then."

"Why?"

"I don't know. She moved away before I could understand why, and she left me hurt. I haven't…I haven't thought about her since."

"When you went to give your lecture in Boise," Irene began. "And came back late…"

"It was because of her. I found her working at a diner, and tried to approach her. To see if she was still my friend."

Irene nodded. She'd noticed the slight tremor in his voice as he spoke, and saw how his gaze shifted toward the windows. He said nothing for a minute, and she waited.

His gaze was tired, she noticed. Soft. Maybe even angry. She realized he'd been out on the balcony again, and a mournful murmur gave away in her heart.

He went out on the balcony to think a lot these days. He went out when the night was at its darkest and coldest, always slipping quietly out of bed like parting death. He would stand there all night above the city and just stare at nothing. Sometimes Irene felt him go; sometimes she didn't. On those rare occasions where she felt his absence, she would see him from their bedroom and watch him while curled on her side. She was afraid for him; just so, so afraid. And always, after watching him for what seemed like hours (though perhaps it was just ten minutes; perhaps it was an eternity), Irene would approach him from behind, wrap her arms around him, and tell him with her body that she was cold, and that she wanted him to come back in—that she was cold.

*He's always just so cold when I hold him,* Irene thought quietly as she stared at him. *Whenever I hold him, whenever I curl myself against him, he's just so cold. Daniel, my love—I shiver so much when holding you. I love you so much.*

"What do you know about me, Irene?"

"Daniel." The question hurt her. "I know that I love you. I know that I love you and will always love you. I know that in America they say any marriage that lasts for ten, twenty, or even thirty years is a lifelong achievement, but every day with you is wonderful enough for me."

She lifted her bare feet from the floor and tucked them under her. It was a submissive and docile posture, one that Daniel often saw when she was upset or scared. Her arms hugged her chest and her fingers held onto the sleeves of her robe, holding herself. He often went to her and held her when she did this, warming her and letting her know that he was there. But now he only listened, and waited for her to speak again. He got up again and moved to the windows.

"I know that you've lived in Seattle all your life and that you've wanted to be a writer for a very long time. I know that you finally succeeded in your dreams while just out of college. I also know that was the time you developed your theses and theories that so many scholars use today to teach. I know that when we first met I was in love with you because I found you to be intriguing and different from all the wannabe asshole art critics that attended my shows. You never patronized, you were never condescending, and you were just…just honest with my work. When we met, you were just done writing the first screenplay for your third novel, and had asked me out on our third encounter together. Remember?"

"I remember, Irene." His voice was toneless but kind.

"You were quite evasive on our first date," she said. "I found it amusing more than I did pitiful, and liked how you always kept your face away from me whenever I tried looking at you."

"Gentlemen tend not to stare," he said half-jokingly and half-seriously. She smiled at that and nodded.

Yes—gentlemen tended not to stare. And during their first time together beneath the wet haze of Seattle rain, his eyes had been elusive and unclear, always glancing to the side whenever she tried sneaking a look at them. He never stared, never ogled or leered, but merely gazed, and what he gazed at was something she always wondered about. His gaze (and oh, how much warmer these memories were when compared to thoughts of suicide!) was far and wide while his conversation with her was casual and light. And yet, there were times when he studied her, let his eyes fall on her, so quick and brief, it was almost like flickering candlelight, and Irene would feel a pressure point of fright creep through her.

Those first dinners together above Seattle's lights had been magical; those evenings spent together beneath the rain had been lovely. His gaze at her, whenever caught straying, made her flush with heat and agitated her breath, sometimes even stirring a restless passion inside her. He traced the soft outlines of her neck with his eyes, studied briefly the naked curve of her shoulders, and watched carefully the moving shape of her lips whenever she spoke. And when she laughed, he'd always smile in return, his expression solemn, almost bitter, as if he were hiding something incredibly sad.

"What is it you see when you look at me, Daniel?"

This question had come after a month-and-a-half of dating and courting. Within an hour, they would be in his penthouse suite making love beneath the dimmed lights.

"You avoid my gaze for a reason. What are you so afraid of?"

"I don't know what you're talking about, Irene."

"Yes you do, Daniel. Right now, what you just did. What are you afraid of?"

He hesitated. He said, "I'm afraid of someday losing you," and placed his hands on the table. "I avoid your eyes because I'm afraid of losing them. It's just that simple."

And just like that, perhaps due to the euphoric intoxication of the night (no doubt too mixed with their drinks stirred by the late humble hour), he had taken her upstairs to where the stars seem to hide, and had found both in her and the night a wonderful refuge.

*Look at me, Daniel,* Irene had whispered. He had been close to climax then. Irene had felt it, felt *him,* and had felt his entire body burn on top of her—*in* her. *Look at me and don't be afraid.*

He had. And from that moment on, Irene realized she really did love him, would *continue* to love him even if he were to hurt her. He was too good to hate—just too warmhearted and too good to hate. In that moment where she climaxed beneath him, suffocated hot and warmed wonderfully by his breath (*so good. Just so deliciously good*), she herself had become afraid, and had realized that her fear was a consequence of her falling in love with him. Love had been made that night, physical and pure, something that was rare and delicious as a ripened fruit found in summer rain, and Irene remembered thinking how emotionally frail he was despite his calm and mysterious demeanor, how his love that night had been a plea as well as a gesture.

*This is the source of all of his novels,* she thought hours later when waking up in bed with him at her side. *Everything he writes comes from that unknown source of his past. Someone hurt him, and he's never since then been able to forget it. He's never been able to forgive* himself.

"I also know that much of the stories you write are primarily based on your experience of love and friendship," Irene said, coming back from the memory, "or at least, the loss of love and friendship."

"A very telling trait of the man as writer."

She got up and held him from behind, lacing her arms around his waist and feeling cold wood against her feet. Her slippers were in the bedroom. "What do we do now, Daniel?"

"I don't know."

"The marks on her neck—"

"I know, Irene."

"There are belt marks on her backside, and other bruises on—"

"I know, Irene. I know." He turned toward her, held her by the waist, and leaned in to kiss her. "I saw them. I know they're there."

"She still loves you, Daniel."

He kissed her again, this time on the forehead, and slowly backed away, letting his arms fall to the side. He had no response, and Irene knew he wouldn't have one.

"We need to call the police," she said.

"We will, but not now. Not tonight."

"Daniel, if this is a case of domestic abuse and we're sheltering—"

"We don't know what it is because we haven't properly talked about it. We haven't properly talked about it because we haven't yet spoken with the right person, because she's still asleep. Give it time, Irene. If it can be avoided, then the police shouldn't be involved."

"You're scared for her."

"Yes."

"You want to protect her."

"Yes, Irene."

"You care for her."

"Yes." There was a pause. "I do."

They went silent. Daniel turned away. He walked to the kitchen and Irene quietly followed, hearing the thin shuffling sound his slippers made against the floor. She took a seat at the kitchen island and watched as he sought something in the fridge.

"You and Arévalo tomorrow…"

"I can cancel it."

"Daniel, don't. You promised. You *need* to meet him."

"There are other important things at the moment, Irene."

"Oh? So important that you'd throw away a project you've been working on for two years? So important that you'd give up your dreams and effort of writing a screenplay you've so longed to complete?"

He moved from the fridge and approached the island. He poured himself a glass of juice and drank it down.

"Arévalo's doing a lot by coming up here," she said, hoping that her voice sounded patient enough. "You can't cancel on him like that."

"There's always Bosworth if I can't make it with Arévalo."

"Bosworth is a douche and a bastard," she snapped. "You said so yourself, Daniel, and you also said you'd never kiss his ass even if there *was* money placed first on the table. Even if it was a few extra grand. Besides, you know how he is: using his eyes to mentally undress me every time he gets a good look. Fucking creep."

Daniel finished his drink. He went silent.

"I know what you're doing, Irene," he said slowly, "and I don't know how to feel. You *want* me to meet Arévalo in the morning; you want me to leave so you can be with her. You want to speak with her. You want to be alone with her."

"Were you in my position," Irene replied calmly, "you'd want the same thing, Daniel. Besides, I'm not going to interrogate her. I'm just going to take care of her and make sure she's okay when she wakes up. You *need* this project, Daniel; *we* need this. And I know it'll make you happier. Were money the issue, I'd be a bit more vehement with my words, but it's your well-being that I care about. I don't want to see you hurting yourself."

"You think I value writing that much?" he asked her. He hadn't meant to sound bitter. "That I would have it harm me?"

"I just know as a fellow artist that art itself can drive the creator. And I just know as your wife I care about you, and only want the best for you. Please, Daniel." Her voice was almost pleading now. "Just go. Make the deal with Arévalo, show him that you're the best person for the job. I'll take care of her. I promise."

"You have to promise me you'll text when she wakes," he told her after a pause. "And you have to make sure that she understands that I'll be back."

"I will, Daniel. I will."

She went to hold him. He resisted at first, and Irene felt his back muscles tense against her, trying to stay strong. But after a moment, he relented, and expressed a weary, hopeless sigh.

"She looks my size," she whispered. "I can loan her my things."

"Thank you, Irene."

"It's late. We should get some sleep."

He laughed. The sound was bitter, and Irene felt it run straight to her heart.

"Irene," he said softly, "even if I were to sleep, I couldn't. Nothing these days can ever allow me a sound sleep."

"I know," she whispered. She placed her face against his back. "I know, Daniel. I know."

# CHAPTER 24

*Seattle / 11:58 a.m.*
*2019*

Jenny opened her eyes.

The first thing she realized was that she was asleep curled on her side in a fetal position, and that her knees were drawn up to her chest with her arms wrapped around her shoulders. The second thing she noticed—*felt*—were the soft bed sheets beneath her body. They were smooth, and the blankets on top of her were incredibly heavy.

The third thing she realized was that she was very, very *hot.*

*Where am I?*

She sat up. At once, a disorienting earth-tilting feeling overtook her, making her moan. The blankets slid from her body and bared her shoulders to the cold. Her head hurt. It—the world—spun painfully on its side in her head and made everything in the room turn blurry. She brought a hand up to rub her head, winced when pain throbbed through her temple, and sat still for a minute staring at nothing. Sweat drenched her neck.

*I know what this is,* Jenny thought dimly. *I know what this feeling of lightheadedness is, this feeling of floating and subtle pain in my head. It's the feeling of freedom; it's the feeling of nausea. It's me feeling for the first time in my life a sense of freedom from having to go downstairs and make breakfast. This dizziness is freedom, and ah, God, it hurts my head.*

The room was wrong. Or rather, it was different, and it took Jenny another dizzying moment to register everything around her.

Heavy drapes covered the windows to her right; morning light spilled through thin slits to the sides and illuminated the bright beige carpet with a brief hieroglyphic show of shadow and light. A grand fireplace made of Negro Marquina black marble faced her from the opposite wall. Above this was a large tapestry mirror that reflected the other half of the room. To her left was another door leading to what she suspected was the master bathroom, and adjacent to that, another door leading to a walk-in closet.

*Daniel. This is his bed. This is his bed, and he…he shares it with his wife now, I guess.*

She moved from the bed and stepped towards the windows. Her feet slid dry and soft against the carpet, and the collective warmth of heavy blankets around her body from before slowly wore off.

She pulled the curtain aside and winced as a white light fell against her face. Small specks of morning commuters zipped their way across the blacktop channels of Seattle's roads; sunlight sparkled against the great bulk of Elliott Bay. Morning commuters made their way through the streets below and looked like brightly colored ants zipping in random directions. They weaved hurriedly in and out through the streets, many carrying handbags and briefcases.

*The blood of machines*, Jenny thought randomly. Gooseflesh broke out on her body, making her shiver. *This is the color of all machines built by man. Not oil, but just…countless and countless amounts of people.*

There was a pile of clothes neatly folded on the bench near the bed. Jenny frowned when she saw them and carefully made her way over. An unsettling feeling filled her as she stared at the pile. Another ripple of gooseflesh traveled across her back.

*So. This is what I have become. After all this travel, this entire journeying through memory and distance, this is what I have become. My body naked like this has been reduced to charity, and I at this moment have nothing to call my own. The bruises, the pity, the sympathy and lies, even the clothes and language…all of these have been given to me, given to my body, and I am seen simply as a naked vessel standing waiting to be used.*

She picked up a pair of jeans and examined its size.

*I really am a body in the purest sense of the word. I can't even control how I look anymore. I am a body right now—I am a woman. How can standing naked in a room filled with no one watching hurt so much?*

The thought was somber. Jenny threw it away when she felt it, and tossed the jeans aside. There were other clothes for her: a white t-shirt and black cashmere cardigan, a long-sleeved gray woolen sweater, another pair of dark-blue faded jeans, a pair of white cotton panties, a small-sized bra, and a few bath towels. There were even slippers for her at the foot of the bed. Jenny stared at all of this and brought her arms up to hold herself, wrapping her arms across her breasts in a small X.

*I am not his wife. I am not her, and I won't ever allow myself to be her. I am not her body, and I won't wear the clothes she provides me with. I may have her face, and she may have mine, but I will not be her. If I have to be a vessel in life, then fine, then let me at least be my own vessel, my own body…my own bruises.*

*I'm sorry Daniel. I am not your wife. I'm not.*

Her suitcase was near the foot of the bed. That was good. She knelt down after a moment and began opening its main compartments. She pulled out the first things her hands found and tossed them onto the bed. She bit her lip for a minute.

A shower. She could use a shower. And this time when she showered, she wouldn't use hot boiling water. She could do that, at least.

*** 

She was out of the shower a few minutes later and walking through a dimly lit hallway leading to the living room. Carpet was here, and that was good. She had refused the slippers offered to her and had decided to walk barefoot instead, not wanting to wear what was once already worn. Or at least, not by her. She had on a pair of jeans that were her own and had put on a long-sleeve turtleneck sweater. They felt good on her body, and, moreover, familiar. Ahead, somewhere in the living room and where Jenny thought the kitchen was supposed to be, a familiar smell of warm bagels and eggs filled the air.

*When you see him, be calm, and remember that he has a wife now. The woman clothed you, offered you her bed, and now she's even attempting to feed you. Remember this, Jenny. Remember that he has a wife now.*

The living room was a large one, opening alongside the western wall and allowing all of Elliott Bay to majestically loom in through the giant windows. Hanging red drapes bordered the windows while white light skidded across the hardwood flooring. Another fireplace stood against the northern wall here. A flat-screen TV hung above it.

She made her way towards the kitchen and saw a woman at the counter making breakfast. Her back was turned. Just as she was about to say something, the woman turned around, and Jenny stopped. They stared at each other.

"You must be Jenny," the woman said. "It's nice to meet you. I'm Irene."

Jenny opened her mouth to reply. What she initially wanted to say, she didn't know, and let out an airless croak instead, feeling the words dry pathetically on her lips. She said unevenly: "I—yes, nice to meet you too. Irene."

They peered awkwardly at each other. Jenny gazed at her eyes and noticed a Chinese slant to them. A steady hiss of cooking eggs punctured the silence.

"I'm sor—"

"Are you—"

Jenny stopped herself, embarrassed. She watched as the woman—*Irene*—offered another polite smile (although it was forced; Jenny could tell it was forced), and heard her say: "I'm sorry. Please, go ahead."

"I just wanted to apologize for last night," Jenny said. "For the way…for the way things went. I'm sorry if I disturbed anything." She paused. She asked in a quiet voice: "Were you the one that carried me?"

Irene nodded. In that nod, Jenny understood she wasn't accepted here, and felt a defeated sigh grow inside her.

*She doesn't trust me yet,* she thought. *I'm not yet considered a threat to her, but I'm obviously not her friend yet either. I don't blame her. If I saw a woman entering my house in the evening asking my husband for help, I'd be suspicious too.*

At the last thought, a sardonic laugh entered her head, shouting wildly: *Ha! Yeah right, Jenny. You'd secretly be* relieved *if Tom found another woman to enter his life! Remember all those nights you used to dream and wish he'd sleep with another woman? Remember how awful and twisted those thoughts were?*

She shuddered. Tom. She hadn't thought about Tom in a while, not since…well, not since

*(yellow cunt)*

yesterday or something. Or had it been two days ago?

"Daniel helped me. He carried you to the living room and removed your clothes so you wouldn't catch a cold. He helped me carry you to our room where I dried you off."

"Oh. Daniel. Is he…"

"He's at a meeting right now, but will be back a little after one. He said he'll try to be back sooner if he can."

"Oh. Okay."

Another awkward silence fell around them. Jenny unconsciously brought her arms up and held herself. Irene noticed, but said nothing.

"Are you okay now?" Irene asked. "Now that you're awake and showered?"

"Yes. I'm feeling better now. Thank you. For everything, I mean."

"Did you see the clothes?"

"I did. But I…I just wanted to wear some of my own clothes today. Thank you, though."

Irene scanned her. Jenny felt her eyes travel across her body, and waited. What she saw then surprised her, and she relaxed her arms a little, letting them fall to the sides. A hint of respect seemed to go through Irene's eyes.

"Would you like something to eat?" she asked. "Although Daniel isn't here, we can get to know each other a bit before he gets here. I promised I'd take care of you until he returns."

"Yes, please. Sure."

Irene gestured for her to take a seat near the windows. There was a nook there with a small, round table, and when Jenny sat down, she felt gentle sunlight fall against her neck. Irene told her breakfast would be ready shortly. Jenny realized as she sat down that this was the first time someone was making breakfast for her. At least, the first in a very long time, anyway. The thought wasn't so unpleasant to realize.

*** 

"I hope you like scrambled," Irene said as she brought over a warm dish and placed it in front of her. "Again, a quick apology for not being able to provide what you may like. It's a bit impromptu. If there's anything you'd like differently, then please, don't hesitate to ask."

Jenny nodded. She stared down at the plate. White fresh steam rose from a messy clump of yellow eggs; three slices of shriveled bacon accompanied the side. When Jenny saw all of this, cramps folded her stomach, and she nearly doubled over and retched.

"I'm so sorry," she began, "this…this all looks so wonderful, it really does. But…but I can't eat this right now. I'm so sorry."

Irene raised her eyes. She had been eating a toasted bagel and was about to open her mouth for another bite. Now she closed her mouth and stared, questioning.

"I'm not trying to be picky, and I'm not trying to be insulting or anything, but…but, like, I just *can't…*"

Irene placed her bagel down. She waited.

*Of course,* she thought quietly. *The turtleneck sweater she's wearing…the way she has it on her body. It's tight-fitting and form-shaping, covering all of her neck and the entire length of her arms. It's to hide her bruises; it's to conceal the fact that there are fingermarks on her neck and belt marks on her back. Even the bruise on her face eluded me this morning. How could I have forgotten? Why didn't I realize sooner?*

Irene shuddered. A vague sense of shame filled her.

"I…I used to work at a diner a lot," Jenny was saying, "and it used to smell horrible there. Just so horrible. Every morning when I'd come home from work, I'd always have smells of eggs and coffee in my hair, and my clothes would always stink. My hu…my home started to smell like it too, and it would just get into my bed so often that it became disgusting. It just became so hard to get out of my hair. I hate the smell of eggs, and I hate the smell of coffee. I just can't stand smelling breakfast food anymore. I just can't."

Silence passed between them. A doleful look passed through her eyes, making Irene shiver a second time.

*He really was a bastard to you,* Irene thought stilly. *A sick fucking bastard. If only you knew how many belt marks I counted on your body last night, Jenny. If only you knew.*

Irene pushed her plate away. "Well then," she said, trying her best to smile, "we should find something else to eat then, right?"

"If it's…if it's okay with you. Yes, please."

"Would you like to eat downstairs then?"

Jenny looked at her, puzzled.

"There's a lounge off of the main lobby that serves sandwiches and drinks," Irene explained. "It's called the GreenDay Lounge. It's nice down there. Mellow. They have soup too."

"Oh. Okay. Yes, please, that would be nice." Jenny bit her lip. "About…about the eggs and breakfast—"

Irene waved her off. "It's fine, Jenny. Don't apologize. We'll just save these eggs for another time."

"Thank you. I'm sorry for troubling you so much."

Irene got up and threw her bagel away.

# CHAPTER 25

Irene had texted Daniel while Jenny had been in the shower. He'd texted back immediately asking for her condition. There could be no deny: When she saw the haste at which he replied, Irene had felt a spark of jealously flow through her, and had wondered whether or not he'd kept his cell phone on all morning next to him. She had texted back that she was fine, and that the two would meet soon. She was making breakfast then, and she told him not to worry.

Now, riding the elevator down to the main floor of the Empyrean Tower, Irene realized that she had left her cellphone upstairs, and was not at all surprised at her feelings of indifference over the matter. An indiscernible part of her called such indifference selfish, while another part of her taunted her for being a coward. None of these voices—both hers and hers alone—made much sense to her, and neither greatly bothered her. Daniel was kind, and he was far more intelligent than most men could ever hope to be for themselves—but in Irene's heart, she knew his love and concern for the world was ultimately encumbered by his sex, and knew that he could only view the many struggles of women with an anxious and troubled look. Condescending perhaps, yes, but life hardly cared which side one took. For this was the heart of the matter, as Irene believed it; this is what connected both of them as they rode the elevator together and kept their silence:

womanhood, and this attempt to define it.

*Slut, Xiaoli*, a voice whispered to her. *You look like a slut in those shorts of yours.*

Irene shivered. The voice came out of nowhere, like a phantom draft blown against naked ankles. She looked to the side to see if Jenny had noticed, and saw that she hadn't. Her gaze instead was turned away, taken by the dull dings of the elevator numbers.

Her mother—it had been her voice she'd heard. Why or how she was hearing her in the back of her mind now, Irene didn't know, but felt another cold shudder pass through her. Her mother was dead.

*Were my mother here now*, Irene thought coldly, *she'd go mad with rage seeing the similarities between me and this Korean woman standing next to me, and accuse my white American husband of a Freudian act of infidelity. She would curse him, say that he was using me as a surrogate for his unconscious fantasies, and force me to leave him.*

The elevator came to a gradual stop. Before the doors opened, Irene thought: *I would rather kill myself than turn into a woman like my mother. Whether it's severe poverty, or cursed with a life-threatening condition, I would rather be all those things than turn into my mother. Like young men realizing the deficiencies in their fathers and suddenly hating them, women too must realize the vanity of their mothers, and in turn ultimately loathe them. Only with an emotional miracle do we escape our parents. It's a miracle at all that we can escape* ourselves.

The thought was bitter. It brought a hot sensation to Irene eyes, and she had to briefly tilt her head back before stepping out of the elevator.

"Is there anything particular you'd like?"

Jenny raised her head. They were seated at a booth together near the salad bar. "Whatever's cheapest," Jenny said quickly. "Please don't spend too much on me."

Irene walked away and came back with two bowls of salad and bottles of orange juice.

"Daniel tells me you once attended the U-Dub," Irene said.

Jenny nodded. It had been years since she'd heard the abridged name of her University. Nostalgia filled her. "Yeah. It was a long time ago."

"Did you have classes together?"

"No. I studied psychology while he studied English. We rarely saw each other."

"What specialization in psychology?"

"I never finished college."

Irene raised her eyes at her, curious. There'd been a despondent tone in her voice.

"How about you?" Jenny asked. "Are you from around here?"

"L.A., but I moved here to Seattle from Boston."

"What was in Boston?"

"Graduate school. I studied psychoanalysis there."

"Oh. What made you come to Seattle?"

*(slut xioli you look like)*

"I graduated from UCLA and decided I wanted to travel," Irene said, calmly. She took a bite of her salad and chewed. Her hands shook. "I went to BGSP in Boston and eventually came back to Seattle for the intellectual community. I attended the U-Dub for another degree."

"What degree?"

"Drawing and Painting."

Jenny looked at her. She asked: "What did you major in at UCLA?"

Irene hesitated. "Bioengineering and Painting."

Jenny stared. She said nothing, and took a drink of her juice. She averted her eyes.

"That's quite an accomplishment," she said finally. "Not many women can earn four degrees these days. Good for you, Irene."

"Jenny."

She raised her head, and Irene watched her, sorry, saying patiently: "I'm not here to interrogate you. Or intimidate you. You understand that, don't you?"

"I...Yes. I guess I do."

401

"I told Daniel that I'd take care of you until he comes back. I *promised* him that. Moreover, I promised myself I'd get to know you to better help you. I'm not here to sabotage you or undermine you. You need not be so defensive around me."

Jenny looked at her. She thought for a minute, and pushed her empty salad bowl away (she'd been ravenous). She said: "Fine. I suppose you're right. I'm sorry though. I...I had a rough night last night."

Irene nodded.

"Did you leave college to move back to Korea?" Irene asked.

"No. My father, he...he left his company shame-faced, and we had to move away. We had to go far away from here and that's why I never finished college."

"Mother?"

"My mother left me a long time ago. My father never remarried."

There was a brief pause.

"Do they still hurt?"

Jenny looked at her, confused.

"The bruises, I mean. The ones on your back. And your face." Irene paused. "I won't force you to talk about them, but I think it'll be easier if you do. With me, anyway. First."

Jenny stared down at the table. "There's nothing to talk about," she said quietly. "I'm fine, Irene."

"Jenny."

She recoiled, suddenly, acting as if Irene had reached over the table to touch her. Irene frowned at her and peered intently in her direction.

"Look. I know I'm asking much by asking you to tell me about your past, and I know we've known each other for less than an hour. But I think I deserve to know a few things, especially because of what happened last night."

A low blow. And with it, a grimace so pained, so hurt, that a dark frown spread through Jenny's face. Irene quickly added: "I'm sorry, but I have to know. I won't force you, and you have every right to ignore me, but I think I deserve it, Jenny. As a woman, I think I deserve it."

Jenny shook her head. "I don't have to tell you, and you don't deserve to know. But I understand that you're asking for his sake. To protect him."

Irene nodded.

"From me."

"Yes," she said. It hadn't been a question. "Both."

"You won't interrogate me, but will mark your territory against me."

"You'd do exactly the same thing if you were me, Jenny," Irene said gently.

"Is that you speaking, or the psychologist?"

Irene frowned at her. "It's the *woman* in me," she said sharply. "It's me, Jenny. You know it is. Someone like you should know when womanhood transcends simple titles. I told you: You can trust me."

Jenny went mute. She lowered her eyes a second time and refocused them on the table in deep thought. Irene waited, patient, and took another glance at the bruise on her face.

*I'm pitying you right now,* Irene thought faintly, *and feeling guilty for pitying you. But at the same time, I'm glad that I can pity you, Jenny, glad that I have the privilege to pity. But I also hate you. I hate you because you remind me of me, and hate you that you make me feel guilty for my pity. I have Daniel now, do you understand? I have him, and I love him, and he loves me too. But when I have these thoughts toward you, I realize I'm no better than that fucking husband of yours that used to beat you, and so, I hate you. I hate you when I just want to be another woman for you. I'm concerned for you, Jenny. But my concern can only paint me who I am in your eyes.*

*I could have been you, Jenny. With your face and your bruises, I could have been you. I wish you were my friend earlier in life.*

"I grew up in a world of two languages," Jenny began. "At home, I spoke Korean, and at school, I spoke English. Living in America made me exist in between two worlds where I was seen as Korean by Americans, American by Koreans, and Korean-American by those who needed further categorization.

403

I was a stereotype and I was an expectation. At home, I was disliked and viewed with prejudice due to my gender and because I was the only child. Outside, my Korean friends loathed me because I refused to submit to cultural norms governing my 'Korean-ness.' I was fetishized; I was discriminated against. Alongside this problem of language and ethnicity was a problem of sexuality. I was a girl; I was a woman. I had to weigh the burden of being a noun that was further divided into smaller categories: 'woman'; 'Asian-woman'; 'American-woman'; 'Korean-American woman'; and 'Korean-woman.'"

"Multiple identities," Irene said.

"No, that's not it. It's already *knowing* your identity, Irene; it's knowing already who you are as an individual. I knew who I was and what I wanted to become as a girl. But this world, through its culture and its social expectations, constantly tried to conform me and force me to be what I wasn't. I had no multiple identities because I already *knew* who I was; it was culture that tried to force me into multiple names. Inside my mind, in my own *heart*, I was me, but outside—out on the streets, in the eyes of society, according to fashion, according to Hollywood—I was 'Korean,' a 'girl,' a 'woman,' some noun that had specific connotations regarding her sex, her eyes, her background, her ethnicity, whatever. Things I couldn't control."

"Hegemony," Irene said for her.

Jenny nodded.

"You speak as if you realized this and kept harboring it all your life," Irene began. "But if this were true, I wouldn't think you'd be with a husband that beat you. I wouldn't think you'd submit yourself to someone that gave you bruises."

Jenny turned her head away, hurt. Irene bit her lip, sorry for the way she delivered her words. She glanced down at Jenny's hands and saw a naked ring-finger. A band of white skin laced the finger.

"Yes," Jenny said quietly, "I know. I know what you mean.

"I moved away after my freshman year and went to Boise with my father.

After a few years, my father passed away, and everything around me just fell into ruin. I became scared. Life didn't make sense after leaving Seattle, and I just didn't know what to do with myself. I just gave up everything that was once me, and just let life overtake me. I didn't care. I just let life come and change me into whatever it saw fit, never once turning back to look at Seattle.

"I married Tom because I was scared. It's…it's that simple, I guess. I left Seattle afraid, and out of fear, let myself submit to everything in life. I became afraid of my own strength as an individual, became weary of the fight, and just…just let someone live for me. I wanted someone to take care of me, be there for me, and just do things for me. The bruises he gave me hurt, but they were safe. Do you understand, Irene? They hurt, but as long as someone was there to define me, take care of me, speak for me, *live* for me, I was safe. I…I was safe."

Jenny lifted her hand and touched her bruise. She did it unconsciously, barely aware of what she was doing. Her eyes were distant and glazed over.

"In life, we have an infinite number of choices we may make. We have complete freedom for who we are as individuals, and have no excuses for our failures. But sometimes life attempts to restrict us; sometimes language and society attempts to impede us. Cliché will tell us what is right, hegemony will tell us what is common sense, Hollywood will reinforce perception and stereotype, fashion will dictate what is beautiful and ugly, and life…life will just make us weary so that we no longer fight for our freedoms. Our individuality."

She lifted her head. She gazed at Irene and caught her eyes.

*You really did love him once,* Irene thought quietly. *I can hear it in your voice. The way you speak, the way you craft your words…you really did love him once. I can hear his voice in your words.*

"I pity you, you know," Irene said. She stopped herself, startled. She took a moment to pause and then said: "That bruise on your face…when I see it, I pity you, and realize just how privileged I am. When all I want to be is your friend, I realize my pity sets me apart from you. Luckier than you."

"I know, Irene."

"Will you hold resentment against me?"

Jenny shook her head. "No. I don't think I could do that. To you, anyway. Doing so would prompt self-pity, and I've had enough of that in life. Your pity is nothing new."

Irene frowned at her. She said, "I know where your thoughts are derived from, and I'm going to tell you what I told Daniel a few years ago when we had this discussion. Pity is not always a theme to be disdained and loathed; it can be a precursor to charity and kindness too. With your experiences and understanding of the world, I understand your need for freedom, and understand how a pitying gaze could be detrimental to an individual's identity. There are the gazes, the expectancies, the categories, the archetypes, and the schema. All this to you means bondage."

"Yes," Jenny said.

"And for Daniel, it means an inequality of social being."

Jenny nodded. A warm feeling of hurt filled her chest at the mentioning of Daniel's name. She realized that Irene had had the privilege of fully indulging herself in his mind during all these years, where she'd simply just gotten a glimpse of them at their youngest when he was still just a boy.

Flickers of jealously stirred in her heart.

"You and Daniel always focus on 'pity' as if it were a pessimistic premise to be held rather than an optimistic alternative," Irene said. "Daniel always focuses on the effect the Pitied has on the Superior Pitier, but he hardly ever speaks of the *affect* the Pitier may have on the Inferior Pitied. I admit that the dichotomies distinguishing between the pitied and the privileged cannot be eliminated in this world, but that doesn't mean a determinist approach has to be instilled.

"In recognizing each other, there is a dichotomy, and in this dichotomy, there is pity. Yet the privileged need not despair over this fact of pity, and the pitied need not loathe the pitier. Every moment in life is a choice to choose,

406

and in this moment of recognizing each other, the Pitier can choose to help and love the Pitied. One need not despair over the dichotomies and inequalities that exist in this world."

"What you're suggesting is a social and moral obligation of the privileged," Jenny said.

"No. What I'm suggesting is a possibility."

"Such possibilities hardly manifest in reality."

"I know. But because it's there, there at *least* is hope and a kindness with pity."

"But those that are assisted will always be considered as the inferior subject."

Irene shook her head. "You don't know that, and to assume so is to adopt a determinist mentality that is opposite of self-determinism. People will change; they will evolve. One who is seen as the Inferior now can be seen as the Superior later. This is the piece Daniel always misses when declaring his theory."

"People will change," Jenny said, "but there will always be more to be pitied in this world. Classes, races, peoples—dichotomies will always suggest to us an opposite and an inferior. Society is never equal."

"Yes," Irene said quietly. "I know." She smiled thinly to the side, thinking something sad and bitter. "And *this* is what Daniel always refutes me with."

Jenny asked sharply: "Do we say to the world, 'Let us pity the world and love those inferior to us'?"

"No," Irene said. Her voice had gone quiet, surprising Jenny. "We don't. I don't know what to say to the world. I only know this: Without pity, I

*(slut)*

wouldn't know how else to love this world. Call it whatever you want, Jenny, but pity—as the first precursor to kindness or disgust—can also evolve into love. And with love, there is always something great for humanity to achieve."

Jenny stared at her. She didn't know what she was referring to.

"You don't pity me out of kindness," Jenny remarked. "I can see it in your face. I say it gently, but you don't pity me out of kindness."

"No," Irene said. "I pity you out of fear. But with this fear, I can choose to care for your well-being. I have the choice to choose how much I love you."

"And yet, I'll still be submissive before your gaze and acts of charity."

Irene nodded. "Yes. I know. This dichotomy can't be eliminated."

"Is fear the only reason you choose to feel concern for me? Or is it an obligation to Daniel?"

Irene looked at her. She said softly: "It's about being a woman, Jenny. I empathize with you because I'm a woman, and I know what it means to be a woman in a world of

*(sluts)*

language."

Jenny stared at her. She said nothing, and simply studied her face, watching as she brought a napkin up to wipe her mouth. Irene placed the napkin down and returned her gaze.

"I'm not a martyr," Jenny said slowly. Tears filled her voice. "And I can't...I can't be a symbol for others."

"I know, Jenny."

"You can't glorify me simply because you're afraid of something you've never encountered."

Irene nodded her head. "I know."

"I just want my life back."

"I know, Jenny. I know."

"*Can* I have it back?"

At this, Irene turned away and bit her lip. She said slowly: "Jenny. There's...there's something else you need to know. About...about all this."

"What?"

"I'm...I'm two weeks late on my period."

Jenny frowned. She didn't understand at first. She opened her mouth to say, "I don't—", and then stopped herself, drawing a blank. Coldness crawled up her back. The saliva in her mouth turned dry.

"I…I mean, is it…have you confirmed?"

Irene nodded. She said slowly: "I took a pregnancy test. Today after Daniel gets back I plan to drive myself to the clinic and confirm it with a personal doctor. I haven't told Daniel. I wanted to surprise him and tell him when the timing was right."

Jenny laid her hands on the table. She swallowed, grimaced, felt her throat muscles convulse, and said lamely: "Congratulations."

"I'm telling you this because I don't want to hurt you," Irene said. "Do you understand? For his sake and yours, I don't want to hurt you. I don't want to hurt or hate you, and I think it's important that you know so that…"

"So that I don't ruin your marriage," Jenny said. Her voice was flat. "So I don't take him away from you. Or think that I have a chance."

"So that you understand that he still loves you, but that he has another role to fulfill now. A father."

Jenny winced at the word. Irene noticed.

"Are you scared?" Jenny asked after a long pause. They'd both taken time to stare at their hands on the table. "For the baby, I mean?"

Irene looked at her, confused, not understanding what she meant. But then she noticed the concern in her eyes, and nodded.

"Yeah," Irene said faintly. "I think I am. In fact, I think I'm

*(raised a whore)*

terrified."

They went quiet. Irene took one final sip of her drink and placed it aside.

"Jenny."

"Yeah?"

"Let's go now. Daniel should be back soon."

They gathered their things and threw them in the trash.

Irene had expected silence on their way back up. Instead, it was Jenny who broke the silence.

"My husband taught me how to throw a baseball last year," she began. "He taught me while we were at the park together, and taught me how to use my shoulder. He used to call it his Mean Pitch. Which is funny, cause I always heard it as his Mean Bitch, but...whatever. He used to practice hours with me until I got it right, and used to do it until my whole body got sore. It was like a total body workout. I got good at it though, and it was enough that he became really happy with me."

Irene nodded. She didn't know where this was going, but kept quiet anyway.

"Last night—or, I mean, a few days ago, I can't remember—I did something to get him mad, and he...we got into a fight. Only instead of it just being a normal fight, it was a big one, and I could tell that he was...that he was really angry with me. I think he meant to kill me."

They gradually reached their floor.

"That night when he meant to kill me, I knocked him out by throwing a heavy cream bottle at his face. I threw it straight at his forehead and right between the eyes. I may have even broken his nose or something. I for sure loosened some teeth. I think I even gave him a concussion."

"I wish you'd given him a coma," Irene said quietly.

"Yes," Jenny replied. The doors opened, and a sad, distant look appeared in her eyes as she turned away. "I wish that had happened too."

They stepped out of the elevator together.

# CHAPTER 26

So. This was it. This is how it felt. This is how it felt to be breaking up with someone. This is how it felt to be losing the person you thought you loved. It hurt. This pain felt deeply in the chest? It hurt, and it hurt in a dull, vague, aching way, akin to finding fresh January snow on a derelict road. Had it been an episode with the half-familiar instances of screaming and shouting, Junghee might have felt better. But no. There was only slight mid-March rain falling against his face, and the familiar movements of bodies moving around him as he stood in the center of Red Square.

"But *why?*" Junghee asked again, his voice a shrill whine. "Can't you at least tell me *why?*"

"I told you, oppa. I just want to be alone right now. I can't take having other people in my life. The time's just not right for me."

He released another exasperated sigh. His breath came out full and white from his lips and rose steadily through the air. Jenny watched him intently from the side and brought her arms up to hold herself. She was tired this morning.

"Like, are you asking for a *break* or something?" he asked her. His voice had climbed to another octave. It gave his overall voice a high, almost girly sound. "Because if that's all you need, like, I can give it to you—"

"No, oppa, not a break. Real. What I'm asking you is real. I need to break

411

up with you."

"But *whyyy?*"

That voice again, high and whiny. Jenny grimaced when she heard it and turned her eyes away, embarrassed.

"I still don't get what you want. Like, do you want to be alone *from* me and be with someone else, or like, alone from *everybody* else? And why does being alone mean having to break up with me? Can't I just give you time and space to *think?*"

"Oppa—"

"Don't call me that if you don't want to!"

She flinched, a look of hurt and surprise on her face. Junghee cursed at himself and sighed again.

God, where had all of this come from? And why was she acting like this *now?* How did she expect him to figure out what was wrong if she refused to talk to him? Last month she had stopped talking to him totally, and had returned NONE of his e-mails or text messages. And now she suddenly wanted to break up with him? Now she wanted to leave without telling him *why?*

"Jenny—"

"Opp…I mean, Junghee, look. I'm sorry, I really am. You've been kind to me and I really appreciate it. But we're not right for each other. We never were. I don't love you and you don't love me, and neither of us is even mature enough to use that word yet, so let's just…let's just be friends or something, I don't know. I don't hate you, and it has nothing to do with you, but I just can't be with you anymore."

"Is it Eugene?"

She stared at him, a perplexed look on her face. "*Who?*" she asked. "Junghee, I don't even—"

"It *is* him, isn't it?" Junghee brought a hand up to wipe his mouth, scraping his palm against his lips. "That freaking liar! I *knew* he was interested in you that day I brought you to Shutlzy's. I *knew* that guy was freaking trying to get—"

"Junghee, this isn't about your friends! God, can't you see that I'm trying to break up with you?" She stomped her foot down and brought her hands up. "It just has to do with *us*, all right? I just can't handle people in my life, and I just *need some space*. Okay?"

Junghee stared at her. He sucked in his lower lip and scrunched in his face. "Don't go," he said. His voice was pleading now. "Please, Jenny. Don't go."

"Junghee—"

He reached out and took her by the arm. Jenny let him, too tired (as well as too embarrassed) to fling him off. His umbrella rocked to the side as he grabbed her, spilling rainwater down her neck.

"Give me a chance," he said, "please, *noona*. Whatever it is, I can do better. Just give me a *chance*."

*God, now he's even calling me noona.*

*Noona* was a term used by guys to call girls 'older sister.' Junghee was older than her. He was calling her *noona* out of desperation.

"Please let go of me, Junghee. Please don't do this. Just…please."

He let his hand slip away. He stared at her. A fine mist gathered in his eyes and his Adam's apple vigorously worked in his throat.

"I'm going now, oppa," Jenny said to him. "Thank you for everything. I'm sorry for hurting you. You really were kind to me." She paused for a minute. Then, in perfect Korean, she said: "Please don't stand here in the rain anymore waiting for me, Park Junghee. I won't turn to look back at you no matter how sad you are. I'm sorry."

His jaw tightened. Jenny saw the movement and knew that he was gritting his teeth. His nostrils momentarily flared, and his Adam's apple frantically swept up and down in his throat as he struggled to swallow. She took one last look at his eyes (now clouding with dry red), and turned away. She lowered her head as she walked and let the rain trickle down her neck and sprinkle her ears. Her sneakers squeaked against wet bricks. She sobbed.

*Seattle / 3:43 p.m.*
*2019*

Daniel was late. Irene said he'd be back a little after one, but right now, it was almost four, and the autumn sunlight outside was already fading. Which was fine, Jenny thought; she didn't care. She didn't want to care about anything just then, and just simply wanted to be alone with the light as it traveled slowly across the carpeted floor, illuminating folding shadows preparing for sleep. She'd spent the last few hours after lunch rearranging her clothes, and then after that sitting on the bed staring at nothing. Irene had left her by herself, and that was good; Jenny didn't want to talk with her. She just didn't want to talk with anybody.

She sat with the curtains drawn back and her body comfortably inclined against the seating area near the bay window, her feet bared to the falling afternoon sun, the denim of each leg rolled up midway to her calves. She sat back in silence and twirled John's cigarette between her fingers.

John's cigarette had somehow managed to follow her; it'd somehow managed to find her after all this way. She held it between two fingers and lifted it close to her face, smelling the faint residue of un-smoked tobacco. She'd found the cigarette while rearranging her clothes, and had felt her blood turn ice-cold when seeing the stick on top of her underwear. A dozen explanations had screamed through her head when she discovered the cigarette: that she'd accidentally opened Irene's suitcase and had somehow gone through her clothes; that the cigarette belonged to someone else and had somehow found its way inside her bag while she was riding in the Greyhound bus; that maybe someone had planted it there, that maybe it was Tom's, that she was just imagining it, or that she had sleepwalked last night and purchased a fresh new pack from downstairs. But no—all of these were just speculative rants and ludicrous fantasies. What probably had happened was that she'd grabbed the cigarette without thinking about it, packed it with the rest of her clothes as she fled from Tom, and had forgotten about it since. It was the only explanation that made sense.

*I am bound to you,* Jenny thought listlessly as she twirled the Winston cigarette between her fingers, *in the same way I am bound to language. I don't know what to do; I don't know how to escape. Me saying that I am my own body is false, because in order for me even to say that I am a 'body' or a 'woman' means that someone else must see and hear me. What am I to do with you? Why can't I throw you away?*

She rolled the cigarette between her fingers. In between the shafts of light that spilled through the windows, the cigarette looked harmless and dull, almost comical in shape. And yet at each point there was a rounded end inviting a mouth and flame to…what? Suck? Inhale? To get lung cancer, mouth cancer, bad teeth? Something. To snap it in half, to throw it away, to find the nearest garbage can and just get rid of it—all of these were easy. But by disposing of the cigarette, would her feelings of angst become tarnished, or become even more exasperated?

*To smoke or not to smoke. I guess that's the question. But once I get my answer, what am I supposed to do afterwards?*

She could smoke it. Indeed she could. This was her *freedom* wasn't it? Smoking was her choice. The choice belonged to her and her alone, and yet with this choice—this freedom to *choose*—there came with it a monumental burden that weighed heavily on her mind. For at this moment here, temporarily freed from all aspects of life—sheltered by the walls, hidden from sight, unuttered and unspoken to—she was obliged to do *anything*, and was held back by *nothing*.

*Freedom. I'm free right now alone in this room. Free from language, freed from perception. I can just do anything and have no one define me.*

She shuddered at the thought.

The cigarette was her choice and her choice alone, and in her freedom, she could choose to smoke it, thereby exercising her right as an individual. And if the cigarette represented death, why, couldn't she *still* choose to have death if she wanted? So long as she had the freewill to choose, so long as she accepted the consequences, couldn't she *still* exercise her right as an individual?

*Who would recognize me if I died,* Jenny thought bleakly, *if I in turn couldn't feel their gaze and acknowledge their recognition of me? Isn't this the ultimate form of freedom? To escape all laws of language and perception? But then, by escaping language, how would I know I existed? I wouldn't know that I was an "I" were it not for language.*

Jenny stopped herself. She frowned.

*What the hell is all this bullshit supposed to mean anyway?*

She sighed. A lock of hair fell across her face and she idly pushed it behind her ear. She leaned her head against the window.

"You're not that great, God," Jenny whispered to herself. She closed her eyes and let the sun warm her face. "You can't ever deliberate or hesitate like we humans can; you can't ever make a decision. Because you're so omniscient and omnipotent, no moment of existence for you is filled with surprise or delight. You know everything already; everything to you is the same moment for all eternity. You have no freewill. You experience no indecision that becomes your moment of freedom."

Jenny opened her eyes. She saw the city below her and felt tears well in her eyes.

*God is not great. He can't ever choose for himself whether or not to smoke a cigarette, for he can never choose. I should have never bowed my head to you, God.*

A buildup of phlegm collected in her throat, and Jenny let out a dry, airless cough, swallowing it back down. She stared at the cigarette for another minute, and moved herself from the window. Her feet felt cold.

"Let's see what God has in store for us now," Jenny sighed wearily, walking towards the door. "Let's just see what happens next in life."

She opened the bedroom door and stepped out into the hallway.

\*\*\*

416

Irene was reading a book in the living room. Jenny knew this even though she couldn't see her. She stood in the dark beneath the hallway's gloom and had her arms wrapped tightly around herself. Thin, papery, scraping noises echoed from the living room as Irene read her book; the sounds reminded Jenny of rough palms rubbing against each other.

*We're playing a game now*, Jenny thought dimly. *The main goal of this game is to see which person will make noise first. We're also trying to see who can stand the silence the longest, and see who can stand this feeling of awkwardness.*

The dull sound of minutes ticking from a clock on the mantle; the low hum of the heater blowing against her ankles; the light, shifting sound of bare feet against carpet and hardwood floors (which was, Jenny realized, extremely selfish on her part. Irene had left her slippers in the bedroom for her, and she had still refused to wear them, rendering both their feet cold); and the audible drip of the kitchen faucet. All of these sounds were suffocating, claustrophobic, and piercing. Jenny was sure Irene heard them too.

A loud boom sounded somewhere, and Jenny jerked in surprise. Gooseflesh rippled down her spine. She waited patiently and heard Daniel's voice from the foyer. Her heartbeat quickened.

"Hey. You're back." Irene's voice. From the living room. "How was it?"

There was a pause. Jenny quietly moved to the end of the hallway. She swallowed.

"Fine. It was fine. Arévalo was being a prick, but it's a done deal, Irene. We got it."

There was the sound of scraping fabric and then a light kiss. Jenny closed her eyes. She imagined Irene delivering a congratulatory kiss to his cheek with her arms wrapped all the way around his shoulders. She probably had to stand all the way up on her toes just to deliver the kiss.

"Where is she?"

"Bedroom. I haven't heard from her for the past hour. She might be asleep."

"Are you going to see Kamen at the clinic?"

There was a brief pause. Jenny heard Daniel handing her the keys.

"You don't have to go, Irene. You can stay."

"I've already set it up with Kamen, Daniel. It's fine."

"I know, but you can still stay, Irene. You don't *have* to go. Do you understand?"

There was another slight pause.

"I trust you," Irene said. "I know you won't do anything, and I trust you as my husband. Moreover, I trust *her* too. She won't do anything, Daniel. I know she's not the type to hurt others."

His kissed her. The sound was full and echoed from the foyer down to the hallway, forcing Jenny to swallow.

*She's pregnant, Daniel,* Jenny thought bitterly. *You're going to become a father soon. You as that boy I remembered—you as that friend I once had—you're…you're going to become a father soon, and you're going to become something I can't even imagine. You're no longer going to be my friend where I got to define you. You're going to become a father—Irene's word.*

Hot tears welled up in her eyes, sudden and quick. The force was unexpected, and Jenny had to momentarily turn her face away and bring a hand up to smother her sobs. She cried in the darkness and blocked out their voices from the living room.

"I'll be back in a few hours," Irene was saying. "I need to drop by the studio real quick."

"Come back soon."

There was one last kiss, some last words of goodbye, and then the final shut of the door.

Jenny waited. She collected herself and forced herself to breathe in deep, heavy breaths. She wiped her face, straightened her shoulders, and slowly stepped out into the living room.

# CHAPTER 27

*Seattle / 3:50 p.m.*
*2019*

There was a video on YouTube that parodied Asian mothers. There were many, but only one stuck in Irene's mind as the most significant. She had watched it with her friends long ago as a child when YouTube was still in its heyday of "Thumbs up!" and again a second time as a student at the Boston Graduate School of Psychoanalysis. The video—per the usual of Youtube idiots who wanted to draw autonomous attention to themselves in a world filled with post-modernist tendencies—showed an Asian man dressed as a woman (an Asian woman) harshly berating his/her two children (Asian children). The skit was a funny one, and for Irene, at least, it was funny because it was brutally honest and true.

The clip was short. It ran for only five minutes, and, throughout, showed different scenes of the "Typical Asian Mother." The video invoked typical FOB stereotypes of the Asian "Tiger Mom," and invoked (realistically, Irene thought) all the slurs and errors of broken American-Engerish.

In one scene, the "mother" is shown standing in the living room with her daughter's report card. She screams, "What this?! A *minus?* You bitch! Why not A plus, you whore!" and throws the report card at her daughter's face. Another scene shows the mother struggling to type on the laptop, screaming off-screen: "Honey! *HONEY!* Laptop not work! Turn on for mommy! Honey!" Another scene, finally with the son (and Irene had noticed that oddity too. She'd wondered why the majority of the "Typical Asian Mother" stereotypes had consisted only of daughter and mother, and rarely of mother and son), had shown the mother talking loudly on the phone with the son sitting morosely in the background. The mother had gone on to say: "Oh yes, my son so good boy! He so smart, he more smarter than your son! My son will go to medical school and become doctor and have lots of money, and your son will work at McDonalds for life! Haha!" (Another scene involving the daughter and mother had shown the mother walking into the daughter's room, seeing a poster of some famous rapper/singer on her wall, and the mother scoffing loudly: "Why you like black men? You want black men in life? Why not nice smart Asian man? Black men will shoot you!")

Of all of these scenes, there was one that Irene remembered the most, and she remembered how it had abruptly caused a spreading of gooseflesh down her arms when she first watched it. The actress playing the young girl had walked downstairs wearing white denim shorts. She opened the door to go outside, was just about to step out, when suddenly the "mother" entered the scene and shouted: "You look like slut in those pants! Go change! Why you want to look like slut today?"

Her friends had laughed a lot at that one; Irene had laughed with them.

*I pretended to laugh a lot then,* Irene thought as she turned the corner leading to the elevators. She was alone, and her flats played off the walls as dull echoes. *I remember how easy it was for me to fake laughter back then, and remembered how naturally it sounded to everyone around me. To me too, I guess.*

Her mother had called her a slut once. She had, in fact, called her more than a slut, and had called her more on multiple occasions. It seemed to be her favorite word when needing to destroy her self-confidence. Sometimes her shorts were too short; sometimes her thighs were too big. Sometimes she showed too much skin, and sometimes the lipstick on her lips—or eyeliner around her eyes, or earrings on her ears, or heels on her feet—made her look like a cheap prostitute. Why was she going to wear heels today? Why was she wearing a skirt to school? How come she looked chubbier this morning, why wasn't she upstairs in her room studying? Shouldn't she go running today, shouldn't she spend a few more hours on the treadmill?

Slut. Her mother liked calling her a slut. In front of her friends, in front of her peers, once even in front of her Homecoming date…she was just a slut to her mother. It didn't matter if it was uttered in English or Mandarin— her attractiveness in school just always made her a slutty slut. In Mandarin, she dressed like *an accompanying bargirl*.

*Bitch*, Irene thought coldly. She felt tears in her eyes and suddenly had to close them. She leaned her head back and swallowed, rocking back and forth on her feet. The elevator neared her floor. *I've called you this many times before, mama, and I do so knowing that it hurts. It hurts because I still love you. Do you understand, mom, do you understand, you old hag? I hurt because I still love you Why couldn't you and papa just love me as I was?*

She came downstairs one hot summer morning wearing denim shorts and a halter top. She was going to hang out with Janice, she told her mother; they were going to the mall and to the beach afterwards.

"If you're going to go outside in public, you need to change into pants, Xiaoli," her mother said (even now, after all these years, Irene still wondered whether or not her voice sounded like her mother's when speaking her native Chinese, and she always shuddered at the thought).

"But Mama, it's almost *eighty-five degrees*—"

"I won't be known as someone who raised a slut in this family, Xiaoli. Change into something more appropriate. Now."

"Mom! I am *not*—"

"I said *go change into something more appropriate!* Don't argue with your mother, Xiaoli!"

She had gone upstairs to change. She had gone upstairs to cry too, but had let the tears fall only after she closed (and locked) the door behind her. She wore jeans that day, and Janice had asked if she was hot. She said no.

*And then there was the time when I had bought running shorts to work out in*, Irene thought. *The first thing she said to me when I put them on was, "You look like a slut in those shorts, Xiaoli," and ever since then, they were known as my slut pants. Slut thighs,*

421

*whore lipstick, prostitute eyeliner. Skanky mouth. I was nothing but trouble for you,*
*mama, and sometimes I wonder how you were as a daughter. Did you get slapped in the*
*face with a ruler too whenever you decided to defy your mother? Did she deride you on your*
*choice of clothes too?*

Was it ever a wonder that she finally sprouted some wings and finally
decided to fly away after college? Now look at her; just look at her now. Four
degrees to her name that had no real meaning except for the ones dealing
with art and painting. What more did her mother *want*?

*I bet she'd like to see me all tired-looking and haggard from drinking too much,* Irene
thought bitterly as she stepped into the elevator. The doors closed behind
her. *I bet she'd love it if she saw me lost and confused, throwing up in the morning with*
*my hair messed up and my eyes red. Papa would like that too probably. I bet she'd liked it*
*too if she saw me reluctantly browsing over brochures with the words "Alcoholics*
*Anonymous" on them, or see Daniel almost hitting m—*

Irene stopped herself, startled. The elevator wasn't moving. She'd gotten
a shock out of the sudden silence, and realized she'd forgotten to press for
her floor.

*Jesus. Come on.*

She reached out with one finger

*(god why am i trembling?)*

and pushed for the underground parking garage. The elevator hummed to
life. Irene stepped back against the wall, leaned her head back, and closed her
eyes.

$$***$$

She had left him upstairs to test his loyalty—there was no denying the truth.
In doing so, Irene hated herself, and felt a warm feeling of self-pity build up
in her chest as she rode the elevator down. She meant it when she said she
believed in Jenny's sincerity, and was honest when she believed in his trust.
And yet…

*I've known her for less than twenty-four hours,* Irene thought as she stared up at the numbers, *and I know she's still in love with my husband. She still carries his memory in her heart like I do. Only she's more desperate than I am. Hurt. I left them upstairs to test both of them.*

The thought was bitter. Just how long had they been together that they still needed to distrust each other like this?

*His hand,* Irene thought suddenly. *I still remember that one night where he hurt his hand.*

The memory re-played in her mind like fresh fireworks ripping through the sky. His knuckles…he'd badly bruised them that night. He bruised the bones, split the skin, and even fractured half his wrist when he slammed his fist against the wall. There had been no pain at first, no howl of agony. All there'd been at first was a deep look of flaming rage, a disgruntled snarl, and a calm, almost maddening look in his eyes as she begged him to stop and cowered against the wall. He hadn't hurt her that night—physically—and emotionally he'd only bruised her. Whoever it was Jenny had run away from, Daniel wasn't like him; he just wasn't. He would never hurt her like that. *Ever.*

*Stop it. Oh please, just stop it, stop comparing yourself to her, stop comparing husband and lives. You're lucky, you're fortunate, you've found someone good in life, and fine, just leave it like that. Why do you keep comparing yourself to her?*

Irene shook her head. Beads of sweat formed on her forehead.

*He would never hurt me,* Irene thought firmly. *He would never go behind my back, never use me. He'd never*

*(cheat the word is cheat)*

*hurt me because of what happened that night. He broke his hand for me, and in doing so, I saw his level of devotion to me. He'll always just love me no matter what.*

Sure, sure. Of course. Right.

She had surrounded herself well during her years in Boston and had made the acquaintance of many reputable figures. Names such as Freud, Jung, Adler, Sullivan, and Lacan had all become part of her newly established society. It was here that she'd developed other habits too, things like having sex on the beach, flirting with Scotch whisky, sipping on some gin martinis, enjoying some late night Woo woo (which was Sex on the Beach without the orange juice, apparently), and everything else in between. Her studies, just like at UCLA, were solid, and she got along well with all her peers, impressed all her instructors, kept good notes during fieldwork, and was just the typical Overachiever-Asian-Girl everyone was fond of (she was the *only* Asian girl in all her seminars, apparently).

Life during the day was boring, so life during the night was wild. Flirting with Rum and Coke during late after-hours was a recurring motif, and anything with a hint of gin or vodka in it was pleasantly divine. But oh, Sir Scotch whisky—*there* was a man she could depend on. *There* was a man who listened to her whenever she needed to talk, a man who let her just speak for *hours* and hours without end. He was much better than Sir Jack Daniels (who was so weak he made her want to puke), and just a tiny bit better than that crazy Piña Colada gal. He let her forget about her mother whenever they were together, and let her drink endlessly without thought of the next morning. He was a *man,* and he was damn strong. Her mother need not come between them, he told her; they need not have her interfere with their relationship, and she need not busy herself with overwhelming guilt in her heart, or those pesky, salty 2 a.m. tears she always had. He always left her tired and hung over the next morning, but that was fine. He rocked her world at night, so not seeing him in bed every morning was an acceptable quality. He probably had other women to please.

Passion; it was passion that finally drove her to move to Seattle. While psychoanalysis offered a unique twist in studying culture and theory, it did not provide a satisfactory appetite for what truly fueled her heart. And what fueled her heart was simply painting.

She would meet Daniel three years after moving to Seattle. In those three years alone, she would establish herself as a brilliant and promising talent. The name on her MFA wouldn't even be dry yet when offered her own private exhibit, and congratulatory champagne in delicate, long-stemmed champagne flutes would become her newest habit. (Of course, Scotch was still her friend. Until she met Daniel, Scotch would always be her bestest of bestest friends). *City Arts Magazine* would generously call her a genius while *Art in America* enviously craved to know where she obtained her prodigious technique. The *Seattle Times* and *Seattle Met Magazine* would call her works masterpieces. Was she in favor of these minimalist landscape paintings because she saw a natural, sublime beauty to them? Or was she inspired by her upbringing as a Chinese woman in painting her minimalist masterpieces? (Irene, with a tired roll of her eyes: "Actually, I'm more inspired by Russian painters like Alexei Savrasov and Sylvester Shchedrin than I am with anyone or anything else. I don't believe artistry needs solely to be reduced to ethnicity.")

Seattle. Seattle was the place where her passions grew and became fully realized. It was in Seattle that her mother's shadow slowly diminished, and it was in Seattle where she met other men different from Sir Scotch whisky. It was with Seattle's intellectual culture and artistic community did her passion for the arts grew, turned wild, and set ablaze.

The night Daniel had fractured his hand had come three months after he'd proposed to her. Irene remembered the memory well: One doesn't forget a night in Paris on New Year's Eve with the Eiffel Tower silhouetted beneath a glowing sky, nor the rare, sincere smile a gal sees on her beau's face when he hears the words *"Yes, yes, of course I'll marry you!"* over the loud roar of bursting fireworks. She'd come home that night three months later tired and happy from their last rounds in the Seattle area together; she'd come home that night tired and happy into their new home at the Empyrean Tower.

She'd come home that night with news of her mother having passed away.

"Irene. Get up from the floor."

She sat on her knees sobbing on the kitchen floor. She was naked except for Daniel's dress shirt around her shoulders. The refrigerator door stood open in front of her, its white light spilled across her face. Shadows stretched her shape across the floor and bled into the darkness behind her.

She was sobbing. Tears spread down her eyes and mixed with the plastered strawberry yogurt on her lips; runny yellow yokes from broken eggshells smeared her feet and legs. An avalanche of food had spilled out of the refrigerator before her, the lasagna from last night smeared across the floor in thick glops of meat. There were other things around her, other scattered bits of food, other heaps of junk: the puddle of milk near her feet, the baked salmon overturned on its side, the bags of cereal spilled across the floor, the Jell-O, the rummaged cellophane wrappers with half-eaten cookies and crackers inside. There was even a carton of ice cream melting next to her, its box-like shape turned upside down and oozing from the corners.

There was vomit on the floor. Daniel saw it clearly lit by the dim glow of the refrigerator. It was black-purplish vomit. It was wine vomit.

"Irene."

She ignored him. She had a wine bottle in her hand and was taking great gulps from it and letting it spill across his shirt in lazy drips. A cabernet sauvignon or pinot noir, she couldn't remember. She only knew that it was red, deliciously red, and that it had a smooth, exquisite taste. There were two other bottles next to her, both of them empty, one having been a white sparkling Riesling, the other, maybe a chardonnay. Both had been gifts offered to her at the show this evening. Both had been finished straight from the bottle.

"My mother's dead," Irene said. Her voice was flat. She brought the bottle to her mouth and swigged it down. "That was my dad on the phone, and he said...my mother's dead. She...she died of some virus, or something, I can't remember. Maybe stomach flu. Or stomach cancer. She was in the hospital for five days."

Deep hollows formed on her cheeks; white skin stretched skeletally across her face.

Just hours before they'd been making love in the dark and she'd been

426

giggling and laughing, sighing with hiccupping pleasures. Just hours before she'd been smiling and shaking hands with a dozen art patrons from different societies, announcing to them the genius of her work and establishing herself as an elite among their world. That she could be sitting here now, thigh-deep in spilled food, wallowing in pity with tears down her face, drinking herself to oblivion…the image saddened Daniel. It just so, so saddened him, like hearing the despairing cries of a young daughter wishing that she were thinner or more beautiful. Seeing her like this was like a dagger to his heart. He pitied her.

"Get up from the floor, Irene. It's cold. You need to come back to bed."

She shook her head at him. She said, "I don't *wanna*," and pouted her lips. "You're not my mom. You're not fucking *her*."

"Irene."

She got up anyway. There was a slight gait to her walk as she approached him, a heavy drunken swagger. Her bare feet crushed the unbroken eggshells on the floor and gushed out mucus-yellow beneath her toes. She still carried the wine bottle in her hands. When she spoke, her breath fell on him like soft noxious fire, making Daniel stagger backwards. It was a mephitic smell; it was the smell of poisonous grapes ripening in the sun before they burst.

"You want to know what my papa asked me on the phone?" Irene asked him, her voice clear but incredibly sluggish. "He said…he said to me, 'Why aren't you near your mother's bedside as she's dying? Why aren't you here with your family? Aren't you our only daughter?'"

"Irene—"

"And then, my uncle…he said, he…he said that all my family was there, and that I was the only one not there, and that, didn't I feel bad *that I wasn't there?* I'm their only child, their only *daughter*, and I'm not *there?* I was at an art show getting drunk with my husband—that's where I was! I was in Seattle drinking champagne and shaking the hands of millionaires! Ha-ha!"

She giggled at him, spewing more of that noxious fume in his face. He was shirtless, and the warmth of her breath caused gooseflesh to break out on his skin. He could smell vomit in her breath, smell the hot, sour, putrid fragrance. Her shirt was opened, the small swell of one left breast briefly exposed between the folds of fabric. When Daniel saw it, he noticed a trickle of wine had fallen there, touching the nipple.

"Give me the bottle, Irene" he said again. "You need to sit down. We'll discuss this later in the morning when things are better. Okay?"

She threw her head back and cackled at him. The move was so sudden that her hair whipped him in his face. His shirt flew open and both breasts suddenly became bared, exposing splotches of wine. She began laughing and giggling in Mandarin, saying only a few words he could understand (*stupid, silly, little boy*), and then she cried back in an ear-deafening shrill: "It *is* morning right now, Daniel! Can't you see what time it is? It's already two-thirty in the morning! If you want to talk about something, then talk about it with me here!" She stared at him. She said, "*Nǐ huì shuō yīngwén ma?*" and laughed deliriously again, bringing the bottle up for another drink.

Daniel reached out and clutched her wrist. He pried the bottle away.

"*Give me th—*"

"Enough. You're done now, Irene. Either go and cry in the bathroom or come back to bed, I don't care. But you're done drinking. No more for you."

She glared at him. Her face scrunched together like a little toddler's and a fat stubborn pout formed on her lips.

"*Fuck you,*" she spat. Then she really did spit, launching a spray of spittle from her lips. "I don't give a *rat's ass* what you tell me to do. You're not…you're not my mom, so fuck you. Go to hell." She spun around. She headed back towards the fridge. "There's more where that came from anyway."

Daniel reached out and took her by the wrist.

"Irene—"

"DON'T FUCKING TOUCH ME!" She threw his hand off. "Don't you *dare!* You think you can control *me?* You think that I *care?*"

She slapped him. Daniel flinched backwards and caught the tips of her nails. They slashed across his cheek and left four red lines across his face. Fire burst out on his cheek.

"Don't you ever—*ever*—grab me like that again, do you understand? All because you're a *man* you think you ca—"

He grabbed her arms and pinned her against the wall. The move was fast, incredibly fast; Irene barely had enough time to register that he moved at all. She felt his hands take her, felt them forcefully *swing* her, and then felt the cold roughness of the wall suddenly press up against her. She yelped in surprise. The impact forced all the air out of her lungs and she briefly banged her head against the wall. She heard the wine bottle clattering loudly from somewhere in the darkness.

"Hit me again Irene," he whispered. His voice was fast and low, warm on her face. "Hit me again and see if it'll end the pain. *Hit* me again and see if your mom will forgive you."

"Dan—"

He shoved her against the wall. Irene let out a cry and felt his fingers tighten on her arms. He'd rocked her head back, banging it a second time. He wasn't hurting her, but he was scaring her, he was scaring her badly, and she was scared of not being able to breathe, of not—

"I know the stories of your mother, Irene. I know that you love her and feel guilty for having lost her. I also know that you wish you'd been there for her, and that you wish she had loved you." He lowered his face at her. "But what are you doing killing yourself? Why are you drinking yourself into oblivion? Are you that *stupid?*"

Tears trickled down her face. "You're not my mom," she sobbed. "You're not *her* Daniel, you're not—"

"*You're not my daughter either!*"

He slammed his fist against the wall. Irene shrieked and heard his fist collide next to her ear. She shrank from his gaze and stared down at her feet, feeling tears drip from her nose.

"You are *not* my daughter, Irene! And you are *not* someone that needs to

429

prove herself to me. Do you understand that? *Do you?* Do you think I fell in love with you just so that I could *pity* you? Do you think that by falling in love with me I'd love you like your mother never did? I love you because you're *you*, Irene! I fell in love because you're *you*, and not some little idiotic Chinese girl who failed to escape the tyrannical shadow of her mother! I'm not here to love you out of pity, and I'm *not* here to pity you just because you never gained a motherly love. I love you because I'm me, and in loving you as me, I offer you the greatest love. Do you understand that?"

Irene nodded. She opened her mouth to respond, but uttered a wet, sobbing croak instead.

"Drinking won't earn my pity or my love, and it *won't* bring back your mother. Drinking won't make me see you as a neglected daughter and love you as one. Okay? Your mother's *dead*, Irene, she's *dead*, and you weren't there at her bedside. Okay? You have to live with that guilt, but at least you still love her enough to cry. *This* should be enough to show that you're not her, *this* should be enough to show that you actually loved her. What do you expect by drinking yourself into a coma? Huh? What? Death? Resurrection? Love, life? What, Irene, *what?*"

"I don't know," she sobbed. "I...I just want to forget. The pain. The guilt. I...I just thought—"

He hit the wall again. A grunt of pain spilled from his nose, but neither of them noticed.

"I love you," Daniel whispered, "and I love you so much that I hate seeing you hurt. But even though I love you, I still retain the right to act selfish. So here's my offering to you, Xiaoli. Either quit it, or walk away from me. Pick yourself up, pull yourself together, or just keep acting like the way you are, and walk away from me. Do you understand?"

Irene stared at him. Tears blurred her vision. She could just barely make out his features in the dark. His skin was blue, and she could feel the warmth of his breath against her neck as he breathed on her. She said nothing.

"I'm not going to force you to stop," he continued, "but I am going to tell you the consequences of your actions if you continue. I *will* force you to leave me; I *will* turn away from you, and just have you part of my past. Everything that we've known together, *everything* that we've planned for the future together…it'll all have been thrown away because you were too scared to accept the fact that you are not your mother. Do you understand, Irene? I'm offering you a choice because I love you, and letting you choose what you want because I adore you. Do you get it?"

"Yes," she sobbed. Fresh tears spilled down her lips. "Yes, I do, I understand, I…I understand." She shook her head. "I understand, Daniel, I understand, and I'm sorry. I'm sorry, I didn't…I didn't want my mom to *die*, I didn't want her to *die without me!* I just lost contact, I didn't want to see her, but I never *wanted her to die! I never wanted her to die without me…"*

She broke down. Daniel let her, peeling himself away so she could bring her hands up and cover her face.

"*I didn't want my mom to die!"* Irene screamed. "Even when she used to hit me or call me a slut, I never wanted her to die! Daniel…I never wanted my mother to die *without me!"*

She sank to the floor. Daniel went to her, wincing, and let her cry against his shoulder. His hand hurt, but he gingerly wrapped his arms around her, feeling her wine-stained breast pressed against him.

"I don't have a mom anymore," Irene sobbed. "Oh, *God*, Daniel…I don't have a *mom*. I don't have a mom in life anymore, and I never got to say *goodbye!"*

"I know, Irene. I know."

She wailed against him.

She cried against him for two hours. Afterwards—at nearly four o' clock in the morning, with bright indigo light peeking through the windows— Daniel carefully gathered her in his arms and carried her to their bedroom. He laid her down and watched quietly as she naturally rolled on her side and brought her legs in. He kissed her. He walked back out to the kitchen later and found some ice for his hand.

***

The elevator doors opened.

Irene stepped out and grabbed her keys from her purse. A light fragrance of evaporating rain from last night filled her nose as she made her way through the underground parking lot. Her flats echoed through the garage like empty lethargic claps, and the metallic jingle of her car keys raised the hairs on the back of her neck. Somewhere above her, near the exit/entrance tunnels, loud overhead traffic rumbled.

*Beaumen,* Irene thought faintly as she made her way past a row of cars. *His name was Dr. Brendon Beaumen. I knew it was Brendon something.*

Irene remembered the young doctor well. He had glanced at her several times during their visit, and had let his eyes travel lazily across her body as he tended Daniel's hand. Irene's skin had crawled when seeing his eyes. She wanted to shout at him: *My fiancé does* not *beat me! He's a good man, do you understand? Do you see my face, do you see my arms? Would you like to run a checkup on me, doctor, see where the bruises are? There are none, so stop speculating! He hurt his hand hitting a wall* trying to save me! *Okay? I will say it for the whole world to hear: I love my fiancé, and he does. Not. Beat. ME.*

The good doctor had accepted their story of a faulty boxing match with an unremarkable nod of silence and offered a few painkillers to ease the pain. Daniel had thanked him. Irene had merely smiled.

"And here we are today," Irene sighed as she approached their car. It was a black 2020 Mercedes Coupe, something that luck (and fortune) had loaned them generously at the beginning of the year. Who said all artists had to starve? "Here we all are with a set of new problems not even Scotch Whisky could solve. Or Freud."

She got in the driver's seat and closed the door. She paused before starting the engine and bit her lip. She stared bleakly out at the windshield.

*I trust you, Daniel,* Irene thought quietly. *I trust you with all my heart. Please be strong, my love. Be strong for me, but also…be strong for us. I can't do this without you,*

432

*Daniel. We can't do this without you. Please understand that we both need you now. We just need you to be there for us.*

Sighing, Irene inserted the key into the ignition, started the engine, and drove out of the garage.

# CHAPTER 28

Years ago, when the drinking had finally stopped—and when their marriage had finally settled into a genuine state of harmony and bliss—Irene had invited him to attend a show with her at the Seattle Art Museum, giving him a rare opportunity to experience firsthand the artistic sublime. Her enthusiasm then had been unusual, and Daniel had grinned constantly at her irritability for having to wait for an answer (he'd prolonged his decision for three days, nearly killing her with agitation). He finally agreed, and she had showered him with delighted kisses afterwards.

That Irene would invite him out one afternoon to simply browse the rooms of the S.A.M. without the need of champagne flutes was itself something sublime and wonderful: Daniel rarely ever saw his wife in jeans when at art museums, and always instead stood by her side while she wore expensive designer evening gowns and glittering jewelry. Her mastery over the arts was a trait universally lauded, and her skills provided only the briefest relief of a normal life when in the public. The champagne, the suits, the ties, the elegantly designed gowns, the traveling, and the occasional need of having to laugh at every bad joke made at receptions—all of these inadvertently had become part of his world upon marrying a lovely woman whose paintings always sold for five figures—six, if the company they were with had generous white old men who liked staring at a young Chinese female prodigy (and, apparently, *a lot* of generous white old men liked staring at a young Chinese female prodigy, Daniel begrudgingly noticed).

Everyone liked to ignore the intellectual and writer, apparently.

Art patrons followed them; innumerable art critics praised them. And once in a while when a cork was popped and a bottle of champagne was poured—and when all the bacon-wrapped shrimp was gone, and all the bad jokes were delivered   Daniel would catch Irene's eyes across the gallery, and she'd silently say: *I know, I know, I'm sorry. Just a few more hours.*

Daniel loved his wife. But he loved her as a person, not as a commodity. Spending an afternoon with her at the S.A.M. as a couple was almost a dream come true.

The exhibition they would be attending was both an occasion and serendipitous event. Mr. Sugawara Tomoaki (and yes—Irene was sure to say "Mr." when addressing his name), just recently deceased, was known in particular circles of the art world as the father of modern romanticism and sadism. In order to celebrate Mr. Sugawara's passing, the Seattle Art Museum—along with other museums willing to host the artist's works as a world tour—had set aside two weeks to showcase Mr. Sugawara's paintings, declaring regrettably that such works would never again touch American soil.

Daniel had hesitated at first. He had a fair exposure to BDSM in art, and had developed a tentative lexicon regarding fetishes, erotica, and the body through his dealings as a scholar intermixed with feminist discourse. But most of the things he'd seen with Irene had been things lacking, and were not at all equal to what the viewer with the imagination demanded. A woman in a skintight clear plastic cat suit was not at all that interesting or intellectually demanding; a man on his knees with a leather mask over his face with his hands tied behind his back was similarly boring. Most erotic art they'd seen had been purely fetishistic and unmoving—Daniel had glanced at them with a minor shrug (Irene had voiced a similar disappointment, apologizing for the lack of ingenuity and sophistication. "I don't understand it either," she said to him one evening as they dined together at Masa's in New York. They'd just come back from another tour of the city. "Perhaps

435

we're missing something that they see, but I don't get how taking multiple shots of a women's legs spread wide open to urinate on the camera is both art and erotic at the same time. Isn't it just the same as capturing someone performing a bodily function? Or someone who's into voyeurism? Does putting it in museum make it art, and does having a *photographer* take pictures of it make it art as well?").

Sugawara though…this artist according to Irene was different. And upon passing through the familiar doors of the Seattle Art Museum, Daniel had discovered why.

Silence greeted them as they entered the gallery. With it were occasional slow threading footsteps and indistinct murmurs to the sides. Daniel frowned when hearing the silence. The sound to him was not respectful or filled with awe, but simply horrified and appalled. As he and Irene walked closer, he began to understand why.

The walls surrounding him were filled with paintings of naked women tied in bondage; hundreds of peach-colored bodies twisted in pain and withered with terror. Many were tied with gags in their mouths while others were submissively curled on their sides in tight fetal positions. Others were knelt submissively on their knees with hot candle wax pouring down their naked backs; others were suspended upside down with their legs spread open. Some were tied like shrimp, others, like pigs with their feet and hands bounded together. Rope tangled through legs and limbs wrapping tight every centimeter of the body. One painting depicted a woman tied to a chair with her legs spread forcefully open; others showed close-up views of women's genitalia. Daniel felt the hair on the back of his neck rise. He felt Irene next to him, and knew that she was disappointed by the stunned silence that was surrounding them. In some sense he was disappointed too, because what he saw there in the room in front of him was…was something spellbinding and exquisite.

They browsed around together, taking chances here and there to whisper in each other's ears. Irene, of course, was delighted, and helped explain to him certain facts regarding each painting. Daniel nodded, feeling again that strange surge of intense curiosity waking from the back of his mind. How was it that a thing like this could sustain itself as art? How was it that those who viewed these paintings felt a visceral sense of disgust and not delight, and what to them would be a delightful substitution for that disgust? There were no gimmicks here, no artificially constructed contraptions depicting false role-plays of submissiveness and domination, no false artists. There was just a brutal deconstruction of the body, the body as 'Body' now, singular and plural, and yet this proper noun rested on this notion of 'Female' and...

His mind went on and on, excited, cold, disturbed. He was suddenly grateful for Irene for having brought him here.

"Daniel?"

"Hmm?"

"Luxemburg just spotted me. I need to entertain a few faces for a while."

"Remember to act pretty."

She snorted at him, laid a playful punch on his shoulder, and left him to browse alone. Daniel let her go, sad that his tour guide was gone, glad that he could brood in silence with his own thoughts. He walked around with his hands in his pockets, carried Irene's purse with him (she always left it with him), and paused every now and then to look at the different paintings.

A painting to the side caught his attention. He turned his feet and walked forward, feeling a cold ripple spreading down his back. He walked as if in a trance, and stared intently at the painting before him.

The painting showed a young girl kneeling on the floor with her back to the world. Her wrists were bounded, and her hands rested securely above the upper swells of her ample buttocks. She sat on her feet and had the bottoms of her soles directly facing the viewer. Long black hair spilled smoothly down her back. Her skin was smooth, young-looking and fresh; it was a dark alien purple that rendered her naked body cold and solemn. She sat against a foreground of absolute blackness and had no gag over her mouth.

It was her face that drew Daniel's attention the most. It appeared just above her left shoulder as a slight gaze back at the viewer. It was a casual gaze, an impassive look, something that barely resembled an acknowledging glance. And yet, still, it captured all of Daniel's attention.

*No other face so far has challenged me so candidly as this,* he thought as he peered closer. *Every other face that I've seen so far has been a face turned away with submission and fear. They've been struck with such apogees of pain and terror that they cannot recognize me. They don't recognize me as viewer, don't acknowledge my presence; they simply submit to me and become subordinated beneath my gaze. But this girl here...this girl here is attempting to defy me, and she is succeeding. She sees my gaze, and, moreover,* recognizes *it. She recognizes my gaze as viewer and thus forces me to recognize myself as a being that is viewing. By having me see myself as a being who perceives, I am made pure, physical, fallible. The omniscient power I once had as viewer is gone and I can no longer objectify freely. Instead my shock of having seen myself is captured in her eyes, and I in that moment have become objectified beneath her gaze. I'm no longer the gazer who sees freely, but now suddenly the gazed upon in this moment of realization of the self.*

Acceptance, Daniel thought; it was a look of acceptance. It was a look of *defiance* hidden beneath an expression of glum acceptance, a slight acknowledging and understanding of fate and being. The look above her shoulder was not a look of wretched despair or even sadness or pain; it was a look of understanding and calmness. The gaze in her eyes declared that she recognized herself as a body and a naked individual, and understood that her hands were forever tied behind her back. Her acceptance of the other's gaze was defiant, for it secretly mocked and challenged those to judge her, subjugate her, objectify her—and fail. By acknowledging the other's gaze, she had defied their objectification of her being; by the serene acceptance in her eyes, she had freed herself from her bounded wrists.

Freedom. This is what the girl's face said as she calmly returned the viewer's gaze over her naked shoulders with pursed lips; freedom.

He had wanted to buy the painting, but of course, that was impossible. When Irene noted his change of mood after the show, she'd asked what was wrong. He explained to her the painting he'd found. She nodded at him, saying understandingly: "That one had caught my attention too. I thought of you when seeing it, and knew it would capture your interest."

Daniel nodded. He thought she was done. But then she spoke to him again, asking a particular question. "Do you imagine her smiling when no one is looking at her?"

"Perhaps. Maybe." He paused. Then: "I do, actually. And I believe she smiles when her back is turned to the world and when she's back facing the dark."

Irene smiled, laying her head against his shoulder. "Me too," she said softly. "I think that too. *Je juge que tout est bien.*"

\*\*\*

The painting. Sugawara's painting with the naked girl on her knees and with her hands tied. This was the image that filled Daniel's mind as he saw Jenny making her way towards him, this was what his mind remembered when seeing the bruise on her face, and *this* was what he thought of when finally seeing her: *Jenny. Oh, Jenny. You're still beautiful. After all these years you're still just so, so beautiful. Why did you ever leave me? What did we do to each other that made us part?*

She appeared from the dark of the hallway and made her way towards him. Her walk was shy…slow. Each step was filled with a soft demureness that made her approach all the more decorous. Her feet were bare, and she held herself beneath her chest with the white sleeves of her sweater covering her hands. A blue band held her hair into a long ponytail.

"Daniel," she said nervously. She tried to smile for him. "Hey."

He stared at her. He searched her face and noticed her bruise. It bugled on the left side of her cheek with an egg-yolk yellow that took up a quarter of her face. It looked like a bee had stung her.

It was beautiful. The bruise that dominated the left side of her cheek…it was a bruise Daniel thought was simply beautiful.

*So. This is a face without makeup, without a mask. This is a face unafraid to bare*

439

*itself to the world, a face that isn't afraid to admit it has blemishes. The bruises on her face, the scars that she tries to hide, the markings on her body—you are so much more beautiful when bared, Jenny. You are just so much more beautiful when showing all of your strength.*

*Don't you ever wear makeup again. Don't ever be afraid to show this world who you are.*

She stopped then, hesitating. "Daniel?"

He shook his head. "Welcome home, Jenny," he muttered softly. He cleared his throat and briefly turned away. He said: "You're as beautiful as you always were. Your beauty hasn't changed a bit."

She looked at him. She bit her lip and nodded, offering a solemn smile of thanks. She turned her head away and wiped her eyes, wishing that he'd come and hold her, knowing that he couldn't.

\*\*\*

"Does it hurt?"

"No. Only when I let it."

"Your husband."

She nodded. It hadn't been a question. She watched carefully and noticed as his gaze dropped down to her fingers. She'd left her wedding ring back in Boise. The band was still visible on her finger.

They were on the couch in the living room together. They sat apart from each other, and Jenny noticed the way he kept a constant gap between them. The gap was wide enough for a body, and it belonged to Irene, and though Jenny felt no animosity, she wished she could hate someone other than herself then. He was being careful, Jenny knew, and the jealously she felt then was as subtle as a blade dipped in water.

"How long have you been married?" he asked.

"Four years. Close to five."

"Do you…"

"No, it's fine. It'll heal by itself." Her hand went up to her face and

440

touched her cheek. The bruise there pressed oddly against the side of her palm. "It's fine, Daniel. I don't need anything."

They sat in silence for a moment. Daniel asked, "Will you tell me what happened?"

She did. She told him all she could since their last encounter at Red Moon's, and told him quickly, quietly, lowering her face as she did so. Throughout it all, Irene's voice spoke up in her mind, saying bleakly: *I'm two weeks late on my period.*

*I guess I really still do love you, Daniel,* Jenny thought as she glanced down at her lap. *How I'm sorry that I didn't get to grow up with you; how I'm sorry that I hurt you and never told you why, and how I'm sorry that things had to be like this. I miss you, Daniel. I miss you with all my heart, and I would give anything—simply anything—to be with the boy I once knew. I miss you so, so much. Why can't I just have you back?*

"Jenny."

She raised her head. "Yes?"

"You're crying."

She looked at him, startled, and brought a hand up to wipe her eyes. "I'm sorry. I didn't...I don't—"

"What about the marks on your neck?" he asked. "Where did those come from?"

"My husband. He...he tried choking me before I could get away."

"Your back?"

At this, Jenny averted her eyes, ashamed. "He used to whip me too," she said quietly. "Whenever I did something stupid or clumsy, he'd get his belt, and he'd...he'd just whip me. This isn't as bad as the previous ones though. This... this one was okay."

Stupid. That last part she said had been stupid, almost with a defensive plea. It sounded like she was asking him to pity her, to—

"Look at me when you speak, Jenny. Don't turn your face away."

She raised her head at him. "What—"

He reached forward to touch her.

Jenny started, feeling the muscles in her body grow rigid. She felt her breath catch and her heart jump against her lungs. She thought he was going to hold her or something, to *kiss* her even, embrace her in some longing hold. But what he did instead was reach out and peel back one loose strand of hair, wiping it away from her eyes.

"Daniel—"

"It's terrible how he's made you view yourself," he said quietly. "It's equally appalling how he's made you afraid to live in this world. You were so strong then, Jenny. Are you really that afraid of yourself?"

Before she could answer, he lowered his hand and cupped her bruise.

Jenny recoiled, almost tearing her face away. Goosebumps erupted through her back and her nipples hardened. His palm...it was light. Firm. He held her.

*I should be offended*, a frantic voice screamed. *I should be offended, I should tell him to stop, I should tell him that this is wrong, should tell him it's like touching a woman's breasts, should tell him Irene—*

"You're still that girl I once knew," he told her. "I'll never see you as anyone else in life, Jenny. But I wish you were strong again. I just wish to God you knew how strong and beautiful you were so you'd be able to face this world again."

She pulled away, tears in her eyes. She felt the light slip of his hand fall from her cheek and leave a cold sensation on her face.

"Don't," she whispered. "Please, Daniel. Just don't."

He pulled back from her. They sat in silence and quietly stared at each other.

"Tell me," Jenny began. "Please tell me, Daniel."

"Yes."

"Was I right to have come back?"

He looked at her. He said nothing at first. Then he slowly nodded his head and avoided her gaze. Tears collected in Jenny's eyes.

"You've hurt me," she began, "more than my husband. Do you

understand, Daniel?"

"I know, Jenny."

"Why did you come back into my life?"

He said nothing. Jenny felt her love for him increase tenfold, and felt more trickling of tears slide down her face. He loved her still. After all these years, he still loved her, and she realized that now. *Felt* it.

"You hurt me," Jenny began again, "because before you, I was hurt in a simple way. When my husband beat me, it was just his fists against my body. I got bruised, I cried, and I always hurt, but at least I healed. No matter how much he hurt me, no matter how much I cried, I always eventually healed, and I knew that

*(pregnant)*

at least I had makeup around to help cover my face. But with you…with you, Daniel, I hurt more than just bruises, okay? I hurt *inside,* I hurt at a place where the skin doesn't heal and where makeup doesn't hide the pain. I hurt in my *heart.* Because of you, I hurt in my heart, and there's nothing I can do to heal that. It just hurts again and again, and you continue hurting it. It just hurts, Daniel—everything about you just *hurts.*"

"And how am I hurting you, Jenny?"

"By lying to me."

"By what lie?"

*(two weeks)*

"By saying that I am strong, and that I can look at the world."

He turned to her. "And how is this a lie?"

She sniffled. She brought a hand up and wiped her face. She said, "You lie to me, because you say that I'm strong enough to look at this world. But the world I look at won't look back at me. The one I want to look at in this world has his head turned. He won't look at me. It doesn't matter how strong I am."

He said nothing. He placed his hand over her knee and clutched her hand. He squeezed it. Jenny squeezed back.

"What can I do to show that I still care for you, Jenny?"

"Give me back the boy I once knew," she sobbed, "and have him near me again. Give him back to me, so that I may remember how I once loved in this world. Give me my life back, Daniel, and show me again what it means to be loved."

He stared at her. He brought his other hand over and used his thumb to wipe her tears. Jenny closed her eyes. She let go of the hand in her lap and brought both of her hands up to clutch the hand that wiped her face. She forced him to cup her cheek and leaned into the warm embrace of his palm, savoring his touch.

# CHAPTER 29

*UW Campus / 2:23 p.m.*
*2007*

The cherry blossoms were in early bloom today.

Petals drifted through the air in a soft shower of pink snow and covered the bricked pathways of the Quad. Emma eyed the petals carefully, and felt a quiet sadness in her heart. She walked through the Quad with her arms hugged around her sides and with her tennis shoes hurried. Long yellow hair rippled against her shoulders as she moved. Sunlight broke through the clouds.

The scene had changed now since winter had thawed and spring had arrived. Before, there'd only been rainwater soaking the pathways of the Quad. Now, however, cherry petals swirled wildly across the ground as dozens of feet passed by. Students lay in the grass beneath the Yoshino cherry trees with their eyes closed and their shoes off, some soaking up the sun. Where before there'd been miserable bodies overladen with heavy raingear like trench coats, windbreakers, ponchos, and down jackets, now there were students wearing halter tops, denim shorts, flip-flops, khaki-shorts, short-sleeve tees, and buttoned-ups. Wind blew through the Yoshino cherry trees, causing a delicate sound that was like sliding paper. More petals fell to the ground.

*I'm going to be late*, Emma thought to herself. Her voice was cold and still.

445

Hurt. *I'm going to be late because I know he always comes ten minutes early. He always comes early.*

She clutched a manila envelope in her hands. His essays were in the envelope. She'd spent the previous weekend reading them, and was now about to meet him at Denny Hall to return them.

She was also going to meet him today to break up with him.

*Are we all just organisms doing nothing on this earth preparing ourselves to die?* Emma thought quietly as she passed by a crowd of bodies. *Every action I see in those around me are all preprogrammed—this I now know. Every style of dress, every mark of fashion, even the very slight movement of passing feet…all of these are inauthentic and almost inorganic.* Preconditioned. *Oh, Daniel. Why did I meet you? Why did I ever fall in love with your mind?*

Nathan. It was Nathan she thought of then—who else would it be? She didn't know why she'd kept his name from him. He'd told her about his sister named Penelope, but she'd never once mentioned Nathan to him. She was too ashamed, maybe. Scared.

Last year they'd been so good together, so…*close*. They'd spent all of last quarter philosophizing and laughing, eating together and reading together. They'd exhausted the Ave and had found secret stairwells in the libraries to spend their mornings together, had even snuck into her dorm together! And during winter break when she'd gone back to Scottsdale to reenergize herself beneath familiar Arizona sun, he'd even web-cammed with her, saying hi once to her mother.

But January…that one afternoon in January. That was the afternoon where everything had fallen apart. And then, Bill's suicide just a month later…

"I'm sorry, Daniel," Emma heard herself say. She sighed. Talking out loud helped hold back tears. Somewhat. "I'm sorry for everything, I guess. I hope you'll forgive me."

Emma sighed again, and thought back to that one afternoon in January.

\*\*\*

"Are you sure you can do this?"

Daniel raised his head at her, surprised, and saw that she'd stripped off her woolen sweater. Beneath it was a simple white t-shirt, and this too she was preparing to remove. She lifted it midway up from her abdomen, the skin beneath it pale and smooth like porcelain—Daniel wanted to kiss it. Her t-shirt was cut low at the neck and shoulders, allowing one slim bra strap to be seen. It was lily-white like her skin.

"Yeah," Daniel said steadily. "Go ahead, Emma. I'm fine."

She looked at him, hesitating, biting her lip and carefully eyeing him. She pulled off her shirt. Daniel watched as she did all of this, admiring the way her hair fell back across her shoulders. It was a lazy stream of gold, a soft fall. He laid in her bed shirtless himself, waiting for her, nervous, the warm feelings of desire in him growing into a strong and hungry lust.

She made her way towards him and carefully climbed on top of him. Daniel's heart raced. He felt a painful erection in the crotch of his jeans and reached out to grab her from behind. She lay on top of him and carefully began kissing his neck.

His hands were nervous; Emma felt it. She was nervous too, and could feel his hands moving unevenly across her body, groping rather than caressing. His hands squeezed her ass from behind, kneading denim swells. She felt that slight bulge from the crotch of his pants again, stiffening, throbbing, urging to be let out.

"Daniel," she whispered. "Take off my bra."

He nodded. He whispered a slight "okay" that neither of them heard, and his hands went up to find the hook to her bra. His fingers fumbled, missed, and then found it again. Her bra snapped off, exposing two small white breasts. Daniel threw the bra aside. Emma leaned forward so that her breasts rubbed against him, and felt again his rough, uneasy hands squeezing from behind.

447

"Emma."

"Yeah?"

"Let me…let's switch positions. Like, if you don't mind or something."

"Yeah. Okay."

They switched, and suddenly he sat on top of her, kneading her breasts. He lowered himself down and began kissing her. He kissed her lips and her neck, kissed her nose and chin, her collarbone, her eyelids, her lips, everywhere. She smelled like peaches. Wonderful, wonderful peaches. Daniel liked that smell. He wanted to *eat* that smell, devour its fragrance, eat it with his mouth, kiss her, kiss her, bring his lips to her breasts, and kiss her. His hands slid down the denim of her legs, found again the firm round swells of her buttocks, and squeezed, feeling, kneading, grasping. Soon he grabbed the waist of her jeans and aggressively pulled them off, wanting that creamy scent again, that hunger, that feeling of smooth twisting legs against him, the taut muscles of her calves, her feet. Kissing.

"Daniel?"

Hurried now, panting. Hungry. "*Yeah?*"

"Do you?"

"Yeah."

"Condom. Please."

He moved off of her, released a loud sigh, and reached for the box of latex condoms they'd bought together at Bartell's Drugstore on the Ave. Emma watched thoughtfully from the side as he opened the small box and noticed how his fingers trembled. She hadn't even noticed when he took off his jeans.

They had discussed doing this two days ago. He was a virgin, and it was obvious by the quick and jerky movements his body gave off. Emma wasn't a virgin herself, though she'd only been with one person in high-school. And even then, things had turned out horribly wrong when her hymen broke for the first time in senior year. Things hadn't progressed well after that.

He was going to be her first. Whether technically or emotionally, it didn't matter. She was equally frightened as he was, and found her fright something exhilarating and delicious at the same time. He wanted her; it was obvious now. He wanted her in a savage way, aggressive and raw, perhaps as something as primal as bloodlust stained with rage. He wanted to objectify her; he wanted to selfishly have her and just…just break and taste her.

Outside, in the cold January afternoon, raindrops pelted the windows, sounding like heavy bones rattling against metal.

"Emma."

"Yeah?"

"Open your legs."

She did. She leaned herself back and parted her legs. She stared up at her dorm ceiling and heard again the drumming of rain. She opened her mouth to ask what he was doing and if he was ready yet, and then suddenly felt his lips kissing her feet. They traveled up her ankles and then her calves, tasting her legs. They found the inside part of her thighs and soon he was kissing her there, savoring her flesh, kissing, kissing. As he kissed, his fingers found her underwear, and this he slowly pulled off, always kissing, always tasting.

"Daniel—"

"Hold on," he whispered. "Just hold on."

"What are you…I thought you said—"

"It's okay. I think I know how this goes."

"Are you…"

He kissed her, brought his tongue and lips against her. And then he was suddenly licking her, tasting her, using his nose and lips and hands inside of her.

Emma felt his tongue in her and reared her head back. She bit her lips together and uttered a low, dry, yet delicious, small hiss of pleasure. A sharp gasp escaped her. Her feet curled. His thumb rubbed the tip of her clitoris, and he kissed her between her thighs again. A pair of fingers slid inside her. She gasped. His fingers slipped in and out, in and out, pulling, reaching, always twisting and feeling. She moaned, felt the tip of his tongue inside her

449

again, and quaked. He suckled and sipped her, licked her, agitated her, stopping only once to brush back her pubic hair with his nose—slurping noises came from between her thighs. Her body twisted and her chest heaved; she brought one arm back and grabbed the edge of the computer desk next to her bed. More cramps folded her feet.

"Dan…Daniel. Wait, hold…hold on."

He stopped. "Emma?"

She shook her head, saying nothing, panting. She opened her eyes. "No. Go ahead. I…sorry."

He looked at her, hesitating, and then slowly moved himself on top of her.

"You're gonna have to help me a bit with this part," he said thinly, offering her a light smile. She could tell he was as scared and exhilarated as she was.

"I don't think it's that hard to figure out, Daniel," she replied. To her relief, he chuckled a little, and lay back on top of her. She wrapped him with her legs. "Go easy, Daniel," she said. "Take it slow, and just…easy at first. Gently."

He nodded. He kissed her some more and played with her breasts, nibbling them. Soon when he was ready, Emma felt him pressing hard against her. He entered her. There was a hiss, a soft wet gasp that made him stop, and then Emma was whispering to him that it was okay, that it was fine, keep going, don't stop. Soon they were rocking back and forth together, Emma hissing with pain and delight, Daniel, breathing heavy and hard.

\*\*\*

Emma opened her eyes.

She saw the wall in front of her and realized she was on her side. She rolled over and felt a cold draft against her shoulders as the blankets briefly slipped from her body. He sat next to her in bed holding one of her novels, his chest still bare, the reading lamp on her desk turned on. Emma grinned when she saw him. She rolled her eyes.

*What a dork,* she thought to herself. *Of course he picks up a book after having sex for the first time. Of course.*

"Reading anything good?"

He turned to her. He smiled when he saw that she was awake, and showed her the paperback. It was *The House of Mirth* by Edith Wharton.

"Hmm," Emma said. "Yummy."

"The taste of Fate and ruin are often yummy when never personally tasted," he replied. He closed the book and set it aside. "Feel good?"

She smiled. "A bit."

"Need to go to the bathroom again?"

"Nope. Fine as spring."

Daniel grinned at her, liking the tangled feeling of her legs next to him. He turned off the lamp. He lay back down next to her and felt her body curl in against him. Her hair smelled oily, and that was good; it was a natural odor, not overly scented with shampoo or artificial sweetness.

He brought the blankets up to cover them and listened quietly as the rain outside bombarded the windows. It was cold in her room, and that too was good: It made lying in bed together all the more wonderful and delightful. She wriggled against him, and he felt the faint pressures of her breasts touch his arm. He felt himself gain another erection as he imagined what her body must've looked like curled into soft shapes beneath the covers.

Lovely. Simply lovely.

"Been watching the news lately?"

Emma opened her eyes at him, surprised. She'd been drifting off. "News?"

"Just wondering if you're still hearing the protesters on campus. They're still there, aren't they?"

Emma bit her lip. She nodded. She didn't want to talk about it, but saw that he was curious.

He was referring to the Riese case that had made national headlines at the

451

beginning of the year. The Riese case involved Anne Riese and her father, William "Willy" Riese. Anne was a seven-year-old girl from Louisiana who was found drowned in her home. Reports stated that William Riese had beaten his daughter out of a drunken rage, attempted to rape her, and had finally drowned her upstairs in their bathroom. The mother, Claudia Riese, hadn't been home at the time. William Riese stated he killed his daughter because he was tired of her "fuckin' retardedness," and wanted to do something about it. Anne had Down's-Syndrome.

"I hear them sometimes," Emma said quietly. "They're sometimes out on the Square at night. I see them mostly during lunchtime."

He sighed. He said mildly: "People become so easily swayed over topics like these. It's sad."

Emma frowned at him. She said: "It *is* a horrible story. People have the right to be angry over something as disgusting as this."

"I'm not disgusted by the events in the story," Daniel said. "I'm disgusted by the way the public is reacting. Sensationalism is the blueprint for everything in America, and I feel that everyone is just becoming overly sensitive to the word 'retard' when considering the story."

Emma sat up in bed. She did so quietly and smoothly, surprising Daniel. She'd been resting her head against his chest just seconds before—the abrupt change in her body language made Daniel frown, and he observed with curiosity as gooseflesh popped across her back. Blankets slid from her body.

"What's so wrong with that word?" she asked. Her voice had become cold. Tight. "What would have been the appropriate word to describe Anne Riese then?"

He said, "It doesn't matter how she's described. Whatever adjective is used to describe her will always conceal the truth of who she was. Moreover, whatever word is used to describe her will always anger a portion of society. Because words for each individual have certain connotations based on the individual's personal experience of that word, there is no universal way to describe anything in this world. Language is never innocent."

Emma nodded, keeping her face towards the dark. Daniel gazed at her from the side, noting again the uneven bumps on her skin. He could see the small groove of her spinal cord running the length of her back, and could see the rounded swell of her right breast from the side. She brought the blankets up to cover herself.

"You're right," she said stiffly. "Sure, you're right. I know you are. But you still haven't answered my question, Daniel. What's so wrong with that word?"

"Nothing. It's just a word. Had the news reports used the word 'retard,' or 'mentally challenged,' or even 'afflicted with a chromosome abnormality,' the meaning would have been the same: Anne Riese was a girl with Down's-Syndrome, and her drunken father killed her because of it.

"The way the public has reacted to this story says to me we are all still more susceptible to language than we are aware of truth. People are right to become angry at the heinous murder of a child, but people rarely ask themselves why they're angry, and to what effect their anger is influencing them.

"Just look at what's happening now across our state and in some parts of the country: Human Rights activists are protesting the news; spokespersons for Special Ed. organizations are making demonstrations against the Riese family. Personal caretakers everywhere are having their voices heard on TV, and families with special-needs children are on every late-night talk show these days. News segments are doing special broadcasts where they're chronicling the history of medical research in America. Not only that, but they're showing documentaries about families with special-needs children, doing reality shows, offering celebrities endorsement deals, and so forth. They've even gone so far as to interview doctors and geneticists to discuss Anne's condition."

"So those who interpret language are at fault then," Emma said.

Daniel glanced at her. He again stared at her backside and noticed the curve of her shoulders. Her backside was cold and lit with a blue hue from the windows that was softened further by the dimness of the room. In the darkness, Daniel saw the smooth texture of her back, and realized that the goosebumps had disappeared.

"Is everything all right, Emma?" he asked quietly.

She turned to him. "Yeah," she said calmly. She tried smiling. "Everything's fine. I'm just interested in hearing what you have to say, Daniel. I like hearing you speak." She paused. She said, "So those who overact to the Riese case are under the influence of language."

"We're all influenced by language," Daniel said. "Some of us just realize it better than others."

"How should we behave to a story like this, then?"

He said: "One should always realize language and ideology if they can. They should be objective as possible when under the influence of language, and not have their minds be swayed from the truth. Language can deceive people as well as direct those towards truth; language can also be used to self-deceive ourselves."

Emma turned her eyes on him. She gazed at him, thoughtfully, and said: "I have this cousin I'm close with. Her name is Suzy. She has a younger brother named Cody, and Cody has autism. Suzy and I are close, and we often talk to each other on the phone. She tells me how her brother sometimes becomes an emotional burden to the family, and how it's sometimes just so hard to cope with parents that never pay attention to her. She tells me how her parents sometimes ignore her, how they give all their attention to Cody, ignore her school activities, and sometimes just pile all the chores on her to do around the house. They love him, every member of my cousin's family loves Cody, but it's just *so* difficult at times, especially for Suzy. Do you understand?"

"What does this have to do with the Riese story?" Daniel asked.

"When you were speaking about how one can use language to deceive themselves," Emma began, "I thought about my cousin. I feel that there's a sense of self-deception that goes on within the family, and just wanted to know what you thought."

Daniel paused for a minute. He asked: "Does your cousin love her brother?"

"Yes. Yes, of course, she always says she does, and so do her par—"

"But despite what she says, there's another part of her that says she hates him, yes?"

At this, Emma went silent, and nodded. She said slowly: "I get the impression that her family is weary these days. More exhausted. Everyone is just exhausted, even though they won't admit it to themselves. They just keep saying how blessed they are and how wonderful it is to have what they have."

"So the family purposefully lies to themselves," Daniel said for her, "telling themselves that they are happy and in love. They don't ever allow themselves to think what is in their mind. They force themselves to smile, force themselves to hide the truth of what is in their hearts."

Images of her father sighing in the attic room afternoon filled Emma's mind then, shocking her to a point of tears. She'd gone upstairs to see her dad and ask what he was doing once, and had spotted him examining an old baseball glove. He'd look handsome in the bright light of the attic. Emma remembered his silhouette being outlined by a soft, lazy golden light, remembered the many dust-balls that floated through the air like miniature free-floating planets, and remembered how tall he'd seemed to her when she was younger, how strong and lovely he'd been, the man that always used to carry her on his shoulders whenever she wanted a piggyback ride, the man that always read stories to her before going to bed, the man that always loved and kissed mommy in front of her. She remembered seeing him in the attic room surrounded by a stack of cardboard boxes, a world full of old dusty things and muted golden colors, and had stopped herself when suddenly hearing her daddy sigh. His sigh had come out loud and sad, almost sounding like a sob, and Emma had stood where she was at the doorway, hugging her doll.

He was examining granddaddy's baseball glove. It was the same baseball glove her father once used as a little boy, and Emma supposed it was the same type of glove her granddad once used when he was little too. As she watched, her father examined the glove in his hands, ran his fingers over the loose stitching, and produced another low, melancholy sigh. Emma didn't like that sigh. It made her daddy's shoulders drop down into a hunch like an old man's. He took the baseball glove and opened one of the cardboard boxes. He placed the glove inside and closed the lid. He stood still for a minute. He looked out at the window that looked out onto the backyard, and swallowed. Emma heard his swallow. It sounded deep and painful, like a large drop of water breaking the surfaces of a hidden lake.

Emma quietly walked away and went to cry in her bed.

Nathan. Her brother Nathan back home in Arizona. He was four years younger than her and was the only brother she had. She loved him for who he was, and supposed she'd always have to. Though inside, she loathed him for who he was, and hated him for how he'd made her father cry that day.

Her brother had severe autism.

"It would be better for your cousin to voice her feelings," Daniel said, drawing her back to the present. "She shouldn't live in bad faith with herself and pretend everything is fine. Let her express her hate; let her say what's on her mind. If she wants to hate her brother, then she should be able to do so. If she wants to love him, then that's fine too."

"But what about the family?" Emma asked. "What if my cousin's family gets hurt by what she has to say or by what she has to admit?"

"I think accepting hurt by a family is what family is about, Emma."

"What if they get angry?"

"Then that family hasn't loved all of its members enough."

She stared at him. She bit her lip. She said: "You're saying that my cousin Suzy should allow herself to hate him if that's what she feels."

"Yes. But only if it's an authentic feeling. She should always allow herself to feel what she feels."

"Why? What good would it do if she admits her hate and disgust? Why can't she just allow herself to go with the language and façade her family has created?"

"Because if she's just constantly taking care of him out of falseness rather than authentic emotion, then her love isn't sincere. And if she declares to the world that she loves her younger brother while really harboring hate in her heart, then she's a liar to her brother and to herself. Worse, she's using her brother as a caricature and excuse for her own cowardice. He's become her scapegoat to turn from the world."

Emma said nothing. She turned her face back to the dark and sighed, letting her shoulders drop. Daniel observed her from the side, noting again the wonderful smooth surface of her naked back. He waited, and was surprised when she lay back down with him, placing her head back on his chest. She closed her eyes.

"Well," she said lightly, "isn't *this* a strange conversation we're having in bed together. How's this for pillow talk?"

Daniel said nothing. He felt her curl against him and brought an arm around to hold her. He stared contemplatively out at the rain.

***

*UW Campus / 2:29 p.m.*
*2007*

"Emma."

She raised her head. "I...yeah?"

"You were saying?"

She looked at him, surprised, and realized that they were standing in Denny Yard now. The yard was empty. They stood facing each other with nothing around them but the summer green lawns and surrounding sycamores.

He looked tired today. His eyes were red and his face was pale. His hair was a mess, and he looked as if he hadn't slept in the past several days. Emma's heart went out to him as she saw him, and knew he was still mourning Bill's suicide. He would probably mourn his suicide for years to come.

"I...I'm sorry," Emma began. "What was I saying again?"

He frowned at her. He said: "You said you had something important to tell me."

"Oh." Her cheeks became hot. "Right. Okay."

She took in a breath. She opened her mouth to speak, but then suddenly went blank on what she wanted to say. She couldn't recall *anything* she'd planned to say to him, and now just stared at him, dumb and mute, remembering their time in bed together. She tried opening her mouth again and then felt tears in her eyes. She swallowed. She said: "Daniel. I think...I think I want to break up with you."

He stared at her. A frown went through his face. He scanned her face for a moment, and said "*What?*" in a low, sharp voice.

"Yeah. I'm...I'm sorry. I just...I'm sorry. I don't know how else to explain, but like..." She shook her head. She swallowed again and offered him the manila envelope containing his essays. "Here," she said. "I've come to return these to you like promised. I've read them, and they're good like always, Daniel. They're always good."

He took the envelope from her. He stared at her. "Emma."

"It's not you," she said. "Really, it's not. I'm sorry if that's...if that's cliché, but it's the truth too, Daniel. I just...I can't stay with you anymore. I just have to step back. It...it just hurts being with a person like you."

A look of hurt came across his face. Emma saw it and turned away, forcing her gaze down at her shoes. Another gust of wind blew, cooling her face. Tears dampened her cheeks.

Daniel stared at her and felt something heavy fill his chest. It felt like an enormous balloon was expanding in his chest now, crowding out his lungs, suffocating his throat. He looked at her and noted the way she rubbed her left elbow as if clutching an old wound. A sweet smell filled the air in his direction as the wind blew, causing that pain in his chest to increase.

Peaches. The smell was like peaches.

"You shouldn't hate yourself just because you hate your brother, Emma."

She gaped at him. She brought a hand to her throat and uttered a low airless gasp. "I don't...what are you talk—"

"It isn't your fault," Daniel said. "If you hate him or are disgusted with him, it isn't your fault. That you hate yourself for hating him shows that you love him, Emma. You shouldn't blame yourself for feeling truth in life."

"This...this has nothing to do with my cousin, Daniel. This—"

"*Bullshit* Emma. Fucking bullshit." Red filled his cheeks. His eyes turned livid, and for one brief second, despite the tired look on his face, he looked handsome. "In January you told me a story about your two cousins when the story was really about yourself. But you suck at lying, Emma—you just *suck* at it. You didn't hear the fluctuations in your voice as you spoke, didn't see the hurt gaze in your eyes, and you most certainly didn't see the *bumps on your skin* as you talked to me. You didn't hear yourself cry while speaking, and you just didn't see what I saw."

Emma said nothing. She simply lowered her eyes and sniffled.

"Just admit it Emma," Daniel said again. "Just *admit it* to yourself, don't keep on lying. Don't care what your family thinks, don't care what your parents will say. You deserve to have this freedom; you *deserve* to have this truth."

"The same type of truth you gave to Bill?"

He looked at her. She looked away, ashamed.

"Daniel. I'm sorry. That...that wasn't what—"

"Bill has nothing to do with this," he said. "It has to do with you. It isn't about your brother, isn't about his autism, and isn't even about your family. It's about being sincere and *authentic* in life, Emma. It's about accepting the *truth*. It's about being free from falseness, and—"

Emma shook her head, silencing him. She said: "Do you remember the parable in Dostoyevsky's *The Brothers Karamazov* about Jesus and the Grand Inquisitor?"

He looked at her. "Don't," he said. "Just don't."

She said, "You've often called those who flee from life cowards for embracing unrealities in life, and to this, I've always agreed with you. But you never talk about *why* we like these things, Daniel—you never talk about *why* in your essays we feel safe with Spider-Man, God, fashion, or everything else that's false in life. We like these things because…because it's safer, Daniel. Do you understand? We can learn how to exist and move in life if we have a reason to *believe*. And if we believe, we can at least accomplish things in life.

"I didn't tell you about my brother because I knew you'd see him for me. Without language, without the lies, I knew you'd force me to see myself seeing him. And by doing so, I'd only be afraid with what you'd offer me."

She bit her lip.

"I need to see myself loving him, Daniel. I need to be able to say that I still love him for my family's sake. I just need to see myself loving others this way."

"So you want to love him out of *falseness?*" Daniel shrieked back. "Did you think I'd help you *pity* him, Emma? Is that what you're saying?"

"No, Daniel," Emma said, shaking her head. "That wasn't it. I just thought you'd…you'd give me the strength to face my fears. I just thought you'd give me truth to see. And you finally have."

"*Goddamn it*, Emma."

He sighed, rocked his head back, and blew an airless curse into the sky.

"I'm sorry," Emma said again, rubbing her elbows. "Maybe you're right, Daniel—maybe no one is strong enough to see truth in life the way you wish it. We…we have to cling onto artificial pleasures to sustain ourselves; we have to take bliss with our ignorance and have to constantly want falseness over truth. In our world, it's so much better for individuals to just go with the flow of things and never question where they're going. It's safer this way. Quieter. With this at least I can…I can call something ugly beautiful and pretend to believe in it."

"*And is accepting what's ugly so horrible too?*" he screamed. Emma jumped at his voice. "You want to call a pile of shit beautiful when it makes you want to vomit? You want to see starving children on the streets and call out Superman to save them? You're stronger than this, Emma—you're fucking stronger than this! Are you going to move through life telling yourself that you're happy, roll a boulder up a hill and pretend it isn't heavy? Christ, Emma!"

"It's the starving mouth that says virtue, Daniel," Emma said quietly. "You know this. I know in your heart you know this, and you know it too that happiness comes in this way. You know pleasure grants more happiness than it does truth. If you feed people pleasure and lies, they will accept any truth."

"Has it ever occurred to you that I might be *wrong?*" Daniel shot back. He clenched his fists together and gritted his teeth. Pain ripped through his jaw. "There are over a billion people in this world, Emma. Have you considered what *they* had to say about your brother—"

"I have. You don't know, so you can't say, but I've asked people, Daniel. I've asked *plenty*, and they always say the same thing to me, always calling me kindhearted and wonderful. But you—you're the only person I've met that told me the truth. You're the only one that has been able to say what I can't."

"Jesus *Christ*, Emma."

They stared at each other. They said nothing for a while, and Emma brought another hand up to wipe her face.

"Say it, Emma," Daniel said. His voice was almost pleading now. "Just say it once. Break away and just say it, don't be afraid. Say that you hate your brother; say that you hate how he hurts your family. Say whatever it is in your heart and be *free*. You can hate him now and love him later, but oh please, just say it. And don't leave me. *Please.*"

Emma shook her head at him. She said softly, "I love my brother, Daniel. And…and no matter how honest your words are—or even how much I have to lie to myself—I'll always love my brother. I'll always have to."

"You're a coward then," he spat. Redness swelled his eyes. "You're not strong enough to be an individual in life. You're just a fucking coward who loves to live in bad faith."

"Yes. Maybe. But at least I'm not lonely. And at least I'm not a murderer."

They stared at each other. Daniel watched her eyes and noticed as they scanned his face one last time.

"And are you going to approach me and kiss me on my 'bloodless, aged lips now'?" he asked bitterly. "Or just walk away?"

"No, Daniel," Emma said gently with a sad, slight, smile, "I won't kiss you. Doing so would be plagiarizing."

"What then?"

"A thank you," she said. "A thank you, Daniel. Thank you for showing me love. And thank you for…for trying to show me truth. I'll always remember you."

She waited for him to say something. He said nothing.

Emma turned away. She whispered *Thank you, Daniel,* one last time under her breath, and wiped her face. She brought her hands up to hold herself and lifted her eyes to the leaves. The leaves had light between them.

The sight was beautiful.

# CHAPTER 30

Daniel gazed at her from the side standing there against the balcony, watching as the sunlight silhouetted her body. Her shadow stretched long and dark beneath the bare heels of her feet and painted the undecorated walls of the living room. It was a shadow distinctively feminine and sinuous; there about it was a hopeless sagging of the shoulders that produced a forlorn stance, an indiscernible gait that came from the slight passing of the sun. *She's shown her backside to me*, he thought quietly as he approached her. *Like before when she tried to turn away from me at the diner, she's chosen this moment to turn her back on me. Only now her turning away from me is without any shame or humiliation, because now she no longer wears makeup. She turns away from me with her face bared—she chooses to turn away from me even when I call her beautiful.*

The thought was depressing. Daniel threw it away when he heard it and made his way towards her.

They'd finished speaking several minutes ago, and since then, had said nothing to each other. She'd gotten up from the couch and had wordlessly walked to the balcony where the sun now played against the outline of her features. She wanted to cry alone, Daniel supposed, and wanted to be with her own thoughts. He was scared for her, and had felt his blood temporarily rise when he saw her lean against the balcony with her hands on the railing. It was so easy to just imagine her slipping over the railing, just suddenly coming undone and falling out of sight, just like—

—just like Bill Bukowski from so long ago.

"Jenny."

She turned around.

Yes, she'd been crying—the tears on her face were still fresh and visible, lit on her cheeks by the fading twilight. The sight reminded Daniel of moth-dust for some reason.

"Can you get me something?"

"What?"

"Do you have a lighter of some kind?"

He looked at her, puzzled. "Why?"

"Just...just because. A candle lighter or something. Or a match."

He went back inside and rummaged through the kitchen cupboards until he found what she asked for. He returned seconds later and handed her the candle lighter.

"Come back inside," Daniel said to her. "It's getting cold out here."

"In a minute."

She pulled something out of her pocket. Daniel frowned when he saw what it was, but said nothing. It was a cigarette.

Carefully, Jenny guided the end of the cigarette to the tip of the lighter. She flicked it on. A dull flame popped out from the tip and briefly wavered in the wind. It looked dull and feeble in the sunlight, a thin scale of orange flickering back and forth. Jenny brought the end of John's cigarette to it and let it catch.

"You smoke?"

"No. Yes. I mean, maybe. It's something I'm choosing to do right now, Daniel."

As he watched, she set the lighter aside and held the cigarette between her fingers. Her eyes glanced briefly at his direction and then back down to the cigarette.

"Don't," Daniel said. "I know what you're trying to do, so don't."

Jenny bit her lip. Her heart picked up in her chest, and her mouth turned sawdust dry. *If you love me*, she thought coldly, *then let me go.*

Jenny brought the cigarette to her mouth. Before she could think of anything else, she inhaled.

Acrid flakes of metal filled her mouth; viscid plumes poured down her throat and irritated her lungs. The taste was like hot embers at the back of her throat, scratching like flakes of burnt popcorn. Soon she was coughing to the side, coughing *hard*. Tears filled her eyes and a burnt rancid odor filled her noise; smoke spilled from her mouth and dried the moisture in her eyes. More coughs erupted from her, each of them dry like thin cutting paper, scissoring her lungs.

Her chest hurt. Her entire mouth and throat clogged with smoke. Sighing, gasping—*heaving* even, panting without knowing it—Jenny straightened herself and readied herself for another drag.

"Jen—"

"Leave me alone," she panted. "Just…go away."

She brought the cigarette back to her mouth. This time when she inhaled she closed her eyes, sucking in as hard as she could.

Coughs wracked her body; poison and heat filled her lungs. Before she'd only coughed and mildly retched; now she violently gagged, heaving uncontrollably, tasting what felt like her own lungs and stomach. She bent over, retched, and felt her stomach muscles cramp with pain. Jenny heaved and felt her lunch with Irene this afternoon churn inside her with a wet, sliding, disgusting sensation. A sour taste of burnt paper filled her nose.

"Jesus Christ, Jenny what—"

She tried to push him away but felt his hands take her by the wrist and pull her to her feet, steadying her. Tears blurred her vision and her legs wobbled. She was dizzy and couldn't tell where the world was anymore. Daniel gripped her by the shoulders and shook her, jarring her already kaleidoscope world.

"What the hell do you think you're *doing?*" he barked at her. "Jesus Christ, Jenny, what are you trying to *do?*"

She pushed him off. The move was weak and light, but he dropped his hands away. "Leave me alone," she muttered. She tried to speak but ended up coughing instead. "Just…leave me alone, Daniel. Let…me have this."

She brought her hand back to smoke again. Daniel caught her by the wrist.

"Do you think this is *funny?*" he asked. "Do you think this will change anything, Jenny?"

She swung at him. Daniel stepped back, catching both of her wrists.

"Let me *go!*" she screamed. "Stop touching me!"

"So you can keep on killing yourself? So you can go on and puke out your *lungs?*"

She tried pushing him away again, cursing.

"This is *mine!*" she shouted. "Do you understand that, Daniel? This is *mine*, and *I'm* the one choosing to smoke it. It's my life now, okay? You can't control me!"

She brought her hands up and covered her face. She began sobbing. The cigarette between her fingers wavered and left a thin trail of smoke.

"All my life I've been controlled," she cried, "all my life I've been told what to do, what to wear—all my life I've just been a thing that people hit when angry, people to make fun of because I looked different! And now when I get a chance to be free…when I get a chance to finally decide what I want to do…you…you tell me to stop Daniel, you tell me *I can't do it!*"

"This isn't about—"

"No! You don't get it, you don't understand! My life's been hell, Daniel, and it's been so because I can't even be my *self* anymore. I always have to look a certain way to people, I always have to act. Even when I was younger I always had to act, and now that I've become a woman in life I have to cover my face with makeup. You don't get what it means to wear a mask or have to dye your hair, don't get what it means knowing your body is a vessel for hurt. You just don't get what it means to be caged, Daniel—you just *don't.*"

"I know what it means to be lonely," he said, "and I know how much it hurts being an individual in this world. I know how much it hurts wishing you had someone to love you."

Jenny shook her head at him. "No," she sobbed. "No you don't, Daniel, not anymore. You have Irene now, and she'll always be there for you because she loves you. I know. She loves you so much."

She brought the cigarette to her lips again. Her hands shook, and she had to pull it away, swallowing. She showed him the cigarette.

"This is me," she sobbed. "Do you understand? This is me right now, this is me reduced to nothing. I've...this is the only time I've ever been free in my life, the only time I get to *choose*. In my freedom, I am responsible, but I still choose to do *this*. I am forced to be a woman and a body, and I can't even have the world look at my face anymore. But *this*—this is mine, Daniel. I can choose *this*." She wiped her eyes and sniffled, feeling mucus in her throat. "Will you stop me, Daniel?" she asked mutely, almost challenging. "Will you...will you take away my freedom to save me? Or will you allow me to be free and smoke? To kill myself?"

"Self-loathing won't change my care for you," Daniel said. His voice was cold but loving. Hurt. "And it won't restore the past."

"I know. But it's the future I want, Daniel. It's...it's the future I need to know."

They stared at each other. Jenny turned away, bringing the cigarette back to her mouth. She closed her eyes, readying herself, breathing in the cold air, air that was like exquisite glass against her naked neck. She was sure this time she would vomit if she took another drag. She would puke, curl over and retch, spew out a yellow stream of acid and food, feel the horrible burn on her lips, and taste that sourly from-inside-the-body smell. Another onslaught of coughs would probably overtake her, but fine—that was fine. She wanted to do this. She *could* do this.

She brought the cigarette back to her lips and steadied herself. She closed her eyes. She felt her fingers trembling and finally in—

Daniel grabbed her shoulders and spun her around. Jenny's eyes snapped open.

"Don't!—"

He took the cigarette from her and flicked it aside. It sailed over the railing.

"WHAT ARE YOU DOING!"

She brought her hands up to hit him. He grabbed her. Jenny screamed, a feral cry, and cursed at him, spat at him. She felt his hands tighten over her wrists and tried to kick him. He moved in close to her and held her, absorbing her attacks.

She wailed against him. Against his body, against his chest, Jenny let herself go, and just wailed, sobbing uncontrollably. Her cries came out muffled against his chest and sounded like agonized moans. She couldn't breathe. Tears collected in the back of her throat and caused her to cough, forcing her to hiccup out her sobs. Her throat was raw, hurt from screaming and shouting—her knees buckled, and suddenly he was holding her tighter, keeping her from falling.

"*I hate you, Daniel,*" Jenny moaned. "*Oh, God, I just hate you! You're just like my husband. You're just like him when he says he loves me. You're just like him!*"

Daniel said nothing. He held her and felt her tears soak his shirt. The feeling was warm, hot and sticky like honey.

"Come inside, Jenny," he whispered to her. "Just come inside and be with me. Just stop crying and come inside."

She made no reply. Daniel led her back to the living room and watched sadly as she wiped her face. She walked away from him.

# CHAPTER 31

Daniel stood in the dim yellow glow of the porch light and stepped back when he rang the doorbell. He sucked in his gut and straightened his shoulders. He felt a little stupid, but at least his hair wasn't gelled tonight. And at least he was in jeans again.

Jenny opened the door and smiled when she saw him. She had on a plain black woolen sweater and dark faded jeans. "Ready for prom?" she asked happily.

"Ready," Daniel replied, returning her smile. He revealed what he'd been hiding behind his back and presented her with a bag from Burger King. "Let's go to prom, shall we?"

\*\*\*

"Not-uh!" Jenny shouted at him, laughing. "Are you serious?"

"Yeah. I'm being real."

"No *waaay!* That's so lame of them!"

He shrugged at her, saying: "High-school's one of the lamest places to be on earth."

"Yeah, but *still.*" Jenny shook her head, doing a disapproving *tsk, tsk, tsk.* "And I used to think that *everyone* in IB was smart. I can't believe they don't get it was a joke!"

He'd just finished telling her about the latest gossip to come out of the world of IB at Evanston-Woods High. Apparently, Todd Phongvonsa, the only Laotian-student in all of EWHS, had declared to the world that he had a list of ten girls he was going to take to prom. He also stated that he was going to treat them all out to Jack-in-the-Box for dinner. Vanessa Hunting, just absolutely *disgusted* at the thought of having prom at a fast food joint, had begun a personal crusade against Todd, and was now spreading slanderous rumors wherever she could. Vanessa was the ringleader of all the IB girls at EWHS, and her words were as wicked as her easily inflamed jealousy.

The truth? Todd was already taking Kimberley Hu to prom, a nice Chinese girl in Daniel's calculus class, and they had plans to dine at the Space Needle.

"*Lame!*" Jenny cried to the side, laughing again. "Vanessa and all those other girls who are hating him are *lame!*"

"It's all over on Facebook too," Daniel said, grinning at her. "Vanessa and a bunch of the girls in IB are making this Facebook page and just saying crap about him. The 'I Hate Todd Phongyonsa' page."

Jenny burst out laughing. "*Fail!*" she cried. "Smartness in IB is just *fail!*"

They laughed together, handing each other another round of fries. They were at Brackett's Landing again, of course, and were parked a few meters away from the sand. Invisible black waves assaulted the sandy shores while a cold crescent moon hung in the sky. The smell of warm French fries and burgers was heavy, and Daniel had slightly lowered the windows so Jenny could hear the soft slap of waves in the distance.

It was a good sound.

"Does he have an actual list?" Jenny asked him, still intrigued and smiling. Her smile was kind in the dark, a wonderful glimpse of something rare and pretty. Daniel felt something in his chest sigh when seeing that smile. "Or was he like, just making it up?"

"He has an actual list."

"And it has actual names on it?"

"Names that aren't *real*," Daniel said, grinning. "Like, maybe two or three of them are real and are in some of our classes, but they're all in on the joke. All the other names are just random Asian names he made up, names that can't be verified. He went to the library and printed out a dozen copies. He's taped them up all over the hallway."

"That's freaking *awesome*," Jenny cried. "I bet Vanessa really blew it after *that*."

"Yeah. Right now, Vanessa and everyone else are practically *giving* Todd stuff to feed off of for new material. Pretty genius if you ask me."

Jenny smiled. She reached for another fry in the bag between them and munched away in the dark. "Where is Todd from, anyway?" she asked.

"He's Laotian."

"Laotian? What's that?"

"Um. I don't know."

They laughed at each other, and soon fell into a happy silence.

"Graduation is coming up next week," Jenny said after a moment. "Nervous?"

"No. Not really. At least, I don't think so."

Jenny glanced at him, knowing that he had more to say. He always had more to say, and the way his voice dropped just now…she just knew he had something more to say. Something deeper. Something good and from the heart.

"I'm more sad than I am nervous that we're finally graduating," he said. "In fact, I'm really sad. We worked so hard during high-school, and we did so much. After all those nights of studying, those hours of going through notes and doing the readings…it just feels so odd giving it up now. I don't know what life's going to be like now that we no longer have people telling us what to do."

Daniel laced his hands behind his head and leaned back in his seat. He glanced at the dark clouds outside and sighed a heavy sigh.

Yes, he was sad. It wasn't a difficult emotion to admit, but something that simply hurt when realized. In just a few days, graduation would occur, and a new phase of life would begin. And in this new beginning, an old phase of life will have ended. In these forthcoming days, who would he be? What decisions would he make? And, moreover, which friends would stand by his side as he entered this new world?

The thought of graduation was absolutely sickening and terrifying to think about; it was as horrible as hearing the death of a loving parent.

"You're going to really miss high-school, aren't you?" Jenny asked him. Her voice was kind and warm. Gentle. "Like, really."

"Yeah," Daniel said, not hearing the crack in his voice. Jenny heard it. "I am. I guess that means I really enjoyed my time at Evanston. But it's bigger than that, you know? Moving on in life forces me to look at myself in life and ask who I am, who I want to become, and what I want to do in the future. It also asks me to reexamine myself in terms of the past and ask whether or not I've done anything great."

"'Monday is gone and Tuesday is soon to come,'" Jenny said. "'After all that has passed, what can I say I have done?'"

Daniel looked at her. She shrugged.

"It's something someone at my church made up," she explained. "It makes me think about life and makes me wonder if I've done anything great for myself."

"Yeah," Daniel said. "I ask that question a lot too."

"Not very many of us get the opportunity to ask if what we did in the past was great," Jenny said, "and not very many of us get the chance to self-reflect asking who or what we want to be in life. Not very many of us can even think about the future."

"I know, Jenny."

"Will you be great, Daniel?"

He looked at her, surprised by the question, but then said evenly: "I don't know. And to be honest, I don't care. I just want to have people surrounding me that I care for and love. That's all that matters in life—that's all that'll ever matter."

They went silent. Jenny gazed at him from the side, forcing his attention toward the waves. He looked handsome.

"You know what I'm going to miss the most?" she asked quietly.

"The football players and the jocks."

She laughed at him, punching him on the shoulder. "No way, I hate guys like that. What I'm really going to miss is the smell, you know? Like, the fresh morning smell that's always there in the hallways when you enter through the doors, or when you enter a certain classroom in a certain section of the building. Or like, when you sit down in the library and can smell the carpet, and the magazine and books on the shelves. And when it rains, you can sometimes smell the sidewalks too. It's a fresh smell. Almost like spring and leaves. Sometimes you can even smell the rain through the windows if you're close enough."

"Yeah," Daniel said quietly. "I know what you mean, Jenny. I know exactly what you mean."

"Can I ask you a question, Daniel?"

"Yeah."

"Do you think it'll all be worth it? With school and everything? Like later on in life?"

He thought for a minute. He said: "There needs to always be something worthwhile in life. No matter what, there needs to be something. And this is why the bravest of us and the humblest of us would scorn the thought of Heaven. If there is an eternal life after death, then life on earth isn't worth living at all. Neither is love. With the impeding knowledge of death, we can choose to cherish and love, and in that moment that we know is so short, appreciate our love. But with the thought of eternal life, love and friendship simply become an accessory—they are no longer worthwhile. Nothing is humble about eternal life."

Jenny nodded. She settled back in her seat and brought her jacket up to cover herself. "Heaven is a place filled with friends you can love," she said quietly. "A place without friends to love is Hell."

"Yes," he said. "I think that too."

They lay there together and listened to the waves. Ahead, a view of stars shone through the clouds in the distance.

# CHAPTER 32

She was crying.

Jenny snapped opened her eyes and realized her cheeks were wet. The pillow cradling her head was wet too, and she sat up with a jolt. She brought her hands up to wipe her face and felt loose strands of hair matted to her cheeks. When her fingers touched her cheeks, the skin there felt soft and tender, making her wince.

She glanced around her and saw the curtains swaying with an invisible force in the corner of the bedroom. The windows were opened. She'd left them partially open before going to bed and had forgotten to close them.

*Ghostskin*, Jenny thought coldly. *I've been watched over by ghosts as I sleep, and all that's left as I try to find them again is their skin. It's just their skin that I see.*

She shuddered. She brought a hand up to rub her head and felt a tight sliding sensation in her throat. She was thirsty.

*What am I doing here?*

She pushed the covers away. She moved to the side of the bed and sat with her feet touching the floor. She closed her eyes, held her head in her hands, and felt as something dull and heavy pounded in ears. She breathed for a minute and then opened her eyes.

*Why was I crying?*

She exited the room and entered the dark hallway leading to the living room. Once again wooden floorboards scraped her threading feet as she walked, and a cold draft blew against her ankles. Jenny entered the kitchen area and stopped at what she saw. A brief feeling of hot guilt flowed through her. She bit down on her lip and winced.

A plate of smoked salmon pasta waited for her on the kitchen island. A plastic covering had been placed over the plate, and a brief white note had been set on top of it.

Jenny swallowed when she saw the dish and silently strode past. She found a glass cup in one of the cupboards and poured herself a glass of water. She drank it down, washed the cup, and stared at the darkened kitchen. Sharp clock-ticks filled her ears from somewhere in the dark.

*Don't speak while eating, Jenny-ah. Close your mouth while you chew.*

Tremors broke out through her body. Jenny gasped out loud in the dark and brought a hand up to her neck, suddenly cold.

Her mother. It had been her mother's voice. And with it, a feeling from the past so strong, so nostalgic, that fresh tears formed beneath her eyes.

*Don't speak while eating, Jenny-ah.*

"Omma," Jenny said. A wet sniffle broke from her lips. "Oh God, omma. I still remember you. I still remember you after all this time."

The memory that replayed in her mind was one that was kind and brief. She was eight years old in this memory, and she was seated on the living room floor eating a small bowl of rice with her mother. Her mother was on the couch behind her speaking on the phone. The TV was on, and it was turned to her favorite cartoon channel. It was warm in the house—this Jenny vividly remembered. Snow had blanketed the streets outside while frost collected on the windows. Her father was out shoveling snow in the driveway, and orange flames had danced in the mouth of the fireplace. School was canceled that day.

"Mom, look! A Christmas parade! They have a Christmas parade on TV!"

She pointed at the TV and turned to get her mother's attention.

"Mom! Omma-ni! Look!"

Her mother nodded towards her, waved her off, and said, "That's nice,

476

Jenny," before resuming her conversation on the phone.

Jenny pouted. She didn't say anything, and turned her attention back to the TV. There were lots of people on the TV, and there were balloons too, big balloons, balloons of all kinds. There was a Santa Claus balloon and a Rudolph the Red-Nosed Reindeer one, and even Frosty the Snowman too! There was even Snoopy dressed like Santa with a funny white beard and a bag of presents over his shoulder!

"Omma! Look! Snoopy looks like Santa! He and Santa are celebrating Christmas together!"

Her mother covered the phone with her hand. "Jenny-ah," she said patiently. "Please don't shout when I'm on the phone. It's very rude."

Jenny stared at her mother, pouting, and turned away with a fresh stab of hurt in her chest. She knew she did something really bad whenever her parents used the word "rude" with her. If she spoke too loud in the presence of her parents when they were with other grownups, she was being "incredibly rude." If she forgot to say thank you or didn't bow her head properly before her elders, she was being "very rude." And when she talked back to her teachers or sometimes whined or complained, she was being "obnoxiously rude."

Rude, rude, rude. She was just always rude.

"Sorry, Omma," Jenny whispered. She sniffled, and scooped a spoonful of rice into her mouth. A warm flush of hurtful tears crawled down her chubby cheeks. She scooped another spoonful of rice into her mouth and swallowed, feeling guilty for making her omma mad.

"Jenny-ah."

She turned around. Her mother sighed at her and came down to kneel with her on the floor. She placed the phone down and brought her hands up to cup her cheeks. She wiped a few tears away.

"Don't speak with your mouth open, Jenny-ah," her mother said. "Close your mouth while you chew."

Jenny pouted at her, again, and nodded her head. "Because it's rude?" she asked sobbingly.

"No, Jenny," her mother said tiredly. "Because you're my daughter, and I don't want to see you choking. Understand?"

Jenny stared at her, her eyes wide and cheeks fat. "Okay, Omma," she said quietly. She sniffled, and then tried to smile. "I understand. *Je-song hamnida.*"

Her mother smiled at her, an exhausted and almost frail look on her face, and went back to her phone on the couch.

Daughter. She had been her *daughter* then, and it was only now that Jenny remembered.

*She probably just wanted me to stop making noise while she talked on the phone,* Jenny thought bitterly to herself. *She probably just said that last part to keep me from feeling bad.*

Still. But still.

Jenny stared at the plate of salmon pasta in front of her and felt another cold ripple spread through her. Irene had made it for her. She had made it while she'd slept in her bed. It no doubt was something Irene made for her out of kindness and charity, and was no doubt something she had done out of worry.

*Have I been a fool all this time?* Jenny thought. *Have I really traveled through life so bitter I haven't taken time to look at those around me? My mother. Abigail, Nora, John, Irene, and…Daniel. God, what have I become, what have I done? In my own self-pity, have I just thrown away all those who wanted to be close to me? Have I taken for granted all the great and small things around me?*

Abigail. Abigail and her golden locks and her frivolous habits of speaking nonstop and giggling idiotically to herself—what had she despised about her? What in her heart had made her loathe her, what made her think that she was so much better than her? There was Nora and her bubblegum and magazines, John and his stoic manner in the kitchen, and just about everyone else at the diner.

What had *happened* to her?

*You're my daughter, and I don't want to see you choking. Do you understand?*

"Oh, Omma," Jenny whispered again. Tears swelled in her eyes, and this time Jenny did nothing to wipe them away. "I don't know if you loved me, I really don't, but in that moment, at least I can pretend you did. I can pretend you loved me then, and at least…at least I can say I truly loved you in return. I love you, mom. I love you so, so much."

Her father. Had she been able to say these words to him before his heart attack many years ago? Yes, of course—surely she had. Surely she had. After all, it had just been the two of them after moving to Boise together. After their fallout with Kate, they'd…

Kate. Oh, Kate. That bitch. That horrible, lying, fucking *bitch*. Out of everyone she'd met in life, it was Kate Jenny wished most of all would burn in Hell. And if not Hell, then she wished at least both of her legs were broken and that she was permanently handicapped and bedridden in life at a rundown hospital. She was even worse than Tom.

*Maybe life isn't so complicated after all,* Jenny thought soberly as she made her way towards the kitchen island. She grabbed the plate of salmon pasta and unfolded the note. *Maybe it's only complicated because we make it so. Maybe we make life complicated because we allow our fears to override what our hearts most need, and maybe what our hearts need in life is just friendship. And love. Maybe each of us here just needs to love and be loved by someone else.*

Jenny read the note. The message was brief and the writing familiar. When she read the message, fresh tears spilled down her cheeks and cleaned her face. She set the note aside and cried quietly in the dark. After a few minutes, she found some utensils in the drawer and began dining on what Irene had made for her.

The note had been written by Daniel. It had read: *J.J.*

# CHAPTER 33

Daniel saw her with her arms hugged beneath her chest and knew something was wrong.

She moved towards him with a slow gait in her walk, her footsteps heavy, her pace slow. She kept her eyes to the ground as she moved. Her cheeks seemed bloodless, and her lips were pursed together. It looked like she'd just finished crying.

"Daniel," she said. "Hey."

He studied her. "You look tired today, Jenny."

"Yeah. I know. You look tired today too."

They went silent. Jenny lowered her eyes and Daniel turned awkwardly away. Around them, pink petals tumbled through the air and decorated the pathways of the Quad. They stood close to one of the Yoshino cherry trees partially covered by its shadow. A quiet wind blew above them, ruffling thin delicate branches.

He noticed that her hair was black again.

"Have you finished finals?" Daniel asked quietly. He hated the hesitation in his voice.

"No. My last day is tomorrow. After that, I'm all finished."

He waited. Finally, he said: "Tell me what's wrong, Jenny."

She raised her face at him. She seemed to contemplate something and then shook her head. "I need you to stop texting me, Daniel," she said finally. "And I need you to stop calling me too. Please. It's starting to distract me."

Daniel stared at her. A feeling of cold hurt filled him.

"Jenny."

"You've started calling me a lot last month, and I'm just telling you I need you to stop. Just, please. I can't...I can't talk to you anymore, Daniel. I just can't."

He took a step towards her. Jenny stepped back, stopping him in his tracks. She never stepped away from him before—never. And the way she did it now, so small and timid...it was almost as if she were afraid of him.

"Tell me what happened," Daniel said again. "Just tell me what happened so that I can understand."

"Nothing happened, Daniel. Just...nothing. I just don't want to talk with you anymore. That's all."

"Jenny, please."

She paused. She said: "I made a promise to myself that I won't speak to anyone anymore. And this means you too, Daniel. Out of everyone I can think of, it means you the most. I'm sorry. That's all I wanted to say today."

"You're not making any sense." An urgent tone picked up in his voice, making him sound panicked. "Was it Jon? Did he do something to you?"

Jenny frowned, not understanding who he was referring to. Then she remembered Junghee's Western name, and said calmly: "Jon has nothing to do with this. We broke up in February, and I'm over him."

"This has something to do with winter break last year, doesn't it?"

Jenny looked at him. She nodded.

"You weren't there for me," she said quietly, "and I...I just needed to see you, Daniel. I just

*(rice buns girl!)*

needed you to be there for me."

He said, "You know something happened that night, Jenny."

Jenny nodded. She knew, but didn't believe it, didn't rightly believe in the hurt and the aftermath that had followed it. She read it on the news and read it through her UW email, but still couldn't—or wouldn't—connect him to the incident. If what happened was true, then why hadn't he come to her? If he was in mourning over that student's suicide, why wasn't he mourning *with* her?

*He's found someone else*, a voice whispered. *He's just found someone else to go to first. That's why he's ignored you all these months—he just found someone else. Another girl.*

Maybe. Possibly. It was a thought Jenny had kept to herself since her breakup with Junghee, and it was a thought that made more and more sense as she further analyzed it. He'd found someone else—he'd found another girl to be with. After seeing how she'd abandoned him, after seeing how she'd changed from him, he'd found someone else to help reconcile his hurt, had found someone to hurt *her* with in return. He'd turned from her, just like she'd turned from him, and he'd tried to forget her. And now after realizing how much they'd hurt each other, they…

What? Were meant to be friends again? Fall in love, hold hands and cry? *What?*

"…couldn't contact you that night because I had to give my statement to the police," Daniel was saying. "I couldn't call because I didn't know what was happening."

Jenny looked at him. She said, "Did you find another girl to be with, Daniel?"

He stared at her. His brow furrowed, and Jenny knew the truth.

"What does that matter, Jenny?" Daniel asked, thinking back to last month. Last month had been when Emma had walked away from him. He still remembered her tear-ridden face and the fragrance of her lotion. Peach breasts. "What does it matter? Right now I'm trying to understand why you won't be my friend again, Jenny."

"You know as well as I know it means everything, Daniel," Jenny said, "and you know why I won't talk to you. You know."

His hands tightened into fists. For a moment, he said nothing, and simply glared at her. "And who was it that came back from Korea with her hair dyed and never contacted me?" he asked sharply. "Who was it that pretended I wasn't hurt, or that she was happy with what she had? That she acted in bad faith for several months pretending that she was happy?"

His words fell sharp against her. Jenny lowered her face and stared down at her shoes, accepting his words as much as she could. She replied: "I'm going to tell you what happened to me on the day you decided not to meet me, Daniel. Okay?"

"Fine," Daniel said. "Go ahead."

"When I waited for you at Shutlzy's, I was hoping to wait for someone more than just a friend. I…I was hoping to wait for someone that cared about me. And when you didn't come, I still waited, sitting there for almost three hours. I called and texted you, thought about you, and even worried about you. Eventually I got up and just started to cry when I realized you weren't coming."

"Jenny—"

"No, I'm not finished yet. I got up and left Shutlzy's feeling embarrassed and ugly. Do you understand, Daniel? Do you know how a girl feels when she's stood up? Do you understand how much it hurts to be lied to by a *friend?* I walked away crying and feeling ugly inside, Daniel. I felt freaking *ugly* inside. And then, like, when I was walking through the dark, I suddenly got lost and didn't know where I was, and suddenly those three guys behind me…"

Her voice trailed off. She brought a light hand up to wipe her nose and uttered a dry cough. She went on.

"Those guys. They…they began saying horrible things to me, Daniel, just…just horrible things that made me realize what I *was* to them. They chased me into an alleyway where one of them finally came up and touched me. He put his hands on me and just *grabbed* me all over, okay? And afterwards, everyone just laughed at me and went away, and I spent another ten minutes crying to myself in the dark. It was cold, and no one was there to help me."

"If I knew you'd be in—"

"But that wasn't the worse of it," Jenny said, interrupting him. She brought another hand up to wipe her face. "You want to know the worst part? The worst part was knowing what I was to them—the worst part was seeing myself weak and helpless for the first time. I was *helpless* to them, not just as a girl or a stereotype, but as a *person*. I couldn't do anything. No matter how much I ran or shouted, I wasn't *a person* at that moment, and couldn't have been myself no matter how hard I tried. Do you understand, Daniel? I was just whatever it was they wanted me to be. I was just a body to them. Just…some *thing* to be laughed at and called with words."

Jenny swallowed. She took several seconds to breathe and then collected herself.

"I re-dyed my hair for you," she whispered. "I went out and re-dyed my hair for you, and you…you just weren't there, Daniel. You just weren't there for me."

"Jenny."

He stepped towards her. She took another step back, and Daniel was able to briefly appreciate the lovely contrast her hair made against the falling backdrop of white petals. He was reminded of snow for some reason; just hair like snow.

"Will sorry change anything?"

"No. Nothing will change the past. You know this, Daniel."

"Jenny, please. Don't do that. Just…don't."

She said, "I need to go, Daniel. I'm sorry. Please don't call me anymore. Give me time to think or something, and like…like, just leave me alone for now. I need to be alone."

"All because you're afraid of getting hurt in life again, you suddenly want to throw away the whole *world?*" Daniel asked. His voice had risen. "Jenny, come on, don't be like that. Don't be such a coward, don't be so weak. I'm sorry, okay? All because I wasn't there for you once doesn't mean you have to be so self-righteous and selfish. Get over it, and just—"

Daniel stopped himself, stunned at his own words. He stared at her and saw a look of hurt on her face. Worse than that—what he saw then on her face was a look of betrayal and dismay.

"Jenny. Please. I'm…I'm sorry. God, I'm so sorry. I didn't mean…I'm sorry."

"I have to go now, Daniel," Jenny said. "The bus is coming. I'm going to be late if I miss it. I parked my car at the Park and Ride."

"What can I say to make you stay?" he asked. His voice was pleading now. Desperate. "Jenny, please. What can I say to make you stay with me?"

She took a step back from him and brought her arms up to re-hold herself. She said faintly: "Goodbye, Daniel. Maybe I'll talk to you later, but…but for now, don't follow me. And please don't contact me."

"You're moving away from me because you're afraid," he said. It was a last-ditch effort. "We can still be friends again, Jenny. We can still *be* together, and you won't have to be afraid. I promise."

She stared at him. "Daniel," she said. "The reason I'm moving away from you is *because* we can still be friends. I thought…I thought you understood that."

Daniel said nothing. He gazed at her one last time and watched as she turned around. He took several steps to follow her, but then stopped suddenly when a flush of tears welled up in his eyes. He stared after her, blurry-eyed, and turned away.

# CHAPTER 34

*Seattle / 11:09 a.m.*
*2019*

Irene heard her in the kitchen before she saw her.

She was washing dishes in the kitchen. No, that wasn't right. She was washing just *one* dish this morning, and as Irene neared, she realized it was the dish that she'd prepared for her last night. As she watched, Jenny rinsed the dish under the sink, dried it off, and placed it in one of the cupboards overhead. She dried her hands and turned away.

"Jenny."

She spun around. Hair fluttered around her shoulders and briefly rippled like silk under the sun.

"Irene," she said. "I'm sorry. I didn't mean to wake you."

Irene stepped into the kitchen. She studied her, and saw that she was dressed in casual blue jeans and a light cotton sweater.

"Where are you going, Jenny?"

Jenny bit her lip. She offered a gentle smile. It was a sad smile, something that was warm and small. The sight of it brought an ache to Irene's heart.

"Thank you for dinner and lunch yesterday," she said softly. "I…I didn't get to properly thank you. For that, and also for taking me in. Thank you."

Irene scanned her face again and noticed something in the foyer. It was her suitcase. A pair of leather boots was set next to it, and her jacket was slung over the coat rack.

Panic filled her.

"If you go," Irene said suddenly, "you'll hurt him. He'll see it as you abandoning him and turning away from him."

Jenny shook her head. "No. If…if I stay, I hurt him, and I become a burden to both of you."

"Jenny."

"No, Irene. You know…you know it as well as I do. I can't stay here any longer. I just need to go. For you. And him. I just have to go and leave. We both know this."

"Yesterday you told me you weren't a symbol for others and weren't trying to act out of martyrdom," Irene said sharply. "Now listen to yourself. Now listen to the way you're trying to glorify yourself."

"I'm just leaving, Irene," Jenny said back calmly, "and I…it's something we both know I have to do. And you want me to go. This I know. It would be better if we both just moved on in life. Better if he moved on."

"And where do you expect to go?" Irene snapped. "Where do you expect to go once you walk out that door?"

At this, another sad look passed through Jenny's face, softening her eyes. She said after a moment: "I'm going back to the place where I grew up, I guess. It's not far from here. It…it should still be there. It's a place I've never really truly forgotten. It's still there, I think."

Irene took a step towards her. She didn't know what was happening, but could feel the situation slowly drifting away from her. She should get Daniel, but he was still in the shower. And wasn't this right? Wasn't somehow all of this *right*? She already knew she wouldn't go and get Daniel; she already knew that she would allow her to walk away, allow her to leave, because…because why?

*Because he still loves her,* Irene thought to herself, *and because she still loves* him. *They both still love each other, and in doing so, she has to leave. And because I love him, Daniel, my husband, I'll allow her to go. I'll allow her to go and bear the weight of knowing both of their loves.*

There was no malice with this thought, no sense of poisonous jealously. Instead, there was just a cold feeling of sadness and remorse, akin to hearing the death of a beloved friend. Irene raised her eyes and caught Jenny's, suddenly understanding, but not wishing to understand. Yes, they'd been in love once—and perhaps in their hearts they still truly were. How he managed to have room in his heart to love so much, Irene didn't know, but now suddenly pitied him. *All* of them, she pitied all *three* of them. It was just so much easier to hate in life. At this moment here, standing before the woman she'd helped feed and clothe, Irene suddenly realized it was so much easier to hate in life, and wished that she had enough strength to hate herself.

"If you go," Irene said, tears sounding in her voice, "I'll stop you, Jenny. For his sake and yours, I'll stop you."

"No, Irene. You won't. And I know you won't try. You won't because…because you care for him. I also know you want me to leave, Irene. To move on with your life."

Irene swallowed another taste of tears in her throat. In the bright early light that came filtered through Seattle's gray skies, she saw watery droplets in Jenny's eyes, and knew that this was going to be the last time she was ever going to see her. This would be the last time.

"I need to go now," Jenny said. "Thank you for everything. Please don't tell him. And please just take care of him." She glanced down at her stomach. Irene turned her head away, ashamed. "Make him happy, Irene," Jenny said. "Just make him happy in life and give him another reason to love this world again. Please just give him that. You know this to be the greatest gift you can give him."

Irene said nothing. She watched as she turned towards the door again and bit her lip.

"Jenny."

Jenny stopped at the door and turned around. "Yes?"

"I wish…I wish we could have been sisters. Friends, at least. You…I think it would have been wonderful to have known you. I think it would

488

have been so good to be your friend."

A gentle smile went to Jenny's lips. It was the same smile from before, soft and incredibly sad. It was enough to make the tears in Irene's eyes finally fall.

"We are, Irene," Jenny said kindly. "We are friends. We are sisters. You *are* my friend."

Irene nodded. She turned her face away and heard as she put on her boots. She heard the dragging of her suitcase and then the final closing of the door. When it was all over, the only things Irene heard were the soothing sounds of muffled traffic from the street below, and the sounds of the shower raging down the hall.

# CHAPTER 35

"Whoo-hoo! Graduation baby! *Graduation!*"

Cheers erupted to the sides. Daniel winced when he heard the noise, but felt himself smiling anyway. A feeling of cascading energy and excitement rushed through him. Those around him raised their voices to fervent cries that rattled the gymnasium's walls, and soon the entire senior class of Evanston-Woods High was making its way through the doors leading from the gym to the Great Hall.

Graduation. Graduation was just three days away. Today marked the completion of their final rehearsal.

"Class of oh-six, baby!" Anthony Pagaliluan cried next to him. "Class of oh-six! Best year ever!"

"Yo, Captain!" Francis Lagabas wrapped an arm around him. "You gonna join us at the beach tonight?"

Daniel raised an eyebrow at him, puzzled. "Beach? No. Why?"

"We're gonna be burning all our notes, Cap! No more IB! No more IB! NO MORE IB!"

The chant got picked up by the crowd. Soon everyone was laughing and cheering, including Daniel. Fists pumped the air and feet stomped the ground; screeching voices tore out from excited lungs and rocked the walls. Daniel glanced at those around him and felt his heart swell. It was a painful yet comforting ache, akin to the loving embraces of a parting friend. Yes, high-school was ending now, and yes, he was frightened of the future. But right now, at this moment here, surrounded by so many that he knew, seeing them so happy, hearing them laughing and crying…his heart went out to them. His heart went out to *all* of them, and oh, how wonderful it was to be young at this moment. At this moment here, surrounded by so many of his peers—how wonderful it was just to be young. And how wonderful it was to realize the time and be happy because of it.

*This is the last time*, Daniel thought quietly to himself. *This is the last time I'm going to be a high-school student; this is the last time I will ever see these walls as something confining and restricting, something lovely. When I see these walls again, I'll be older.*

It didn't matter. Nothing mattered at this instant other than understanding the moment in which they all existed. To have loved, to have laughed, to have cried…why was there such great fear of the future when in the past every moment had been *lived?*

Tears swelled in Daniel's eyes, thick and sudden, and he had to suddenly step back from the crowd and watch them from afar as they passed by. Their voices carried low but strong through the hallway, sounding like heavy raindrops during summer. He watched as they held each other and laughed, watched as a few wiped aside subtle tears and leaned on each other for comfort.

It was a beautiful scene. It was a scene that hurt his heart so, so much.

"Going to stand here all day and take in the sights, Daniel?"

He turned around. It was Thu Nguyen.

"School's over, you know," she said. "We have lives to live outside of this place"

"That may be true," he said, mildly, "but not everyone here will be able to live their lives once out of this place."

Thu smirked at him. It was a friendly smirk, both challenging and acknowledging.

"Still hoping to be a writer?"

"Always."

"Well good luck with that then. See you one last time this Saturday at graduation."

Daniel watched as she walked off. He noted the slight sway of her pendulum earrings, the tight spread of wrinkles against the surface of her leather skirt, the clanking sounds of her high-heels, and remembered suddenly how her eyes had momentarily flashed at him before turning away. *Yes, Thu,* Daniel thought quietly. *Good luck to you as well. Good luck with everything in life. Perhaps we'll meet again someday.*

"Daniel. Captain."

He turned around. It was Kooper.

"You did it, Cap," Kooper said as he approached him. "You've finally made it. Congratulations."

Daniel smiled at him. He took a step towards him and extended his hand. After a moment's hesitation, Kooper took it, and squeezed. He wore his varsity jacket.

"*We* made it," Daniel said to him. "We both made it, Koop…Steven. We made it together."

"I couldn't have done it without you, D."

"You would've and will," Daniel said. "We all will. Eventually."

"You've always been the man," Kooper said. "Always have been, always will be. No matter how much people may cheer for me, it'll always be *you* they cheer for, Daniel. I love you, dog. No homo. You know?"

Daniel grinned at him. He dropped his hand.

"I'll see you this Saturday," Kooper said. "And I'll be screaming my lungs out for you when I see you walking that stage to get your diploma. You hear?"

"I hear you, Kooper."

"I'll be looking for you in the audience too."

Daniel nodded. He smiled. Warmth spread beneath his eyes.

Kooper smiled at him one last time and turned away, his eyes red, his posture when moving away straight and tall. He no longer swaggered.

Daniel stuffed his hands in his pockets and moved himself away from the gym. Ordinarily he would have made his way towards the exit doors and gone home, but now he made his way towards the library instead, purposefully dragging his feet along. His heart was light, and his mind buoyant. It seemed like he didn't walk at all, but rather, simply floated, drifting farther and farther away from the noises behind him. He came to the library doors and stood still for a moment, observing the emptiness around him. From outside, afternoon sunlight shone through the court-facing windows and painted his shadows against the walls.

*The last time*, he thought. *This will be the last time. As a student, as a boy…this will be my last time ever standing here as someone once young.*

"Daniel."

He spun around. "Hey," he said. He smiled. "Glad you could make it."

Jenny smiled at him. The smile was light but sad, appearing doleful in her eyes. Daniel frowned at her.

"You look good when you smile," she said gently. "You should do it more often, Daniel."

He looked at her. "What's the matter, Jenny?"

She shook her head as if he'd asked a silly question, and ended up sniffling instead. She said: "I just wanted to say congratulations. To you and everyone else. You guys worked hard, Daniel. You deserve to be happy." She paused. She said: "I won't be walking with you this Saturday. I…I have to go to Korea tomorrow. I won't be graduating with you."

He stared at her. "What are you talking—"

"I mean, I'll be graduating, but I won't be walking, Daniel. The school's going to send me my diploma. I just won't be at the ceremony. I won't be walking."

She said this last part with a soft croak in her voice. A loose strand of hair fell across her face, covering her eye. She wiped it back.

"When will you be coming back?" he asked.

"I don't know. After summer, maybe. Daniel…" She bit her lip. "Today is the last day I get to see you. That's what I'm trying to say. This is the last day I'll get to see you for…for a few months at least. For a while."

"Your family?"

She nodded. "Yeah."

Daniel studied her features, saying nothing. The disappointment he felt was cold and heavy, like a pile of bricks dropped in his stomach. He glanced at the light outside and realized they were in the same location where they'd first held each other. Had that been just a year ago? It felt like lifetimes ago. He wondered vaguely whether or not her blood was still somewhere on the floor, and realized it didn't matter.

"I'm sorry if I've ruined plans for you this summer," Jenny was saying. "And I'm sorry I won't be able to watch you walk during graduation. I know it's a big deal for you."

"It's fine," Daniel said. "Don't worry about it."

He hesitated. He gazed at her.

"Jenny. Here."

"Yeah?"

He approached her. He held her.

Jenny gasped at him, surprised, but then immediately leaned in against him. His arms folded around her shoulders and held her tight from behind. She placed her head against his chest and closed her eyes, rubbing her face against the soft cotton of his chest. She sobbed.

"I'm sorry," Jenny whispered. "I wish I didn't have to leave you, Daniel."

"Shh, Jenny. It's fine. Don't cry about it."

"Don't be mad."

"I'm not. You know I'm not. You'll be back soon anyway. Right?"

"Yeah. But still. I wish we could've spent more time together."

A cold feeling swept through Daniel, making him shiver. He knew what he had to say. He hesitated only because he knew that by doing so, he'd break this moment of holding her, and let time retake what temporarily was theirs. In this moment, she was his, and she felt so, so wonderful in his arms.

"Jenny," he began. "Do you want to go to the beach?"

***

*Seattle / 11:25 a.m.*
*2019*

"Where *is* she, Irene?"

"Daniel…please, don't—"

He grabbed his jacket and quickly shrugged it on. He grabbed his wallet from the kitchen counter and ran towards the door.

"Daniel—"

"Just tell me where she is. Just—"

He stopped at the doorway and saw tears on her face. He paused, slowly went to her, and gently grabbed her by the shoulders. He held her.

"Irene," he said. "Come on. Shh, don't cry. Please just don't."

"You love her," she said. "You love her still after all this time."

"I love y—"

"I know. I know you do, but still…I don't want you to go, Daniel. Ah, God, *please*, I don't want you to go to her."

Daniel lowered his face and kissed her. He kissed her face and tasted her tears. When she tried turning away, he took her by the chin and kissed her again, keeping her close. He wanted to hold her, take her in his arms, tell her it was all right…but all he could do was kiss her out of fear, afraid that she would convince him to stay.

"Tell me where she is, Irene," Daniel said again. His voice was brisk but warm. "Just tell me."

"Let her go, Daniel," Irene sobbed. "Please. Just…stay with me. Don't go to her. *Please*, Daniel."

He grabbed her gently by the face and pressed his forehead against hers. Irene felt his fingers trembling and knew he was struggling to stay calm.

*Hit me*, she thought suddenly. *Oh please God, just let him hit me. Let him hit me*

495

*and feel sorry about himself, let him hit me and apologize. Please God, I'm sorry, but make him like her husband. Make him into a bastard and let him hit me, let him hurt me so that I keep him with me.*

Irene reached out and held him from behind.

*Don't go, Daniel. Oh, please, don't go. Let me use your own goodness against you, let me…just let me hurt for you.*

"Irene."

"If you go," she whispered, "if you go to her…I'll…I'll see it as a decision, Daniel. Do you understand? I'll see it that you chose her over me. I'll see it that you went to her and left me alone here."

He kissed her between the eyes. "I love you," he breathed. "And no matter what you think, I'll always love you. And I *will* come back, Irene. No matter how hurt you'll be, I will come back. One last time: Where *is* she?"

"She said she was going back to her childhood place," Irene said. "She said…she was going back to a place she always remembered, and that it should still be there. Some place special. Someplace…*her*."

Daniel released her. He moved fast and alert, as if suddenly being pulled away rather than turning from her. When Irene opened her eyes, she saw him already at the door, putting his shoes on.

"Irene—"

"Go," she said. She turned away from him and wiped her eyes. "Just go, Daniel. Don't…don't talk to me. Just go and find her. I know you want to."

Daniel stood in the foyer and stared at her. "Listen to me, Irene."

"Just *go*, Daniel. Just…go. Come back if you want. I don't care anymore."

Her words pierced his heart. Daniel said nothing. He turned away from her and opened the door. He paused, and then quickly closed it behind him.

Irene sighed. She went to the couch in the living room and sat down. She closed her eyes.

*Edmonds / 2:39 p.m.*
*2006*

"The beach?" Jenny asked.

"Yeah," Daniel said. "Sure. Why not? It'll be the last time for you, right?"

"Yeah. I guess." She looked at him. "You want to go now?"

"Yeah," he said kindly. "Let's go now, Jenny. Let's go now."

# CHAPTER 36

Jenny gazed outside the window and thought to herself: *So. A city in the morning truly is beautiful when waking with the sun. Like seeing the naked face of the one you love waking next to you, a city seen with the morning light is a promise of a new day. We will always suffer in life; we will always mourn. But each new day can give us a reason to love and cherish as well.*

She was headed north on I-5 crossing the spanning bridge-way that rose high above the blue waters of Lake Union. Bright sunlight sparkled on the surfaces of the Lake and then disappeared again. The clouds were plenty today and occasionally eclipsed the sun with strips of gray. Behind her, Seattle's uneven stiletto-shaped skyline diminished from view as the 511 Sound Transit bus took her farther and farther up north. The bus was cold, but that was fine—Jenny had her jacket placed over her chest and her arms hugged around herself. Beneath her, black massive tires rolled steadily on and on with an indistinct hypnotic hum.

*I wonder if I'll ever see this city again,* Jenny thought quietly, closing her eyes, *or if whether or not it will continue existing into the future without me. Seattle. You've been so kind to me, my friend. If I take a part of you with me in my heart, will there be those who become jealous of me?*

It was Kate that Jenny thought of then as she sat there with her eyes closed and her head leaned comfortably against the windows. In thinking of her, a hot flare of rage lit in her heart and then quickly died away. She remembered how she first met Kate after seeing her standing in the kitchen of their old home. She'd been wearing her mother's apron and slippers that day. She'd also been holding onto her father's hand.

Kate. That bitch. That lying, cunning, deceiving bitch. If there was anyone worthy of her total hate, it was Kate. Katie Chung. Chung Kyung-soon.

*You hurt my father, you fucking slut.*

At this, Jenny's eyes popped opened, and she winced at the brief light that cut through the clouds. After a moment, the light was gone again, swallowed by gray sky.

*You hurt him, and you just left us hurt and miserable. It was because of you we had to move away; it was because of you I had to leave everything I once knew. It was because of you I left Dan…I left Seattle, and everything I once loved.*

Had it been the very same day she'd spoken to Daniel for the last time in the Quad at the UW campus? Jenny was sure it was. She'd told him she didn't want to be friends anymore on that day, and she'd left him standing alone beneath the pale petals of the Yoshino cherry trees. She'd come home that evening distraught and in tears; she'd come home that night to find Kate fucking in bed.

*Fucking,* Jenny thought coldly as she gazed solemnly out at the windows. *I caught you fucking my father once Kate, and then I caught you fucking again. On the very same afternoon I left my only friend in this world, you had to destroy everything I knew.*

She sighed. The anger was no longer sharp now, but just something that burned quietly in the corner of her heart. It was a flame she had let burn for years, she supposed. It was a memory that could never be extinguished.

Sighing heavily a second time, Jenny brought her jacket up close to her chin, closed her eyes, and let her dreams overtake her.

*Edmonds / 7:19 p.m.*
*2007*

She slid her car into the driveway and turned off the engine. She sat still in the darkness for a minute and breathed out several haggard breaths. Her eyes stung. She'd managed to drive home without crying, but her vision had turned blurry when driving on 99. Now that she was parked and off the road, she let out a quiet moan, brought her hands up, and covered her face.

"I'm so sorry," she sobbed. "I'm so sorry Daniel, but I can't. I just *can't*. Not with you. Just not with you."

She sniffled. She wiped her eyes after a moment and then finally raised her head.

The lights to the house were off. Jenny frowned, but didn't think anything of it until she was out of the car and carrying her backpack. She paused at the door and felt sweat form on the back of her neck.

Why was her house so *dark* this evening?

*Why are all the lights off when Kate always comes home early?*

She checked the driveway and saw Kate's Audi parked next to her Mazda. Her father still worked late nights at the office, and he only came home when everyone else was in bed. Kate always returned home early to make dinner, and she always left the lights on. Always.

*What's happening? Why does this feel wrong? Why am I suddenly so cold?*

Jenny bit her lip and craned her neck back to look at the second-story windows. The windows overlooking the driveway were dark and covered with curtains. Every window on the second floor in fact had the curtains drawn, but something about these curtains seemed more deliberate, ominous, darker than the rest. The windows that overlooked the driveway belonged to her father's room.

*Please God,* Jenny thought. *Don't let it be what I think it is.*

She turned away from the door and rounded the corner of the house. There, Jenny unlatched the door leading to the backyard and made her way to the porch deck. She approached the glass doors that led into the kitchen and cupped her hands around her face. She peered inside.

The kitchen looked undisturbed and the living room was clean. Kate usually left pots and pans in the sink and sometimes set her purse on the kitchen counter. There were none of these things, and Jenny shivered again.

*Her car's in the driveway, but where's her purse?*

A red light blinked on the wall of the kitchen. It was the answering machine. Kate hadn't come to check any of their calls.

Shivering, Jenny pulled out her house keys and unlocked the door. She slipped out of her shoes once she was inside and dropped off her backpack. She quietly made her way through the living room and crept up the stairs. She paused midway and looked behind her. Kate's shoes were in the foyer. Next to them was a pair of dark leather Italian shoes for men.

Her father didn't have shoes like that.

*Let me be wrong, God,* Jenny thought desperately again. *Please just let me be wrong. Don't let this be what I think it is.*

A splinter of light glowed from beneath one of the doors in the hallway. With a sickening feeling, Jenny realized the light belonged to her father's room. She crept down the hallway and knelt beside the door. Kate's voice sounded behind the door. With it was the deep sound of a man's voice grunting and panting. They spoke in Korean.

"…doing tonight?" a voice asked

"…school…no sound…door downstairs."

"Everything…with the lights off."

A quiet sound of giggles followed. Jenny wiped her nose and felt something dry in the back of her throat.

There was a small crack between the double doors. Jenny crept closer, peeked inside, and felt the hairs on her neck rise.

Two white naked bodies lay on top of her father's bed. One of them was lean and muscular and had his backside decorated in neat hieroglyphic glows of shadows caused by the dim lamplight. The other body was Kate's. She was

501

laid out wide and spread out beneath him like a giant white starfish. The man bent over her and kissed her breasts. He kissed her face and then kissed her neck, making slurping sounds, drinking her. Kate's legs lifted and wrapped around his waist. She reached over and grabbed him by the neck. Her feet hung in the air like two dangling white plums, and she giggled at him, saying something Jenny couldn't hear.

*You're cheating on my dad, you bitch,* Jenny thought coldly. *You're lying on the same bed that he sleeps in every night, and you're letting some stranger fuck you while you laugh like a fucking dog. I trusted you. I trusted you so, so much.*

"When?" the man asked. His voice was low. "Why not now?"

"When I can, oppa," Kate replied. She sighed, reared her head back, and turned her face aside as he began nibbling her breasts. "He…he has a daughter. But soon. I'll do it soon."

There was a sigh, a grunt, and then the wincing sounds of creaking bedsprings as the man lowered himself on top of her. He began thrusting into her, increasing the rickety sounds of the bedsprings. Bubbly squeals erupted from Kate's throat. She sighed deliciously beneath him and let out a pleasant moan. Short jerky gasps filled the room.

Jenny wiped her nose and reached into her pocket. She didn't know what she was looking for until her fingers finally touched it. It was her cellphone. Hesitating, she brought the phone out and held it in front of her near the crack between the doors. Images of her father having sex on the couch from last year filled her mind again, making her stomach turn. Just what went on behind her back between these walls when she *slept?* Jenny held the phone out and zoomed in on Kate's naked body. With a trembling hand, she pushed the RECORD button, held her breath, and waited.

"Oppa," Kate whispered. "Faster. Go a bit…go a bit faster."

His thrusting increased. Kate's feet bounced wildly around his waist like two white obscene pompoms. Her mewing turned into high octave squeals and filled the room. There was the constant creak of straining bedsprings, the meaty slap of thighs, and the squishy *thulp-thulp-thulp* sounds of hard meat

502

entering wet layers of skin. As Jenny watched, sweat formed on the man's backside, gleaming smoothly in the half-dark.

She stopped the recording after one minute and carefully turned away. She tiptoed through the hallway and quietly crept down the stairs. She found her shoes in the kitchen, grabbed her backpack, and slipped back outside into the backyard. Once outside, she sighed, and turned her head to look up at the stars.

*What do you want me to do, God?* she asked tiredly. *Now that I'm here, born on this earth, just what do you want me* to do?

There was no answer. Jenny wasn't expecting one. With another heavy sigh, she left the backyard, rounded the corner of the house, and went to move her car.

***

*Edmonds / 8:33 p.m.*
*2007*

Jenny watched as the man left her house and strode to his vehicle in the Stewarts' driveway two houses over. The Stewarts were on vacation. That made sense. It would've looked suspicious to have a foreign vehicle parked in their driveway for the whole neighborhood to see, even if it *was* during the evening. So long as the attention was brought to another household, it didn't matter where his vehicle was kept. Jenny herself was parked across the street several houses down. She'd been careful to find a spot that looked inconspicuous, and had driven in and out of her cul-de-sac for several minutes trying to decide what to do. It wouldn't have made much sense for her to keep her car in the driveway for him to see—Jenny was sure Kate had described to him what her car looked like.

*Get out of here,* Jenny thought darkly as she sat behind the steering wheel. *Just get the fuck out of my house. Hurry up and go. You're not welcomed here.*

The man got into his car, started the engine, and zoomed away. Jenny started her vehicle and drove back towards her house.

Kate was in the shower. That made sense too, didn't it? Jenny heard the loud thunderous drone of the showerhead upstairs and removed her shoes in the foyer. She closed the door behind her and quickly ran upstairs to her room.

After twenty minutes, Kate finally exited the bathroom.

"Kate?" Jenny asked as she knocked on her father's door. "Are you in there?"

"Be ready in a minute," Kate shouted. Her voice was pleasant and warm. Jenny bit her lip when she heard it.

She stepped back and waited, cramps in her stomach. Adrenaline rushed through her veins and caused the hairs on her arms to stiffen. She had no idea if this was going to work or not.

*His sperm is in you,* Jenny thought coldly as she stood in the hallway. *If he didn't wear a condom, his sperm is all over inside you, and you fucked while lying in my father's bed.*

"Jenny," Kate said happily when she opened the door. She smiled. "You've finally come back. How was school?"

Jenny licked her lips together. She said, "I…I need to show you something," and pulled out her cellphone. She switched over to her video files. "I just need you to look at this for me," she said dryly. She found her latest created video and pushed PLAY.

The image was dark at first. Eventually the pixels came together, and a grainy image of a naked man kneeling on his knees in bed could be seen. There were two, long, naked legs wrapped around his waist. The angle slowly shifted, and soon Kate's body entered the shot, fully naked and white on her back. Her breasts jiggled up and down like small mounds of Jell-O as the man rocked himself on top of her. Gasps spilled from the cellphone speakers. The gasps were womanly and high, sounding like complaining kittens. Eventually the gasps—rusty due to the recording—turned into quick squeals of delight. The sounds climbed higher, sharper, and soon became stretched out wails and delicious moans.

Kate's smile disappeared beside her. As Jenny watched, her eyes widened and her breath caught—every muscle in her face just seemed to freeze. Her eyes bulged out wide on her face.

"Where did you get that?"

Jenny closed her cellphone and backed away. She swallowed.

"Get out of my house," Jenny said. "Just fucking pack your things and go, Kate. I don't want you here anymore. Fucking leave or I tell my father."

Kate stared at her. Her eyes narrowed into daggered slits, and she said tonelessly: "Give me that cellphone, Jenny. Give it to me *now*."

Jenny shook her head. She slipped the cellphone into her pocket and sniffled. She said: "You're a slut. Just some fucking slut that entered my dad's life and tried to win my trust. I hate you. I *trusted* you. I was even starting to like you until you…until you *fucked* on my dad's bed. You're here just for my dad's money and property. That's all you're here for."

Warm tears formed in her eyes.

"Why did you have to mess everything *up?*" Jenny whimpered. "With so much crap happening in my life already…why did you have to go and do something like this?"

Kate's lips pressed together. She said nothing for a minute and just stared, hands clenching to her side. "Just give me the cellphone, Jenny," she said, "and we'll talk about this later, okay? What you saw…it…what you saw was a bad thing, okay? Just a mistake of sorts. Okay? It was just a mistake, something that—"

"Liar! You're nothing but a fucking *liar*, Kyung-soon, and you're lying to me *and* my dad! Just get out of here before I tell my dad about what you did!"

"You annoying wretched little *brat*." She spoke in Korean. "I said give me that cellphone! Give it to me NOW!"

Kate jumped at her. The move was so fast Jenny barely had time to register that she was even moving. Long wrenching claws grabbed her hair as she tried to duck away and slammed her head against the wall. Pain exploded through her face; her right eye refused to open. Jenny shrieked out loud and brought her hands up. She snarled. She pushed out with her hands and pathetically punched Kate in the stomach, shoving her away. There was one last searing bolt of pain as Kate stumbled backward with a fistful of hair.

"Is he your boyfriend?" Jenny asked, panting harshly. "Is he like someone you met online or something? Is he someone younger than you?"

"*That's none of your bu*—"

"You're a *whore!*" Jenny gasped, "and when my dad finds out about the video, he's going to drive you out and—"

Kate leapt at her again. Jenny brought her hands up and felt a windmill of slashing nails slice her face. She screamed, felt Kate's hands take her hair again, and this time drove a random knee straight into her stomach. There was a loud *augh!* sound, and soon Jenny was free, stumbling blindly away. She turned around and struck her hip against the sharp edges of the hallway table; another bone-shattering bolt of pain ripped through her. Jenny screamed. The pain bloomed through her left hipbone and traveled all the way down her thigh. Her feet tangled together, her legs lost balance, and she went down sprawling. The floor rushed up and slammed her dead-center in the chest. It was like taking a hammer blow directly to the sternum: the ribs in her chest folded, her lungs squeezed tight, and all of the air disappeared from her lungs. Darkness swam in her vision. She tried lifting herself back up and could only manage to crawl.

"When your father hears about this," Kate said coldly behind her, "he's going to punish you, Jenny! He's going to punish you for invading other peoples' privacy, and there's going to be no one to protect you!"

Jenny tried to pick herself up, failed, and flopped back down with a sob. She cringed with agony when trying to move her legs. Kate knelt down and grabbed her by the hair. Jenny hissed through her teeth and felt tears gush down her face. She wailed out loud. Hands rummaged through her pockets and pulled at her jeans.

Kate moved off of her. Jenny rolled onto her side, grimaced, and clutched her thigh. As she watched, blinded by tears and hair, Kate ripped apart her cellphone and threw the battery away. She took out the SIM card and placed it in her pocket. She tossed the phone to the ground and stared. A cold calculating look of contempt passed through her eyes.

Jenny gingerly picked herself up. She cried as she moved and heard her knees pop. Her left hip throbbed with pain and sticky tears smeared her face. She gasped at Kate, and said steadily: "I still want you to leave, Kate. You don't deserve to be in this house."

"You're in no position to tell me what to do," she snapped. "How dare you even *think* of undermining me, Jenny. I cared for you after all this time, and *this* is how you treat me? You're lucky I don't tell your father every night to drive you out of the house!"

Jenny grimaced, felt something in her leg give out, and grimaced again. When she went to touch the place she hit her thigh, she winced, and felt a fresh bruise already forming.

"If you don't leave," Jenny said back calmly, "then I'm going to keep the videos I uploaded on YouTube and Facebook. I'll keep them online and tell my friends about them."

Kate's eyes widened. Her eyes popped out fat on her face and her mouth dropped open.

"You…you wouldn't *dare!*"

She rushed past Jenny and shoved her aside. Jenny fell back against the wall and watched silently as she strode past.

Kate burst into Jenny's room. Her eyes frantically searched the area and then fell onto her computer near the windows. Her blood turned cold.

A YouTube video was running on the monitor screen. It was on repeat, and was the exact same video Jenny had captured on her cellphone just hours before. The image was in high quality, the bodies in the video now rendered smoother and with greater detail. Kate's face was easily visible.

"No! Take this down! Take this down *now!*"

Kate ran to the computer and exited out of the video. She scrolled to the bottom and felt her heart stop a second time. There, in the description box, were the words: *Katie Chung a.k.a Chung Kyung-soon. J.D/MBA Harvard University 2003. Edmonds, Washington. Works at Geo New Foundations Inc., Seattle. Being herself.*

Along with that was the same description written in Korean.

"Delete this video," Kate ordered. "Take it down now!"

Jenny hobbled into the room, wincing. Sweat plastered her face. "I'll take it down if you leave, Kate," she panted. "Get out of here, and I'll delete *all* the videos I uploaded."

Kate glared at her. "Just how many videos did you *upload?*"

"If you go, I'll go into my Facebook and YouTube accounts and delete them. I'll take them off my computer and make sure no one sees them. But only if you go, Kate. Only if you get out of here in the next ten minutes."

"Do you think you can *threaten* me?" Kate shot back. "A little girl like you talking back to *me?* You don't even know what I am *capable* of, Jenny! To exploit someone like this while taking a video of them without their permission! The legal consequences of your actions have just ruined you!"

"Legal or not," Jenny said, "it's your professional reputation on the line. So sue me, see if I fucking care. We'll see who hurts more in the fallout when everything gets over. We'll see if you can work again as a professional woman. Also…" She reached down and clutched her thigh, wincing. "You physically attacked me. I have the bruises to prove it. Not to mention you broke my cellphone."

Kate glared at her. An ugly blue vein crawled out from the corner of her temple.

"All those years at law school and business school," Jenny said. "What's more important to you, Kyung-soon? Getting back at some little girl like me, or preserving your personal and professional reputation? How many people do you know in the business world that respects you? I have nothing to lose. Girls my age do crap like this all the time and get in trouble for it, but women like you fall hard once pushed off the edge. What will it be?"

"You're fucking blackmailing me, you little slut."

"I know."

Kate stood up. She calmly walked over and stared down at her. In that moment, Jenny's mouth turned dry, and the first real quivers of fear went through her. The way she stared at her and coldly scanned her face…it felt like she'd missed something. Just…something.

"I don't take kindly to being blackmailed," Kate whispered, still in Korean. "And I will *not* be pushed around by a snotty and spoiled girl like you."

"Well I'm sorry," Jenny replied. She was trying to sound brave. She swallowed. "And I…I don't like it when people hurt my appa. *Or* when my trust gets misused."

"If I leave this house," Kate said, "how do I know you'll remove those videos?"

"You won't. But at least it's better than just letting them stay up on the Internet with you living here. I told you: I'll delete them. Whether or not you believe me is up to you. You have no choice *but* to believe me."

Jenny swallowed. She badly had to sit down somewhere.

"If you don't leave," she said quickly again, "I won't just leave them on my Facebook account. I'll…I'll send them out to other places too! I'll put them all over the web for the whole world to see. I'll send them to *every* organization that has a website, both in English and Korean. Your life will be ruined, and you'll never work in this country again!"

Kate's jaws tightened. For a moment, she said nothing, and just simply stared. Then: "What you're doing is illegal, and I hope you know it. But I also hope you know I'm going to take matters into my own hands for having been pushed around by you." She smiled. It was a cruel smile. "When your father is ruined, when he is hurt and lost, know that it was all because of *you*, Jenny. Know that *you're* the reason for ruining your father's life as well as your own."

Jenny said nothing. She realized then that if Kate decided to fight her again, she'd lose, and end up as a bloody pulp on the floor. She was stronger and taller than her, not to mention much more athletic, and had the reassured arrogance of an educated Asian woman that liked seducing other men. Moreover, she still had her father's loyalty on her side, and still had enough cunning intelligence to hurt her. When Jenny glanced down at her hands, she saw jagged fingernails broken at the ends.

"Call your father if you want, dear Jenny," Kate said, almost sneering. Her voice came out as a mocking coo. "See if it'll make a difference. Two can play it at that game. I had plans to leave this fucking pigsty soon anyway."

She reached out with a hand. Jenny jerked backwards in surprise and hit her shoulders against the door. Kate laughed at her, tapped her nose, and drew back a lock of her hair. Jenny shivered when feeling her nails.

"Get out," Jenny gasped. "Get the hell out of here, or I'm—"

Kate slapped at her. Her hand came out of nowhere and struck her across the face. A loud *SMACK!* erupted from Jenny's cheek and her head snapped to the side. A cloud of black hair flooded her vision and a sharp gasp escaped her lips. Hot trailing tears stung her face.

"Be quiet," Kate sneered. "You're ugly when you talk, Jenny. Just be quiet."

Kate caressed her face one last time and walked away.

Jenny stared after her, her cheek still raw. She watched quietly as Kate reentered her father's room and tasted salt in her mouth. She appeared a few minutes later dragging a black suitcase into the hallway.

"I guess this is goodbye," Kate finally said. She smiled, sending another alarming fear through Jenny's chest. "It seems your family has a habit of running out the ladies of the house. Perhaps it's your family's destiny to raise whores under one roof."

Jenny's eyes widened. "*I am not a whore!*" she screamed. "I'm not the one sleeping around and bringing random people into my house!"

"Jenny. I wasn't talking about *you.* I was talking about your mother. But don't worry. Sooner or later, you'll follow in her footsteps. It's what every woman part of your lineage seems to do these days."

"*My mother isn't a wh*—"

But she was gone, having disappeared from the hall and making her way down the stairs.

Jenny sobbed. It was relieved sob that came out like a whimpering croak from her throat. She went over to her bed and sat down. Her thigh still hurt.

She sat still for a minute and listened as the door downstairs swung open. After a few seconds it, closed, and silence filled the house. The rumbling roars of a starting engine erupted from the driveway of the house, and soon Kate's Audi was screeching loudly into the night.

Jenny closed her eyes for a minute, listened, and then fell backwards onto her bed with a heavy sigh. She opened her eyes and stared at the white ceiling above her. She whimpered. She swung her lower body onto the bed and curled onto her side, bringing her hands up to cover herself. She cried.

"I still have one more final tomorrow," she sobbed. "I still have one more final, and I don't even know half of the material. I'm going to bomb my final."

Laughter collected in her chest. It built up to bubbly giggles in her throat and then finally spilled out as mad cackles that filled the room. The noise echoed crazily through the house and eventually turned into hiccupping chuckles. Eventually, the laughter died off, and all that was left were weak, pathetic, sobs.

"Ah, *God*," Jenny moaned. She closed her eyes for a minute and curled her legs in. She was cold. "I don't know what to do now. I really don't. It would just be so much easier if I just died."

She laughed again and just lay there on her side, wishing for the night to be over. After a while, she removed herself from bed, stumbled to the bathroom, and took a long hot shower.

# CHAPTER 37

"We're here, Jenny."

Jenny opened her eyes and felt a warm light touch her face. She looked outside the windows and saw a pattern of gray clouds mixed with blue in the sky. Waves sounded in the distance. It was a pleasant sound, Jenny thought, and made her imagine the slipping of garments from naked skin in the summer morning. Salty sea-breeze hung damp and fresh in the air. They'd taken Daniel's car again, and Jenny supposed she must've dozed off a bit as they traveled to the beach. It must've been a light doze, though, because she remembered thinking dreamily to herself: *This is home; this is a place where my heart belongs, and this is where I must someday leave. Life is changing now, and I have to grow up. It hurts to leave this place and it hurts to know that it'll only be part of my past as memory, but...maybe this is life. Maybe this is part of love and memory.*

She'd looked over to the side and stole a glance at Daniel. His attention was politely focused ahead on the road.

*This is home,* Jenny had thought distantly again. *This is a place where my heart can belong even if it may hurt. This is the definition of home; this is what friendship means.*

"Jenny?"

"Yeah," she said slightly, undoing her seatbelt. "I'm awake."

They got out together and walked towards the sandy pits that made up

Brackett's Landing. It was low tide today: Unearthed sand dunes and organic sea junk dominated the shoreline and looked like recently discovered treasure. Seagulls cried out in the distance.

"It really is beautiful here," Jenny said as she stepped down into the sand. Daniel followed, not really saying anything. There was something quiet yet solemn in her voice. Something poignant. "I can't believe none of us see this more."

Daniel came next to her and stood by her side. He hesitated, and moved in close to her so that she knew he was there. Jenny moved next to him, and let their arms brush.

*Monday is gone,* Jenny thought faintly, *but oh, how wonderful it was. How wonderful it was to have experienced it with someone by my side, how wonderful it was to have loved and been loved. At this very moment now, standing at the shores of the beach with the gray sky and cold wind, how wonderful it is to know that someone will always be there for me. To simply love me.*

"I'm going to miss you once you leave," Daniel said quietly. "I…I hope you know that, Jenny. I'm going to miss you a lot."

"I know, Daniel. I know."

She searched for his hand. He took it, and firmly squeezed. She lay her head on his shoulder.

"Daniel?"

"Hmm?"

"Do you really think this place is beautiful?"

"Yeah, Jenny. I do."

She said softly, "If I were to die, I'd like to be reborn here. I'd like to be reborn nowhere else but here."

He hesitated. He heard the unfinished question in her voice, and was afraid to ask.

"Alone?" he said.

"No. Not alone, Daniel. If I were to be reborn alone here, it wouldn't be Heaven."

She closed her eyes. She leaned against him, and Daniel stood there supporting her. Jenny felt the cold sea-breeze wind blow at them from behind, and smelled the heavy aroma of salt and ocean in the air. She felt brief sunlight on her face whenever the sun poked through the clouds, and felt beneath her feet the shifting grainy sands. But most of all, she felt Daniel there beside her, holding her there and keeping her close, his shoulder her support, his hand warm and strong. There was something sad here as well, but it was something small, not yet defined. It was good holding him like this—good to be his friend.

*I don't ever have to be afraid in life anymore because of this moment,* Jenny thought. Solemnity filled her heart. And with it, a feeling of acceptance. *No matter how much I suffer in life, I no longer need to be afraid because I can know for sure I once was cared for in life. That I once was loved.*

*Thank you, Daniel. Thank you for everything. Thank you for being my friend.*

She sighed against him. Yes, it was good holding him like this. With all that had happened, with all that *would* happen in the future, it was just good to be holding him like this, by his side, as his friend.

Just good.

***

*Edmonds / 12:56 p.m.*
*2019*

"Jenny."

She turned around. Her eyes widened.

*Daniel,* she thought. *He actually came for me. He came all this way.*

He made his way towards her and ran through the sand. Wind rushed through his hair and blew it to the side. A livid expression grew on his face as he approached but disappeared when he was next to her. He seemed tired in the dim morning glow. Scared. He looked like he'd just finished running a thousand miles just to find her.

"Why did you *leave?*" he gasped. "Jenny…why did you leave without *telling*

514

*me?"*

"Daniel."

A cool breeze blew in their direction. Jenny's hair wavered endlessly with it and fluttered around her shoulders. She regarded him with a thoughtful gaze and then smiled at him when noticing his frown. It was a frown all too familiar and one that she recognized from her childhood. It was the frown of the boy she once knew and loved; it was the frown of the boy who once carried her to the girl's bathroom when her nose bled, and that had sat with her at the beach whenever she was troubled.

It was just the frown of the boy she once loved.

"You came looking for me," Jenny said softly, still smiling at him. "Thank you. I didn't…I didn't think you'd come for me."

He studied her. He collected his breath and gasped, feeling heat rushing away from his face. He glanced past her shoulder and noticed her suitcase in the sand. Her jacket was neatly folded and placed on top of it. Her boots were next to the suitcase as well. She stood barefoot in the sand waiting for him.

"Please," Daniel said when he turned back to her. "Please don't. I know…I know what's happening, so please Jenny…don't. Just come back with me. Don't leave me again. I can't bear you leaving me again."

She went over and cupped his face. Daniel looked at her, surprised, and realized he'd been shaking. He grabbed the hand that was against his cheek and leaned into it, closing his eyes.

"I never stopped loving you, Daniel Fischer," Jenny whispered, "not even in those moments where I forced myself to forget my past. You were always there with me, always in my mind. Always in my heart. I've never forgotten you. And I never *will* forget you."

"Jenny. I—"

He stopped himself, turning away, unable to finish. He swallowed what felt like jagged rocks in his throat.

"I can force you, you know," he said finally. "I can force you to stay,

Jenny. I can keep you here if I wanted, make you be with me. I can force you to physically stay with me if I tried."

"And in doing so," she said for him, "will you ever receive my love in return?"

He shook his head.

"Are you so selfish with your love that you'd confine me, Daniel?"

"No," he said. "God, no. But I can't have you leaving me again, Jenny. I just *can't*. Not after having found you again. Not after…not after seeing how beautiful you've become."

She smiled at him and reached down to take his hands. She brought them to her lips and kissed them. Around her, waves crashed harshly against the shoreline. Seagulls cried out in the distance.

"Jenny."

"Wait, Daniel. Just…wait."

She stood on her toes and wrapped her arms around his neck. She placed her head on his chest and closed her eyes. Daniel took her from behind and held her, immersing himself in her hair.

"I love you, Daniel Fischer," Jenny whispered. "And I'm so glad that you're my friend in life. I'm just so happy for everything."

"Jenny, please." Tears threatened his voice. "Don't."

"I love you," she whispered. "And I just…I just wanted to thank you. For everything. But most of all Daniel, I want to thank you for showing me courage in life. Thank you for showing me the strength needed to love this world. Thank you for showing me courage."

Tears spilled down his face. Jenny felt them on her cheeks and realized she was crying too. The tears were warm and kind, sticky, like honey.

"I love you, Jinyoung," Daniel whispered, "and I will always love you. I've always loved you."

Jenny smiled. She sobbed against him one last time and pulled herself away.

Daniel pulled her back, held her in his arms, and kissed her. He kissed her

516

fully on the lips and tasted warm salt in his mouth. Jenny held him back, letting his arms take her, squeeze her, grab her from behind. She felt him against her and held her breath, feeling his lips soft and wonderful.

After a moment, he let go, and stood gazing at her face.

"I'll watch you," Daniel said, "and I won't ever turn away from you, Jinyoung. I'll always be here for you no matter what."

Jenny smiled at him. She nodded. "Thank you, Daniel. I…I love you too."

She turned from him. She directed her gaze towards the water and felt a relaxing breeze at her shoulders.

*This is it, I guess,* Jenny thought to herself. She smiled at the waves and moved towards the shoreline. *It feels good to be back home after all these years. It feels so good to be with those I love and the place I grew up in. This place belongs to my heart, God, and no one, not even you, can take it away from me. So much has happened in my life, and as I look back on all of it now, I realize that I am happy. Just so, so happy.*

Cold waves touched her toes. Soft sand shifted from her feet, and white bubbling foam broke over her ankles.

Oh, how great it was to be loved in this world. It made all the suffering and bruises worthwhile, all the hurt, poverty, and disease bearable. It made it possible for the bruises to heal, and made it possible for the individual to take pride in their lives. Love like this was so rare and yet so sublime when found, a love that cared unconditionally and purely. In this world, could not one still laugh even in the face of despair? So long as one had the strength to stand, the audacity to try, the will to *achieve*—and the courage to love—could not one accept their despairs and realize the possible joys that came with it?

Her mother. That one moment where she'd told her not to chew with her mouth open and had wiped her cheeks…couldn't this be how she remembered her? Or her father…that one night when he'd returned from work. Couldn't she still love him as a father despite all the hurt he caused? Nora, Abigail, John, Ted, all of those at Red Moon's Diner…and Tom. She was indebted to all of them just as she was indebted to her parents. And then there was Irene. And Daniel.

*Maybe this is what life is,* Jenny thought calmly as another wave hit her legs. *Maybe in life we are born to love so that we may smile at death when remembering all of our moments in life. A heart truly loved by another is just so much greater than all of the wealth bought in this world—I accept my death readily, and smile without fear knowing that I once was loved.*

The waters pulled at her waist. Jenny's feet stumbled and lost their footing. She turned around.

Daniel stood on the shoreline behind her. He stood there as promised and watched her longingly, lovingly, holding a forlorn yet understanding expression on his face. He would watch her until the end, she knew; he would watch her and never leave her. This Jenny knew.

"*I love you, Jinyoung!*" he cried out behind her. He brought his hands up and cupped them around his mouth. "I'll always love you. No matter what, I'll always love you!"

Tears welled in Jenny's eyes. Her feet lifted from the sand and soon she was paddling against the waves. *Goodbye, Daniel, my friend,* she thought. *It was so good to love and be loved by you. It was just so, so good.*

Seagulls cried out in the sky. Their shrill calls to each other reminded Jenny of her father, and that was because…because…why?

*Because that was the first time I ever saw him crying,* Jenny thought. *It was the first time I'd ever seen a grown man cry, and it was just right after I had that fight with Kate.*

Yes, that was right—she'd caught her father sobbing loudly on the doorstep that night. He'd come home distraught over something at work and had just slumped down in front of the door with his jacket off, his tie loosened, and his hair in complete disarray. His sobs had called her down from her room, and when Jenny opened the door to see what was wrong, she'd said—

\*\*\*

"Daddy?"

Her father sat hunched over on the doorstep, his shoulders heaving, his back trembling. Sweat soaked the areas under his arms and marked the lines of his back; his briefcase was placed to the side and his jacket was thrown to the ground, the dim yellow glows of the house lights casting his shadow deep and large against the grass.

Jenny paused at the doorway and felt something prick the skin along her back. Her father's hands covered his face and loud agonized moans filled the air. Jenny shivered. She closed the door behind her and went to him, wincing as her bare feet touched cold pebbles.

"Daddy? Appa?"

Yongsook rubbed his face. He swallowed and produced a meaty gurgling sound that caused Jenny to grimace. She sat down next to him and winced when her bottom touched the ground. The bruise on her thigh was as large as a grapefruit.

"Jenny," Yongsook said.

"Yes, appa. I'm here."

"Come here. Your father wants to hold you."

Jenny leaned against her father's bulk and felt his arms wrap around her. She smelled cologne on his shirt and peppermint in his breath, but there was no alcohol, thank God.

"Are you my daughter, Jenny?"

"Yes, appa."

"You'd never hurt me."

"No, appa. Never."

Her father sniveled. "I'm sorry," he began, "I'm sorry for everything. I've ruined our family and I've mistreated you as my only daughter. I've failed to take care of our family and have just ruined everything. I don't deserve to have you, Jinyoung. I just don't deserve to have anybody in life."

"*Daddy, don't!*"

Jenny planted her face against her father's chest and wept against him. Tears swelled in her eyes with abrupt force, and before Jenny knew it, she was sobbing as hard as her father.

"Don't say that, daddy," Jenny said. "Don't say that anymore. I'm here. I'm your daughter. I'll always be your daughter."

Her father said in a trembling voice: "I have to leave soon, Jenny. I have to leave and find another place to live. I can't stay here in this city anymore. You'll have to understand this for me, Jenny. I have to move away."

Jenny shuddered. Kate's voice, loud and clear, suddenly spoke up behind her, saying coldly: *Two can play it at that game.*

"Is it Kyung-soon?" she asked.

Her father looked at her, alarmed, but then slowly nodded. "She's an evil woman, Jenny," her father said. "I should have never…I thought that she…but I'm a fool, Jenny. Your father's a stupid, stupid fool. I should have never let her enter our lives."

He sniveled again, and Jenny kept silent. She watched as her appa cried and did her best to comfort him. She leaned against him, offered him her embrace, and just let his arm wrap around her shoulders.

"Did Kate post a video of you two together, appa?"

"How do you—"

"She sent it to your company, am I right? To your boss, maybe? Did she send it so that everyone in the company knows?"

Her father stared at her, red-eyed, palm-prints on his cheeks. "Has she threatened you, Jenny?" her father asked.

"Only on the phone," Jenny said quickly. "Is that what happened, daddy? Did she do something to you at work?"

Her father nodded. He said, "She did everything like you said. And then she called me afterwards, and we fought for…we fought for a long time. I don't know what to do anymore. I just don't know what to do."

Her father wept a second time, but this time Jenny didn't offer her support. She just sat next to her father and stared blankly at the grass near her feet.

So. This was the revenge Kate had been talking about. This was what she meant after all this time. Of course there'd be other sex videos of her and her father. Why hadn't she anticipated that?

"Daddy?"

Yongsook said breathlessly, "I have to leave soon, Jenny. Your father has to go away. I don't know when, but it will have to be soon. I can't work here anymore. Everything for me is just ruined here."

Jenny hesitated. She said: "Take me with you then."

Her father turned to her. "What?"

"Take me *with you*," Jenny said. She grabbed onto her father's arm. "Daddy…appa-ji. Please. Take me with you. Let me come with you wherever you go."

"Jenny—"

"I can't stay here," Jenny said, crying suddenly. "I don't want to stay here anymore. I hate it here. I don't want to be alone, and I don't want to be abandoned by another parent. Daddy…*please.*" She cried against his shoulder. "Take me with you. I don't care where it is, but let me be with you. I'm your daughter, and I'll always be your daughter, and I love you. So *please.* Let me just come with you. You're the only family I have."

Yongsook stared at his daughter. "Why?" he asked suddenly. "Why do you want to suddenly be with me? What could someone like me offer you when I've only treated you with so much cruelty?"

"I just don't want to be abandoned," Jenny replied. It was Daniel she thought of then as she said these words. Daniel and his kind regard and his deep frown, his love towards her and his friendship. It was Daniel she thought of then—it was the scene where she'd turn away from him in the Quad beneath the Yoshino cherry trees and left him crying beneath the falling petals.

"I just don't want to be alone," Jenny said quietly again. "I'd rather be with you than live by myself, appa. You're my father—I can't abandon you."

Yongsook wrapped his arms around her and squeezed her tight against his chest. He sniffled loudly against her ears and Jenny closed her eyes, hearing the sound of his heartbeat.

"I was wrong," Yongsook wept loudly. "I was so *wrong* to ever despise you, Jinyoung. I was a fool to believe that having a son could better my life when in reality just having you in my arms has saved me. I'm sorry. Your stupid father is so, so sorry. I love you. Your pathetic excuse of a father loves you, and he will do everything he can to protect you."

Jenny nodded. She whispered, "I love you too, daddy," and wept silently in his arms. She—

***

*Edmonds / 12:56 p.m.*
*2019*

Daniel watched as she disappeared beneath the waves and reappear again a second later. She was farther out in the water now and only visible whenever the waves receded.

*I love you,* Daniel thought quietly, *and this is my gift to you, Jinyoung. This is my last love for you.*

Jenny turned around as if hearing his thoughts and was hit with another wave. The water crashed above her head and moved swiftly to drag her down. She was cold, but the feeling was more soothing than terrible. She turned around again and gazed back at the shoreline. She smiled at him. Another surge of warmth and love filled her heart.

*This world really can be beautiful so long as someone has a reason to love another in life,* Jenny thought. *There really can be a reason for joy in life even if in life there is pain and suffering. The people we call friends, the people we choose to love for their choosing to love us first in return—these are all the greatest moments in life. Just…love, I guess.*

It was a thought Jenny kept sound in her heart even as the last of her remaining strength faded from her body, and even as the last unrelenting waves of Puget Sound finally engulfed her.

*Goodbye, Daniel,* she thought calmly. *Goodbye, my friend. I love you. I will always love you.*

Jenny opened her eyes and saw the sky overhead. The clouds had briefly parted and were now with slanted rays of gold that streamed downward from the sky. Jenny thought they were beautiful when she saw them.

She smiled.

# CHAPTER 38

Seattle / 1:19 a.m.
*Two days later…*

He sat alone in the living room with the lights off.

Irene hesitated when she saw him and stood in the hallway with her arms wrapped beneath her chest. He sat motionless in the dark with his eyes closed. Behind him, Seattle's glittering city lights spilled through the glass windows and spread midnight shadows across floors.

"Daniel?"

He turned towards her. Even in the dark, Irene could see the wrinkles beneath his eyes and the lines that stretched his face. His eyes were red, his brow, furrowed. His face looked ten years older.

"Oh, Daniel."

She went to him and heard the shuffling sound of her slippers against the floor. The lights that surrounded them tattooed his face with an eerie glow and made it seem as if he were in a permanent frown.

"Daniel."

"Shh, Irene. It's fine. I'm okay."

She went to him. She held him. She sat beside him and held him, wrapping her arms tight around his neck and placing her face against him. The tears were immediate and sudden, spreading hotly down her face.

"I'm sorry," Irene whispered. "I'm *so sorry*. If I had known, if I had *any* thought of what was going to happen, I would have…I…I…"

Daniel wrapped his arms around her and kissed her. Her tears tickled his neck and her breath warmed his cheek. He whispered: "Shh, Irene. Don't cry. It's not your fault."

"You're so *hurt*," she sobbed. "I can see it Daniel, I can see it in your face. I'm so scared for you. I'm so scared that this hurt won't ever leave you, I'm so scared that it will stay with you forever in your life. I'm so sorry. *God*, Daniel. I'm so *sorry*."

"Irene—"

She wept against him, forcing him into silence. Daniel did his best to hold her.

"I love you, Xiaoli," he whispered, "and I will always love you. Do you understand?"

"Yes," she sobbed. "I...yes, I understand. I love you too, Daniel."

He moved himself from the sofa. Irene watched, wiping her eyes.

"Daniel—"

"Stand with me," he said, taking hold of her hands. "Stand with me for a moment."

"But—"

He pulled her gently off the sofa, and, still holding her hands, knelt down on one knee. He began kissing her hands.

"Daniel."

"This is how I first proposed to you," he said quietly. "Do you remember?"

"Yes. I remember."

His lips traveled from her hands to her wrists. Irene stood where she was and closed her eyes, rocking back and forth on her feet. He gently grabbed her by the waist and brought her closer, peeling her shirt back. He began kissing her midriff.

"Daniel."

"Have you thought of names for the baby yet?" he asked.

Irene gaped at him. She took a step back and placed a hand on her stomach as if he'd touched her with something sharp.

"How…Daniel…how—"

"I know I'm a stupid man," he whispered. He smiled sadly at her from the dark and reached to take back her hands. "But when my wife starts acting a bit different around me—and when she begins speaking more and more about her time at the clinic and starts eating extremely healthy—I tend to notice."

He brought his lips to her stomach again, kissing the white snowy shell that was her midriff, feeling the taut firm surface of her skin.

Irene knelt in front of him. She grabbed his hands and peered intently at him from the darkness. She whispered: "You are *not* a stupid man, Daniel Fischer. You are my husband, and I love you with all my heart. But right now, I need you to be strong for me. I need…*we* need you to be strong for *us*. Please, Daniel. I can't do this without you. Don't abandon us, don't go away. I'm nothing without you. I just *need* you."

"I know," Daniel whispered. "I know, Irene. I know, Xiaoli. I know."

She held him. Daniel held her back, feeling another soft flow black silk-hair against his neck.

"I am always with you, Yu Xiaoli," he whispered. "And I won't ever leave you. I'll be by your side no matter what. I love you. Do you believe me?"

"Yes. I believe you, Daniel. I believe you." She paused. "Are you angry?"

"No, I'm not. I love you. And I will always love you. And I am always happy with you. No matter what."

Irene nodded. She cried against his shoulder and felt the warmth of his body. She realized he was warm then, and that his body felt good against her.

After a few more minutes of holding each other in the darkness, they moved to the bedroom and slept together, warm and safe in each other's arms.

# THE THIRD INTERLUDE

## Final Thoughts

<u>July 28, 2010</u>

A month has passed since graduation. <u>I am with a quiet solace in my heart.</u> My friends have left me; they have fled from life. They have found peace with their fantasies and found callouses on their hands from their labors. Where am I now, now that I am alone and with my dreams fulfilled? Who am I to them that has published his first novel at the tender age of twenty-three? I am nothing but a monstrosity to them for speaking my mind and refusing to wear masks in life; I to them must be a thing envied. I to them must be a <u>vilified god</u> that has accomplished his dream.

I am sad.

***

<u>September 22, 2010</u>

My thoughts turn more and more towards life and what I'm meant to do with it. I want to love, but to whom do I say this to? I want to think, but what society will accept me? Nevertheless, I will transcend. I will make it my ultimate goal in life to transcend the wretched scorn of my contemporaries, and will make sure I will never fall trap to life and its labors. I promise myself <u>to never become weary.</u>

***

<u>September 30, 2010</u>

To grow, love, learn, and then to work towards death is a cliché and typical ideological pathway every American takes. It is a pathway I refuse; it will be one I transcend. With all heart, I will never sigh like my "friends" when they speak to me of their labors. I hope to never roll my eyes like them when realizing they missed another car payment, when they forget to meet another deadline at work, and hope to never think about my past like them where they say: "How? How have I ended up like this?" and, "Who? Who has loved me in life? And why did I throw him/her away?"

I will transcend. As a writer, as someone that *must* write, I will transcend somehow, someway. No man in a mask will tell me how to live or be a man, and no amount of weariness in life will weigh me down. My heart is hard now; I have lost all my friends. I have nothing to lose.

***

October 13, 2010

Should you read this someday, either as a published work or journal entry, know that I have written these words for you. My words now, in the present moment as an emerging author, are words influenced by you. And my words later, as a future-writer someday happy in life, will be reflections of our memories together.

I muster courage to live and breathe in this world.

I muster courage to simply be my*self*.

The Fall of Fashion*

"A style of dress emerges from a film; a magazine promotes night spots which launch various clothing fads…the fetishism of commodities reaches moments of fervent exaltation similar to the ecstasies of the convulsions and miracles of old religious fetishism. The only use which remains here is the fundamental use of submission" (sec. 67).

--Guy Debord "Society of the Spectacle

Thao Le's stumble at this year's London Fashion Week was more than just a klutzy fall over two untrained feet: Her stumble instead exposed all the necessary social codes used to maintain fashion as a 'natural' reality. Gasps followed her graceless tumble; mouths gapped at the collapse of the statuesque Vietnamese goddess. It was not Le's wellbeing or even identity that concerned the world, but rather, the revealing of a reality without the clothes where all actions thenceforth became bared, naked, and left brutally honest. The truth could be no simpler: The world of fashion is a farce. Its 'truth' to us exists only because society has accepted its signs and mythological codes. Moreover, Thao is not a goddess, but rather, something far better: a human being. Her unfortunate (and rather amusing) unsightly stumble down the walkway helped only to reinforce these false cultural values while simultaneously revealing them.

---

* The following is a short essay written by Daniel Fischer in 2016 after having been specially invited to attend Fashion Week in London. The essay focuses on fashion model Thao Le's unfortunate stumble and the many mythological codes that constitute the fashion world. The essay was published in *The Verstand Journal*.

Parts of the essay are written with a facetious tone indicating the author's personal relationship to Thao. The two in fact are close friends in life, where an element of tongue-and-cheek can be detected throughout. One can only assume that the author wrote the essay as a friendly way to tease Thao.

The world of fashion is a farce. Nowhere else is there a spectacle comparable to Hollywood where all individual identity is suppressed, eliminated, and blindly submitted. One needs to simply examine Thao's arrogant strut down the walkway to see this. Her walk is elegant and envied; she is viewed with social awe. The audience is hushed and left in darkness where their existence to themselves is temporarily forgotten and loaned to the models on stage. The commoditization of Thao's body, face, flesh, and name, propagate a sense of social superiority.

But the goddess trips; she flaps her arms inelegantly to the sides, tangles her feet, yelps out loud, and falls to gravity. At this moment of tumbling, words such as "beauty" and "elegance" are replaced with "human" and "clumsy." We as the audience gasp at this moment of revelation for we suddenly realize the depths of our deception: We had believed the models on stage to be infallible; we had allowed ourselves to adorn them with a language befitting of elitists and gods. What was the reason for this belief?

The models in Fashion Week are no more different than Sartre's unfortunate waiter. Like the waiter, each model must act and *be* a model in order for society to recognize their presence. Anything outside this quality of 'model-ness' would be to diminish the illusion of Fashion Week and begin to treat these women as individuals—such a thought is unheard of in Fashion Week. Thus, it is with bad-faith do these models put themselves before us to be seen where every step, gaze, and turn of the head is exaggerated, reminiscent of the desperate Hollywood actor, and foolishly elaborated upon. "The public," Sartre accurately states, "demands of them that they realize it as a ceremony; there is the dance of the grocer, of the tailor, of the auctioneer…a grocer who dreams is offensive to the buyer, because such a grocer is not wholly a grocer" (102). The model is thus not allowed to 'dream' when posing as a model. Moreover, she is not allowed to think, to gaze back, to assert her identity, and must passively be to us what is expect of modeling—to simply be *gazed upon*. Any model who wishes to speak as a woman no longer remains as a model; she instead suddenly breaks from her role as an objectified object and now must be objectified as something else.

This notion of bad-faith elucidates an even more insidious theme surrounding the spectacles of Fashion Week. Though Sartre does not discuss the social status of women, his ontological comments constituting the individual's existence with Others coincides with Berger's own insightful understanding of women's predicament. Thao's shock occurs to us because her stumble reveals her presence to herself:

I have just made an awkward or vulgar gesture…I neither judge it nor blame it. I simply live it…but now suddenly I raise my head. Somebody was there and has seen me. Suddenly I realize the vulgarity of my gesture and I am *ashamed*…By the mere appearance of the Other, I am put in the position of passing judgment on myself as on an *object*, for it is as *an object* that I appear to the Other. (Sartre 302, emphasis added).

Once again, it is through bad-faith do these women allow themselves to be called models, and it is with the audience's participation do these qualities of 'modeling' become complete. But Thao stumbles, and her fall to us disturbs our social understanding of 'proper' fashion. Moreover, Thao herself is left 'ashamed' and vulnerable, for now she must see herself as a *non*-model before the eyes of the Other. She is stripped of her 'model-ness' when seeing herself viewing herself, and is ultimately left exposed before our eyes, naked and freed.

The insistence of women being nothing more than viewable objects is a theme readily accepted and unconsciously promoted within the spectacles of Fashion Week. Fashion, as a social phenomenon, is a genre meant to be simply *looked at*. Those who wear the garments of fashion either as an art form or seasonal trend must physically carry this burden of being seen. Without words to speak or actions to declare, the fashion model must perform her function as a 'model' and do nothing else. In doing so, she must continually be aware of herself being seen by the Other while never hoping to contradict or speak back to the Other. She thus is made submissive into her role, silent, decorated with language and garments not of her own creation—she simply is objectified. This objectification moreover extends beyond the modeling stage where women continually must 'see' themselves in society when in the presence of men:

A man's presence is dependent upon the promise of power which he embodies…the promised power may be moral, physical, temperamental, economic, social, sexual—but its object is always exterior to the man…by contrast, a woman's presence…is manifest in her gestures, voice, opinions, expressions, clothes, chosen surroundings, taste…to be born a woman has to be born, within an allotted and confined space, into the keeping of men…a woman must *continually watch herself. She is almost continually accompanied by her own image of herself.* (Berger 45-46, emphasis added).

Women are furthermore not freed by fashion. On the contrary, because fashion demands to be looked at, those who wear the garments of fashion must be displaced twice as much by their clothes. Names become irrelevant during this gazing moment, for it is the clothes the fashion model must showcase, and it is the clothes the audience is trained to recognize. The many layers of clothing these models wear—symbolically and physically—eliminate more and more layers of identity just as does a kimono suppress layers of individual emotion for the 'artisan.'

One might simplify this by saying: *men act* and *women appear.* Men look at women. Women watch themselves being looked at…the surveyor of women in herself is male: the surveyed female. Thus she turns herself into an object—and most particularly an object of vision: a sight. (47)

This notion of being seen and objectified through bad-faith in the world of fashion is also seen in fashion magazines. The models that appear in these magazines are not real, nor are they themselves. Instead, modifications have been made to their bodies to appeal to an idyllic social paradigm of what is 'desirable,' 'feminine,' and 'perfect.' Each of these models have been 'touched up': they have been modified, repainted, re-digitized, and re-lightened. The entirety of fashion magazines thus no longer becomes an artistic artwork of photography or expression, but rather, a showcasing of the most cunningly and most subtle made alterations to the human body. *Elle* in its 25th Anniversary U.S. edition in 2010, for example, chose Academy Award winning actress Gabourey Sidibe to pose on its front cover. In doing so, public outrage occurred when many accused *Elle* of altering Sidibe's skin tone. This was made in contrast to Sidibe's front-cover pose in *Ebony* March of 2010 where the actress's skin seems much darker. In addition, Bollywood actress Aishwarya Rai Bachchan was seen on the cover of India's *Elle* 2010 December edition with a lighter, paler complexion that many accused was unlike the actress's natural skin color. In August of 2008, *L'Oreal* became the center of controversy when it was accused of whitewashing—that is the term—American singer Beyoncé Knowles's skin for one of its campaigns for a Feria highlighting kit. Other issues remain, such as American singer Rihanna's pose on *Vogue* for its October 2011 edition, Indian actress Freida Pinto's skin portrayal for *L'Oreal's* cosmetic products beginning in 2009, and so forth.

While all the ethnocentric, racist, and sexist qualities of these magazines are bluntly obvious, what is disturbing to witness is the *readily acceptability* of which these magazines circulate through culture and become consumed. While one can choose to recognize that no fashion magazine is representative of real women, mass audiences still consume these magazines, purchase them, emulate them, and hope to dress like them as if they were truth. The individual who purchases fashion magazines intelligent enough to recognize these racists and sexist tendencies acts in bad-faith: She knows absolutely the model on the cover is not real, but simply modified and done up—and yet, she still purchases the magazine anyway, unconsciously submitting herself to the poisonous social codes embedded in its pages. The aforementioned examples also elucidate another troubling plight of women: that they are 'imperfect' as women in reality, and must be 'perfected' in magazines for fantasy. Thus they are society's objects than they are themselves as women, for their images are altered in order to meet society's standards of 'perfection.' Even when Jennifer Lawrence declared to the

world in 2013 that her image on *Dior* was Photoshopped, many still cheered
for Katniss Everdeen in the next installment of *The Hunger Games* rather than
demand her true face. Falseness had prevailed over this demand for truth;
America had once again fled back into a world of fantasy.

With all things, fashion is a language, and every language is a system of
signs. The cut of a skirt, the clanking of high-heeled shoes, the flapping of
elegantly designed gowns—these all signify something more than what their
definitive denotations suggest: They connote a spectacle in which all things
have become a commodity. And yet, despite this language, fashion is ever
rarely unique, and, like Hollywood, it is always the same. In order to appease
the general masses, Fashion Week, despite its elitism, maintains itself with a
tasteless repetition. This repetition is understood through the semiotic
structures of mythological languages and linguistics, where, with the help of
Barthes and semiology, the mundaneness of fashion is elucidated:

The fashion industry, after all, depends greatly on a series of 'myths' in order
to produce an innocent façade which, in fact, acts to speed up
consumption...clothes, generally, take a long time to wear out. The myths of
the fashion system exist to speed up consumption, to lock people (women in
the main) into an annual system which can generate consumption through a
vocabulary of interchangeable, layered and repeatable functions. (Allen 47)

Barthes' simple formula for dismantling the language of fashion relies on the
Object of signification, the Support of signification, and a Variant. In this
formula, "Skirts (O) with a full (V) blouse (S)" has exactly the same signified
meaning in "A cardigan (O) with its collar (S) open (V)" (47-48). Thus the
cut of a skirt or length of a gown is never different when expressed in
language, for fashion will always be constricted to this matrix of language and
uttered with only slight nuances with *parole*. A cardigan cut one way and then
another will always be a cardigan; fashion—and style—always remains the
same. "Dresses remain each year, obviously, but their Variant, whether they
are long or short, pleated or tapered, closed with a zip or with buttons,

allows the fashion system to perpetually recreate and regenerate its messages from a simple stock of elements" (Allen 48). As a commodity, Fashion Week seeks to reduce the human value of its products for it refuses to recognize its use-value with regard to human labor. The materials and energy needed to produce these garments are diluted even further by less-than-human models that strut the runway—their sell value comes to us only through false visualization and repetitive language.

Thao Le's stumble revealed all the inconsistences of a perfect world made by fashion, and the gasps that followed her (seemingly painful) stumble reinforced these inconsistencies. One does not stumble as a model, declares the gods of the fashion world; one does not act like "that." For those of us who gasped, we had unconsciously accepted these commandments as something sacred, and had become frightened at the appearance of reality. I, however, applaud Thao's stumble, and am glad to have seen her 'naked.' Fashion is a farce, and it was only through this unfortunate event was there pleasure in seeing this farce exposed. The glamorous qualities of expensive high-heel shoes and sparkling gowns can only do so much for a woman before eliminating her identity beneath the clothes she wears—one is far more beautiful when stripped of culture and left standing naked as an individual.

Come on Thao, dearest and loveliest friend—pick yourself up in life.

## Works Cited

Allen, Graham. *Roland Barthes*. London: Routledge, 2003. Print

Berger, John. *Ways of Seeing*. London: Penguin, 2008. Print.

Sartre, Jean-Paul. *Being and Nothingness: A Phenomenological Essay on Ontology*. Trans. Hazel E. Barnes. New York: Washington Square Press, 1992. Print.

O what to me the little room
That was brimmed up with prayer and rest;
He bade me out into the gloom,
And my breast lies upon his breast.

O what to me my mother's care,
The house where I was safe and warm;
The shadowy blossom of my hair
Will hide us from the bitter storm.

O hiding hair and dewy eyes,
I am no more with life and death,
My heart upon his warm heart lies,
My breath is mixed into his breath.


--William Butler Yeats
"The Heart of the Woman"

# EPILOGUE

Her head rested on his shoulder.

"Is this a dream?"

"Maybe."

"Am I dead?"

Daniel looked at her, dubious. They'd been standing and admiring the waves together. Her question had broken him from a deep thought and caused him to stir. Moreover, it had been a dark question, something that had caused him to frown.

"What are you talking about, Jenny?" he asked quietly. "You're right here with me."

Jenny opened her eyes and lifted her head, realizing she must've dozed off again. She'd been dreaming. She looked outward towards the waves and saw that the sky had darkened a bit with clouds.

"Daniel."

"Hmm?"

"Can I ask a question?"

"Sure."

"If...if I were to die, would anyone miss me?"

A frown cut through his face. His tone grew serious. "Why are you talking like that, Jenny?"

"Just answer the question. Please."

He said: "There will always be someone to miss you, Jenny. There will always be someone in this world that will miss you if you leave."

"Why?"

"Because—" Daniel's throat caught. He gazed at her thoughtfully from the side and then offered a smile. It was a sad smile. It was an understanding smile. "Because they will have loved you, Jenny," he said finally. "Those that will miss you will be those that have loved you."

She smiled at him. It was a grateful smile, one that hurt Daniel deep down in his chest. A sudden urge of wanting to hold her filled him.

"If I were to leave, Daniel," Jenny whispered, "would there be people waiting for me?"

"Yes, Jenny. There will always be those waiting for you. Those that loved you will always wait for you."

"If…if I were to leave you Daniel, would you wait for me?"

Daniel nodded. His jaw tightened and his throat hurt. In his heart, something deep inside seemed to break, reddening his eyes. "I'll wait for you, Jenny," he whispered. "However long it may take, I'll always wait for you."

She smiled at him. She turned away from him.

"Jinyoung," she said.

"What?"

"Jinyoung. I said my real name's Jinyoung. Not Jenny."

"Jinyoung." His voice broke. "A nice name. A pretty name."

"No. Not really. It's just a typical name."

Daniel smiled at her. It was another thin and sad smile, and Daniel would have given anything in the world then just to have her turn around and see it.

"I'll be here, Jinyoung," he said quietly. "I'll be here waiting for you."

Jenny nodded, but didn't raise her eyes at him. She made her way over towards the shoreline and stopped momentarily to remove her shoes. She peeled off her socks and rolled the legs of her jeans up midway to her calves.

Gray clouds had covered the sun overhead; brief blue poked through. She made her way towards the water and felt clumpy sand rub her feet. Small rocks pricked her soles and other small white shells of long-dead animals broke beneath her heels. She reached the shore's edge just as another rushing tide was coming in, and shuddered when a mind-numbingly cold wave slapped her feet. Water sprayed up to her calves.

"I'll wait for you, Jinyoung!" Daniel cried behind her. He'd cupped his hands over his mouth. "I'll always wait for you!"

She turned around and saw him standing there on the shoreline, still looking longingly after her. *Daniel,* Jenny thought quietly. More waves surged against her, numbing her legs. *Oh, Daniel. You've been my one and only friend in this world. You've been the only true person to really love me. Thank you. For everything.*

*I love you too.*

Waves tugged at her calves, forcing her forward. She tittered for a minute, nearly lost her balance, and found her footing again.

The water was at her stomach now. Jenny looked back and smiled one last time at him. She gazed at him, hoping with all her heart he knew how much she loved him. He did not wave or call out to her, but merely smiled in return—a smile that, though Jenny couldn't properly see at this distance, she was sure was sad and loving. Her feet lifted from the sandy bottom and her body was lifted up by the current. She was drifting now. Waves smacked her face.

"Goodbye, Daniel, my friend," Jenny whispered. "I love you. I will always love you too. Forever I will always love you."

The waves submerged her head and forced her below the surface. Jenny fought them, swam out far as she could, and felt for one brief moment a horrible fright as she saw the eternal gloom of the water. She almost panicked then, but then saw the sky overhead open with a brief glow of sunlight. Light broke through.

*Beautiful,* Jenny thought. The waves forced her downward. *Everything is just so beautiful here. All is well.*

Jenny pushed forward with her last remaining strength and smiled when she looked at the sky.

The light had come through and parted the clouds; shafts of light spilled through.

The sight was beautiful.

# ABOUT THE AUTHOR

DISKO PRAPHANCHITH was born in Laos, Vientiane, and moved to the United States as a young boy. He graduated from the University of Washington in 2012 and holds a Bachelor of Fine Arts in Creative-Writing and English. He is well-versed in subjects involving literary theory, post-structural discourse, critical practice, and philosophy. He currently resides in Seattle, Washington. *Courage* is his first novel.

26448777R00305

Made in the USA
Charleston, SC
08 February 2014